ARCHIVES

THE THRILLING LIBRARY:

ARCHIVES

BY
NORMAN A. DANIELS
AND
E. HOFFMANN PRICE

INTRODUCTION BY
TOM JOHNSON

THRILLING PUBLICATIONS
2017

TABLE OF

CONTENTS

INTRODUCTION

TOM JOHNSON

I N THE Fall of 1939, the same year that *Secret Agent "X"* and *Operator #5* ceased their long runs at Ace and Popular Publications, respectively, Ned Pines' Standard magazines launched *Thrilling Spy Stories*, which featured a new character called the Eagle. Written by Norman Daniels under the house name of Capt. Kerry McRoberts, the hero is Jeff Shannon, America's top secret agent. It is also the year that Leo Margulies, the head editor for the Thrilling line, appeared to have been trying to revive some of their floundering titles. From 1939 to 1941, several new characters would appear in a burst of creative juices that had to come from editorial committee: the Black Bat in *Black Book Detective,* the Crimson Mask and Candid Camera Kid in *Detective Novels,* the Purple Scar in *Exciting Detective,* the Ghost and Masked Detective in their own magazines, and the Eagle in *Thrilling Spy Stories.*

Whether their main titles were slipping in sales, or the publisher was just looking for a way to increase sales with new characters, is hard to tell. But the influx of new characters came at a bad time. The war in Europe and the Pacific was about to cause havoc in the pulp publishing industry with a paper shortage. This new burst of energy was short lived, and very few of the new characters survived past a few years. The Eagle only lasted for five stories and disappeared without a murmur. But it was an interesting series.

Like Secret Agent "X," the Eagle was a Lone Wolf secret agent, though his main foe is the Nazis, not American gangsters. He is tall, maybe 28 or 29 years of age, neatly dressed in a blue suit, and described thusly: the collar of his white shirt was immaculate, the tie just the right color. He has brown hair and friendly blue eyes; as the Eagle, he is known the world over, from Tokyo to Berlin—known and feared! In the first story he was given a love interest, but the editors kept her mostly off stage, as a foil to the beautiful women the Eagle attracted during his adventures. She did take a starring role, however, in the story, "The Stolen Gas Gun."

That story has a peculiar ending probably worth mentioning. In the second to last chapter, the Eagle suspects a higher up in American intelligence to be a spy, and makes certain arrangements. At the end of the chapter, the Eagle has been captured, knocked out by gas defending himself and his fiancée. But in the final chapter, the climax has all happened offstage and is disclosed in a conversation with the Eagle and his superior. It's as if the story were running long and they had to make a severe cut.

Norman Daniels would eventually become a pretty good writer of spy thrillers, as his 1960s *Man From A.P.E.* and *Baron of Hong Kong* paperback series show, but in the 1930s and '40s, he was more at home dealing with American gangsters, and the occasional Nazi saboteurs. The Eagle was a fun series, but Daniels wanted to write the stories as he would typical gangster novels, and at times they may have missed the mark as spy thrillers. The series might have fared better at the hands of G. T. Fleming-Roberts. One thing they sorely missed were the femme fatales that Fleming-Roberts introduced so easily to his spy stories, and Daniels would later bring into his own spy stories, but not yet.

Still, for whatever its failings, Norman Daniels was a top-notch writer, and his stories are always fun to read, and so too are the adventures of the Eagle.

We know that Leo Margulies always had several stories on hand when he released a new title, or at least had a call for submissions among his stable of writers. Although the series was eventually given to Mr. Daniels, there were undoubtedly stories submitted by other authors. One such title was very likely "The Black Dragon" by Capt. Kerry McRoberts (Will Murray thinks the author is actually E. Hoffmann Price), which appeared in the February 1940 issue of *Popular Detective*. The story involved Japanese interests in the Philippines. G-2 is not mentioned, and the name of the agent is changed from Jeff Shannon, but we are told he was called to the Philippines recently. Unfortunately, for some reason the story was not included in the series, and was a stand-alone spy adventure.

When the Eagle series ended, Norman Daniels had a few plots left over. One story, "The Last Train to Freedom," was very likely the sixth entry in the Eagle series. Published in the October 1943 (it was submitted in October 1942) issue of *Detective Novels*, the story actually takes place in 1941, prior to America entering the war, but after Germany has occupied France. The character of the Eagle is changed to a consular clerk (sometimes called an agent) from somewhere, who penetrates occupied Paris to warn Americans to get out. But he is too late, the Gestapo has already arrested the Americans, and are holding them for exchange of German prisoners elsewhere. From there, the story becomes a simple murder mystery, with a touch of intrigue.

Undoubtedly, there are more unused stories out there, masquerading as something else. We may never know the full history of the pulp houses and their main characters, but after all these passing years since the demise of the magazines, we are still learning some of their secrets.

Happy Reading!

Tom Johnson
Seymour, Texas
May 23, 2009

STORM OVER THE AMERICAS

CHAPTER I

MYSTERY PLANE

THE SENTRY on duty near one of the great locks of the Panama Canal was the first to hear the distant roar. He shaded his eyes against the afternoon sun and peered skyward. He had keen eyesight, this sentry, or he'd have never spotted that minute speck high above him. It was a plane—and a big one if the sound of her motors was any indication.

The sentry stepped into a small shed and used the telephone.

"Plane flying overhead, above the banned area," he reported. "Too high to make out her identity."

On hearing those few words, powerful glasses were turned toward the sky. A dozen fast pursuit planes took off and climbed rapidly to intercept this plane which flew above territory long barred to any aircraft except military ships. A huge sound device was put into operation. Everywhere, there was activity!

Then, as the fast pursuit ships gained altitude, the unknown craft suddenly went into a bank, nosed back and roared away. An hour later the pursuit planes came back to their landing.

"Sorry, sir," a flight lieutenant reported to his commanding officer, Colonel Judson Foster. "It got away from us. That ship was probably equipped for stratosphere flying. I caught a glimpse of her and by her design I'd say she was some kind of a bomber. There was no identification on her wings."

"It's damned suspicious," Colonel Foster growled. "All planes in this vicinity know they can't fly over a barred area and this ship didn't even carry any identification insignia. It smells like trouble to me. Where did that ship come from? Why did the pilot defy military regulations and fly her over the canal? It's a matter for Washington. That's all, Lieutenant."

Ninety minutes later Colonel Foster studied a code message from the Secretary of War. He decoded the message behind locked doors, with a sentry on guard.

COLONEL JUDSON FOSTER,
U.S.A. PANAMA CANAL ZONE:
MESSAGE RECEIVED. AGREE PLANE HIGHLY SUSPI-
CIOUS. CONTACT AGENT JEFF SHANNON AT HOTEL
ARRIDO, PANAMA CITY.

Foster touched a match to a corner of the message, watched it burn to ashes and swept these into his waste basket.

"Jeff Shannon—the Eagle," he muttered. "It must be important if he's down here."

FOSTER CALLED the Hotel Arrido and was connected with Shannon. "Oh, yes, Colonel," a calm, modulated voice answered him. "I received a message, also—to hold myself ready to help. What can I do?"

"A plane, without identification, flew over the barred zone a few hours ago. Looked like some kind of a stratosphere ship. I don't like it."

"It flew south, I suppose," Shannon said quickly. "Yes, I rather guessed that, Colonel. I'm on my way to Caracas, Venezuela, now, on a search for two agents who went there three months ago and vanished. I've an idea your mystery plane ties up with activity down there. Thank you for the tip. I'll try to check on that angle."

"You'll take the next plane, eh?" Foster answered slowly; "Watch yourself. I rather think those foreign influences in Caracas won't relish the intrusion of the Eagle."

There was a chuckle at the other end of the wire. Colonel Foster hung up, leaned back in his chair and stared vacantly into space.

"If what I think is happening," he muttered, "it will take all the speed, power and ruthlessness of an eagle to clean up the mess."

The officer started up as from outside there came a single shot and a command for someone to halt. Then two rifles opened up. Colonel Foster rushed out of his quarters and found a sergeant lowering his automatic slowly. The sergeant snapped to attention.

"Sorry if you were disturbed, sir," the sergeant said. "A sentry saw someone lurking outside your office, sir. Looked as though he might have been eavesdropping. He got away and from the glimpse I had of him, he seemed to be one of these natives who are always hanging around. Probably nothing to it, sir."

Colonel Foster restrained the impulse to leap into action. Nothing would be gained by showing his suspicions. There might be other spies around. He touched the peak of his cap in a salute.

"As you were, Sergeant. Instruct your men to watch closely for anyone who acts suspiciously. However, it probably was only a native trying to see if he could steal something. Good night, Sergeant."

Colonel Foster walked slowly into his quarters. He barked a summons for his orderly, had all windows closed and the curtains drawn. He stationed his orderly at the front door with instructions that no one was to be admitted. Then he got on the telephone to call Hotel Arrido. But Jeff Shannon had already checked out.

He studied the plane schedule to Caracas, and groaned. The Eagle would be taking off at this very moment. Too late to warn him now.

Colonel Foster replaced the instrument, his throat dry, his forehead moist with perspiration.

"Heaven help Jeff Shannon now," he muttered. "They'll pick up his trail in Caracas. One shot is all it will take—or one stab from a knife."

Colonel Foster knew how spies worked. He had served in the A.E.F. during the entire World War. And his fears for the safety of this crack agent of his country, known as the Eagle, were very real.

THERE WERE five passengers aboard the night plane to Caracas. The forward seat was occupied by a man of about forty-five, paunchy, pompous-looking and quite at home in the air. Across from him sat another passenger who was as gaunt and thin as the first man was stout. His cadaverous cheeks looked like those of a mummy. He seemed nervous and avoided looking out of the window as much as possible.

Number Three passenger was a young man of about twenty-eight or nine. He was neatly dressed in a blue suit. The collar of his white shirt was immaculate, his tie just the right color. He had healthy looking brown hair and blue eyes that were pleasantly friendly. The newspaper in his lap was opened to the sports page.

Directly across from him sat a tall man with a trimmed Vandyke. A monocle was screwed into his left eye and he was intently reading lengthy documents that he took from a briefcase. He paid no attention to those around him.

Passenger Number Five had been the steward's greatest problem in the last twenty flights. Number Five was drunk. Not stupidly drunk, nor belligerently, but with just enough alcohol in his system to make his spirits as buoyant as the plane that roared southward.

One of the agents put a gun against her head.
"You will surrender or I will shoot!"

"M'name's Claney," he told the world at large, "I'm a good guy, I am. Ev'body likes me. I like ev'body. Even you, steward. Say, don't you carry anything to drink on this jalopy?"

The man with the monocle turned and gave the steward an annoyed glance. The steward did his best to quiet the boisterous passenger, then hurried to the pilot's quarters in response to a signal.

He emerged with a radiogram in his hand. He walked over to the bearded man, bowed, and handed him the message.

"For you, Señor Lachner. Ah—*gracias.*"

He slipped a coin into his pocket and returned to his problem of keeping the obstreperous Number Five quiet. The bearded man who had been called Lachner read the message and frowned. He removed a small book from his briefcase, glanced around with suspicious eyes as he lifted the documents he had been reading, to conceal the little book. He opened it, studied the radiogram and began comparing certain words.

It took but a few moments to decode the message. He growled a low oath as he read it.

U.S. INTELLIGENCE AGENT KNOWN AS EAGLE
ABOARD YOUR PLANE. IDENTIFY HIM. AT LANDING POINT
HIM OUT AND HE WILL BE TAKEN CARE OF. BE CAREFUL.
HE IS DANGEROUS.

Lachner replaced his documents and the code book in the briefcase.
The message he crumpled into a ball and thrust into his pocket. At the
first opportunity he would burn it. He leaned back in his chair and
studied each passenger intently, paying particular attention to the noisy
celebrant in one of the aft seats.

Passenger Number Five arose suddenly, pushed the steward out of
his way and staggered forward, apparently heading for the pilot's quarters. As he passed Lachner, he reeled. Lachner jumped up to prevent
the man from falling into his lap, but what happened then was worse.

THE REELING man's legs became tangled with Lachner's and
both crashed to the floor of the plane. Evidently under the impression
that he was being attacked, the man who had called himself Claney
began to fight.

The young man seated in a chair opposite Lachner got up, seized Claney by the collar and jerked him to his feet. The steward took charge of him. Lachner, half stunned by the fall, groaned and sat up. The considerate young man took his arm and aided him to his feet.

"Fool!" Lachner growled, and shot an angry glance toward the protesting young passenger who had upset him. "He should not have been allowed to go up. He is dangerous."

"You're right," agreed the young man helping him into his chair. "Quite right, but I don't think he'll bother us again. The steward's on the job now."

Lachner gazed at the self-styled Claney thoughtfully. His dark eyes narrowed in hate. He folded his arms and allowed his right hand to slip beneath his coat and touch the warm butt of an automatic slung under his arm. Lachner was in a mood to kill.

The neatly dressed young man across the aisle favored Lachner with a warm smile, settled back in his seat and loosened his collar and tie. He closed his eyes and dozed.

Lachner kept staring at Claney, then had a sudden inspiration. His hand shot toward his coat pocket. The code message was gone!

"*Ach,*" he muttered, "he is a stupid one. But he cannot get away and at the landing field we shall work far too quickly to allow his escape."

The plane droned on through the night, and was over the Caracas landing field when the warning signal indicated that it was time for safety belts to be attached. The passengers roused themselves from the lethargy that comes of long journeys. Lachner fastened his belt, turned his head and looked directly at the objectionable Claney who seemed to have fallen into a stupor.

The plane circled the field twice, then nosed down.

It taxied along the runway smoothly and rolled to a graceful stop. Lachner quickly unbuckled his safety belt, seized his briefcase and was the first passenger to reach the door. He stepped out, looked around as if he expected to meet someone, then shrugged.

He moved aside, put a cigarette between his lips and held his lighter toward the tip of it.

But he didn't light it until the inebriated passenger was helped out of the plane by the steward. Lachner had carefully watched all the others emerge. The gaunt man had been greeted by two women who escorted him to a car. The paunchy man had shaken hands with a dark-featured South American and had immediately begun talking of margins and profits. The neatly dressed young man had been the third to emerge. He had surveyed the field with the look of a disinterested connoisseur of airports and then walked blithely into the darkness.

Claney, apparently still intoxicated, almost fell out of the cabin door. He stood on the ground, swaying and grinning inanely. It was at that moment that Lachner snapped his lighter into glowing life and nodded his head slightly toward the plane.

THREE MEN, standing well in the shadows, moved forward. They quickly surrounded the man Lachner had indicated. Two of them took his arms in an apparently friendly fashion, but the drunk winced under the pressure and tried to squirm free. The third man stepped directly behind him. There was a surreptitious movement. Only someone watching intently would have noticed that a blackjack slapped across the captured man's neck.

He seemed to wilt, his head lolling to one side.

The three men increased their pace, hustling their unconscious burden toward a car parked well off the runway. But the young man they had in tow seemed possessed of a unique ability to throw off the effects of a blow. Almost instantly he began to fight. The man directly behind him growled something in a foreign tongue, whipped a knife from a sheath under his coat and drew the blade back for a murderous thrust.

A single shot roared out. The man with the knife howled with pain and looked down at his hand as the knife fell from numbed fingers. The hand was dripping blood.

Somewhere a policeman shouted. Others came rushing toward the scene.

The three would-be killers jumped into their car and sped away. The bewildered Claney stumbled around, muttering to himself.

And deep in the darkness that surrounded the flying field, the nattily dressed young man in the dark suit who had been one of the plane's passengers slowly put a smoking gun back into his pocket. He opened a crumpled bit of paper and studied the words on it. To almost any other pair of eyes those words would have meant only that one Franz Lachner was to contact his firm in relation to the shipment of certain samples to a customer immediately.

But this young man was a master at codes. Without referring to any code book, he got the true meaning of the message. It ordered Franz Lachner to discover the identity of the Eagle who would be aboard the plane and to signal certain agents who would be waiting at the airport so they would make no mistake and capture the wrong man.

"BAD," THE neat young man muttered in the darkness. "Very bad. They knew I was on my way as quickly as I did. Means a thorough organization, plenty of men and money to operate it. Looks like the Secretary of War was right. This will be a dangerous job."

He calmly rolled the radiogram into a ball, flicked it into the night and strolled away, whistling softly.

When a problem so difficult as to defy solution presented itself, the Eagle usually whistled. He was sure there was always a loophole somewhere; that the best of spies leave crevices in their plans where he might get a fingerhold and pry open the whole rotten affair.

CHAPTER II

THE EAGLE SHOWS HIS HAND

PETER FARROW, consul at Caracas, Venezuela, was studying coded reports from the United States. He was extremely busy. With war ready to break out both in Europe and the Orient, the work of consular officials had become exacting. Farrow was tired, but there was far too much to be done before he could snatch a few hours' sleep.

He raised his head, listening, as his secretary's voice reached him from the outer office. She was trying to stop someone from entering, for Farrow had given orders he was not to be disturbed. The consul arose and walked to the door. It was opened before he reached it. A tall, immaculately dressed young man was grinning at Farrow's secretary and gently pushing her aside. She stepped away when Farrow appeared.

"Hello there!" The unexpected visitor grinned into Farrow's stern face. "You look like my old geography teacher. Come on, wipe that crusty look off your face and let's sit down and have a cigar."

The visitor edged by the astounded consul, walked around Farrow's desk and dropped into the chair there. He parked both feet on the edge of the desk, found a box of cigars and helped himself to one. He extended the box toward Farrow.

"Please sit down and have a smoke. It's good for the nerves. Oh, yes—you out there in the other office—close the door and don't listen at the keyhole. Also, don't admit anyone else and no phone calls, do you hear? No phone calls."

The secretary bobbed her head and said, "Yes, sir." Then she glanced at Farrow and turned a beet red. She quickly closed the door.

Farrow stepped over toward the desk. The frown on his face died away and turned into a broad grin.

"No need to introduce yourself, my friend. I've been told too often that the Eagle makes himself right at home no matter where he is. Welcome to Caracas—and to enough trouble to keep a dozen eagles busy."

"Tell me all about it," said Jeff Shannon, and sent a spiral of smoke ceilingward. "And— Oh, yes! There's a young fool locked up in one of your Caracas jails by now. He was in the same plane with me and I expect he got himself pinched. Get him out! You see, there was a gentleman named Franz Lachner aboard. He received a code message to the effect that I was to be identified and fingered for some of his men who would wait at the airport to kill me. This young fellow was pretty tight and by his actions he made Lachner think he was the Eagle. All I had to do was sit back and look bored."

Farrow parked himself on a corner of his desk and looked at this amazing young man whose reputation had spread across the entire world. As the Eagle he was known from Tokyo to Berlin; known and hated—and feared.

"Here it is," Farrow said quietly. "A couple of G-Two agents showed up here three months ago. I know they arrived, but they didn't even have time to report to me before they were obliterated. Maybe they are dead—maybe just prisoners. This isn't the United States and I can't be too curious, you understand. And you'll be in the same predicament. Plenty of luck and some good clear thinking helped you get away from their first welcoming committee. You may not be so fortunate next time."

THE EAGLE looked up and smiled.

"Interesting. What else?"

"What else?" Farrow grunted. "That's all. Absolutely all! And isn't it quite enough—to have a couple of our agents vanish like that? I can't give you the vaguest clue as to what happened to them. But something must be doing here. Some activity is going on that we can't put our fingers on. That's why those agents were sent here."

"Have you noticed any odd-looking planes flying around?" the Eagle queried. "Bombers? Probably equipped for stratosphere flying? Know of any?"

"Stratosphere flying?" Farrow exclaimed, surprised. "Of course not. The only planes I've seen are Venezuelan ones and they're all made in the United States. This man Franz Lachner—I don't know much about him either, except that he seems to be a big shot Nazi. He's supposed to be a trade agent for Nazi Germany, but if he received that code message, he certainly must be a spy. But there is one thing you must get straight right at the start, Shannon. You're entirely on your own. This isn't the United States and you can't call in the army, the navy or the marines to help you. If you fail—that's the end of it. I can't make a formal complaint because the Venezuelan government hasn't asked for your aid."

The Eagle

The Eagle grinned amiably and nodded, "I know all about that—and I also know just how dangerous men like Lachner can be. My job is to find those two missing agents and I mean to do it. If anything else crops up to interest me, I'll take care of that as well."

Farrow's lips compressed tightly. "Don't be too sure. Oh, I've heard of the way you work, how fearless you are and the results you get. But dammit, man, the world is on the brink of war! This isn't a game of tag any longer. It's…. Oh, what's the sense of me telling you all this? You are as well aware of it as I am. I didn't mean to go off the handle like this. But you're so damned cocksure—so certain you can—"

The Eagle's feet plunked on the floor and he sat bolt upright.

"I'm certain all right, old man. Very certain! Because we're in the right. We're fighting a grim menace of dictatorship, death and ruin. With right on your side you can't lose, if you've the courage to back up your convictions. And you may know this about me also. I always work alone. I have never called for help yet. If help presents itself, very well. I use it. If not, I fight my own battles. Now let's get down to facts. Who seems to head these Nazis here?"

Farrow sat down with a sigh. "This Franz Lachner you spoke of—he's as high as anyone, I suppose. Anyway, they kowtow to him. There is a German beer garden which he and his kind frequent. I don't know what they do there, but it certainly looks like a good meeting place. Here is another thing. Recently there seems to have been an unusual influx of German tourists. I can't understand it. Caracas is no swanky tourist resort. People of other nationalities don't come here as a rule."

"Interesting," the Eagle repeated softly. "Thanks, Farrow. I probably won't see you again, but if anything vital crops up, I'll let you know. Don't mention my name in reports to Washington. You haven't even heard of the Eagle."

HE WAS gone an instant later and Farrow settled down to a limp degree of calmness.

"Amazing young man," he told himself. "So damned amazing I wouldn't be surprised if he did get through. Luck to him. That's the only help I can give."

The Eagle stepped into a street barren of life. It was the siesta hour. He pulled down the brim of his hat to shade his face from the merciless sun and walked slowly toward his hotel. Saluting the desk clerk, he walked to the third floor and quietly made his way to his room. He paused outside the door and listened intently. When he was certain no sounds came from within, he inserted the key, turned it and kicked the door open. At the same time he leaped back in case some trap had been set.

The Eagle had encountered such traps many times before. And he was well aware that Franz Lachner was no fool. By now the Nazi spy might have realized that the man who had called himself Claney really had been under the weather and not acting; that the quiet young man who had sat across from him was the real Eagle. And the Eagle had already sized Lachner up as a man who would not hesitate to take desperate measures.

The Eagle closed the door, locked it and removed his coat. He flopped on the bed, dead tired, for the few hours he had been in Caracas had been busy ones. During that short period of time he had learned for himself almost as much as Farrow had told him. Also there were clothes hidden in the room that would transform him into a German tourist.

The Eagle was anxious to get started, but he realized that if he went abroad now, he would be regarded with suspicion. No one stirs in Caracas between noon and mid-afternoon unless there is an urgent reason.

The Eagle's pose seemed to drop from him as he relaxed. He was once more plain Jeff Shannon, crack secret agent of G-2, unofficial operative of the F.B.I. He had entered the work with several years of training in the State Department and the code offices. He knew most of the tricks that spies used. He could read ordinary codes almost as easily as he could English and harder ones broke down under his diligent attacks.

Tucked away in his agile mind were facts that would have amazed the instigators of foreign propaganda and sabotage. Jeff Shannon knew many of the more important spies by sight and he had studied their careers intently and with considerable relish. For Jeff Shannon hadn't become the Eagle until he was as well versed in this grisly business as any man alive.

After a reasonable time he removed his clothes and donned those which he had secretly purchased. They closely resembled those worn by these so-called tourists he had observed. With peroxide he made his brown hair a distinct blond shade and let his disguise go at that. To the Eagle, disguise meant more acting a part than making up for it. He could speak German fluently and was certain he would get by.

He waited until late afternoon before he strolled out of the hotel. There was a row of chairs on the spacious porch. One stolid-looking man occupied one of these, sitting apart, obviously lonesome. The Eagle walked over and sat down beside him.

"IT IS a long way to come for a glass of beer, *mein Herr,*" he said sadly. "I do not like this country—the heat and the flies. Nor do I like the lack of discipline here."

"Ach!" the other agreed readily. "It never changes, this barbarian land. Once before I was here, as an engineer supervising the building of a bridge in southern Brazil. It was the most difficult task of my life. I swore I'd never return, and now—"

He spread his hands in despair and gave the Eagle a wan smile. The Eagle showed none of what instantly registered in his brain. Here was a man, typically a tourist, who stated he was an engineer, hated the country and yet returned. Why? Was he under orders?

"It bores me," the Eagle answered in smooth German. "Nothing to do but drink beer and sleep. Is that any life for an honor graduate of Heidelberg? Me—an electrical engineer of renown?"

"I know, I know," the other man answered with a sigh. "I feel the same as you, *mein Herr,* but like you I can do nothing about it. Perhaps we can find comfort in a glass of beer now, eh? At least, they saw fit to import plenty of it—direct from Munich. I am Eric von Maden, and you—"

"Paul Osterode," the Eagle promptly replied. "Let us drink to our meeting."

CHAPTER III

MURDER ORDERS

WALKING ACROSS the street, they headed north and landed in a typical German beer garden. Somewhere, in a back room, a male quartet was singing a German folk song. Pudgy bartenders were scurrying back and forth with beer steins.

With this German at his side, the Eagle felt reasonably secure. His friend was known and the others would accept the Eagle on the basis of his acquaintance with von Maden. They sat down and ordered beer.

Suddenly the buzz of conversation died away. Two men had entered the beer garden and they were certainly not in the favor of the Germans there, who eyed them with open hate. The Eagle recognized one of the newcomers instantly as an Austrian who had fled his country before the barbed wire of a concentration camp could close about him.

"He has his nerve," the Eagle whispered to von Maden, "showing his *Schwein's* face in here. Something should be done about it."

"*Ach*, but this is not Germany. However, I have heard rumors that he nears the end of his rope."

The Eagle felt a twinge of genuine sympathy for this slender, middle-aged refugee. By force of circumstance he had been driven out of his own land and now, even in a foreign country, he was menaced by the same men from whom he had fled.

He glanced idly around as there came a stir at the doorway. Franz Lachner strolled in, acknowledging greetings with nods of approval. The Eagle tensed. For if Lachner studied his features intently enough, there was bound to be trouble and in this obvious hotbed of Nazis it might prove extremely dangerous to the Eagle.

Lachner, moving about among the tables, suddenly spotted the two men who had entered only moments before himself. His face grew red in rage. He clapped the monocle to his eye, strode over to their table and looked down at them.

"There is no room here for you!" he snapped. "Get out!"

The two Austrians merely looked up at him and shrugged.

"This is not Germany, *Herr* Lachner," one of them said blandly. "We have as much right to be here as you, and even though we don't like the people in this café, we do like the beer."

Lachner's right hand rose swiftly to administer a slap. But someone tapped him on the shoulder. A man in a brown tunic and Sam Browne belt saluted, opened his tunic pocket and brought out a sealed envelope, which he handed to Lachner.

The Nazi leader ripped open the flap, read the message, then scrawled something on it and handed it back to the messenger. The messenger started for the door while Lachner turned back to finish his pleasant little interview with the men he considered enemies.

Joan

Twice he slapped the older man across the face. In a flash both Austrians were on their feet. Beer steins began flying. The messenger, on his way out, paused to enjoy the fracas and lend his strident voice in condemnation of the two enemies.

The Eagle had hoped for this. He sidled toward the messenger, holding a stein of beer in his hand. Suddenly he flung the contents of the glass into the messenger's face, raised the stein and slugged him over the head with it.

BECAUSE THIS happened near the exit and everyone else in the room was crowded around the unfortunate refugees, no one noticed it. The Eagle seized the messenger before he slumped to the floor. He extricated the envelope from his pocket, dropped the man into a convenient chair and slipped out of the place.

He walked rapidly across the street, clinging to the shadows of the low buildings, and thanking his luck that it was a dark night. He was climbing the steps to his hotel when the confusion in the beer garden really became serious. Someone had discovered the messenger, slumped over a table.

The Eagle removed his disguise quickly, secreted the clothing and applied a brown stain to his hair. He donned a bathrobe, lit a cigarette and sat down to study the message. It was in a difficult code. He opened his Gladstone bag, looked up to be sure curtains were drawn and the door closed tightly, and from a cleverly hidden pocket removed a code book. He decoded the message rapidly and the import of that note made the Eagle draw a sharp breath. It read:

> To His Excellency *Herr* Franz Lachner:
> Urgent! Plans for stratosphere bomber stolen from War Ministry. Shipped to Caracas care of one James Kirke who may be only a cover address. Investigate! If Kirke is espionage agent, he is to be removed. Obtain plans at all costs. Believe someone will make copy of them, secretly return them and hope they have not been missed. Quick action is imperative.

It was signed by a name that unconsciously brought a chill to the Eagle's spine. For the Gestapo were taking an active part in the set-up here, whatever it was, these many miles from Germany!

The Eagle sprang to his feet. Lachner had okayed the message indicating that its orders would be carried out immediately. Now, with the messenger slugged and the message stolen, Lachner would act fast. The Eagle had no time to lose.

He was almost ready to go into action when he heard authoritative voices demanding entrance to some of the rooms down the hall. He flung off his clothes, donned pajamas and a bathrobe and propped the pillows against the headboard of his bed. He lay down, picked up a newspaper and began reading. The message he had stolen was already ashes and washed down the sink.

Someone banged on his door. He got up, rumpled his hair and opened the door. Two Venezuelan policemen stepped in, followed by *Herr* Lachner and the messenger.

"Señor"—one of the policemen saluted respectfully—"we are sorry for this intrusion, but there has been some trouble. This man"—he waved toward the messenger—"was attacked and a valuable diamond stolen from him."

The Eagle nodded in polite understanding.

"And you search for the robber, of course. You may examine me and my room, señors. I have nothing to hide."

Lachner, standing near the door, eyed the Eagle narrowly, something more than a hint of suspicion flashing in his eyes. The Eagle seemed to see Lachner for the first time. He bowed in his direction.

"Greetings," he said. "You're the man who was upset in the plane, aren't you? Don't tell me that diamond was your property?"

LACHNER SCREWED his monocle in place and bowed stiffly.

"Unfortunately that is so. But of course, *mein Herr,* I do not suspect you. It is only known that the man who committed the robbery originally came from this hotel."

"He is not the man," the messenger broke in. "I am sure of it."

There were more apologies and the quartette bowed themselves out. The Eagle turned quietly back to his bed, slid under the covers and resumed reading. Although his every impulse was to swing into action fast if he wanted to save the life of this James Kirke, he knew better than to give himself away this soon. Lachner would have him watched. The keen, sly mind that was Lachner's had more than guessed at the truth when he had seen Jeff Shannon.

Yet, the Eagle realized that with any delay whatsoever, James Kirke, whoever and whatever he was, might be murdered. The message indicated that the stolen plans concerned a stratosphere ship. That was a tie-up with the mystery plane that had flown over the Panama Canal.

The Eagle swept the covers away, jumped to his feet and transferred a gun from his Gladstone bag to his pocket. Damn the consequences! A man's life was at stake.

He opened the door of his room cautiously, took a quick glance into the corridor and drew back. A burly man was posted near the landing. One of Lachner's men! The Eagle tiptoed over to the window and peered out. It was a dark night and his window overlooked the rear of the hotel. If Lachner had left a guard in the corridor, certainly he must have left one to watch the Eagle's window as well.

Switching out the light he softly raised the window. He would be a perfect target if there were guards out there and they had orders to shoot him, but he had to risk that. But from all he could make out, no one seemed to be watching the rear court.

He ran back to the bed, stripped off the sheets and fashioned them into a rope. Cautiously he let this drop out the window, and waited for a moment. Nothing happened. He swung out the window then and began letting himself down the improvised rope, hand over hand.

Then the Eagle's heart stopped beating for a second. A man was standing just beneath the swinging rope of sheets. He had a gun in his hand and it was aimed straight up, centering the Eagle in its sights. Apparently this spy had been under cover and had wisely bided his time until the Eagle tried a getaway.

The Eagle let himself down a few more notches, certain that the spy was not aware he had been seen. About a dozen feet from the ground, the Eagle let go. Before the astounded spy could yank the trigger of his gun, the Eagle's body struck him. He went down with a crash, but was up again instantly and looking for the gun which had flown out of his grasp.

Instead of the gun he found a lithe young man crouched and ready to spring. The spy was a powerfully built man with stubby, bowed legs, thick arms and big hands that were clenched into fists. He discarded ideas of finding his gun. What harm could this slender opponent inflict? One smash with his big hands and the result would be practically the same as that of a bullet.

HE GROWLED and started a savage rush toward the Eagle. But he kept on going—for the Eagle leaped aside so agilely that the spy had no opportunity to check himself. When he did, there was a fury waiting for him, a fury that rapped a dozen painful blows to his face.

The spy opened his mouth to roar for help. A fist hit him on the throat and changed the roar into a weird bleat. He spread his big arms, leaving himself wide open, but depending on his ability to take it, so he might get close enough to wrap this dancing, feinting devil in a rib-crushing embrace.

The Eagle knew better than to permit this to happen. He slugged a well placed blow to the face and danced back. In a moment he had the spy groggy. Then the Eagle stepped close and finished it with two blows to the face.

As the spy crumpled to the ground, the Eagle raced toward the rear of the court, scaled a fence and reached the street behind his hotel. Now he had to determine who this James Kirke was and where he lived. Lachner would already be on his way after the man.

CHAPTER IV

GIRL WITH COURAGE

JIM KIRKE was bent over a draftsman's desk on which several blueprints were pinned. Tracing paper was fastened in place and he was making a careful copy of the plans before him.

About thirty, he was dark-eyed and chestnut-haired, with a wide forehead and a chin that jutted aggressively. His mother had been a native of Venezuela and from her he derived his dark Latin eyes. His father had been from the United States. It was well after midnight. He rubbed his eyes and yawned. Another hour and he would be finished with one of the most important tasks of his career. Señor Hernandez, head of the Venezuelan Military Intelligence, would be proud of that work.

Behind Jim Kirke, portieres, masking a window, stirred as if a breeze swept them. Then they were parted, slowly, cautiously. Silently as a ghost, Franz Lachner slipped into the room. Monocle screwed tightly to his eye, cane thrust beneath one arm, he reached under his coat and drew a gun. Treading softly he approached Kirke from the rear. He shoved the gun out as the young man turned his head, and Jim Kirke slowly raised both hands.

"You are wise, my friend," Lachner whispered. "A sound out of you and I shall be compelled to blow your head off. Ah, I see you have the plans for our new plane. It was a clever bit of work, getting them, Señor Kirke. Very clever, worthy of my own agents. But your man fumbled a bit and we discovered he had shipped them here. You, as an intelligence agent for the Venezuelan Government, would have reaped a rich reward if you succeeded. Now remain just as you are while I take back the plans."

He unpinned the tracing paper, stuffed it into his pockets. With almost the same motion, he covertly extracted a knife as he placed his cane on the drafting table.

Lachner's lips drew back in a snarl as the knife was upraised, poised for a swift descent. And at that moment Jim Kirke, who had not seen the knife, noticed the shadow thrown across the board. He began to turn his head. The knife came down, but Kirke managed to yell before his voice was abruptly cut off as the blade penetrated his heart.

Like a very tired man his head came down to rest against one crooked arm lying across his drawing board.

Lachner whipped the blueprints from beneath the dead man's body. There was blood on them, but he paid no attention as hastily he rolled the blueprints up. There were others he wanted, and instantly he set to work looking for them. Intent on his search he was suddenly jerked back to actuality by a soft, yet grim voice.

"Don't move! Stand up and raise your hands! I.... Jim! Jim! Oh, what have you done to him? You've killed him! He's dead!"

Lachner swung around slightly and kept his hands high. A beautiful blond girl was standing near him, with a heavy gun in her fist. Moreover she seemed to know how to use it.

Joan Kirke sidestepped to where her brother lay dead. She raised his wrist gently. There was no pulse. She faced Lachner again.

"You filthy, murderous spy," she accused, her voice choked with emotion. "You killed my brother—knifed him in the back! We have firing squads down here for men like you. Keep your hands raised and don't move! I'm going to call the commandant!"

LACHNER GULPED. To be beaten at all was bad, but to be outwitted by a mere girl would make him a fool in the eyes of his followers. Then Lachner's worries ceased. For another man was creeping into the room—one of his own men, a man with closely cropped hair and thick lips drawn back in a silent snarl.

Joan seemed to sense her danger. She whirled around, but too late. The apelike invader made a flying leap toward her and Lachner instantly galvanized into action. The gun was wrested from Joan's hand. Her senses reeled as Lachner slapped her across the face. She clutched at the edge of the desk for support, but did not scream.

"*Ach,*" Lachner grated, "you came in time, Otto, but after this you will work even faster. Another moment and this little fool might have shot me."

"If I only had!" Joan groaned. "If I only had!"

Lachner studied her a moment and shook his head sadly.

"It is too bad that one so lovely and young must die. But you would report me to the commandant and have me arrested."

Lachner drew a gun from his pocket, snapped back to the mechanism. Joan turned deathly pale. It was coming! She would have no more chance than Jim. In a moment this gun would roar and she'd join her brother in death.

The gun leveled and Lachner showed his teeth in an evil leer. His finger tightened on the trigger. Then the one light in the room went out and an instant later a gun roared. Lachner's hissing breath turned into a scream of pain. His gun flew from his grasp as his hand went numb and dead.

The other spy saw a shadowy form near the door, shouted a guttural challenge and swept forward with knife upraised. But that shadowy form moved so fast it seemed to possess wings. The spy ran straight into a right jab. It smacked against his jaw with a bone-breaking sound. The spy called Otto crumpled and fell to the floor.

Taking advantage of this moment, Lachner spun around and raced for the open window through which he had gained entrance. He dived through it headlong, landed on the dirt outside. But he scrambled to his feet quickly and vanished into the night, leaving a trail of blood from his wounded right hand.

Back in the house, Joan stood tense, waiting for the final outcome. She couldn't see the man who had saved her life, but she could hear him bending over the spy he had knocked cold. Finally he straightened up, walked over near the door and turned on the light.

Lachner

"Hello," he said pleasantly. "Looks like I showed up just in time."

Joan couldn't hold back the tears any longer. The Eagle, glancing beyond her, saw the knife protruding from Jim Kirke's back.

"No," he said gently. "I was too late. Much too late. I'm—terribly sorry."

Joan fought back her tears.

"Who are you?" she demanded. "Why do you say you were too late? Did you know this was going to happen?"

The Eagle nodded somberly. "I knew—and I came as swiftly as I could, but *Herr* Lachner beat me to it. He"—he nodded toward the dead Kirke—"was your brother, wasn't he?"

SHE NODDED, mutely. The Eagle walked over to the corpse and made a quick examination. Then he eyed the spy, groaning on the floor. He bent down and administered another punch. The spy went limp again.

"Miss Kirke"—he led her to another room and helped her onto a davenport—"I know you're brave enough to face facts. This is war—if you haven't already guessed it. We're fighting an organised band of spies who stop at nothing to gain their own rotten ends. Killing your brother wasn't necessary. All they wanted were those plans which your brother was trying to copy in order to counteract the deadly uses to which they would have been put. Now they'll try to kill you—before you can get any action out of the local authorities."

"I can get action," Joan said spiritedly. "You have even named the man who killed my brother. I'll identify him, and I know his fate."

The Eagle sighed. "Yes, I know too. A brick wall at dawn—if you can prove it. But Miss Kirke, you must admit that I saved your life and that you owe me a favor."

She looked up at him. Somehow she trusted this clear-eyed young man.

"Go ahead. I'm listening."

"Then forget about Lachner. If he is removed, there will only be a lot of trouble between your country and his. And you would find it difficult proving your case against him. So why not let this gorilla I knocked out take the blame? Say he killed your brother. He's just as responsible, being here with Lachner. Lachner won't dare interfere."

Joan Kirke's eyes blazed. "You're trying to help Lachner out of this. You're a friend of his."

"No, no!" the Eagle insisted. "Lachner would rather see me cooling off in a morgue than anything else I might think of. He hates me as much as I detest him and his kind. But if Lachner is put away, there will only be another to take his place. Plans might be altered. We wouldn't know just where we stood. With Lachner working more or less openly as he does, we have a chance to get him—right. There are other lives than your brother's which are menaced, Miss Kirke."

Joan Kirke raised her head. "I don't know who you are, but you wouldn't have shot that—that devil and half killed his hireling if you weren't on Jim's side of the fence. I trust you."

"Thanks," the Eagle said softly. "My name is Jeff Shannon. Your brother was a counter-espionage agent for Venezuela. I have a similar job for the United States. You and I fight for the side we think is right. That happens to be the exact opposite of Franz Lachner's ideas. You knew your brother operated against Lachner and his kind. He must have told you something. Can't you help me—in any way?"

"Yes, I'll help you, Jeff Shannon. But I must report my brother's murder to the police. And Señor Hernandez is entitled to an explanation—the whole truth for him, Jeff Shannon. You will have nothing to fear. The United States and Venezuela are friendly and cooperative."

The Eagle nodded. "Very well. But only Señor Hernandez—and swear him to secrecy. Now—had your brother learned anything significant?"

She leaned toward the Eagle, in her eagerness forgetting everything else for the moment except his question.

"THE PLANS for this stratosphere bomber," she whispered. "Copies were sent from Caracas to the War Ministry in Berlin. Jim said they had been traced on paper made in Venezuela and were original plans. Therefore they must have been drawn here. That's all I know. Jim didn't tell me too much. But wait—there is something else. Jim was busy watching these German tourists who have come to Caracas lately. I know he was suspicious of them. There is an old yacht club a mile above the harbor. Jim was watching that. He said many of the tourists went there and that shortly after they sailed away."

The Eagle held her soft hands for a moment and looked straight into her eyes.

"Hernandez will wonder just who Jeff Shannon is. Tell him he is—the Eagle! I think then he will gladly follow my request for Lachner not to be arrested, nor the civil police told of what actually happened here. Meanwhile, be very careful. Lachner knows you can identify him and he'll not stop at another murder. Contact Hernandez, turn this spy on the floor over to him and then let no one in the house. I'll try to return as soon as possible."

He smiled at her understandingly and was gone. The Eagle's mind was spinning. Somehow these German tourists, these mystery plans for a stratosphere ship and an abandoned yacht clubhouse tied together. Somewhere in that maze lay the clue to the whereabouts of the missing G-2 agents.

And there was more; much more. The plans for that ship had been developed in Venezuela. Perhaps actual ships had been built and tested. But where? Not in Caracas or any of the surrounding towns. Airplane manufacture always requires a great deal of space.

The tourists! The Eagle's mind clicked. It takes skilled technicians to build and plan airplanes. The German, von Maden, was an engineer. The Eagle recalled other tourists he had observed. They all seemed to be of a high type of intelligence. Most of them wore glasses which undoubtedly indicated close, detailed work. They had no women or children with them. Were they here to take part in the buildup of some gigantic and secret war machine? Did they really sail away?

Joan sat immobile for perhaps three minutes after the Eagle's departure. She was alone now—with her dead brother and a spy who was still out of the picture. But Joan was afraid no longer. In her eyes were smoldering fires. Her small hands clenched. She arose and went to the telephone.

CHAPTER V

CHECKMATE

THE EAGLE slipped back through the darkness, watchful lest Lachner had left spies to strike from cover. But he was not disturbed.

As he reached the more important streets of the city, he heard sirens and knew that Joan Kirke had reported the murder. His thoughts were centered on her during his walk back to the hotel. He had never met a girl like her; a girl who could face facts and still retain her composure so well.

The hotel lobby was deserted. A sleepy desk clerk and a bell-hop looked up and relaxed again when they recognized him as a guest. He walked up the stairs, turned into the corridor leading to his room and there he paused. From beneath his door came a sudden flash of light.

The Eagle drew his gun, snapped the safety off and walked gently toward the door. He didn't open it. Perhaps Lachner himself was there, with a horde of his spies, setting a death trap.

The Eagle listened intently. His room and his possessions were being given a complete frisk all right. Lachner had certainly wasted no time. But the Eagle knew there was nothing among his possessions to indicate that he was an operative of the United States G-2. The Eagle rarely carried identification, depending on his wits to get him out of difficulties.

He backed away slowly, keeping his gun ready for action. There was a supply closet halfway down the corridor and he made his way toward it. The door was not locked and he stepped inside, leaving the door open a crack.

Twenty minutes went by, then three men emerged from his room. By the disappointment evident on their faces he knew that they had discovered nothing significant. They hurried along the corridor, passed within three feet of the Eagle and turned down the stairway.

The Eagle went in careful pursuit. When the spies reached the street, he watched them through the windows of the lobby. They started off, walking fast, choosing the darkest portion of the street to shield them from observation. Although the last of the trio kept looking over his shoulder, he saw no signs of pursuit for, although the Eagle was already on their tracks, he was a master at the art of shadowing.

They turned into a path leading to the rambling front porch of a big mansionlike house. Apparently there was some kind of a warning signal or a guard posted at some inconspicuous place, for the three were instantly admitted without knocking.

From a place of vantage across the street the Eagle estimated his chances of getting inside this spy's nest. It was bound to be a dangerous procedure, but that was no deterrent to the Eagle. He lived for danger.

Transferring his gun to a side coat pocket, he stole through the yard of a deserted house next door. He ducked as a dark form loomed up and a man dressed in uniform, with a gun strapped to his hip, strolled by. A guard! There would be plenty of these without question.

As noiselessly as a cat, he prowled the estate, selecting a means of entering the house. Once a flashlight split the darkness as a guard made a routine inspection of the premises. But satisfied that everything was peaceful, the guard turned back to the house, walked over to a side door and without using a key, entered. The Eagle grinned.

He reached the same door after ten minutes had elapsed. It opened under his touch and he found himself in a small hallway from which stairs led to the floor above. He tiptoed toward them. It was better to be certain that Lachner and his aides were in bed before he began an extensive search of the offices and files.

AT THE head of the stairs the Eagle paused to listen. He heard gruff voices below on the other side of the landing where the main stairway was. Crouching behind the balustrade, he observed Lachner and two aides emerge from a room, line up and formally salute. A fourth man came out, nodded pompously and headed for the main stairway. He turned around just before he started up and saluted.

"Heil," he said with a cold smile.

"You have done well, *Herr* Lachner. The Ministry of War will be pleased."

"Thank you," Lachner bowed low before this man. "The Baron Wesener is very kind. And mark you, this is but the beginning, Your Excellency. Before we are done, this continent will tremble beneath our wrath."

The pompous man addressed as Baron Wesener nodded, saluted once more and clicked his heels. Then he started up the steps.

It had hit the Eagle like a blow in the face when he heard this man's name. Baron Wesener! High in the Nazi War Office, a confidante of generals and statesmen. His presence alone attested to the importance which the War Ministry placed on this mysterious South American adventure.

The Eagle cautiously tried a door, found it open and stepped into a bedroom. A huge swastika was suspended from the wall over the massive bed. This, then, was probably the guest room and the baron was more than likely headed for it. The Eagle walked softly toward the door, flattened himself beside it and when it swung open, he was concealed from view.

Baron Wesener slammed it shut without looking around, sat down and began drawing off his military boots. Suddenly he jerked erect, for the muzzle of a gun was pressed against the back of his fat neck. A voice, low and ominous gave him orders.

"The baron would be wise and remain healthy if he does as I say. Stand up, walk over to that wall and keep facing it! The slightest deviation from my orders will mean death."

The baron's excess fat began to quiver. These men were all alike, the Eagle thought swiftly. The more power they held, the more pompous they became and the more they feared death or violence themselves. This Baron Wesener was a downright coward.

The Eagle smiled as he stepped over to the bed, dragged off a sheet and began tearing it into strips. With the strips he bound the baron tightly, gagged him and then pushed him into a chair, binding him to it.

"The baron shows more wisdom than his outward appearance indicates," the Eagle said with a chuckle. "You have saved your own life. Now I must warn you that if you make any noise I'll be forced to come back and kick your fat face in."

The frightened look on the baron's face indicated a numb submissiveness and the Eagle quietly left the room. He went down the corridor to the front entrance.

The house was plunged into darkness now, but a man stood watch at the front door. Not for an instant did he avert his gaze from the tiny window that overlooked the path. Getting him was a simple matter. The Eagle used the butt of his gun and caught the man before he crashed to the floor.

NEXT HE sought out the room from which the baron and Lachner had emerged. It was dark, but he first pulled down all curtains, boldly turned on the lights and looked around. Files lined two walls, and there was a built-in bookcase crammed with volumes pertaining to the science of war. He glanced into some of the files and grunted. They were careful dossiers concerning every important South American official.

Then the Eagle found his first significant clue. A map, folded and somewhat worn, was in one of the filing cabinets. He spread this on the desk and studied it intently. It showed various routes to the mountains. Trails were outlined clearly, distances that could be traveled by car were indicated and spots marked to show where the rest of the journey must be made afoot. One circled spot was labeled "Colonia Tovar."

It outlined certain guard posts. And there was something else. A line had been drawn due north of the circled spot and part of the shores of Lake Maracaibo had been outlined. An attempt had been made to remove all signs of this supplementary map. It meant something, but the Eagle could not figure out just what.

He wanted to examine this house and leave it without making his presence known. Therefore he refolded the map, placed it back in the filing cabinet, then moved toward the big flat-topped desk in a far corner of the room. To reach the drawers he had to pass between a small cabinet that looked like a radio, and a huge wall safe—and the instant he passed by, he sensed that he had cut an infra-red alarm signal ray.

A guard at the rear of the house gave a lusty shout, whipped out his gun and ran toward the front hall. He saw his colleague slumped unconscious on the floor and shouted this news.

The Eagle raced to the big windows, pulled aside the curtain and swore softly. Two men armed with rifles were parked outside. Apparently Lachner had given explicit orders as to just what should be done if this alarm signal went off.

The Eagle thought quickly, and acted even more swiftly. There was a small door at one end of the room which led, he figured, to the narrow corridor off the side hallway. He raced toward it, and in a moment was silently creeping up the side stairway.

There was confusion below a few minutes later as the Eagle, chuckling, stole back down the side stairs and slid through the small door he had used shortly before. He heard Lachner hurrying down the main stairs. He was shouting orders on his way.

"Perhaps it's that fool of an American! I have been suspicious of him. Guard every door and window. Paul, you come with me—and keep your gun ready. If you see this man, stop him, but do not shoot to kill. I want a talk with him before he dies."

Lachner was halfway down the hall when a cheerful voice called out to him from the living room.

"Hey, Lachner, why don't you come in? I'm getting impatient."

Lachner growled an oath, signaled his men and they closed in on the door. Two of them leaped into the room, rifles poised. Lachner, certain

"Don't move—stand where you are and raise your hands."

that he was now well protected, drew himself erect and strode importantly into his own living room. He stopped in sheer astonishment at what he saw.

BEHIND HIS own desk, which no one beside himself could occupy under orders of severe punishment, sat the slender young American. Lachner's box of privately blended cigars was open and he saw at a glance that the intruder had not only lighted one, but had also stuffed his vest pocket full of them.

"Not bad, Lachner." The Eagle surveyed the glowing tip of his cigar. "After I smoke a few of these, I might actually get to like them. Come on in. Sit down. Or don't you know how to receive a guest?"

Lachner's eyes blazed as he rapped out a string of Teutonic oaths. Clenching his hand into a hard fist he strode toward the desk. Two of his men kept the Eagle covered.

"Now, now," the Eagle derided, "you're surely not thinking of starting a fight, Lachner. A man of your age, and with your physique ought to consider the consequences. I'm betting a good sock over the kidneys would put you under. Too much beer, that's what."

"You—you—" Lachner found his voice finally. "You insufferable pig! Get out of my chair! Get away from my desk—or shall I have my men kill you immediately?"

The Eagle shrugged. "It wouldn't do your rug any good and if your marksmen should miss, they'd only bore holes in that nice paneling on the wall behind me. Please sit down, *Herr* Lachner. I've only come for a chat."

"You have come to spy!" Lachner roared. "To steal! To murder me while I slept. You are nothing but a common thief—a murderer."

The Eagle raised his hand languidly and pointed to Lachner's bandaged right hand.

"Mosquito bite, *Herr* Lachner? Or perhaps a bit of lead poisoning? Did you refer to me as a thief and a murderer? I haven't killed anyone— yet. Nor have I stolen. Can you say the same?"

Lachner turned pale, then crimson. He motioned his two guards to stand back, stepped toward the desk and, scowling heavily, sat down on the edge of a chair facing it. The Eagle puffed leisurely on his cigar, shoved his chair back a few inches and propped his feet on the highly polished surface of the desk.

"Shoot, Lachner," he drawled. "Oh, no? Not the guns now, eh? That comes later, doesn't it? You wanted to talk to me about something I heard you say. Well, here we are all nice and cozy. You've got perhaps twenty or thirty armed men to see that I don't harm you"—he grinned dryly—"I've got a little ace in the hole to see that they don't harm me. So why not talk calmly and without antagonism? You wish to learn things from me, I'd like to ask you a few questions."

"Who are you?" Lachner growled. "What are you doing in my house? I have a legal right to shoot you."

The Eagle waved a deprecating finger. "But you wouldn't, *Herr* Lachner. Because if you killed me, there would be complications. Oh, very serious complications. No—don't bother to interrupt me. I'm not referring to what the local authorities might try to do to you. I'm thinking of Berlin and the War Ministry. They wouldn't like it if Baron Wesener suddenly vanished while he was on a tour of inspection and a guest in your own home."

Lachner jumped to his feet. He spun around and howled orders. They were relayed to other men posted in the hallway. Heavy feet pounded up the stairway. A voice yelled back the news. The Baron Wesener was gone!

LACHNER WALKED over to the desk and slammed his fist down on it.

"*Schwein!*" he raged. "You shall die for this! What have you done with the baron?"

The Eagle flicked off a good-sized chunk of ash on the rug, returned the cigar to his mouth and grinned contentedly.

"He's safe, for the present, Lachner. And mind who you call 'pig' even in your own language. I've a sensitive soul and I might— Well, it's highly possible the baron won't return. Do you gather my meaning? Now be good enough to send your trained gorillas out of the room so we can talk in private."

Lachner's eyes burned into the Eagle. His lips worked and his hands clenched and unclenched as he tried desperately to stifle his rage. He studied this insolent young man for a moment, then gave the orders for his guards to withdraw. Although this young puppy's words were careless and light, although he taunted Lachner, the Nazi leader had a glimpse of the intruder's eyes. They carried no mirth in them and they made Lachner shiver slightly.

"That's much better," the Eagle said. "Now *Herr* Lachner, there isn't much I mean to ask you because you'd only answer me with a mess of lies. I'll simply tell you a few things. You and your men are trying to build up an empire in South America. An empire ruled by might and violence. In the event of another major conflict you hope to paralyze all industry down here, prevent Brazil from shipping out her very necessary raw materials which will be so useful for your enemies. You hope to bribe and murder your way to a real power in South America. There can be no other reason for your presence here. Well—you can't do it. Hear me? You can't, because I'll stop you."

"You will stop me!" Lachner thundered. "You insignificant puppy! With a flick of my finger I can have you exterminated."

The Eagle laughed heartily. "True—quite true—but you forget the baron. No one but myself knows where he is and if I shouldn't return to him, he'd starve to death. I wouldn't want to be in your shoes if that happened. Let's see…. They call them concentration camps in your country, don't they? In medieval days they had a far more vivid name for them. Torture rooms! Well, we've had our little chat I think I'll be on my way.

"Oh yes, you want to know where the baron is, don't you? Here's what we'll do. You send one of your best men with me. Mind you, he mustn't be armed or I won't like it. He can drop me off at the hotel and I'll give him a written message as to where you will find His Excellency."

"Bah!" Lachner roared. "Am I fool enough to agree to a proposition like that? You would betray me the moment you were out of this house. No! You will tell me first or I shall take care of you. You cannot get out of here."

"And the baron can't get out of where he is. We're stalemated, Lachner. You've got to trust me and you may be sure I will keep my word. Now—shall we go?"

THE BEARDED German arose and bowed stiffly.

"Very well," he snapped. "It seems that you have outwitted me for the moment. I believe that you will return His Excellency to me, for if you do not there is no way to escape my vengeance. We shall call it, as you say, a draw."

The Eagle rubbed his chin, grinned and put on his hat.

"Of course, *Herr* Lachner. And I hope you will heed my warning because you'll be carefully watched from now on. The slightest show of violence in either Caracas or any other South American city will bring quick punishment directly on your shoulders. You're not fooling me, you know. I've guessed your little game."

Lachner's lips compressed. He screwed his monocle into place, bowed and clicked his heels again. Then, with a gracious sweep of his hand, he escorted the Eagle to the front door. He assigned one man to accompany him.

CHAPTER VI

LACHNER'S TRICK

S TEPPING OUT into the night, the Eagle shoved his hat to the back of his head and whistled blithely as he strode down the street. His guard remained close to him.

Lachner watched them vanish into the night and smiled contemptuously.

"*Ach*, a clever young one but impetuous. Like other enemy agents he has jumped to the conclusion that I am here to establish myself as a dictator. How foolish unless…. *Herr Gott*, if he has but seen that map!"

Lachner rushed back into the living room, yanked open the filing cabinet and drew a long breath of relief. His map was still there and untouched as far as he could see.

Twenty minutes later the Eagle's escort returned, panting from his fast run. He handed Lachner a sealed envelope, saluted and withdrew discreetly. Lachner ripped open the flap and read the message. There was a prominent vein in his forehead that throbbed out the beat of his heart when he was aroused. It beat so fast now that Lachner felt dizzy as he read:

My dear *Herr* Lachner:
You will find His Excellency rather uncomfortably situated in the closet of his own room with some dirty clothes covering him. I might have taken him away to a safer spot, but he carries around far too much lard to make such a move practical. Why in thunder don't you German agents go on a diet?

That was enough to make Lachner turn gray with rage, but the signature brought rasping oaths to his lips.

"The Eagle!" he roared. "So he *was* the Eagle! Here—in my very hands and I let him go! But before morning the Eagle will be safe. Otto—Paul—upstairs with you. His Excellency is confined to the clothes closet of his own room. If you were not such dunderheads, you would have searched it carefully. You will pay for your carelessness. Go!"

It had been only a short time before that when Jeff Shannon had waved Lachner's agent-guard out of his hotel room, sat down and laughed until tears rolled down his cheeks. It did his soul good to bring these overbearing, lordly officers down a peg or two. He was remembering Lachner's face. It had been the most ludicrous puzzle that the Eagle had seen in years.

But the Eagle didn't discount Lachner's wily nature. The German agent would attempt something else—and soon. Before that occurred, the Eagle had to know certain things. There were those tourists, for instance. More and more he realized that they were anything but what they seemed.

Then the mystery plane and those plans. Somewhere there had to be a spot where the forces of this undercover war could operate. He recalled the map in Lachner's files. Eagerly he extracted a detailed map of Venezuela from his own briefcase.

He located the section which had been outlined on Lachner's map and his finger pointed to a town with a name all out of proportion to South America. Colonia Tovar. Tovar was the name of an old and respected German family. Then it came to him. Of course, the lost colony! He had heard it mentioned before, often, but it had slipped his mind.

THERE WERE footnotes with the map and he checked these. The full history of the mountain colony was given. Four generations ago it had been settled by a small German colonist group and since then, by isolation and self-imposed laws, it had remained a true German colony. The descendants of the original settlers were as completely German as the most Teutonic inhabitant of Berlin.

Their customs were retained, the language and the religion.

"Germany is where Germans are," the Eagle murmured softly. "That is the theme song of the Nazi. Therefore, it's possible they have invaded this mountain colony and set up their machinery for war at that spot."

The Eagle went down to the desk. The night clerk was still dozing, but the single bellboy was busy somewhere. For fifteen minutes the Eagle asked questions.

"*Si*, Señor, it is known as the lost colony," the clerk agreed. "Always we have known of it. The people—they are law abiding and good people. They raise their own crops and live completely alone. There never has been any trouble."

The Eagle was covertly glancing over the desk clerk's shoulder. In the mail slots, he noticed a letter with a German stamp affixed to it. The number of the room was that of the one occupied by one Marenbach, a tourist.

Gazing thoughtfully at a huge map which the desk clerk had spread out, the Eagle pretended he could not see it well. The clerk invited him behind the desk. As he passed by the mail slot, the Eagle's hand flicked out and transferred the letter to his pocket.

Half an hour later, in the security of his room, he worked feverishly over the letter. To all appearances it was nothing but a letter from home and signed, "Your faithful wife, Magda."

Yet that letter intrigued the Eagle. He suspected there was far more to it than appeared on the surface. In the first place it was much too patronizing to be a letter from a wife to her husband. Codes didn't help him any and by checking letter frequencies he determined that it was not code. Therefore the only other alternative solution was that of invisible ink. But heat brought no reaction; nor did acid or alkali help.

The Eagle rubbed his chin thoughtfully, then snapped his fingers, and slipped into his coat and hastily removed his shoes. He opened the door, watchful for any more guards whom Lachner might have sent. Certain he was unobserved, he crept down the corridor, climbed two flights of stairs and stood before *Herr* Marenbach's room. The door was locked and the key in place.

The Eagle used the small blade of a penknife to worry the key loose. He quietly slid a newspaper under the door, forced the key out of the lock and held his breath until he felt certain that Marenbach's rhythmic breathing indicated that he had heard nothing. He pulled the key under the door, grinned a little and had the door unlocked in half a minute.

Grasping his gun by the muzzle he was prepared to use it as a blackjack if *Herr* Marenbach awakened. Swiftly he turned his attention to Marenbach's clothing. He studied the light gray suit, the white shoes and the white cork helmet.

There was one item of startling contrast. In the breast pocket of the coat was a somber black handkerchief. The Eagle wet his thumb, pressed it against the handkerchief and found that his finger was smudged. Stuffing the handkerchief into his pocket he quietly left the room.

BACK IN his own quarters, he quickly drew a basin full of tepid water, thrust the black handkerchief into it and watched the dye run out until the water became black. He dipped the letter into this solution, shook off the excess water, then studied it carefully. The Eagle's knowledge of spy tricks served him well. The dye in the handkerchief was the reagent which brought out the secret writing.

What he found was a map and a few instructions. The map made him whistle softly in surprise. It indicated the trails to the lost colony and showed that Marenbach, an engineer, was expected to smooth out several barely negotiable passageways.

The instructions indicated that Marenbach was to report to his ship before midnight the following day and be prepared to assume his duties at once.

The Eagle glanced at his watch. Four a.m. He was worried about Joan Kirke. Lachner was quite likely to strike through her. And the Eagle felt that she knew more than she had told him. More than that he found that he actually wanted to see her, even if the visit had no significance so far as his work was concerned.

He guessed she would not be asleep—not after all that had happened. Swiftly donning his clothing, he slid his gun into his pocket and walked out of the hotel. But he had no more than reached the street when he skidded to a halt. Six armed men of the Venezuelan Night Patrol, led by a slender young lieutenant, spread out to encompass him. Rifles were turned his way.

"*Buenos noches,* Señor." The lieutenant touched the peak of his cap. "You are in a great hurry, *si?* Perhaps you will tell us your name."

"Why not? Jeff Shannon—from the United States. I've some urgent business—"

The lieutenant clapped a hand on the Eagle's shoulder.

"I am very sorry, Señor. You are under arrest for the murder of James Kirke. You were observed emerging from his home and the man whom Señorita Kirke accused of killing her brother has confessed all. You paid him to assist you in the murder so you might steal certain valuables," the officer told him politely.

Stunned, the Eagle offered no resistance. Here was Franz Lachner's fine hand. Cleverly he had fashioned a trap that would take care of the Eagle for an indefinite period of time. There would be a lot of red tape before he could extricate himself.

It was painfully clear how it had been done. Lachner had simply sent the imprisoned man a message that he should accuse Jeff Shannon of being his mentor. Witnesses had been provided to swear they saw Shannon emerge from the house.

Of course Joan Kirke could help clear him by her testimony. But was she available? This open-handed method of sidetracking the Eagle indicated that she might have been kidnaped—even murdered.

The Eagle was aware that the lieutenant was still talking. He jerked back to reality.

"You will come along quietly, Señor. Precede me, please."

The Eagle barely restrained the groan that sought to escape his lips. Lachner had certainly worked fast. His own spy, the man whom Joan had caused to be arrested, would swear that Jeff Shannon hired him. The Eagle knew that eventually he could squirm out of this mess, but he would have to reveal everything he knew. And meanwhile Lachner would carry out his schemes. Joan would undoubtedly be menaced.

THE EAGLE shrugged. His shoulders sagged in a gesture of resignation. He turned slowly and took about four steps. Then, as the six-man patrol assembled itself, he whirled on the lieutenant, seized him around the waist and yanked his gun from its holster, jabbing the lieutenant in the spine with the weapon.

"Sorry, Señor. If one of your men even raises his rifle, I shall be forced to kill you. Back up slowly, keep in step with me. Obey and you will not be harmed."

The lieutenant realized the futility of resistance. All his men were in front. If they began shooting, their bullets would strike him first and the menace of that gun digging into his ribs spelled death as certain as the next dawn.

Slowly the two men moved back until they reached the mouth of the dismal alley running beside the hotel. There the Eagle neatly tripped his prisoner, wheeled and raced away in the darkness. A few shots were fired, but the bullets missed by a mile. He passed through several yards, keeping his nose pointed toward Joan's home. The Venezuelan authorities would never think of looking for him there, and he had to see Joan.

When he reached the house, he found it dark and the front door locked. For a moment his heart skipped a beat. Then he reassured himself. Joan was probably on her way to the garrison to be ready to identify the murderer of her brother.

The Eagle sped around the side of the house, kicked in a cellar window and slid through it. Gun in hand, he made his stealthy way to the upper floor. The silence of a tomb greeted him. He located Joan's room, turned on the lights for a fraction of a second and let loose an audible groan.

Silent evidence pointed to a quick departure. Whether it was forced or voluntary he did not know, but he did know that no matter what Joan did or where she went, Lachner's spies would be on the watch for her.

The Eagle sat down heavily and for the first time in many months felt the depths of actual despair. Finally he forced himself back to some semblance of calmness. He had work to do. Important work! From the look on Lachner's face he had fooled him completely. Lachner thought that the Eagle had assumed, as had everyone else, that his activities were confined to Caracas and the coast line.

But the Eagle knew he must somehow reach that lost colony and do it quickly—before Lachner turned loose his dogs of war. All thoughts of Joan must be thrust aside ruthlessly. Thousands of lives were at stake, the happiness and prosperity of millions. No matter how he felt toward this girl, whom he had known but a few hours, he had to carry on. And to do this he required rest.

The Eagle walked over to the bed and flung himself down on it. In three minutes he was fast asleep.

CHAPTER VII

FOUR IN DANGER

WHEN LATE morning sunlight awakened the Eagle, he sprang up with an angry imprecation at himself for oversleeping. Then he settled down to do some clear thinking.

He couldn't venture out in broad daylight for every *alguacil* in Caracas would be looking for him. He was positive now that Joan had vanished and could be of no help in establishing his innocence. He simply could not permit himself to be arrested.

Downstairs he found food and ate it mechanically. He spent the afternoon outlining his plans until they took a definite form in his mind. They involved danger and they undoubtedly would take him away from the place to which Joan had been taken, but with the Eagle, duty came before all else.

He waited until well after darkness before he ventured out and then kept to the quieter streets, tensed for a quick race to safety if an *alguacil*—a policeman—spotted him. He reached the center of the city finally and stole toward the rear of the German beer garden where the fake tourists passed their time.

Several of the so-called tourists were being feted in a back room. The Eagle saw them arise suddenly and raise their glasses in a salute. *Herr* Marenbach seemed to be the guest of honor. So! Then somebody in command evidently was sending Marenbach to assume his duties even though the German had not received official word from Germany. Perhaps they believed the letter had been delayed.

The German bowed himself out the door half an hour later and headed due north along the waterfront. As he progressed, the German seemed to grow more wary and the Eagle discovered his task of shadowing difficult.

Then abruptly, he recalled Joan's story of the mysterious yacht club. Marenbach was heading there! As all the other pseudo tourists did, just before they sailed.

The Eagle darted to the right, made his way over silent streets and kept his eyes open for patrols. For he had the Caracas authorities as well as Lachner to worry about. Then he saw his destination, a low, apparently deserted club.

But was it deserted? The Eagle heard the faint slapping of muffled oars. He dropped to his stomach, wriggled over to a bank and gazed down at the beach. Two dories, loaded to the gunwales with boxes of heavy goods, were being rowed ashore. Men were waiting and the cargo was quickly transferred to a truck. As it rumbled away, the Eagle saw *Herr* Marenbach loom into sight.

Two men stepped out of the darkness, guns in hand and Marenbach stood stockstill while they searched him. He showed them certain papers and was passed on, to vanish into the darkened clubhouse. An eagerness to see the inside of that place gripped the Eagle and only by an effort did he resist the impulse to invade it. Because he realized that if Marenbach got away now, he would have to begin all over again.

The German emerged after almost an hour. He looked around carefully as if he had been warned to watch himself, then hurried back to town. But behind him stalked an unseen Nemesis—the Eagle.

A little later when Marenbach, armed with identification papers and his traveling bags emerged from the hotel, he headed straight for the waterfront. As he passed a narrow, dark street, he felt a light tap on his shoulder. He turned and a fist rammed straight against his jaw. Without a sound the German collapsed.

Working with frantic speed, the Eagle carried him into a deserted shack and rapidly divested the man of his clothing. He donned this, but realized there was no time for further disguise.

WHATEVER HAPPENED now rested with Lady Luck. He tied the German securely, gagged him and left him in the shallow cellar below the shanty. It would probably be hours before he was discovered.

Examining the stolen identification papers, the Eagle saw that they were in order, and hurried toward the pier. A fast launch was waiting. He stepped into it, merely nodded to the officer in charge and stood at the prow as he was carried out to the harbor where a liner was anchored. Venezuelan officials, at the dock, had passed him without a glance. His papers were enough.

The ship's captain met him on deck, saluted respectfully and assigned him to a cabin.

"At two o'clock, *Herr* Marenbach, you will go aboard a dory and be rowed back to shore," he informed. "A car will await you for transportation to the airport. By morning you will be at your destination."

The Eagle paced the narrow quarters assigned him. If Lachner or any of his aides should by any chance arrive with further instructions before time for the ship to sail everything was lost. It was an unaccustomed feeling—and uncomfortable—but the Eagle was nervous, apprehensive.

Aboard ship preparations were being made for a quick sailing. Then, shortly before two in the morning, a knock on the door informed the Eagle that he was to get ready at once.

Ten minutes later he was being rowed ashore by two husky men who said nothing to him. A car picked him up at a broken-down old pier, whisked him through the city, through a narrow lane among trees and let him out in a small clearing beside a transport plane that was poised at the end of a runway for a quick take-off.

The place did not seem to be an ordinary landing field. It was well away from the city, cleverly hidden by surrounding thickets. Men were busy piling crates of goods into the plane and the Eagle discovered he was the sole passenger.

Things were going almost too smoothly. During the flight over the mountains, the Eagle kept thinking of Joan Kirke. Where had she gone? Was she in Lachner's hands, a prisoner?

Then, with the dawn, the Eagle had his first glimpse of the lost colony. Nestled among the valleys of the Andes it looked like a slice of southwestern Germany. It was a quaint and apparently flourishing place. A landing field had been recently cleared away and the plane was circling toward it. The pilot nosed her down, rolled across the field and came to a stop.

Instantly a dozen men in black uniforms appeared. The Eagle, watching them through a window, gaped in astonishment. They were Gestapo agents, operating openly here. They swaggered with each step, bustled other people out of their path and quickly surrounded the ship.

The Eagle stepped out, holding his breath. Lachner must have some means of contacting this colony, he was thinking, and if the real *Herr* Marenbach had gained his freedom, Lachner would have a grim reception prepared for the Eagle.

But there were only salutes and low-voiced instructions from the rotund leader of the Gestapo.

"The freedom of the village is yours, *Herr* Marenbach, but you will hold yourself ready for further orders," he said crisply. "You know what there is to do and we can lose no time. Until you are summoned then—"

He stepped back and saluted. The Eagle returned the gesture, and began hating that stiff-armed thrust of obedience to a cause he detested.

BUT THEY had taken him at face value. He was free for the time being, though he realized it would not be for long. Meanwhile, though, if he could locate their ammunition plants, their plane assembling factories, he would at least have something to report.

Glancing over his shoulder he saw that the plane which had flown him here was rapidly being unloaded. One box fell from the hands of a worker. It cracked open and the Eagle had a glimpse of an airplane motor part. Then the Gestapo, surrounding the ship, closed in. The laborer was unmercifully beaten before he was driven back to his work.

"This," the Eagle told himself, "would be a bad place to be trapped. Those Gestapo look as though they miss roughing up people—and would they go to town on me."

He strolled through the village, amazed at the exact replicas of German cottages. The people even dressed as German farmers. They were a proud, clear-eyed, blond race, but the Eagle detected signs of covert fear in the women and in some of the men. He began to think that perhaps they resented this invasion of their Fatherland replica in a new world.

Then it was that the Eagle received one of the greatest shocks of his career. As he passed by a small market place, a girl sauntered out. She was dressed like a peasant with a wide, brilliantly colored skirt. Her hair was long, worn in two braids hanging down her back. She smiled.

"Joan!" The Eagle's lips formed the word, but he did not speak.

She took his arm and they walked slowly along until they were well into the hills where the Gestapo rarely bothered to venture.

"How did you ever get here?" the Eagle asked. "What in the world happened, Joan? I can't understand—" He had unconsciously spoken to her as "Joan" because that was the name by which he thought of her in his mind. As simply she called him by his first name.

"It wasn't difficult, Jeff," she said. "I've known of this colony for years. As a little girl my mother used to bring me here for vacations. The people know me and trust me. They resent the intrusion of the Gestapo agents and all this activity. All they ask is the peace and quiet they've enjoyed for more than a century. I come back each summer and visit. When I'm here, I dress and act like the inhabitants. It isn't far by auto if you know the trails. When I told Hernandez what happened, he ordered me up here."

The Eagle looked up sharply. "Ordered you? Then, like your brother you are also a secret agent, eh? Have you discovered anything, Joan? Are there ammunition dumps here—and assembly factories?"

"No, Jeff. I've asked a few discreet questions and I've looked around. There are no factories here. It's nothing but a stop-over. They ship their crates of parts here, then they are transferred somewhere else. Even the inhabitants of the village know nothing and they don't dare ask questions. The Gestapo have been here but a few weeks and they have already established a concentration camp. Men—women, too—just vanish if they so much as criticize any move made by these agents. I saw you get out of the plane. Oh Jeff, it's terribly dangerous here! They'll realize you're an impostor. These men are devilishly clever."

THE EAGLE led Joan over to a rustic wall, hoisted her on top of it and sat down himself.

"I couldn't quit now, Joan," he said soberly, "any more than you could. According to my theories, this colony is probably bristling with war planes and factories. I must find out where they assemble those planes and manufacture the bombs. I can't stop until—"

He stopped short with a sudden exclamation. That map he had seen in Lachner's living room! There had been a line to Lake Maracaibo.

"I've got it!" he said tensely. "This, as you suggest, is merely a stop-over. Listen, Joan. So long as I'm accepted as *Herr* Marenbach, I can go right ahead. They'll take me to this other hidden city where I'm supposed to work in chemical laboratories. You stay here. Somehow I'll manage to get word to you. Is there any way to get a message back to Caracas?"

Joan shook her head. "There's only a radio station, set up by the Gestapo for communication with Lachner. Oh, Jeff, please be careful! I—I can't help but think of what happened to Jim—to my brother. I—I'm afraid for you now."

The Eagle took her hand and pressed it gently. "Joan," he said firmly, "you and I hold in our hands the opportunity for stopping murder, sabotage, and possibly even invasion of this continent. Today the world is crammed with discordant issues. We've got to work for the issue we believe is right. If you and I refuse to risk our lives, later on millions of men will risk theirs with no choice as to whether they want to or not. Can't you see?"

"Yes—yes, I see. I guess it's the only thing that has kept me going since that other night. But Jeff, what can we do? How can we possibly fight all these men? They have all resources at their command, while we have nothing."

The Eagle tapped his temple significantly. "Except for what lies up here. Now listen—you know this country or can find out about it. How far is it to Lake Maracaibo, and where is the trail?"

"It's about thirty miles," she said slowly. "But Jeff, Lake Maracaibo is isolated from civilization. There can't be…. Wait, Jeff! I think you're right. *Frau* Hensinger told me only this morning that she wondered what tractors were doing plowing their way through the wilderness. Those men are making a road. It must lead to Lake Maracaibo. Jeff, we're on the right track!"

He nodded. "And what to do about it? They'll ship me up there, watch me like hawks and pretty soon I'll be exposed. Then what? Still, I must take the chance. With you here and able to get back to Caracas without much trouble I've an ace in the hole. Be ready to move immediately, Joan. I'll send word the moment I'm sure of things. Stay clear of these Gestapo, and—"

The Eagle stopped abruptly. From below, in the village proper, came the shrill notes of several whistles. He started up.

"It's an alarm!" he said tensely, "And only one thing could be responsible. They've discovered I'm not Marenbach. They'll have witnesses to show that you seemed to know me and they'll take you, too. Joan, we're going to Lake Maracaibo—and there's only time enough for you to reach your friends in order to get us food. I'll stay here, behind this fence. The Gestapo won't learn of our meeting until later. Hurry!"

She sped away, cutting across the fertile fields toward the outskirts of the village. The Eagle dropped behind the fence, saw to his gun and pumped a slug into the firing chamber.

The Eagle knew how these men from the Gestapo worked. And he knew that once he fell into their hands, hope could be abandoned!

CHAPTER VIII

PRISON CAMP

ALMOST TWO hours elapsed before Joan returned. She carried a basket crammed with food and fear was plain in her face.

"They're searching everywhere, Jeff!" she said in a rush of words. "They've got patrols out—have even conscripted the villagers to create a ring around the whole area. But I have friends here, as I told you. I've taken them into my confidence and they want to help. We travel due north. There are no Gestapo agents there—only natives. We can slip through the ring. They won't see us because they don't want to, these friends of mine. But we must hurry!"

They beat their way through forest and over towering hills. They saw no signs of the ring of men thrown about the village. The Eagle had an idea that these simple people deliberately avoided seeing them so they would tell no lies if questioned by the Gestapo.

All day long they made their slow progress up the tortuous sides of the Andes. There was food enough and water in plenty. Joan held up well and gradually these two discovered that there was more than friendship between them. Yet neither spoke of it. There was a gigantic task to be done, a dangerous piece of work that might take their lives before it was completed.

They rested by night and with the dawn toiled forward again. A compass, provided by one of the villagers, was their guide. At noon of the second day they topped a high peak and looked down at the smooth, blue water of Lake Maracaibo. They were at the extreme southern end of the huge lake, where primitive wilderness held sway. But did it? The Eagle pointed into the valley. A thin column of smoke arose like some skinny finger seeking to defile the clouds.

"It's there," he said softly. "From now on we must be careful. They'll have guards thrown out, especially since we made good our escape from the village. Joan, you didn't hear anything of two Americans being held captive, did you? I don't believe I told you, but two agents preceded me down here and they vanished."

"There are no such prisoners in the village or I should have known of it," she told him. "Perhaps they brought them here to the lake. Jeff, what are you going to do now?"

"I don't know. First I must have a look at the armaments industry they've created down here. As I see it now, there is only one solution. Outright destruction of the whole place."

They maneuvered warily after darkness set in. Then they moved forward faster until they reached the fringe of forest behind which lay the insidious activity of the foreign spies. Jeff parted a few branches, glanced through them and drew in a quick breath. He had expected to see a complete picture of preparation for war, but nothing on the scale that presented itself now.

A broad flying field was to the left. Hangars were wide open and more than a score of heavy bombing planes were being inspected by mechanics. There were twice as many fast pursuit ships, with their wings barren of identification.

To the right towered a frame building into which a line of men carried shells and aerial bombs. All about were men in full uniform. Here they had no need to hide their true identity. The grim insignia of their nationality was boldly displayed. Barbed wire fencing hemmed in the entire place and guards armed with rifles patrolled every foot of it.

JEFF SHANNON groaned. "I'd sell my life for one bomber with her racks filled. Getting into that place will be harder than breaking out of Alcatraz. We've got to find the gate and study the guards."

He took Joan's hand and they crept along the protecting edge of the forest until they had made a half circle of the place. The Eagle saw the gate at last. Four guards were posted atop scaffolds that commanded a view of the whole clearing. From each scaffold bristled a machine gun and powerful searchlights were ready to be trained on any invading force. He saw, too, how camouflage concealed the airport and the small factories. A plane flying directly overhead would have noticed nothing unusual.

"It would take a well equipped regiment to attack this place," the Eagle whispered. "Joan, it doesn't look as if there is a way of getting into the place."

"Can you fly a plane?" Joan asked, and when he nodded silent assent: "Then let's try to steal one. Perhaps—"

"Wait!" The Eagle held up his hand. "Joan, look down there just outside the gates. In that little grove. See? Two men—Americans." He almost shouted. "Why, that's Bob Traynor and Frank Bailey! If we could only get them working with us. They're shackled to those posts, but I can get them free. Come on—there's no time to lose."

With Joan at his side they crept forward. Within the Eagle a tiny voice kept telling him to beware. But he could only see those two men, helplessly staked out like cattle. Two more American men would be of great help, also, and these two would know the ins and outs of this encampment.

"Jeff," Joan said anxiously, "it may be a trap. Why aren't there any guards near these men?"

"I don't know," the Eagle said. "But we've got to chance it, Joan. You stay here. Take my gun. If anything happens, try to shoot a clear path for me. Don't worry—I'll make it."

"Good luck," she whispered.

The Eagle crept on hands and knees until he was within twenty feet of the two stakes to which the American agents were tied. It was gloomy there now, because some of the lights had been turned out. The Eagle drew a pocket knife, opened the largest blade, then darted into the clearing intent on cutting the two men free and escaping before anyone was even aware of his presence.

Suddenly Joan screamed. Her cry was cut off as though a hand had been clamped across her mouth. But the Eagle did not pause. He reached the side of the Americans and saw that each man was gagged with adhesive. They could not shout a warning.

He swung around, crouching. A line of men with rifles were emerging from the darkness to hem him in on all sides. Then he saw Joan being half carried, half dragged between two black-clad members of the Gestapo. One of these agents held a gun against the back of her head as he shouted to the Eagle:

"You will surrender or I shall shoot!"

The Eagle sighed, and raised both arms high....

IT SEEMED hours later when the Eagle stood before a long table behind which sat uniformed officers of this hidden armaments town.

They were resplendent in swords, pistols and medals. Their high-crowned caps were perched jauntily on closely cropped heads. A man of about fifty seemed to be in command, from his insignia, a major-general.

"Now," this man said gruffly, "you will begin by telling us how you found this place. No lies—they will be punished. And remember also that this girl who came with you is likewise a prisoner. Upon her we shall inflict the punishment to be meted out to you in the event that you do not cooperate with us."

"Very well," the Eagle said.

He grinned at the dozen men, walked over to the desk and sat down on the edge of it. Two Gestapo agents rushed up to him, dragged him back and slapped him soundly across the face.

"It won't be so long," he said quietly, "before I return that slap—and my hand won't be open when I do it. Now, if you want me to talk, let go and step back. I don't like the odor of you. Reminds me of a sty."

For a moment the Eagle thought these two meant to shoot him on the spot. But harsh orders from the major-general sent the two agents back toward the door.

"Stand at attention and answer these questions," the Eagle was told. "We have already communicated with Caracas, so you will gain nothing by lies. How did you know this place existed, and how many other persons know of it?"

The Eagle shrugged. "Can't say for sure. I told—let's see—Señor Hernandez and the American consul. *Herr* Lachner was extremely careless in leaving maps around. I had a look at one of them and—Well, I got here, so I must have known the way."

"And the girl?"

The Eagle made a wry face. "One of the peasants in the lost colony. I was in a spot there and persuaded her to help me get away. After that I couldn't shake her. She insisted on coming all the way. Just a stupid girl who should be milking cows—not mixed up in an affair of this kind."

"We shall soon know," the commandant snapped. "*Herr* Lachner has been ordered to report here at once. If you have lied, you shall face a firing squad. And Lachner will know who you are."

At a signal the two Gestapo agents dragged the Eagle out of the room, across the entire length of the improvised town and hurled him into a barbed wire enclosed space about twenty feet square. Bob Traynor, Bailey and Joan were there, huddled in a group as far away from the guards as possible.

The Eagle watched the gate close in his face and grinned at the leering grimaces of the Gestapo men. Then he brushed his clothing casually, threw back his head and whistled a lilting tune as he walked toward his companions. He sat down on the ground and looked around.

"Nice little place you have here. Exclusive is the word—and completely away from any curious eyes."

Traynor laughed. "That's right. Boy, it's tough trying to live with sentries watching every move you make. I'd rather be in solitary confinement. Well, you're here—so we might as well know all about you. I suppose you were sent down to look for us?"

"How in the world did you find the place?" Bailey queried.

THE EAGLE eyed both of them. They were gaunt from lack of sufficient food and sleep. Their hands were calloused, their bodies dirty.

"Make you work for your keep, eh?" he remarked. "Prisoners of war and prisoners of industry at one and the same time."

"They make us work in a coal mine they found over on that hill. The rest of 'em are too high-hat to do work of that kind, so with a bayonet ready to stick us every now and then, we dig the coal and haul it out. They maintain a nice little electrical system with it. Oh, there's every modern convenience here."

The Eagle hunched himself closer, gave Joan a wide grin and spoke quietly.

"Listen, boys, I'm Jeff Shannon. Maybe you've heard 'em call me the Eagle. Well—no barbed wire fence ever held an eagle on the ground. I'm going to fly out of here."

"How?" all three asked in a chorus.

The Eagle heaved a great sigh. "I don't know—yet. Have to grow my wings first. But—we don't leave here until this place is obliterated! Wiped off the face of the earth!"

Traynor shook his head slowly. "You don't know the half of it, Shannon. They taunt us with their plans. Listen—they intend to wait until there's a war on the other side of the pond. If the United States tries to help any of the enemy nations, the Panama Canal will be bombed first. Then Mexico and the United States itself, within flying range of these new stratosphere bombers—and let me tell you, that's plenty. If Brazil, Chile, Argentina or any other Latin-American nation decides to take a hand, they get the same treatment. See that big shack over there? It contains enough bombs to blow New York off the map. Over there, behind that camouflage of trees, are long-range cannon. They can be flown, piecemeal, to suitable points and turned on the various cities down here. All hell will break loose if they ever get started, Shannon!"

Joan took both of the Eagle's hands in her own.

"Jeff, can we do anything?" she pleaded. "Is there any hope at all?"

"Tomorrow," the Eagle said, "Lachner comes. When they find out who I am, they may decide to eliminate all of us, or put us to work in the coal mines until we drop of exhaustion. Lachner rather has it in for me, and I don't think his ideas of vengeance are any too kindly. So we must act quickly. Are there guards around here all the time?"

"All the time," Bailey said mournfully. "If we even step toward the barbed wire fence, they aim their rifles at us. Don't think it would take much to make them shoot, either. Day and night they keep four men on duty, watching us."

The Eagle was staring toward the dark sky. Above the prison camp wires were strung, and at one end of the camp a pole supported them. The Eagle's eyes narrowed.

"Is it possible that when the guard changes, they relax vigilance for a minute or two?"

Traynor answered eagerly. "Yes. Those going off are usually so tired they walk away before the others get here. The whole bunch meet near the gate at nine—well after dark. The guards on day duty work a fourteen-hour shift. I've heard them grumbling about it often enough."

"Then we can do nothing until tomorrow," the Eagle said. "We'll have to risk Lachner's appearance. Joan, you ought to get some sleep. You others, too. We'll need all our energy tomorrow night. For I've a plan."

CHAPTER IX

THE WAY OUT

GRAY DAWN was just breaking when Traynor and Bailey were aroused and herded out of the barbed wire camp at the point of bayonets.

Joan and the Eagle were unmolested, but he knew that when Lachner arrived, their time would come.

Shortly after noon they were given a bowl of weak soup and some dry bread. The Eagle nibbled at his chunk of bread and grinned at Joan.

"All the comforts of deluxe hotel service. They even wait on us, Joan."

"Oh, Jeff!" There was a choked sob in her voice. "How can we ever get out of here? When Lachner finds out you're here, he'll order you killed! Even if they don't kill us, we'll be forced to work like slaves. Look at Traynor and Bailey! They're just walking skeletons."

The Eagle's grin died away. "You've got to keep your chin up, Joan, darling," he said. "We're not licked until they throw sod in our faces. I'm hoping for just one break—that Lachner's temper won't run away with him."

An hour later they heard a bugle blare. All work ceased for the moment and the men lined up, rifles grounded, shoulders thrown back. From the trail came a party of eight with Lachner in the lead, astride a wiry little mule. He saluted the commandant, inspected the small army, then walked over to the barbed wire fence enclosing the prison camp.

The Eagle arose, ambled over to the fence and stopped only when two bayonets touched his stomach. He saluted Lachner with a wry grin.

"So we meet again, *Herr* Lachner. You don't happen to have one of those cigars about you? I didn't get around to smoking all of them, and when we're back in Caracas I'll give you one in return."

"That man"—Lachner pointed an accusing finger—"is the Eagle! The most dangerous of all agents employed by the United States. I shall not rest easy until I see him riddled with bullets."

The Eagle moved his head in acknowledgement. "That's real praise coming from you, *Herr* Lachner. But I'm quite satisfied. Men like you and I expect to die violently some day. This is a little earlier than I had planned it—but who are we to buck Fate? I'd much rather be dead than slaving in those coal mines like Traynor and Bailey are forced to do. Whenever you're ready for the fireworks, just whistle. I'll be along."

One of the Gestapo agents clicked his heels and bowed.

"*Herr* Lachner, it is not for me to suggest, but we need more coal and we do not have the men to mine it. This man might help, eh? Then later on you could take care of him as all spies should be taken care of."

"*Ja!*" Lachner snarled. "Let him work the mines. Work him twenty hours a day. The woman—put her to work in the kitchen. Let her wash the dishes. Feed them swill. Let them suffer."

"*Ja, Herr* Lachner." The Gestapo agent started for the gate. Lachner stopped him with a command.

"Not now, you fool. First I would talk with this man. He knows much and he will tell. Give me one hour, then bring him to me."

The Eagle whistled again as he strolled back to Joan's side and sat down.

"Nice fellow, isn't he? I thought that by telling him I'd prefer death to working in that mine he'd give me a taste of the mine. Psychology, my dear. An interesting and useful subject."

BUT JOAN could stand no more. She broke down, huddled in his arms and he let her cry until there were no more tears. Then he kissed her gently.

"Didn't I say I'd fly out of here?" he reminded her whimsically. "What does an eagle have wings for? Now you won't be bothered until tomorrow, so get all the rest you can. Me—I've an appointment with His Majesty, and if he presses me too much, I'll talk. And what he'll learn! I'll stuff his ears so full of blarney it will make his head spin."

It was almost dark when the Eagle stumbled back to the prison camp after his set-to with the bearded German spy. His guards forced him through the gate and urged him forward with cruel kicks. The Eagle's face was bleeding and raw. The marks of Lachner's big hand were still evident.

Traynor and Bailey started up, to rush to his side. The Eagle pursed cracked lips and whistled again. Joan helped him into a sitting position, moistened the hem of her skirt in a bucket of tepid water provided for them, and gently washed the blood from his face.

"*Herr* Lachner," the Eagle said softly, "is no gentleman. He had two men hold me while he did this. I didn't like it and I told him so—which made him all the sorer. But he and I are not finished, my friends. Gather around closely so those guards won't be able to see what we're doing."

The Eagle thrust a hand under his shirt and took out—one gauntlet. The kind worn by the officers of this hidden town.

"All for that I took Lachner's punishment." He grinned crookedly, for his face was somewhat out of shape. "One measly little glove which to me looks exactly like a pair of eagle's wings. Tonight's the night, boys—Joan. Lachner's staying over, probably to encourage my coal digging a bit. But my hands are tender. Nothing like my feet. They're quite tough."

The Eagle leaned back and removed his shoes. They had crepe rubber soles and heels. He pried away one sole, ripped it off the shoe and held it against the gauntlet.

"Fits perfectly, eh? Now, Joan, here is where you come in. A woman should weep and sew for her boys in the trenches. Please don't weep. Just sew—this rubber sole onto the outside of the gauntlet. You'll have to use grass— No, wait! Let's all take a stroll around the limits of our prison. There's bound to be bits of wire. Get all you can and don't let the guards see you."

They separated, but thirty minutes later again were huddled in a group. Using pieces of rusty wire, Joan fastened the rubber sole of the Eagle's shoe to the gauntlet he had stolen. The camp was settling down for the night. In about an hour the guard would change.

"Listen, carefully," the Eagle said. "When our charming hosts withdraw from their posts, it must seem to them as if we're huddled together exactly as we are now. But I'll have to leave for a moment or two. The rest of you make it seem I'm still in the party. If things go wrong, you carry out my plan, Traynor. You are the strongest. Ready?"

They nodded. This was desperate work, but no more desperate than was their situation. No one spoke again until the guards, stationed along the fence, withdrew to turn over their duties to the new shift.

THE NIGHT was pitch dark and few lights were on. Most of the inhabitants of the town were feting Lachner. The guards had grumbled about their tour of duty preventing them from joining in the festivities.

Suddenly the Eagle scurried away on all fours. The darkness swallowed him up. The others held their positions so that should any of the guards look back, it would seem that all four prisoners were in one group.

The Eagle reached the pole just inside the barbed wire fence. He wrapped both arms around it and shinnied up it like a monkey. He reached the cross piece over which the wires were strung and donned the gauntlet, with the crepe rubber fastened around it.

The wire that Joan had used was carefully pushed deep into the soft rubber so that none of it was exposed. Without hesitation the Eagle grasped one wire. He tested its strength, knew he could not tear it down. Then he dug into his pocket and took out the knife. He had been searched, but only for guns. The knife had not been appropriated.

Holding this firmly with the rubberized gauntlet, he sawed away at the wire. It parted and one end fell to the ground. He held his breath for fear it might touch the fence and create a brilliant blue flame. But it dangled two feet away.

Perspiration poured down the Eagle's face. He had carefully selected a wire leading to one of the small factories, now darkened. If he had cut the wrong one and doused the lights in the other buildings, his whole scheme would have gone awry.

He slid down the pole and rejoined the others before the new guard shift had taken their places.

"Got to work fast," he said. "Here's the dope. Taunt the guards, get them good and mad. Coax them near the fence. Got the idea? Let's go! Spread out—each of you take one guard. Keep his attention."

The Eagle walked briskly over toward the pole he had climbed. In the darkness he slipped on the glove once more, seized the trailing wire and quickly fastened it to the fence. Then he walked over to where one guard rested on his rifle, staring blankly into space.

"Hello," the Eagle said in German. "For a minute I thought you were a tree stump. You smell like one—the kind that are left in marshes, I mean."

"Quiet!" The guard raised his rifle. "Do not approach closer or I shall give you a taste of my bayonet!"

"You wouldn't dare," the Eagle taunted. "You haven't the nerve. I might grab it and turn your own rifle against you."

Deliberately the Eagle walked closer. The guard growled a curse and thrust his bayonet between the barbed wire. The Eagle dodged aside agilely and made a derisive sound with his tongue. The guard lunged forward, intent on making this American spy squeal. That lunge brought him up against the barbed wire fence. He dropped his rifle and collapsed without a sound, dangling over the fence like some bullet-riddled soldier far out in No Man's Land.

Scooping up the rifle, the Eagle whirled around in time to see two other guards lolling against the fence. The fourth had his rifle to his shoulder and Joan was centered in his sights. The Eagle raised his bayoneted rifle high and raced toward the man.

THE GUARD swerved his gun, but before he could press the trigger, that rifle was sailing through the air at him. He tried to duck it, but the Eagle had figured on that and purposely sent the blade in a low line. It hit the man in the middle of the chest.

He fell forward with a groan, and lay still.

The Eagle raced back to where the power line was hooked to the fence. With his rubber-lined glove he quickly untwisted it, wound it around the pole, then raced over to join the others.

"Got 'em!" he said gleefully. "Now, Joan, you make for the hills. Don't argue—do as I say. Traynor, you and Bailey follow me."

Joan hesitated a moment, but obeyed. On her way she stopped long enough to pick up a rifle. The Eagle smiled, but there was no laughter in his eyes.

Slightly in the lead of Traynor and Bailey, he dodged between buildings, a rifle ready in his hands for quick use. He held up a hand suddenly and the others crouched near him.

"There are guards around the arsenal," he said in a low voice, "but we can't afford to wait. Someone may see those men on the barbed wire fence. Now here's the dope, Bailey, you make a line for that small shed a hundred yards to the right. Traynor, you stay right here. I'm going into that arsenal. I may come out in little pieces and then it's up to you mugs to get Joan away. Do you understand?"

"Listen, Shannon," Bailey said, "Joan's in love with you. Backing that up is the fact that you're invaluable to the service of our country. Me—I'm just a no-account operative who got himself into a mess. Let me go!"

"And have all the fun?" the Eagle asked wryly. "Nope! I got you out of that prison camp and you owe me the privilege of blasting this city of war to the skies. Beat it—and cover me when I start to run for it."

Bailey touched his forehead, grinned amiably and made his dash to a point of vantage from where he could cover the Eagle without exposing himself. Traynor sighted his rifle experimentally, drawing a bead on the guard who stood fixed post at the entrance to the ammunition dump.

"Ready?" the Eagle asked

Traynor nodded, and his finger grew white against the trigger. Bailey waved encouragement from his position and then leveled his own rifle. The Eagle gripped his gun with strong, eager hands.

The bayonet glistened dully and the Eagle's eyes narrowed to slits. His chances of coming out of this were few. Yet it was his job, and one by which most of the world would benefit. He couldn't fail!

CHAPTER X

RUIN

FALLING INTO a crouch, he broke into a sprint. He crossed a small parade grounds and was within twenty feet of the sentry when the man realized this onrushing ghost meant no good. He raised his rifle, but its stock had barely touched his shoulder when two slugs smashed through his head. Traynor and Bailey had fired simultaneously.

Two other sentries came rushing toward the Eagle. He shot one of them through the shoulder. Traynor's gun blazed and the other went down in a sprawling skid. He didn't move again.

The Eagle paused just long enough to yank an automatic from the holster of the nearest sentry. He threw aside his rifle and headed for the entrance of the ammunition dump.

A powerful searchlight was turned on, sweeping the grounds in an attempt to pick out the cause for the shooting. Traynor and Bailey ducked the light, but it held the Eagle in its glare for a fraction of a second. Two of the machine guns at the main gate made the earth dance around the Eagle's feet. But he reached the doorway to the building and the machine gun became silent. It was tantamount to suicide for the gunners if they let bullets smash into the explosives stacked in that building.

Two men emerged, guns ready. The Eagle's automatic blasted the first one, sent him reeling back against his mate. With a leap the Eagle was upon both of them, using his weapon as a club. Then Traynor and Bailey lost sight of him as he entered the doorway.

There were two more shots, reckless shots for they came from within the ammunition dump. An officer, pistol in hand, was heading a squad of four men toward the place. Traynor picked him off and also took care of one of his men. Bailey shot with methodical calm, and the detail retreated swiftly.

Inside the ammunition dump, the Eagle was forced to shoot point blank at a burly guard. Then a small man in a white smock tried to interfere. The Eagle rushed him, sent a roundhouse blow to the face that knocked his man out.

He stopped then to examine the place. Stacked on a bench beside him were the long-handled throwing grenades used by the Germans. He thrust as many of these as possible into his pockets and beneath his belt.

The silence outside worried him. He wondered if Traynor and Bailey were dead, if Joan had escaped. No matter now—there would be no one to harm her.

Just one of the grenades which the Eagle carried would set off a devil's own inferno. Nothing would withstand the concussion once this place went off. He raced up a rickety stairway to examine the floors above.

The upper floor was stacked with huge aerial bombs and shells. He gaped in astonishment at the huge amount of supplies. There was a window near him and he risked a quick look through its dirty glass pane. The hangars were about a hundred yards away and the field was a scene of frantic excitement.

Then a rifle spat and another blended its roar with the first. The Eagle saw a medal-bedecked officer fall heavily. Traynor and Bailey were still on the job.

Near the floor a ray of dim light from outside attracted his attention. He peered down a shaft that was much like a huge shiny box. It was used to pass bombs down to the men who would carry them to the planes. There was plenty of room to accommodate the Eagle's slim form.

Someone was running madly up the stairs. There would be heroic men among these troops stationed here; men who were willing to die for a cause they believed right. A man's figure showed for a second and the Eagle fired from the hip. The intruder ducked back, unhurt. His gun roared and the Eagle felt a slug smash into his thigh. He tried to back up, but his leg refused to support him and he crumpled into a heap.

The invader, encouraged by no answering bullets, turned on a flashlight. It swept across the Eagle where he knelt, grimacing with pain. With a shout of triumph the German started a rush across the floor. The bayonet on his rifle was pointed downward, ready for a death thrust.

The Eagle raised his gun and pulled the trigger without really being conscious of it. But his aim was accurate. The German's rifle exploded as he fell, but the bullet only plowed through the wall behind the Eagle. The German pitched forward on his face.

Grimly, the Eagle crawled toward the chute, drawing one of the grenades from his belt. He thrust his feet down the slanting side of the chute, gritted his teeth and laid the grenade down gently. He took two more from his pockets and lined them up.

From the sounds outside he knew that the building was surrounded and that once he let go, he probably would come flying out into the arms of a dozen men. That chance he had to take. They were coming into the building, too, egged on by the harsh orders of their superiors from what they believed to be a safe distance. But the Eagle knew that only vast distance would be safe for anyone once this building went up.

He wiped sweat off his face, swallowed hard, then rapidly drew the pin on each bomb and hurled them in three different directions. He gave himself a hard push and went sliding down the shaft. His wounded leg began bleeding faster and darts of agony shot through his body.

The Eagle came out of the chute, sailed through the air for about twenty feet and landed with a thump that almost knocked him out. A dozen men were rushing toward him. He gestured toward the building. The men hesitated, fired a few shots, then turned tail and ran.

The Eagle began rolling over and over, trying to put distance between himself and the ammunition dump.

Then it came. There was a tremendous roar and one side of the building rose into the air as if being carried away by a tornado. A second explosion; then a third. There was a split second of silence while the roar echoed and reechoed over the hills. Then the real explosion came as bombs, dynamite and powder supplies were set off.

The ground trembled. Debris hurtled through the air. And all the while the Eagle kept on rolling. Flashes of fire lit up the night as the explosions continued with renewed velocity. A chunk of board struck the Eagle across the back. He groaned and lay still a moment.

He began inching his way now. One leg dropped off into space. He was on top of a ravine. Men screamed, but their voices were puny above the gigantic crash of the explosions. The Eagle slipped, tried to hold himself in check, but could not. He slid down into the ravine until a small clump of brush stopped him.

The explosions were still going on. The concussions were terrific, but there were no longer any screams. The Eagle sighed like a man very tired. He closed his eyes and waited for the inevitable end....

IT SEEMED hours later when he awoke as someone tried to force cool spring water down his throat. He looked up into Joan's face.

"We're both dead?" he asked, still stupefied.

"We're very much alive, Jeff. I saw you come flying out of that chute and I tried to reach you, but the ravine was too steep. Then you came sliding down to me."

"Traynor—and Bailey?" The Eagle sat up suddenly. "Lachner—and the others?"

"I don't know," Joan answered in a queer voice. "I—I haven't looked up there yet. I—I don't think I want to."

The Eagle tensed. Above them the roar of an airplane motor broke the quiet. The Eagle struggled to his feet, clawed his way to the edge of the ravine and looked out on a scene of complete desolation except for one small cabin plane which was poised at the far end of the runway. Apparently it had been too far away to be damaged by the explosions.

"Shannon!"

The voice seemed to come from miles away. The Eagle clambered to his feet. His wounded leg buckled under him, but Joan was at his side.

The plane was racing toward them. It slowed and Traynor jumped out. He was waving his arms madly. "Shannon!" he shrieked as he ran closer. "We made it! Bailey's got a broken arm and a bullet through his shoulder, but he's able to handle the plane. We've done it!"

"Have you seen Lachner?" the Eagle asked steadily.

"Have we seen him?" Traynor enthused. "He headed for this plane the minute he learned you were in the ammunition dump. The commandant went with him. They were going to take off, leave their men to die. They knew you'd blast the whole place to pieces. But Bailey and I shot our way toward the plane and before she took off, we put a few slugs into her. One of us got Lachner who was at the controls. He's dead—so is the major-general. When the building went up, we were far enough away to avoid the concussion and the debris. Here—let me help you. Man, oh man, won't this make the headlines!"

The Eagle took Traynor's arm.

"Nothing has happened here, do you understand? Nothing! Before these men came, there was only wilderness here. That's all that remains now. We'll fly back to Caracas. Hernandez is entitled to an explanation, and so is the War Department, but other than that—we're mute. Do I make myself clear? News of this kind would only inflame people who might otherwise never think of war and bloodshed. The Germans will never make a complaint—not even an investigation, I'm betting."

"BUT GOSH," Traynor protested, "you risked your life to do this! I'm not seeking any glory for myself, but, Shannon, they pin medals on men for the kind of stuff you did."

"And they pin tombstones on doughboys who die in battle," the Eagle said. "Don't forget that. Our job is to stop this mad business of war making. If we do it secretly, so much the better. Give me a hand to that plane, will you? My leg feels as though it weighs a ton."

Joan was hastily bandaging his thigh when the plane took off. Bailey circled the ruins twice. Nothing stirred except a little smoke that came from between the piles of debris. She shuddered and looked up at Jeff Shannon. "Where do we go from here?" she asked him.

The Eagle's eyes softened and his lips spread in a smile.

"'We' is right, darling. Where do we go? First, back to the States. After that—who knows? But let's forget all that, and concentrate on just us."

II

NETWORK OF HATE

CHAPTER I

BLADES OF BLOOD

A **S HE** munched, he thought over the possibilities which the note implied.

Europe was on the grip of a crisis, not the first and probably not the last. But there had to be an end to that sort of thing some time. Sooner or later there had to be a breaking point. First it had been Austria, swallowed up by the Nazi maw—then Sudentenland, Memel, Czechoslovakia had swiftly followed. Now Poland was on the agenda. Would Poland be the breaking point?

The Eagle finished his rather odd sandwich, paid his bill, and departed. His rapid course took him across the Seine to that rabbit warren of buildings near the *Invalides*—buildings that housed one of the cleverest General Staffs in the world.

Colonel LeClerc greeted him heartily.

"Be seated, *mon ami*. Will you have a cigarette?"

"Thanks, *mon colonel*. Your note indicated urgency. What do you want of me?"

"There are times, *mon ami*, when I marvel at your insight!" retorted the colonel, snapping his *briquet* and offering the Eagle a light. "Also your American desire to get to the point without beating bushes. However, I hesitate to suggest anything that will continue your exile."

"If it's an exile, it's a self-imposed one, Colonel," the Eagle said cheerfully. "Give it to me straight. Is it Poland this time?"

"No, it is not Poland—not at least so far as you are concerned," the colonel replied. "True, the present crisis is deepening rapidly. But there are many fronts and phases in the current threatening world situation. No, my friend. The task I have in mind for you is not precisely a European one."

Colonel LeClerc opened some papers before him on the desk. His face had grown serious and keen, and one could realize that here in the person of this rather pudgy old gentleman was one of France's most supple counter-espionage experts, with a mind like a well-balanced fencing foil.

"*Voici!*" He spread out a map of North Africa. His finger traced the boundary line between Italian Tripoli and the territory of French Tunis.

"Here we have them… Mussolini's forces, heavily manning the Italian side of the boundary—especially strong at the towns Misda, Sinaun, Nasra, Ghadames and Ghat far to the south. On our side of the border is the French headquarters at Duizat with mobile columns of Spahis, Tirailleurs and Mokhazenis patroling the border in advance of our defenses. So far, so good—force and threat of force against force and threat of force! But trouble has arisen behind the lines."

"What's the nature of it?" the Eagle asked.

"A Nazi spy, a capable fellow if ever there was one, is demoralizing our headquarters and creating consternation by his boldness. And his agents are working on the dissident natives. There is even fear"—here the colonel lowered his voice—"that the Senussi are being encouraged to rise again!"

THE EAGLE whistled. The Senussi, that dreaded fanatical sect with headquarters deep in some mysterious place far within the Tripolitan deserts—their power was enormous and their strength a thing to respect. If they were so minded, they could rouse up the credulous North African natives in an incredibly short time.

"Who is in command at Duizat?" asked the Eagle.

"General de Tremond—an old-school soldier. He will cooperate with you. But, *mon ami,* you speak as if you have already accepted the assignment—"

"Who is his chief of staff?" Jeff Shannon interrupted.

"Colonel de Castex."

"Old-school, too?"

"Just a little on the martinet side—doesn't believe in all this foolishness of Information Divisions, counter-espionage and Intelligence work in general. Discipline and the officer's manuals are his watchwords."

"We probably won't get along," said Shannon. "I know the type."

"*J'ai peur que oui!* I'm afraid so!" admitted the colonel.

"And this Nazi spy?"

"Drakenfels—a devil if there ever was one—seems to know every move in advance—evidently speaks the dialects like a native—writes

impertinent letters to the general and his chief of staff and moves at will around the secret fortified areas."

"Interesting character," the Eagle said. "Will you order a plane to be readied for me?"

"I've already done so. I knew you'd consent. Major Henri Desnot, the Intelligence officer on the spot, has been notified of your expected arrival. He reports that the Senussi have established a headquarters somewhere down opposite the Tripolitan border on the Egele Plateau and he is anxious to find it. He is a capable officer, but so far he has not made any headway against the cleverness of Drakenfels."

"Desnot may resent my coming," Jeff Shannon muttered. He knew what an officer's pride was.

Colonel LeClerc shrugged his shoulders.

"I know you will use all your tact to secure his cooperation."

"I'll have to," Jeff said, "but the set-up doesn't look too promising— an American barging in on the work of French officers. Who is Major Desnot's assistant?"

"Captain Rene Martin."

"That's better." The Eagle was relieved. "I know him well. He's good."

"Unfortunately he is too well known to the natives," the colonel reminded him.

"That's true," he admitted. His brow furrowed.

"Colonel," he said after a pause, "you've just given me an idea, a plan. Listen. Have you among your subordinates a young officer who can speak American English and who can at the same time disguise himself convincingly as an attractive young lady!"

COLONEL LeCLERC took the strange request in his stride.

"At least three who can acquit themselves well in such disguise and of the three, one, Lieutenant de Krelis, spent several years at an American Institute of Technology and speaks like an American."

"Good! One more question, then: Is Captain Rene Martin still a bachelor?"

"Yes."

"Good! Send de Krelis tonight by plane, with his female disguise. He is to be my sister, affianced to Captain Rene Martin. Being American, the 'young lady' can go unchaperoned!"

The colonel looked at him long and steadily, his eyes thoughtful.

"Very good!" he said at last. "I see your plan."

"You see only the beginning of it," Jeff Shannon said. "The end I can't even see myself."

"Strength to your wings… Eagle…" Colonel LeClerc said softly as the two shook hands.

CHAPTER II

THE "SWEETHEART" OF RENE MARTIN

THREE MEN plotted in a rug-draped room off the Rue Sidie Esserdou, in the native quarter of Tunis.

The three men, taken individually and separately, would not have caused much comment in that crowded North African city. The two older men were evidently Saharans from the Oases of the Touat, desert-bred Berbers. The third and youngest, swarthy faced and crooked nosed, was also undoubtedly desert-bred, but a Taureg.

These three, seemingly so ordinary, were emissaries of the powerful secret society of North Africa, the Senussi! The eldest of the three, he who was known as Kalfat ben Kaddour, was arguing with the younger man.

"By the Seven Hairs of Kufun!" he swore, tapping his hands on the small tabouret before which they sat so that the coffee cups rattled. "We can strike at him through his woman!"

"Is it certain that she is his woman?" queried the younger man. "Allah alone knows the whys and wherefores of an infidel and his woman! The Bazaars whisper that they are betrothed—though only a Frank could sit shamelessly with his face-unveiled betrothed in a public café."

"Allah alone, who knows the hearts of men, can judge this thing!" said the eldest man piously. "But if, according to Frankish standards, she is his betrothed, so much the better for our purposes! I repeat, we can strike at him through her!"

"Has she no father, nor any male kin?" asked the younger man.

"Aye, a brother she has—a man of some little renown as a fighter and as a master of guile...."

"Of Frankish blood?"

"Nay, of that race from beyond the sea, American!"

"And the name of her brother?" The younger man leaned forward.

"Zzeff Shannon!" retorted Kalfat ben Kaddour composedly.

"And ye would abduct the sister of this one?" The older man, he who was called Amar ben Ali, leaned forward, a trace of excitement in his tones.

The other two looked at him, a little surprised.

"He is renowned not only in Tunis, but the whole of North Africa, this one!" said the worried Amar ben Ali. "Even though he has not been here for a long time—not since the Riff uprisings—he is still remembered."

But the other two were not impressed. The young man was especially eager to achieve this stroke, for it was aimed against Captain Rene Martin, that brilliant young Frenchman who had again and again harassed the secret emissaries of the Senussi and had again and again foiled their plots. For this fanatical sect, made up of elements from all the races of North Africa, aimed at nothing less than the driving of the white man from the entire broad area of Africa.

The two argued with old Amar ben Ali, but he remained unconvinced, so the two made their plans without him. It was known that the sister of Jeff Shannon was sojourning in Tunis. It was known that she was betrothed to Captain Rene Martin, Jeff Shannon's friend. It was known that they were seen in public together. It was decided to abduct the girl and hold her as a power against Rene Martin, the chief stumbling block to the plans of the Senussi.

Amar ben Ali, the old nomad, shook his head.

"When thou settest fire to a forest of canes, beware of the tigers that will be roused!" he quoted.

The manner of the "girl's" abduction was quickly arranged. Selim, the young Taureg, he who had worked for white men and who spoke English and French, was selected for the task. It was known that the girl was a guest at the Hotel Majestic. It was known that she, in common with many Europeans, could be found at the Café de Tunis on the Avenue Jules Ferry at the hour of sundown.

So, Selim, the young Taureg, was delegated to gain approach to her at the hotel, to inveigle her forth beyond the Porte de France and to get her into the Native Quarter.

Once there, it was a simple matter in that maze of streets, to seize her and immure her within one of those typical Tunisian houses, with its heavy doors set in thirty foot walls, one just like another. Once there, it would be a simple matter to slide her out, enclosed in a box which could be taken beyond city limits, loaded on to a car and driven eastward until the camel caravan was met. Then by slow stages she could be taken to the nearest stronghold of the Senussi, the Plateau of Egele, near the border of Tripoli, of which no Frenchman had knowledge!

For the Senussi were well organized. Their secret agents were everywhere. Their means of communication and travel were remarkable. Lately it was even whispered that they had added airplanes to their equipment, and the older and more conservative of this Senussi shook their heads at this as at all the modern innovations that were suddenly being introduced to their fanatic organization.

It was whispered that a new leader had risen among them, a new leader who believed in taking all the improvements and weapons of the white man and using them against their makers.

These three emissaries of that sinister sect finished their conference at last. It was deemed wise to go forth and see this woman whom they were to use as a pawn in the game against France and the hated Roumi, the white man. It was close to the hour of sundown.

The three drifted inconspicuously, into the narrow street, mingling unnoticed with the polyglot population. The street was an overflow from the *suk* of the Vegetable Cellars. Nearby were the *suks* of the Leather Workers and of the Perfumers. Beggars crawled underfoot. Gaunt camels slumbered overhead. There rose a shrill clamor of native voices as the three drifted silently through the streets, avoiding donkeys and two-wheel carts and the restless ebb and flow of this boiling native quarter. Veiled Tauregs stalked through the crowd, Spahis in long cloaks and red tarbooshes clinked musically by. The muezzin's call to prayer rang out from a minaret high over head.

Those three reached the Porte de France at last, and passed through its massive masonry, and kept on down the Avenue Jules Ferry.

They slowed up their long ranging strides as they approached the Café de Tunis, its open air tables filled with the white and scarlet and blue of French officers and the gay colors of the women with them.

AT THE third table from the end there sat a couple. It was Kalfat ben Kaddour who plucked his companion's cloak and jerked his eyes toward the two.

And it was evident to all beholders that those two were interested in little else but themselves. He was a French officer of the finer type of Frenchman, the Colonial Administrative type, the warrior, the man who spends his time not on the boulevards but at the outposts of France's Colonial Empire.

Yes, Captain Rene Martin was a soldierly man, bronze featured and clear eyed. The row of ribbons on his white uniform attested to his record. The red ribbon of the Legion d'Honneur, as well as the green and red of the Croix de Guerre, with several palms upon it. Other ribbons there were, campaign medals and decorations from the North African Government including that of the Nisham of Tunis, the whole forming a bright row of bright double ribbons and medals unusually profuse for a man of such youth and such comparatively minor rank.

Handsome and distinguished looking, speaking English learned at his two years at Harvard, and practiced thoroughly since, it was no wonder that his companion looked upon him with favor.

The companion was a striking looking girl, soft and feminine looking, and there was no doubt in the minds of any of the onlookers that she was what she seemed to be.

The three sinister figures, cloaked and sandaled, slowed their footsteps as they passed, glittering dark eyes staring at the two.

Then the three figures disappeared into the crowd.

Selim had identified his victim!

CHAPTER III

THE EAGLE'S PLAN

"**B** **UT TELL** me more about the Senussi!"

Young de Krelis's voice was deeply interested but low. For a moment he forgot his disguise and reached absently for a non-existent trouser pocket—only to remember in time.

Captain Martin glanced at the sidewalk and the crowd eddying up and down the Avenue Jules Ferry. It was a brilliant colorful scene, but the young captain's brow became clouded as he looked about. He sighed a little, and then as though shaking off some unpleasant thought, turned back to his companion.

After all, young de Krelis had spent all of his short service in France and he must be instructed.

"They're mysterious enough, these Senussi, all right!" said Martin thoughtfully. "You know they are not any single race or tribe, but they are a terrible religious, fanatical sort of secret society with an extraordinary amount of political power. The order was originally founded by a descendant of Mohammed and it had its beginning in Algeria in 1787. From Algeria it crept through Morocco to Arabia and south across the Sahara. Their chief shrine, of course, is at the Oasis of Giarabub. Their great center of education, their *zawia*, is here near the border.

"But the seat of their power is farther south in the desert. They have enormous centers of educational propaganda and homes of teachers. These places always offer hospitality to any wandering Mohammedan and fill him up with food and propaganda as soon as he comes into their dwelling.

"The Italians had a tough time with them. All sorts of fierce battles were fought between the Italians and the Senussi who guard all the ancient trade routes of the desert. It cost Italy over a hundred thousand men and millions of money and even now she only extends inland about two hundred miles. Their frontier extends along a line of oases stretching from Augila to Giarabub. Once in a while a daring aviator skims farther south.

"But if he should have to make a forced landing, God help him! If the Senussi don't get him, the Veiled Tuaregs will!"

"Who are the Veiled Tuaregs?" asked de Krelis.

"They are a fine and powerful race. Their men go veiled, you know, unlike other Islamic tribes where it is the women who are always veiled. They are wonderful fighters, but they confine their activities almost solely to robbing caravans. At this they are extremely adept. It is only when they fall under the sway of the Senussi that they become dangerous. And," the young man ended gravely, "we've heard that they're almost completely under the domination of the Senussi now!"

"You look worried and tired, *Mon Capitaine*," said the younger officer. "Why don't you rest, sip your drink, and forget all your worries!"

Martin sighed. "I wish I could, but somehow the whole thing seems rather hopeless. Here we are, the French, holding the North Coast of Africa on the shores of the Mediterranean! Other empires have held territories here and they have passed! The Carthaginians rose and fell. The Romans followed them. I can show you that ancient Roman road now, with chariot tracks eight inches deep. The Arabs gained a foothold, and then the Turks.

"Now France is struggling to maintain a precarious empire against that great force of nomad peoples who have seen empires come and go throughout the centuries. Everything seemed fairly well under control up until the last month. Then the Senussi, who have been dormant for years, suddenly took a new lease on life! There is strange unrest in the Sudan. The warfare between Berber and Moorish tribes, between Arabs and Tuaregs, has died down and they are united in a common fanatical front against us.

"To make matters ten times worse there is this strange Drakenfels, the Nazi, among us somewhere, day and night—spoiling our counter measures, assassinating our secret emissaries and agents, spinning a network of hate, laughing at us daily. I would like to wring the fellow's neck with my bare hands! It is Shannon's idea that the identity of Drakenfels can be discovered by going to the Senussi. It will be your task to find out who he is."

Martin was thoughtful and silent for a space. Then:

"Your task is not an easy one, my friend. It is a clever idea, Shannon's—to have you disguised as a woman—my fiancée and his sister. They will attempt to strike at me and at Shannon by abducting you. At least we hope so—that sounds funny, doesn't it? Well, we'll follow the abductors. A simple plan, but risky for you."

"I do not worry!" said de Krelis simply.

"That is good. You must also use every means to find out where they take you and attempt to escape or to signal us in some way, in case our spies should lose your trail. Above all find out all you can about Drak-enfels!"

Young de Krelis nodded, his face serious under the shadows of the feminine hat he wore.

"Even now," continued Martin, "the Senussi are probably watching you. I would not be at all surprised if they attempted your abduction this very night!"

"And in the meantime this American will try to find out who and where this mysterious von Drakenfels is?" asked de Krelis.

"He will find him, if any one can," said Captain Martin and rose slowly to his feet.

He escorted his pseudo fiancée to her hotel and left "her" there to await whatever fate held in store.

They were followed by a tall hawk-nosed native clad in a dark burnoose. Selim was stalking his prey.

It was after Martin had left his companion that de Krelis, in his role of a young woman dining alone, left the dinner table and moved to the terrace for a solitary liqueur and coffee.

A MESSAGE was brought and the very chic-looking woman went to the side door to meet a tall, swarthy hawk-nosed young native wearing the robes of a desert man.

"Mademoiselle," said the man in excellent French, *"Capitaine* Martin has sent word by me requesting you to meet him at Number 19 *bis Rue el Arian* immediately. He has finished his duties and wishes you to ac-company him to see some interesting sights!"

With an excellent rendition of a young girl receiving a message from her fiancée, the chic *mademoiselle* wasted little time in obeying the summons. One of the preparations for her meeting with her fiancé was the quiet slipping of a shoulder holster beneath her dress, a shoulder holster that held a small automatic pistol, a precaution that might have startled the young desert man, had he seen it.

The young Tuareg preceded the chic American girl to the street where a car waited.

With great courtesy he opened the door and bowed his companion in.

Taking his place by the driver, he nodded to the man. The car moved out along the Avenue Jules Ferry toward the Porte de France.

CHAPTER IV

THE BRASS HATS

J EFF SHANNON arrived in Tunis two nights after the abduction of the pseudo Patricia Shannon. He came accompanied by Sam Cameron, of the British Intelligence Service. He had looked up Cameron in Paris, knowing him to be there. Sam Cameron was no new friend. The two had been in the Riff Campaign together, and the Eagle knew that Cameron could be relied on. Cameron had obtained leave and the two had set out.

Rene Martin met them, was introduced to Cameron, and when told that he could speak freely, gave the Eagle the news.

"We followed the gang to the edge of the Egele Plateau," he reported, "then night came on and we lost them, our pilots not being able to follow them in the dark. The next morning they had disappeared. Meanwhile I've had a note from this man Drakenfels, may he rot in hell, mocking me and telling that unless I cease all activities for ninety days he will see that my fiancée is done away with in short order."

"Don't worry about de Krelis," said the Eagle. "Moslems don't harm women. I'll carry on from this point. I suppose I'd better call on the brass hats. How about leading me to the lion's den?"

Rene Martin grinned.

"Don't take offense at Colonel de Castex. He's an old martinet who doesn't mean half what he says...."

"Lead me to him!"

Colonel de Castex was tall, angular and bony; smelling of soap, starch and pipe clay. He was obviously all soldier, from his gold braided *képi* to the soles of his boots.

To Jeff Shannon he seemed as friendly as a rattlesnake. Jeff was tired and could have used a few minutes of relaxation. But a colonel is a colonel and Shannon stood straight, clicked his heels and saluted.

As for the colonel, it was plain to be seen that (a) he did not like Intelligence officers, (b) that he did not like Americans, (c) that he disliked the combination of American and Intelligence officer most of all.

"To what am I indebted for the honor of this visit?" he asked frostily.

"I am Jeffrey Shannon, on special duty with the French General Staff. By order of Colonel LeClerc I am reporting to you, *mon Colonel,* for special service." As he spoke, Jeff relaxed a little. The colonel glared at this deviation from the strict position of attention and growled something under his breath. It sounded like:

"Intelligence fiddlesticks. What is needed is a real soldier!"

"This old war-horse is going to be hard to handle," the Eagle thought.

THE COLONEL spoke up, unable to keep uncomplimentary thoughts to himself.

"Can't understand what Paris means by sending a young squirt, a foreigner at that, on an important detail like this! Har-umph! If they insist upon sending me callow youths, I'll have to insist upon having them supervised by senior officers of rank and experience! Orderly, direct Major Desnot to report to me!"

The orderly snapped out a salute and departed.

"Major Desnot," said the old colonel heavily, "is Divisional Intelligence Officer. You will work under his direction!"

This was counter to instructions, but the Eagle decided to bide his time. There was little good to be gained from arguing with this old billygoat. Perhaps this Major Desnot would turn out to be a good guy and he could work without friction.

But his first view of Major Desnot dashed these hopes to the ground.

The major wore gold *pince-nez.* Humorless eyes glinted forth from behind them with all the warmth and friendliness of a plateful of cracked ice. He ignored the hand that Jeff Shannon stretched out to him, but he unbent like an icicle in a furnace when the colonel spoke to him. The Eagle put him down as a hundred percent Yes-Man.

"Major Desnot, you will take charge of this young man and instruct him in what you require of him and inform him of his duties. That's all!"

Captain Rene Martin was embarrassed and uncomfortable, but for the time being said nothing. The major led the two out.

As it happened, Sam Cameron was taking advantage of the interim to snatch a little well-merited rest and lay sprawled on a couch in the outer office, snoring.

Major Desnot stared at the snorer with a cold and frosty eye. Then his jaw set and his voice grew harsh as it rang out.

"It must indeed be difficult for you and your companion to leave the bright lights of Paris and come out here where real soldiers live and risk their lives!"

This was too much for Captain Martin.

"I think Major Desnot is suffering under a misapprehension concerning our American confrere," he said quietly. *"Monsieur* Shannon happens to be a Chevalier of the Legion d'Honneur of France, even though he is an American."

"I see," said Desnot very shortly and led the way to his own office, where he gave what information he had concerning the Nazi spy, von Drakenfels. His information told nothing that the Eagle did not already know.

"NOW, WHAT I want you to do, Shannon," Desnot started very arrogantly to issue his instructions—

"What you want me to do, Major Desnot, has very little to do with the case," said the Eagle very gently.

"Just what do you mean by that?" Desnot barked.

"What I said," returned the Eagle steadily. "I am sent here by higher authority to work independently upon this case. You are required to furnish cooperation, not direction."

Desnot started to rise from his chair.

"We'll see about that," he said, something akin to pleasure in his eye. "The first thing I will have to do is to report you for insubordination."

"And the second thing you will have to do, Major Desnot, will be to pack up your troubles in your old kit bag and face a court-martial back in Paris. Read that, Major!" The Eagle flipped out his confidential orders.

Desnot turned a sickly green as he read them.

"Of course, of course, *Monsieur,* I want to do all I can."

The major had become almost slavish in his deferential politeness. Shannon got rid of the man as quickly as he could; picked out some quarters for himself, Cameron and the tough little French Corporal Sauvage who had been sent ahead by Colonel LeClerc as bodyguard; and threw himself into the job of getting a line on the Nazi spy, Drakenfels.

"What do you want me to do?" asked Rene Martin.

"I'd suggest you change your identity and attempt to pick up the trail of the party that carried de Krelis away."

Rene nodded and disappeared, to turn up an hour later with darkened skin and in the uniform of a sergeant of Spahis.

"I'm flying down to join an *escadrille* of Spahis, who are conducting the search near the edge of the Egele Plateau," he said simply. "So long."

The Eagle, now in French khaki uniform, wasted no time in getting into action. From the regimental intelligence units, who were cordial and cooperative, he secured several men of ability and training, to work directly under him. These he assigned to strategic points, telephone switchboards, regimental headquarters, brigade headquarters and the headquarters of the corps.

The first job he tackled personally was to make a strict examination of all the records and descriptive lists of the officers in the force. From these he picked out several who seemed capable of furnishing leads. The second thing he did was to circulate among the regimental intelligence officers and pick up all the information possible.

IT DIDN'T take him long to figure out that the mysterious von Drakenfels was all that LeClerc had promised. Von Drakenfels had played fast and loose with the entire corps. No one could be sure that he was not still brazenly circulating around the corps area. It was almost certain that he was. Not an order was issued that did not find its way to the enemy. The movement of any body of troops, however small, was known immediately and commented upon caustically not only by dissident natives in the town but by Italian officers across the border in Tripoli. The arrival and departure of any officer of rank was immediately commented upon by scornful letters from this same Drakenfels.

The Eagle saw some of these letters. They were written on French official army stationery in a fine copperplate hand. There could not be the shadow of a doubt that the fellow was actually posing as a French officer! There was no other explanation for the ease with which Drakenfels found out all the decisions taken at various headquarters and the officers' meetings and staff conferences.

Yet in all this mess the Eagle detected a ray of hope, a chink in Drakenfels' armor. Drakenfels was obviously afflicted with the meglomania of the Nazi doctrine and possessed all the supercilious contempt for his antagonists that is such a marked feature of the Nazi beliefs.

A man like that could get over-confident. The Eagle knew human nature. Given enough rope, such men hanged themselves.

It was late at night when the Eagle's first day's work was finished.

He decided to snatch some rest for an hour and then get on the job once again. To be near the center of things, he dragged out a cot he found in an office in the headquarters building, stretched out and took a book from his musette bag with which to relax. It was a series of colorful stories by Rafael Sabatini concerning Cesare Borgia.

Jeff was in the middle of an interesting page when he heard someone enter the room. A heavy voice boomed out.

"Nero fiddling while Rome burns!"

The Eagle looked up to find the Chief of Staff, old Colonel de Castex, glaring at him.

The colonel was across the room in two strides and picked up the book to examine it, snorting like a hippopotamus as he read the title.

"Bah! Reading fiction while a silent battle is going on all around you! 'The Justice of the Duke'!' If there was any justice in Paris they would send someone over here who'd spend his time running down this von Drakenfels instead of reading trashy fiction! What you should be reading, *mon ami,* is a book on how to catch Nazi spies!"

"I don't find much time for reading, Colonel," said Jeff Shannon wearily, "except when I rest. I work pretty steadily at this game and find that my brain as well as my body needs occasional relaxation. Pretty sound psychology, Colonel. Try it some time."

Colonel de Castex snorted at him once more.

"Psychology! Bah! I'll believe in psychology when I see it capture von Drakenfels. The only reading good for young officers is a hard study of tactics and regulations! You'd better get some results around here before you talk so learnedly about psychology! Results! Results are what count!"

Grumbling deep in his throat, the old walrus flung himself out of the room.

The colonel had flung the book down on the desk. A white square of paper had fallen out from the volume. Thinking that it might be a loose page, the Eagle picked it up. His eyes widened as he studied it.

It was written in fine copperplate script.

> My dear Jeff Shannon:
> Pray consider me at your service in your praiseworthy attempts to put an end to my pernicious activities. I am indeed honored that a man of your attainments should be sent all the way from Paris on account of my unworthy self. I am hoping that you will prove yourself of higher mental calibre than the estimable but somewhat inept gentlemen against whom I have been pitted so far. It must be confessed that their clumsy efforts to apprehend me have been so easily evaded that the game is becoming slightly boresome. Accept, my dear Shannon, the assurances of my highest consideration.

The note was signed: "Erich, Graf von Drakenfels."

CHAPTER V

GUESS AND OUTGUESS

J EFF SHANNON studied the note in silence. He dropped the reading of his book for the time being and studied anew the notes he had made on the officer personnel of the corps.

The latter had not yielded very much with the exception of two. One of these was a Lieutenant Karl Mueller, born in Strasbourg of German parents and enlisted in the Foreign Legion where he had eventually gained a commission. The other was a Captain Hugo Wagner who was born in Paris of a German father and an Irish mother. Both of them spoke German flawlessly and both of them were in positions which gave them access to affairs at headquarters. Lieutenant Mueller being attached to the division staff as an assistant intelligence officer while Captain Wagner was regimental intelligence officer of the 2nd Regiment of the Foreign Legion. Both had blameless if somewhat colorless records.

Deciding to have these two men looked into more closely, Jeff went up to the telephone exchange where Charbier, one of his French aides, was installed at the telephone.

"Any news, Charbier?" he asked.

"*Oui, mon commandant,*" replied Charbier, frowning. "About five minutes ago someone called me personally, a voice that I could not recognize. This voice, laughing while it talked, said that if my chief, Jeff Shannon, needs any more reading matter, he'll be glad to supply it. I do not know who it was or what it was all about! I did not think it worthwhile to disturb you over it."

"Next time," said the Eagle gently, "don't hesitate to disturb me, no matter what the case may be. That was von Drakenfels."

"*Mon Dieu,*" the Frenchman breathed.

"Don't feel too bad about it," said the Eagle. We'll—"

He was interrupted by the entrance of an orderly, bearing an envelope from Cameron, who had gone to the message center. Inside was a note from Rene Martin and another note from Cameron attached to a sweat-stained square of paper covered with several columns of words.

"This message from de Krelis came in, brought by a native, an Ouled Moussa from the western hills. I am sending it with the bearer by return plane as it is terribly important— Rene Martin."

"These notes came in on the plane, carried by an unsanitary native who will act as guide to the place where de Krelis is held. The native is eating with the Mokhazenis of the headquarters detachment and is available when you want him," Cameron's note read.

Capt. Rene Martin

The message from de Krelis was in code, several columns of words.

It was the code upon which they had agreed, a diagonal code, in which the date was the key. In solving it, the Eagle first took the date, which added up to seven, then counted seven words from left to right on the top line, which gave him the second position of the code. Then, counting diagonally across the paper, still keeping from left to right, the last word was the ninth from the top.

With this number he went back to the first column, and counting down nine words, he had the first word of the message. Skipping nine words he had the second word. By continually, skipping nine words and going from left to right, he had managed to decipher part of the message when the orderly again came for him, demanding with great urgency his immediate attendance at a staff meeting by order of the Chief of Staff.

THE EAGLE went at once to the headquarters building, encountering Colonel de Castex as he entered the office.

"Behold this!" growled the colonel, shoving a piece of paper at the American officer. "I beg of you to read this, and discover for yourself what is going on at corps headquarters on the eve of an important troop movement!"

The note was written in the familiar copperplate script that characterized all of von Drakenfels' communications.

> Congratulations upon securing the talents of the new sleuth from Paris. Sorry that I have to relieve you of these few unimportant papers, *mais la guerre est toujours la guerre!*

"He's taken the operation orders for the troop movements scheduled for tomorrow!" spluttered the colonel. "Taken them right out of my dispatch case! Do you understand? Right out of this office! What in the name of *le bon Dieu* are you going to do about it?"

"He's a clever man, Colonel," the Eagle said quietly.

"*Mais bien sur!*" the colonel's tone was openly contemptuous. "Tell me something that I do not already know. Your task is to find von Drakenfels without any excuses or alibis! When are you going to do it?" He hammered on the desk top. "Our secret reports are that there are heavy Italian concentrations on the border near Sinauan about two hundred kilometers from here. The stolen operation orders prescribed the movements of our corps in taking up positions opposite that point—"

"In that case it is just as well that the orders were stolen!" the Eagle interrupted.

The colonel's jaw sagged open.

"Wha-what!"

"The orders were based upon false information," the Eagle snapped. "The real concentration of Italian forces is taking place nearly five hundred kilometers to the southward at Ghat, in the rear of the Egele Plateau. Weapons, gold and huge numbers of tribesmen are crossing there and assembling somewhere on the Egele Plateau, from which they will strike northward through Algeria, behind your forces—you will be cut off from your base."

The Eagle noted that other officers had come into the room and that it was filling up with the personnel of the staff meeting.

Colonel de Castex recovered his composure somewhat.

"Bah!" his voice was still contemptuous. "Words—words—what proof have you of these things?"

"Reports from trusted subordinates!" the Eagle answered, and then shrugged his shoulders as he saw the colonel's face harden into stubborn lines. "Very well," he said, "I will go myself and bring back proof of what I say! I will fly down immediately. In the meantime I strongly advise that you send some sort of a covering force to protect that flank in case I'm right."

"Waste of time and men!" snorted the colonel, then remembering the strict orders from Paris relented slightly. "Yes, I'll send a squad of the Foreign Legion down there. There's an old fortress there opposite Khat—the place is called Tazali—the men will be sent down by transport plane immediately—but when are you going to capture this Nazi spy in our midst?"

"Colonel," Jeff Shannon's voice was steady, "you've been trying unsuccessfully to capture him for a month. I have only been here forty-eight hours. All the same, I will have him for you in another forty-eight hours!" And with that he turned on his heel and left the meeting.

He went directly to the room where he had left his musette bag. Someone had evidently opened the bag for the volume of stories he had been reading. The book called "The Mercy of the Duke," was opened and spread face downward at the opened page. He knew he had not left the book like this, and he wondered idly who had been reading it. Picking it up to close the covers he found a square piece of paper underneath it. It was covered with the now familiar script.

My dear Shannon:
Obviously you are a civilian officer in need of the advice of a professional soldier. War is a highly complicated and involved game, requiring intense effort and study in order to master even its rudiments. My advice to you, as a man young in his military career, is to read less of Rafael Sabatini and more of Field Marshal von der Goltz. Follow my advice and I am sure you will find yourself a more worthy opponent than you have been so far. Accept, my dear sir, the assurances of my highest consideration.—Erich, Graf von Drakenfels.

Jeff found time to grin, figuring the Nazi chap must be slightly twisted to waste so much time in running around writing notes to people. He glanced at the book again and idly read the conclusion of the story he had started.

He stood stock still for a space as a sudden idea crystallized in his mind. Suddenly he saw his way clear before him!

But it must wait—his main job now was to verify that important information from the southern end of the *bled*, that ominous movement of tribesmen across the border behind the Egele Plateau.

De Krelis had written his code message under difficulties.

I am held within Rock El Jehado near Well Abu Mizzar in Valley of Vultures near Fort Tawanil—Mustapha ibn Hassen—the Senussi gathering here at border—thousands of men—attacking northward through Algeria—dlrected by someone in Tunis posing as French intelligence officer.

The Eagle reread the taunting note from van Drakenfels. It came over him suddenly that the whole tone of it was triumphant. In a lightning flash of intuition, he was certain that the Nazi spy knew all about de Krelis' message—knew de Krelis's identity and was laughing to himself. It meant that de Krelis's life was in danger—it also meant something else. He continued to decipher the message from the French officer.

"…bearer promised reward thousand francs gold to guide you here…."

WELL, IT was time to get started. The Eagle sent Charbier on an errand. The keen little Frenchman returned after a few minutes with a bundle wrapped in paper. The Eagle finished packing his musette bag.

He dropped by the Mokhazeni barracks for the native, the Ouled Moussa from the western hills, who was to guide him back.

The native had gone, they told him, to the flying field, where he was waiting by the plane that was to carry them back.

The Eagle made his way to the flying field. Before arriving there, he slipped quietly into an artillery shed, and in its shadows unrolled the bundle that Charbier had given him. From a far corner of that shed he issued moments later, shimmering white in the moonlight, magnificent in gold embroidered white silk *khalet* with embroidered silken headcloth. He strode with the lithe freedom and arrogance of a son of the great tent, a man born of high Arab lineage.

He located his plane, standing by itself on the runway. The landing lights were not turned on, pending his arrival. In the shadow of it stood a dark figure.

"Ho, thou in the shadows," said Jeff Shannon speaking in the faultless idiom of the high bred native, "if thou art awaiting the Roumi officer, he is no more, praise be to Allah!" And saying this he waited, inwardly tense but outwardly serene as became a high born son of the great tents.

"Lord, I was not told," said the man deferentially, and Jeff noted swiftly that he did not speak with the accent of an Ouled Moussa from the Western hills but in the manner of a Taureg.

His hunch was right! Von Drakenfels knew! Quick thinking was needed if de Krelis's life was to be saved.

"That is somewhat strange!" replied Jeff, and bent toward the man as though suspicious. "Give then the word, that no mistake can be made!"

The man, swarthy-faced and hook-nosed, was undoubtedly a desert-bred Taureg, being no less a person than Selim in fact. He came out of the shadows.

"There is no mistake, Lord!" said Selim, suddenly anxious to prove himself to this magnificent one. "The word is: 'The harvest of the moon is love.'"

Selim waited for the authoritative stranger to cap the verse of the old Berber song.

"And the harvest of the blades is blood!" added Jeff, the verse leaping to his lips from some half-forgotten memory of the ancient song. Selim again spoke.

"Word came to me within the hour to hasten here and slay this low born slave, this dog of an Ouled Moussa—which I have done—and to join myself with the Roumi officer and travel with him."

"Carrying word—" prompted Jeff, meanwhile quietly loosening his pistol underneath the silken robe.

"Carrying word to the Lord of the Portal of Doom to slay this Frankish woman captive, who is no woman—at once—"

"And the Roumi officer?"

"To slay him after arrival at the Rock of El Jehado!"

Jeff struck swiftly, so swiftly that the man had no warning and went down without a sound except the thud of that heavy pistol butt against his head.

IN THE shadows of the plane, the Eagle quickly divested himself of robe and headcloth, and, rolling them into a bundle, threw them in the cockpit of the plane.

He lifted and dragged the inert form of the man Selim into the rear cockpit and braced him against the seat with his belt—this to enable prying eyes to see that he was duly accompanied to the southward by the native.

These things done, he called to the mechanics. The floodlights were turned, the chocks removed, and the motor turned over.

The chief mechanic informed him that the big transport plane with its squad of Legionnaires had already taken off and was on its way to Fort Tawazil.

With the bound body of Selim behind him in the rear cockpit, Jeff took off and pointed the ship's nose for the desert regions to the south.

The Eagle had sufficient to occupy his mind without worrying about the man in the cockpit in rear of him. There was that matter of the false information of the Italian concentration opposite Duizat. It was plain that it was meant to hold the French immobile while the attack developed elsewhere.

There was also the danger of the trip he had himself undertaken, and the probability that von Drakenfels had sent orders to kill de Krelis by other messengers as well. The ship was traveling smoothly, he examined his controls and the twin guns and their ammunition holders.

There was another worry, and that was the little squad of men Colonel de Castex had sent down to Tawazil—a mere handful, doomed to certain death against that horde of nomads who were surging in through the border.

Night came on as he drove southward, a faint cloudiness filling the sky and starlight giving a dim radiance. His altimeter registered three thousand feet, his air speed indicator showed close to two hundred miles an hour. There was a bank of clouds showing ahead at which he barely glanced.

It was when he darted under the edge of this cloud that he looked up in amazement!

For three shadowy shapes roared down at him out of the clouds, their projectile-like advance preceded by thin, luminous lines of tracer bullets! They were Italian pursuit ships of the latest model!

The hostile guns were chattering death, screaming it in malignant bursts of fire which raked him as they converged upon his speeding ship.

His natural paralysis at this sudden turn of events was only momentary. His hands dropped to the trips of his own guns. His stick moved under his steady grasp. The air swarmed around him with the strange unknown attackers.

He flung his ship out of danger, his guns snarling back at the enemy as he slipped sideways.

For a split second he caught and held the nose of the last of the diving enemy ships in his sights. His guns screamed. Their lean smoking tracers drilled into the enemy ship just forward of the cockpit. They bit into wood and metal and sawed their way backward toward the pilot. The man saw their resistless march and rode his ship to avoid them. He was too late!

THE STREAM of hot metal sliced into him. His ship rolled away, only to present its belly to the rest of Jeff's burst. The enemy ship turned on over, the pilot's body hanging by the belt, as the ship blazed its way down out of the sky.

The other shadowy ships, dimly seen in the starlight, banked tightly and came back to finish their attack. Jeff hurled his way down the airway with his motor full out.

An enemy plane flung itself after him—levelled off and rolled in at him like a projectile. Bullets pecked at his wings. They were dangerously close to the cockpit. He waited until the last second, then edged away and dipped his nose. The other enemy ship flung itself down out of the sky at him—he was in danger of being caught in a slanting fire from right and left.

He dived with power full on. The ship screamed downward with the pull of its powerful motor added to the pull of gravity. Then suddenly he levelled off and shoved upward again. The good French plane trembled under the terrific strain, but her nose started slowly up, until suddenly with a savage rush, it hurled itself skyward like a steel pointed arrow.

And that arrow was pointing at the heart of the nearest enemy ship. The enemy was centered in Jeff's ring-sight. Already Jeff's tracer bullets were drilling remorselessly into the nose of the enemy ship. Whiffs of black smoke spewed forth from the motor. The ship was doomed, and as its pilot faced that realization, the remorseless stream of bullets found their way through to him, and his ship twisted crazily and lurched like a stricken thing down the skyway—tearing downward with a swiftly accelerating speed until the wail of its passing was killed by the immensity of the desert below.

The third ship, which had started a dive, suddenly levelled off, far to Jeff's right and sped away in the darkness, the glow of its exhaust growing smaller in the distance until at last it was lost in the clouds. There was no elation of victory in Jeff's thoughts.

The unexpected attack convinced him of one thing—that von Drakenfels already knew of the mishap to his emissary—that inert figure in the rear cockpit!

CHAPTER VI

THE DESERT FORT

IN THE meantime the transport plane carrying that little group of sturdy Legionnaires had long since moved on southward, and it was well beyond noon when they passed over the tortured and riven outcroppings of the Tinghert area and on to the northern abutments of the Egele Plateau.

Far ahead of them was the tiny fort, scarcely more than a blockhouse, which was their destination.

It was a silent, deserted and sinister looking place as they saw it. It reared itself up, one flank protected by the steep walls of the canyon, the other three sides facing on a plateau that sloped downward through a wild tangle of rocks and shrubs.

There was a stretch of hard sand near the fort which gave landing security, and here their plane came to rest, the heat on the desert floor striking up at them.

The hardened campaigners glanced about suspiciously at the lay of the land, studying as much of it as they could see from the plateau. Then they went stolidly into the fort, laid out their equipment in its single barrack-like building, and gravely set up their automatic rifles in the embrasures of the outer wall.

They were taking no chances, those Legionnaires. They knew the nomads of the desert!

It was Sergeant Barboz who calmly informed the plane pilot that the last garrison of this desolate place had been massacred to a man. He pointed out the graves underneath the wall just outside the wall of the north angle.

The Legionnaires' careful survey of the fort, their scrutiny of the gate and its repairs, the steady and disciplined preparation to put the place in readiness for defense, was an impressive sight.

BUT AN onlooker would have been more impressed had he been able to see a dry valley at the far end of which was a small spring.

It was five kilometers away. Under the shadows of its cliff were encamped all of the warriors of the Ouled Djerir and all of the warriors of the Ait bu Reg.

There were close to nine hundred warriors of the two tribes. Now, the Ouled Djerir and the Ait bu Reg are not ordinarily friendly. But they were united in hatred for the infidel. And that hatred had been sedulously cultivated by emissaries of the Senussi who had been working among them for the past month.

They had jointly given control to Sheik Ahmed el Kagah, who even now sought to restrain the ardor of the young warriors.

"Fools," he said, fingering his gray beard, "I know that our scouts have reported the arrival of this flying ship. But ye do not understand the custom of the Franks. The flying ship comes only to leave its cargo, and a small guard, then depart. The cargo will be of value, and the guard will be small. Better for us to wait until the ship departs."

A murmur of approval went up from the older heads among the warriors. This was sound counsel.

Back at the fort the pilot was in a quandary. He did not like leaving this little handful of men in this desolate place.

"Sure you'll be all right here?" he asked Sergeant Bardoz.

The Legionnaire nodded briefly.

"If we are not left too long," he said significantly, and glanced down over the edges of the plateau.

THE PILOT followed the direction of his glance. He could see nothing. Nor did the sergeant see, although he might have suspected the presence of four watchers whose glittering eyes peered at the fort about seven or eight hundred yards away, hidden like snakes behind the rocks and shrubs.

The pilot shook hands with the sergeant, piled into his ship and took off.

Sergeant Bardoz and his men watched the departure of the transport plane silently from their ramparts.

The men were contented and soon had cook fires going and water boiling.

But the contentment of his men was not shared by Sergeant Bardoz. He stood above the main gate staring long and thoughtfully down at the far edges of that plateau.

He was certain that he had seen a movement of some object among the rocks. He called up his corporal, a stolid Alsatian, Corporal Mollino.

Mollino nodded as his chief pointed out the phenomenon.

"They watch us!" said Mollino, briefly.

It was well along toward three in the afternoon. Sergeant Bardoz glanced up at the sun and around the face of the desert.

"They will not attack before dusk!" he said briefly. "We'll try to get ready for them."

With two sentries left on duty, the sergeant climbed down and made an inspection of the fort.

His chief concern was that pile of cargo taken from the ship.

It was covered over with a tarpaulin. It included boxes of reserve food and ammunition, reserve gas and oil for the plane. Sergeant Bardoz' heart lifted as he found two wooden boxes containing guns.

They were extra machine guns provided at Jeff Shannon's suggestion at the last moment. There were four of them, beautiful, efficient objects, simple in operation.

"Let them come," muttered Sergeant Bardoz. "We will be ready for them!"

As the afternoon drew to its close and the scorching yellow of the desert changed to velvety lavender, the sergeant and his men grew more alert each minute.

The sentries reported seeing what they believed to be the movements of large bodies of men at the far edge of the plateau. The sergeant verified this report, studying the place with his glasses.

In the half light, rocks, and clumps of scrubwood took on unreal shapes. The longer the sergeant stared the more did his imagination endow the sweeping plateau with life. He could actually see creeping forms and hear the rustle of bodies slipping forward over rock and sand.

"I'm getting jumpy," he said to himself.

To reassure him, there came the bellow of an old-fashioned rifle at the edge of the plateau, and a slug flattened itself out against the mud wall, scattering a shower of dust. The sergeant was immensely relieved. From a worried and temperamental human being he galvanized into the steel-nerved fighting machine that the Legionnaire should be.

There was no need to give orders. His men were on the alert, at their posts, fingers on triggers, peering into the darkness which had now descended upon the desert.

The opening shot seemed to have been a signal, for following it there came a rolling crescendo of fire from the far edge of the plateau, a crack and rattle of guns which filled the air with hissing, smacking, whining slugs that thudded and tore into mud wall, iron bound wooden gate and rock foundation.

There was no need to warn his men to save their ammunition. They stood by their guns, waiting.

The sergeant peered forth from an embrasure by the main gate. He knew now that what he saw was no figment of his imagination. The lower end of the plateau had come to life. The ground heaved and undulated with crawling forms, slinking forward snakelike through the gloom. The sergeant had not expected such great numbers. He was not a man to fool himself, once he had sized up the situation. He saw that it was hopeless....

OF THAT gallant fight put up by the handful of Legionnaires there are no records save the rumors within the tribes. But of the strategy of the old sheik there are many stories.

The Legionnaires died like men. And for once, the nomads did not mutilate their bodies. One strange thing they did do, however, at the insistence of the old sheik, was to divest the bodies of the slain of their uniforms.

And shortly thereafter the signs of battle were cleaned away, the wounded cared for, the dead buried. The plateau once more resumed its barren, empty look.

The strangest thing, however, was the fact that sentinels in the uniform of the Legion began once more to pace the ramparts.

Nor could one see, from a short distance away, that there was anything amiss—that these were not real Legionnaires. Especially, one could not fail to see the sinister crowd of men, five hundred of them, waiting silent and still hidden under the firing platforms and the fort's one building.

It was a deadly trap which the old sheik had set—and flying toward it, all unknowing, was Jeff Shannon, the Eagle.

CHAPTER VII

DESERT BATTLE

S **TILL ANOTHER** force of nomads had made camp for the night at a nearby oasis.

They were a section of the Ouled Delim, who, led by a young chieftain named Khebba ben Ayal, had come southward from Morocco to join the Senussi and were headed down from Ain Talba on their way to Ghat.

They were fierce proud warriors, over a thousand men, lean nomads well armed with a heavy proportion of rifles among old muskets and brass-handled swords.

Their evening supper fires were lighted and the subdued clamor of a nomad camp rose in the evening air.

Meanwhile the Eagle was peering down from his ship, scanning the bleak terrain beneath for signs of the small fort, which he had figured from rough calculations to be not more than ten or fifteen miles directly ahead.

It was then that he noted the lights of camp-fires far off to the right. Directly below him he could dimly make out the outlines of a small oasis. He brought his ship down carefully and landed in the smooth sand. A few yards from him the dim outlines of palm trees showed against the starlight.

Beneath them was what seemed to be some sort of a building.

He had almost forgotten the native in his rear cockpit.

For the first time he decided to take a look at him. He could not strike a light, for the slightest sign might disclose him to any prowling nomads.

He felt of the native. There was no trace of blood on the man. His practised fingers ran over Selim's head and face. There was the large welt on the forehead of the unconscious man caused by the pistol butt.

He found his flashlight. Cautiously shielding it, he let it play up and down on the form of the unconscious native. No, there was no other wound. It was as he had thought—the man was still unconscious.

But some steady and persistent sound impinged on Jeff's ears. It was the throb as of drums beaten from afar. There was something barbaric and remorseless about the sound. Borne faintly from the same direction came the shrill whine of native flutes. Evidently there were a lot of nomads in the vicinity.

Walking out from the shadow of the machine, Jeff stared towards the direction of the sound.

Again he recognized those fires, their flickering gleams reflected against the palm trees of that oasis not over a thousand yards or so distant, as nearly as he could estimate in the darkness.

He walked away from the dark blur of his ship in an effort to explore the place in which he found himself.

Some night animal rustled away among the trees as he came up to the palms. The dark mass that he had seen under the palm trees resolved itself into ruins of an old building. It was empty and deserted and its sagging walls looked dangerously near to tottering over. He did not venture too close to it.

Something crashed and thudded in the brush near at hand. Instinctively Jeff leaped aside, flashed forth a single beam of his flashlight, before he remembered the danger.

Then he cut off the beam and was in darkness as he saw the slinking form of a jackal, staring at him, green-eyed and snarling, not ten feet away.

He walked slowly back to his plane.

The drums were no longer throbbing.

The silence left by their cessation of activity became a little ominous and sinister. It was as though some unseen force was watching and waiting.

He wondered if the keen eyes of a Berber sentry had spied the single and cautious flash of his light.

He climbed up into his plane, and sat in the cockpit. There he cautiously snapped a light from a match, bending low down so that its gleam could not be detected, and lighted a cigarette.

Lieutenant de Krelis

Selim was silent, breathing evenly behind him, his head still slumped forward on the cockpit rim.

The Eagle stared out over the desert, trying to pierce the blackness of the night.

He stiffened in his seat as he saw what he believed to be movement far out between this little oasis and that large one occupied by the tribesmen. The eyes can play strange tricks upon one who stares too intently into the unreal light of the moon. He closed his own eyes for a moment and rested his head against the back of his cockpit.

He was certain that he had seen movement out there on the desert.

He opened his eyes again. Refreshed after a few seconds' rest, they reported with startling clearness what he had already suspected.

The dim shapes of men mounted on camels, and men moving forward silently on foot, shone up with startling clearness! Men were coming straight from that other oasis to his right. Another group who had evidently moved along the edge of the desert were coming in from another direction. Still a third group was converging in upon him from the opposite direction. Jeff crushed out his cigarette on the inside of the cockpit.

It was uncanny, the absolute silence of those moving figures.

The three columns were extending out now into a sort of a line and circling the oasis. There were all of five hundred men, afoot, ahorse, and on camel back. The gaunt shapes of the camels could now plainly be seen and the slowly deepening light of the rising moon gleamed on steel.

It needed no analysis on the Eagle's part to make him realize that he was in for a bad time!

He had landed, facing to the south, toward that little fort which he reasoned could not be more than a mile or two on his front.

Glancing again toward that enveloping mass of armed nomads, Jeff noted that the advance scouts were almost within a hundred and fifty yards by now. They came on, those dismounted men, rifles flung across their bodies, peering intently into the obscurity of the small oasis. As yet they probably had not seen him. It was only a matter of a few seconds until they came near enough to make out the dark outlines of his plane.

THE EAGLE had seen enough. He switched on his self-starter. The motor roared into a coughing, barking bellow of sound. He gave it the gun.

The motor deepened into a full-throated hymn of power.

The nomads halted for a second, and suddenly the plane rattled with the impact of bullets. Guns flashed but he could hear little sound above the roar of the motor. He kept his head low and gave the engine more gun. In a moment the plane began to creep forward with the pull of that whirling propeller. There was a flash of white burnooses, the gleam of steel, the glow of rifles fired from nearby.

The Eagle's hands dropped to the trips of his guns.

His tracer bullets leaped forward through the darkness, driving with irresistible force into that mob of close-packed humanity. It was as though a huge knife was slicing through the multitude.

But the ship would not rise! One of the nomad bullets had cut the elevator controls!

The way opened out before the slowly advancing plane. The guns chattered and roared.

Men went down before them, camels jerked and floundered and slumped to right and left.

The plane moved forward with more and more speed but he could not get it off the ground. He gave it more gas. It dashed out of the shadows of the oasis. The guns belched forth their thin messages of death. The wheels of his plane ran into and over still forms that spread themselves miraculously before him. A wall of shouting, screaming men flashed by on either side.

Bullets hummed and sang and thudded into the machine.

Suddenly he was clear! Still on the ground, but clear!

The smooth expanse of desert sand stretched out before him, rising upward toward that plateau which held Fort Tawazil on its farther crest.

Jeff stepped forward, gun out, starting toward the Nubian.

Suddenly the horde of nomads was far behind him. Jeff glanced to the rear. Selim was silent in the rear cockpit, his eyes dull and glazed. A thin trickle of blood ran down his forehead.

The plane was gaining more speed as the powerful engine swung the propeller and lifted it forward. It was making a good thirty to thirty-five miles an hour now. Jeff was hard pushed to use his rudder quickly enough to avoid rock clumps and gulleys that appeared suddenly in his path.

He narrowly avoided plunging into the bottom of a dry gully, some thirty feet deep, the ship careening for one dizzy second on its edge before he jerked it away from that danger spot.

The ship breasted the slope and roared up it as though nothing could stop it.

Ahead of him Jeff saw the squat outlines of the fort dimly lighted by the increasing rays of the moon.

A comforting sight was the gleam of steel from a sentinel's rifle. Jeff glanced from his delicate task of threading his way between outcropping rocks and found comfort in the sight of that figure pacing back and forth so solidly in the moonlight far ahead.

The fort spelled strength and security and a bulwark against attack.

CHAPTER VIII

THE HOLY ONE

WITHIN THE fort itself, keen eyes and ears had listened to the battle of the night.

Faintly borne on the desert air had come the roar and rattle of rifle fire by those marauding Berbers who had attempted to capture the plane. More clearly had come the steady roar of the plane's answering guns.

The noise of pursuit had come closer and ever closer until it had died out and been succeeded by the increasing roar of the motor of the plane.

Those in the watchtower of the fort had reported the approach, too rapid for camel or mounted man or man on foot, of that strange blur in the darkness which was the glow of the plane's exhaust. It had dipped into hollows and risen again on crests, only to dip once more, but it came nearer and ever nearer. What it was, none of them knew, but those older ones among them who had traveled farther and had seen more, decided that it was some sort of an automobile, that strange thing propelled without horses or mules which ran smoothly over the ground at such a terrific burst of speed.

As it came nearer, men saw that it was a lone affair. Therefore there was not more than a single man with it, at the most, two or three. How a French automobile could come this far in the desert, they did not know. But their plans were quickly made under the leadership of the sheik, old Ahmed el Kabah.

"All ye unwise ones who would crane your necks, full of idle curiosity like geese in the market place, remain hidden! Let the strange land machine come in here. No doubt they are certain that friends await them. Once inside the fort, we can quickly dispose of the venturesome Frank!"

His counsel was obeyed. The curious ones retired again into their hiding places in the shadows under the firing platforms.

The gates were swung wide. The sentinels paced their posts, bayonets gleaming in the moonlight.

Nearer and nearer came the strange machine with the reddish glow marking its advance. It dipped down into the hollows. It rose again on the crests and dipped, disappearing from view. There was one small hollow not two hundred yards from the fort. The strange machine dipped into this and suddenly its roaring motor grew silent. Minute after minute passed. The old sheik looked about him. Questioning glances were directed upon him.

"Allah alone knows what has happened!" he said. "There is safety in moving with caution."

And thus they waited, those fatalists, those sons of the desert.

Five minutes dragged into ten; ten minutes into fifteen. And still they waited.

AT THE moment when the plane, drawn forward by the pull of its powerful motor and propeller, breasted the rise that flanked the hollow, Jeff Shannon had glanced at the fort again. His eyes had suddenly grown watchful! He peered forward in the few seconds allowed him before his machine dipped into the hollow. As it descended into that hollow, he cut off the engine. The plane ran along under its own momentum for a few yards, and then slowed up as the incline ended at the bottom of the gulley and the steep farther side rose before it. Just short of the crest it came to rest.

The Eagle was up and out of the cockpit with startling speed. He crawled up under the crest and peered at the fort. Then quietly he pushed himself downward and returned to the machine. For a moment he stood there in thought. Then he glanced at the recumbent form of the man in the rear cockpit.

Selim was dead. With more speed than gentleness, Jeff lifted the corpse out of his seat. Thereafter, it was but the work of a second to unloosen that bundle in the cockpit and dress himself in silken Khalat and head cloth.

This done, he carried the dead body of the Berber to where some overhanging scented bushes provided concealment. Carefully he deposited the form of his traveling companion under these bushes and hurried back to the plane.

There was a small japanned tin box back of his seat. This he pulled out and from its contents he selected a tube. Squeezing out some of the pigments from this tube, he smeared it over his face, reducing its red and white healthiness to a dull brown.

With the hood of the Khalat over his head and his face partially concealed by its folds, he might have passed anywhere for what he now seemed to be, a high born desert dwelling Berber.

The plane had slid backwards down the slope and was resting at the bottom. He manipulated the self-starter. The motor burst into a roar. In a few more seconds the propeller was whirling with increasing speed.

The plane edged forward slowly. With gradually increasing power, it rolled up the incline and out upon the level going, heading toward that wide gate of the fort.

All of a hundred rifles were ready to bark forth their swift messages of death when that whirling propeller pulled the plane up to the walls and then slowed down.

But the rifles lowered uncertainly. The eyes of the old sheik widened. This queer devilish invention of the white man ceased its roaring thundering cough. The propeller blades grew slower and slower in their revolutions as the motor was cut off.

Lean, brown faces stared at the queer sight, but fingers dropped away from triggers.

For the lone man sitting behind those slowly revolving propeller blades was a keen-faced, dark-skinned son of the desert!

Moreover, he was no lowly born son of the desert, but a man who had first seen the light of day in a great tent, a thing self evident from the austerity and arrogance of his pose and the richness of his attire.

Moreover, and this was the greatest wonder of all, he entered that place of hatred and suspicion making the Secret Sign of the Senussi, the three fingers outstretched, and dipped three times in the direction of Mecca!

TRIBESMEN IN ragged burnooses crowded about him, questioning vehemently, but the stranger paid them no heed. His questing eyes sought and unerringly fixed upon the face of the old sheik.

"Peace be unto you!" said the stranger in clear Arabic, addressing none other than the old sheik himself, and disregarding all lesser men.

"And to you, peace!" returned the old tribal chieftain, his lips mechanically forming the customary response of courtesy.

"These, thy followers, crowd too closely upon me," calmly stated the new arrival. "I would be free from their importunities."

The old sheik bowed his head submissively and then raised it and glared at his followers.

"Back, ye Sons of Many Fathers!" cursed the old chief. "Are ye blind that ye cannot see that there is a Holy Man amongst ye!"

The stranger, from his lofty perch in that queer machine, glanced about him questioningly.

"I see," he said, "by the favor of Allah ye hold this fort! But what means this masquerading of True Believers in the clothing of the Franks?"

The old man was eager in his explanation and a little proud. He explained how they had captured the place, and he explained in detail his ruse for ensnaring the airship of the Infidels when it returned.

"Ye have done well, and I will carry word of your wisdom to the Lord of the Portals of Death!"

The stranger inclined his head gravely, as though approving.

"Ye have done well!" repeated the stranger, and then went on: "Tell me, oh Sheik, at what hour do you expect the return of these infidels? At what hour do you expect them to come here to fall victims to your superior wisdom?"

"That will be as Allah wills!" said the old sheik. "But I do not expect them before daylight." The old chief's eyes glanced shrewdly over the bullet dented fuselage of the plane.

"Ye have been molested on your way hither?" he said.

All the while the Eagle had been listening for the sound of pursuit which he knew was inevitable. It had come, faint and far, to his ears, but nevertheless distinct. The sound of many angry men, afoot, ahorse and on camel, swarming to the lower edges of the plateau. He nodded curtly.

"I have been molested by a rabble of ill-begotten ones, marauders of the desert, who know not the Lord of the Portals of Death, and the respect due his

The Eagle brought his gun butt down hard.

emissaries! Even now they follow close upon my trail. Do ye, then, oh Sheik, have your young men to load their pieces and give them fitting reception when they come howling upon my trail like a pack of jackals!"

"To hear is to obey, oh Holy One!" said the sheik.

He raised his voice so that all men heard. The response was immediate. Grunting their satisfaction, the men who had been forced to remain concealed all day swarmed the ramparts and lay cheek to rifle stock as they waited, listening as the clamor of that pursuit grew greater.

FAR DOWN the edge of the plateau a confused mass of men and horses and camels showed itself. Like hounds on a trail, they were following the marks of those rubber tire wheels in the sand. Looking neither to the right nor to the left, they did not see the dead body of Selim hidden under the stunted bushes. They came on, their wild cries growing louder and louder.

The tribesmen in the fort waited, fingers on triggers, as the disorderly mob streamed toward the fort. Nor did it take those warriors of the Ouled Djerir and of the Ait bu Reg long to distinguish the peculiar war cry of their hereditary enemies, the Ouled Delim!

"Better that ye warn your men to hold their fire," advised the austere stranger from the cockpit.

And the old sheik did as he was bade, ringing out his warning to the younger and more impatient members of his tribesmen. The warning was effective, for the men along the walls, impatient as they were to see the carnage commence, held rifle stocks to cheeks and kept anxious fingers still, until the range had decreased to some three hundred meters.

And then some excited youngster started the fusillade. The rifles barked jerkily in response, their staccato stuttering deepening into a swelling roar as gun after gun took up the chorus. A hail of lead whined and poured into the ragged column of the pursuers, a hail of lead that dropped man after man, and sent plunging camels crashing to earth.

Wild shouts rose from the tribesmen behind the walls. Screams of pain and anger answered them from the pursuing forces. The hail of lead intensified in volume and in deadliness as the fanatical survivors struggled onward against that rattling chorus of whispering and thudding hornets that stung and killed.

Human flesh and blood, no matter how actuated, by the fires of fanaticism, could not long withstand that withering outpouring of winged death! The plateau surface became dotted with the bodies of the slain. The surviving tribesmen faltered and turned.

The sheik had great difficulty in making his men cease their frenzied loading and firing. It was not within the compass of his plans to have the plateau littered up with the bodies of the slain. The cessation of that hail of death emboldened the fleeing to slow up their precipitate progress. It emboldened the more stubborn, those nearest the front, to return cautiously, in an attempt to retrieve the bodies of the slain.

No opposition was offered to this, and they grew bolder, until finally they were appearing in groups and clumps of men, silently carrying away their dead. No rifle barked from the embrasures of the court, and it was not long before most of the traces of combat had disappeared, carried limply from the plateau by friends and kinsmen.

CHAPTER IX

THE ROCK OF EL JEHADO

INSIDE THE fort, the Eagle strolled about among the sweaty tribesmen who were congratulating themselves upon easy victory. He paused before one swarthy son of the desert. The man looked up from oiling his rifle and gazed with respect upon the tall man, swathed in the silken Khalat.

"Ye are of the Ouled Djerir?" asked Jeff.

"Aye, Holy One," returned the Berber.

"You have traveled far?"

"Ben Abbes, no less!" returned the nomad.

"Your camels, are they far from here?"

"They are hidden at the Well of Abu Mizzar, at the far end of the Valley of the Vultures, which is hard by the Rock of El Jehado, which contains the Portals of Doom!" explained the man simply.

"So!" Jeff Shannon's voice was perfectly casual. "May ye ride well and far in the service of the Prophet. Peace be upon ye!"

He strode away, an imposing figure in the long robe of the desert. He had found what he wished to know.

The tribesmen were excited over their brush with the other desert nomads. Also, being unused to forts, they were careless. The gates had remained opened, and men strolled in and out.

It was of this situation that the Eagle took immediate advantage. Unnoted in the darkness, he slipped out the gate of the fort, and strolled unconcernedly along the plateau, retracing the route he had followed coming in.

It was not long until he saw and heard men moving about in the darkness of the plateau, the last of those who were carrying away the bodies of the slain and wounded kinsmen. He directed his steps to one of the groups working nearby. The moon was beginning to set and already the plateau was growing darker. It was impossible to tell a man's features or to discern much more than his outline. Counting on this, the Eagle came up boldly to within a few yards of the group.

"Peace be unto you!" he saluted.

"And to you, peace!" returned one of the tribesmen, mechanically.

"One of you who is swift of foot, take word to your chief immediately!" Jeff's voice was commanding. He gave the man no time for questions.

"Tell him this," said Jeff. "The camels and tents of the Ouled Djerir and Ait bu Reg are hidden by the Well of Abu Mizzar in the Valley of the Vultures hard by the Rock of El Jehado!"

A buzz of excitement rose from the group who had heard his word. Visions of valuable loot to be had for the taking rose quickly to their minds. One among them stepped out.

"Who are ye who come bringing this good word?"

"One who wishes you well," said Jeff quietly, and faded back into the darkness.

He walked slowly back to the fort. His absence had passed unobserved.

The effect of his maneuver was soon apparent. There came a shot from above, on the wall, and a sound of camel-men racing close to the fort. Those men outside quickly ran in and the gates were closed.

A long exultant shout came from the camel-men in the outer darkness.

"Ho, sons of nameless mothers!" shouted a voice exultantly. "We ride now to the Well of Abu Mizzar in the Valley of the Vultures to take thy camels and tents even from under the shadow of the Gates of Doom!"

AN ANGRY shout broke forth from the throats of the men he had heard. In a second the whole interior of the fort was in turmoil. Dear to the desert man is his knife and his gun, but essential to his life is his camel. It is his wealth and his unit of wealth.

Nothing could stop those men. They tore down from the firing platform, grasping rifles and swords. The voice of the sheik rose in vain. He was hauled along with the rush of frenzied men.

They swarmed out of the gates of the fort like a horde of angry hounds on the trail. Their voices grew faint in the darkness as they ran shouting on the tracks of the men who would deprive them of their mounts.

In a few minutes the fort was emptied of every living thing except Jeff Shannon. He stood by his ship and looked about him. The gates were open and the place deserted.

Far down the plateau, growing faint in the distance, he could hear the excited shouts of the pursuing tribesmen and the taunting yells of those men who with superior speed were setting forth to loot them of their wealth.

An occasional shot echoed back as the mad pursuers attempted to halt their enemy.

"So far, so good!" thought Jeff.

And throwing off the confining folds of the Khalat, he went to work on the broken cable of the plane. Working with swift, practiced hands, he quickly had the damage repaired. One thing more he had to do, and that was done when he found the tins of reserve gas left by the transport plane that had brought the Legionnaires.

There was a confused murmur of shouts welling on the breeze and the sound of an occasional shot coming from the direction taken by the fighting tribesmen.

From the words of the tribesmen he knew where the secret place of the Senussi could be found on the plateau above him. The Rock of El Jehado, they called it—and another had referred to its appearance "like a great ship." And there was talk of its entrance, called by one the Sword Cleft in the Rock and by others the Gate of Doom.

It was then that the hardest part of his program came. For he had to wait.

There was no doubt in his mind that Rene Martin and his squadron of Spahis would be somewhere in the vicinity. And they would undoubtedly have heard the firing and would be on their way to investigate. He made up his mind to gamble on the chance that they would come before daylight.

He seated himself in the cockpit of his plane and waited.

It was an eerie business. The little desert winds whispered and whimpered about him. The snarls of fighting jackals came from down the plateau. From far off came the subdued murmur of the fighting between the tribesmen—a rear guard action as he well knew, for the Ouled Delim had a good start of their foes.

They would come swirling and fighting to the Rock of El Jehado and it was upon that that he counted to aid him in carrying out his plans successfully.

If only Rene Martin would appear!

The slow minutes dragged on like centuries. In the chill that precedes the desert dawn, he shivered and wrapped the soft folds of his Khalat more closely about him.

It began to seem to him that his was a hopeless wait—Rene Martin might be miles away. To do what he had set out to do he must move quickly or else his chance would be gone. And de Krelis's life hung upon his success, for he had no doubt that the diabolically clever brain of von Drakenfels had seen the necessity of getting word to the Senussi about de Krelis' true status.

Before touching his self-starter he listened again. Then his head went up sharply.

CHAPTER X

THE RED CURTAINS

H E **HEARD** the unmistakable clink of steel against stone! Something moved in the shadows on the plateau. Two dark shadows detached themselves from the deeper gloom and came on. Behind them moved a deeper and bulkier shadow advancing snakelike across the plateau. A surge of thankfulness went through Jeff Shannon.

He called out in French. His hail was answered immediately.

There came a clatter of hoofs—suddenly the darkness was alive with Spahis—Rene Martin was grasping his hand.

"What has happened?" asked Rene eagerly.

Quickly Jeff told him. "And now there is no time for talk, Rene. Have your men scatter and pick up all the burnooses they can find. Conceal all military trappings. You and your men will be of the Ouled el Seif—from the Draa Plateau—I am your leader—we come to join the Senussi—my name is Abdul ben Jeffa. I go now to fly after these fighting tribesmen—you follow with your two hundred men. Perhaps, God willing, we can make shift to enter the Rock of El Jehado, capture this leader and rescue de Krelis—*c'est entendu, mon vieux chou?*"

"Yes, it is understood, old friend!" grinned the Frenchman and turned to his men, telling them.

There rose a jubilant murmur and grunts of satisfaction from the lean desert-bred Berbers who were the Spahi cavalrymen. It was a role they loved.

Jeff climbed into his plane, leaned down from the cockpit.

"The sign is 'The harvest of the moon is love,'" he said, "and the countersign—'the harvest of the blades is blood!' I go now, follow me quickly as you can!"

He woke his motor into life, horsemen cleared out of his way, he gathered speed and was in the air.

It was a matter of minutes only to catch up with the fighting tribesmen and pass over them. They were moving slowly, lean wolves harried by lean wolves, toward the Valley of the Vultures and the Rock of El Jehado, and already were within a quarter mile of the place.

In the first faint rays of dawn Jeff saw it, looming like a great battleship at the head of the desolate valley.

There was an oasis hard by, and near this Jeff came down, finding, as he had reasoned, that it was the oasis that guarded the camels and horsemen of the followers of the old sheik. There were women and children here and a few old men, listening apprehensively to the sound of fighting coming ever nearer. Jeff had concealed his plane in a hollow of the sand dunes and now strode masterfully among them.

Startled at the apparition of this tall, richly-clad prince of the desert, they quickly saddled a horse for him and he galloped toward the rock, looming up silent and sinister above the sands.

Nearing it, he saw the long cleft in the cliff.

He rode arrogantly toward the place, noting that a swarm of Nubian guards were about the entrance, peering and listening to the tumult of fighting which was rolling steadily nearer.

They were huge men, with serene black faces rising above cloaks of fine white wool, lined with green and gold, caught in by broad belts of red leather in which were thrust the ivory handles of knives and revolvers. Across their backs they bore excellent rifles of Belgian make.

"'The harvest of the moon is love!'" Jeff gave the sign, low voiced.

"'The harvest of the blades is blood!'" echoed the leader of the Nubians mechanically, and strode forward, respectful.

THE RICHNESS of Jeff's attire and the arrogance of his bearing had its effect on these men. One sprang to hold his horse while he dismounted, another aided him to the ground and they bowed low as he announced himself.

"Send word to your master that I am the Sheik Abdul ben Jeffa, of the Ouled el Seif—the Sons of the Sword—from the plateau of Draa and that I bring two hundred swords to him. Tell him that the Ouled Delim even now come to attack him, having revolted, and that my men are battling with them. Make haste and I will follow!"

A tall Nubian ran ahead, entering the narrow opening, and two others fell in behind Jeff as he strode into the gate and up the winding chasm. It was evidently the former bed of a stream, but it had been smoothed out and made passable by the hand of man. It was well guarded. Jeff noted loopholes set within the rocky walls, commanding each turn and twist of the ascending passage.

They came at last to a lovely garden and a cool, dark building before which eunuchs with drawn swords stood on guard. Within all was cool and quiet, Moorish arches, disdaining by their grace the weight they bore, gave vistas of long galleries.

At the end of the longer of these galleries there was a sort of throne beneath a great arch, a throne that gave upon a view of the exquisite garden with its pools and fountains.

With a swift indrawing of his breath, Jeff Shannon gazed upon the man who sat upon the throne.

He was dressed in black silk, embroidered in gold, and wore a purple sash about his waist.

The face was coarse and fleshy, with deep pouches under the eyes, and the man's stomach bulged outward over the folds of his sash.

Behind him stood two Nubian slaves, naked to the waist, leaning on broad-bladed swords. A brown-skinned girl waved a peacock feather-fan above the man's head.

Mustapha ibn Hassen was high in the councils of the Senussi. There was power and cruelty in the man's heavy lidded eyes, as he peered at the tall stranger before him.

"Peace be unto you," said the Eagle gravely.

"And unto you, peace!" the man's voice was flat and toneless.

"I am the Sheik Abdul ben Jeffa," continued Jeff, "and I bring two hundred swords of the Ouled el Seif to join your forces!"

"So men have reported," said the man above him with no flicker of interest showing.

At that second came an interruption. A Eurasian, a tall, thin man in white robe, came soft footed, and, bowing low before his master, handed him a folded slip of paper.

The Eagle's impassive face gave no sign of his perturbation as he watched the fleshy face of the man above him. Mustapha ibn Hassan's face was also expressionless as he read the message.

THERE CAME out of the shadows behind the throne a silent Nubian swathed to his eyes in white burnoose. In his belt of red leather he bore a length of silken cord, the type of silken cord used for strangling criminals. The heavy dull eyes of Mustapha ibn Hassen rested upon this man a second.

"Go, thou," he said, "to the harem quarters and bring forth the Frankish woman—who is no woman. Bring that one here that I may see justice done before my eyes!"

The Eagle showed by no change of expression that he heard or understood. The message from van Drakenfels had come through at last! Did that fateful piece of paper contain also warning of him? He would soon know.

Yussuf, the Strangler, bowed low and departed. The Eagle noted the direction of his going—and waited.

As he waited, he did some fast thinking. This Mustapha ibn Hassen was reputed to possess the *baraka*—divine protection against harm. Bullets would be turned aside from his flesh and sword blades shatter against him harmlessly—or so his followers believed.

The heavy eyes of Mustapha rested fleetingly upon the man before him.

"Ye do well," he said in his flat, dull voice, "ye do well to come so far to serve the True Faith. But now ye must rest and refresh yourself. Later we will converse. I send now to disperse this rabble that clamors before the gates. Do thou partake of food and rest until I send for thee."

He glanced obliquely at one of the tall Nubians nearby.

"Take the honored guest to the Room of the Red Curtains," he said, "and see that in all things he is well served!"

There was a second's flicker of the Nubian's eyes that warned Jeff, but he gave no sign. Bowing low, he turned and followed the Nubian, who led him in the *same direction* taken by Yussuf the Strangler.

At the end of the hall, they turned into a narrow corridor at the left. The Eagle, grave and unperturbed, kept step with his companion.

They came at last to a broader hall that ran the length of the building.

The Nubian halted before a pair of heavy red curtains that separated the hall from some inner room. There was a strange light in the man's eyes.

Jeff Shannon half turned as though to push aside the red curtains and enter. Then, with the speed of a black panther and with all its intensity of controlled power, he twisted and came up under the Nubian's outstretched arm, his fist driving with the force of a battering ram at the man's head.

The Nubian staggered. Before he had time to recover, Jeff propelled him through the curtains.

There came a stifled grunt, the sound as of a butcher's ax striking the chopping block, and the thud of a falling body!

JEFF BACKED away from those sinister red curtains and walked sedately down the hallway until he heard approaching footsteps. Hiding behind the shadows of a Moorish pillar, he saw those whom he sought approaching.

The tall Nubian, Yussuf the Strangler, was driving before him a figure in the costume of a white woman. Young de Krelis's face was set in hopeless lines. His hands were tied behind him. There was the mark of a blow on his cheek.

The Eagle loosened his pistol in its holster and stepped forth as Yussuf came opposite his hiding place. The startled Nubian dropped hand to belt for his knife as the Eagle struck. The heavy pistol butt crashed above the Nubian's ear. The man went down without a sound.

There came a swift, thankful gasp from de Krelis. In a thrice, Jeff unbound him. The two dragged the Nubian's inert form behind the shadows of the pillars. Here they swiftly divested him of his burnoose and de Krelis donned it.

Mustapha ibn Hassen half rose from his seat as two men appeared suddenly beside him. One of them was the white-robed, young sheik of the Ouled el Seif whom he had sent to his death not five moments ago! The other was a slighter, smaller man in a burnoose obviously several sizes too large for him.

It was then that things became blurred to Mustapha ibn Hassen, for the slighter man pressed a pistol to the head of the Nubian and there was a muffled shot.

At almost the same second Mustapha heard, as though afar off, the echo of another shot and a searing pain shot through his body and he fell illimitable depths into a sea of forgetfulness.

The body was thrown into the darkness behind the thronelike chair.

The two shots, muffled purposely by close pressure of pistol muzzle against cloth, were evidently not heard, for men's minds were on the turmoil outside the gates below. The Ouled Delim and their enemies had been thrown backward by the arrival of a new force, grim riders who swept across the desert face and swarmed about the gates of the Rock.

Unnoted and unhurried, the Eagle and de Krelis strode down the winding ramp, coming at last to where the horsemen below recognized them.

CHAPTER XI

MURDER

F **AR TO** the north, the town of Duizat was practically deserted. Colonel de Castex, stubbornly convinced of the truthfulness of the "false" information he had received, had prevailed upon his general to move his entire force down into that system of trenches already constructed along the border facing Italian Tripoli, trenches especially strong opposite the Tripolitan town of Sinuan. "The Little Maginot Line," the French called it.

The Italians, of course, had immediately massed troops on their side, and there were large forces of Italian Colonial Infantry, as well as many tribesmen from the hinterland of Tripoli and the southern reaches of the Libyan Desert.

It was well toward the evening of the second day since Jeff Shannon's departure when the telephone bell rang in Sam Cameron's dugout, a dugout he shared with the Intelligence officer of the *Deuxième* Tirailleur Regiment.

"By the Lord Harry, I'm glad to hear your voice, Jeff!" Cameron exclaimed. "When did you get back? Just now? Listen, guy, I've got that requisition, Form 18B, all filled out and ready for you to sign. Where are you? Righto. I'll be over at once."

Cameron hung up, grabbed his hat and was out of the dugout in a split second.

Jeff Shannon, with Rene Martin and young de Krelis near him, hung up the phone, trying not to show his excitement. For the phrase used by Cameron meant that he had had some important information that he could not trust anyone to deliver but himself.

Jeff was elated. After all, there were only a few hours left for him to make good his promise to run down the Nazi spy, von Drakenfels. And judging by Cameron's cryptic report, the net was evidently closing around Drakenfels!

They were occupying the Machine Gun Battalion P.C. Jeff listened to the talk of his companions with half an ear, waiting for the appearance of Cameron. Minute after slow minute dragged along until twenty minutes had passed. Jeff glanced at his watch.

"Where the devil did that call come from?" he asked the man at the switchboard.

"From the *Deuxième* Tirailleurs," returned the man stolidly.

"How far is that from here?"

"About five minutes' walk!" returned the orderly.

Another ten minutes passed. Jeff could not stand the strain of waiting any longer. He went out and headed toward the *Deuxième* Tirailleur P.C. Halfway there he rounded an abutting wall in the communication trench and was halted by a group of stretcher bearers and a doctor, gathered about a form lying huddled on the ground.

One look was enough.

It was Cameron, the back of his head blown out.

The job had been done with a pistol, fired from near at hand, for there were powder marks on the head.

Cameron had been murdered just where the trench turned at an angle. It was plain to be seen that the assassin had lurked around the turn and had fired as Cameron had passed by, hurrying on his way to the Machine Gun P.C. with his important information, whatever it was.

JEFF HAD assumed as a matter of course that the telephone wires were constantly tapped. But this fellow von Drakenfels was uncanny. Not only had he kept Cameron under surveillance but he seemed to have known instantly, in spite of the code message, when the Englishman had started out with his information. Von Drakenfels had struck with brutal swiftness.

Investigation disclosed that no one had seen the murder. The body had been found by a passing ration detail.

News travels fast in a military command and Jeff could sense the rising anger of the men as they became aware of the fact that the Nazi spy had added another murder to his already long list.

Jeff hurried straight to Cameron's quarters.

Here he found everything in disorder. The contents of Cameron's musette bag were scattered all over his cot, his notebook was gone and his code diagrams had been taken. On the table, secured by an empty wine bottle, was the inevitable note. Jeff snatched it.

"Sorry," it read laconically, "but this fellow unfortunately made himself a nuisance. So far, you, Jeff Shannon, and your aides, Captain Rene Martin and de Krelis, are safe. I don't consider any of you or your combined brains worth wasting a bullet upon! Yours cordially, von Drakenfels."

Jeff pocketed the note. It was important to find out what Cameron had tried to report.

One of the Machine Gun officers had seen him about two hours before he was shot. He reported that Cameron had brought up a prisoner, a native soldier out of a Mokazeni unit, at the point of a pistol, and turned him over to a guard of two military gendarmes.

"What's become of the prisoner?" asked Jeff.

He had been sent to Corps Headquarters accompanied by the two gendarmes. No one seemed to know what had happened after that.

It did not take much time, however, to locate the two military gendarmes. Their bodies, stabbed again and again by what seemed to have been a trench knife, were found in an empty dugout between the Machine Gun Battalion P.C. and Headquarters.

Of the prisoner they had been escorting there was not the slightest trace. He had seemingly disappeared into thin air.

Reports of the two additional murders ran through the trenches. Hate for the mysterious von Drakenfels filled the air.

At Headquarters old Colonel de Castex, bristling of mustache, snorted:

"What is it now! Your boasted forty-eight hours is nearly up! What are you going to do—wait until every man in the corps is murdered before you find that von Drakenfels?"

The Eagle restrained his anger.

"Colonel," he said, "I'll have to ask you to call a conference of all the corps Intelligence officers tonight at ten o'clock to meet at the Machine Gun Battalion P.C."

The colonel growled at this but nevertheless made a note on his memorandum pad.

"Why you want a conference I do not know," he said, "and besides the Machine Gun Battalion P.C. is too close to the enemy lines to assemble so many officers."

"That is exactly why I am holding it there, Colonel!" said the Eagle cryptically, and left.

SEVERAL OF his helpers were assembled when he reappeared at his quarters.

"What about those two fellows, Lieutenant Mueller and Captain Wagner?" he asked.

"I went through Captain Wagner's dugout," said Corporal Sauvage, "and I found his pistol barrel fouled from a recent shot and only four cartridges in his magazine instead of five."

"Good! Keep on watching them both! Keep your eyes and ears open. If my hunch is right, von Drakenfels is getting scared, and he'll try to commit another murder or two or I very much miss my guess."

"Perhaps *Monsieur le Commandant* will himself keep an eye open," suggested Sauvage, soft voiced, and Jeff remembered that this man had been especially detailed to watch over him by Colonel LeClerc.

"I'll be careful," he said. "The first thing I'm going to do is investigate the trench sector held by the Machine Gun Battalion. Along there our trenches are nearer to the enemy than at any other part of the line. Keep in touch with Charbier at headquarters. Turn up at the conference at ten o'clock. Dismissed."

Supper hour had come and gone and darkness was descending.

The Eagle went about his task. He was completely unaware that word had already gone forth demanding his death. How it went forth no one seemed to know, but it was preceded by a buzz of excitement through the corps. Word came to almost everyone simultaneously that *the Nazi spy had at last been sighted and recognized!*

It came by telephone and by word of mouth, it flew on mysterious wings so rapidly that in a very short space of time almost every man in the corps was seeking for the man described so carefully in the message. The description ran as follows:

"The Nazi spy, von Drakenfels is posing as an American in the Intelligence Division," went on the warning, "he is tall and well built, with tanned face and good features and blond hair. Don't take any chances with this man as he is exceedingly adroit and dangerous. Shoot him if he puts up the slightest resistance or protest!"

It was a diabolically clever move. The Eagle went cheerfully on his way, towards the Machine Gun Battalion sector, ignorant of the fact that an almost perfect description of him had been broadcast to the entire corps as the description of a man who should be shot down like a mad dog, on sight.

ATTACK

EVERY **SOLDIER** in that corps was so filled with rage at the Nazi spy that he was determined to take the law in his own hands should he meet with the fellow who had caused so much grief. But Jeff Shannon went on his way ignorant of the danger that surrounded him, thinking of the conference that he had called for ten o'clock. Everything hung on that conference according to his plan, for he was certain that von Drakenfels would be there.

The hard thing would be to make the Nazi spy reveal his true colors, but the Eagle had a plan to effect this and had made his arrangements to carry it out.

He rounded a trench wall. Just then a flashlight was played upon him.

Suddenly strong arms grasped him and an automatic pistol was shoved into the pit of his stomach.

"Hands up!" rasped an unpleasant voice in his ear and he obeyed quickly.

The beam of the flashlight played for a second on his face and form. Then it was flashed off again.

"*Mon Dieu!* We've captured the *salopard!*" rasped the unpleasant voice again, and the pistol muzzle was shoved more deeply into Jeff Shannon's stomach.

"Who are you! Speak quickly!" ordered a voice out of the darkness.

"I'm Jeff Shannon." Jeff's anger got the best of him. "*Salopard* yourself! Holster your gun!"

An ominous silence greeted his words. It sent a chill through him.

"There's no doubt about it!" announced a strange voice in the darkness.

"Tall, blond hair, tanned features," rasped the unpleasant voice again. "*Monsieur* le Nazi spy, we have found you at last!"

"You men are crazy!" Jeff exploded. "What is this, a joke?"

"Not so crazy that we don't know a spy when we catch him!" retorted someone, then addressing his companions: "What shall we do with him?"

"He's pretty clever—better make him harmless before he starts some of his tricks—let him have a bullet in the belly!"

"Hadn't we better take him to some officer?" asked the man who held Jeff's right arm.

"Why delay the inevitable?" argued the man with the pistol. "Let him have it now and do the explaining later."

"Listen here, you men," the Eagle said. The gravity of his situation was dawning on him. "You're making an awful mistake. Take me to an officer and let me identify myself."

A silence greeted his words.

"He speaks very good French!" said the man who held his right arm.

"What do you suppose a clever Nazi spy would speak? Esquimaux?" jeered the man with the pistol. "Let's kill him and get it over with!"

The pistol bored into Jeff's middle. He stood with every nerve and muscle paralyzed, waiting for the smash of that bullet.

"Take your medicine like a man, Nazi!" said the unpleasant voice, and then the fellow swore. "The gun is jammed!"

SHANNON'S FACULTIES cleared as if by magic. He brought his arms down from over his head and struck blindly into the darkness, putting the full force of his weight behind the blow.

Someone went down before him. A yell went up and more forms appeared in the darkness. A huge fist swung at him, scraping his face cruelly. He drove at the bulk of someone in front and smashed again until the man collapsed with a grunt of pain. Hands were clawing at his shoulders and he spun about and struck in the darkness.

There came suddenly the ring of an authoritative voice. There came a flash of light. At that second Jeff felt a jarring blow and passed out.

He felt a dim sensation as of being dragged, and was dimly aware of a confused roaring sound in his ears. Again he became aware of the light, a glow which became stronger and stronger until at last he could dimly make out his surroundings. He found himself tied in a chair with a row of half-seen faces before him and some one dousing cold water on his head. A voice was speaking above him.

"So it seems pretty conclusively proved that we've got our man at last," said the voice. "First we have his forged orders bringing him to the corps. Secondly we have found upon his person a notebook in German. Thirdly we have found these codes which are unknown to us and are undoubtedly the secret codes of the Nazi General staff!"

Jeff focused his uncertain eyes and made out the gold *pince-nez* of Major Desnot who was standing above him, holding some papers in his hand.

Looking about him he saw that he was in the Machine Gun Battalion P.C. and that the place was filled with Corps Intelligence officers, among whom he saw Lieutenant Mueller and Captain Wagner, both of them staring at him unwinkingly.

"You can see," Major Desnot's voice went on, "that this fellow answers perfectly to the description of him broadcast this evening.

"Have you anything to say, Captain von Drakenfels?"

Major Desnot turned his gold *pince-nez* on Jeff, his cold eyes gleaming like icicles behind them.

There was hard suspicion and no mercy in the eyes of the officers staring at him. Jeff Shannon could read no pity in any face.

"What time is it?" he asked, strangely enough.

Some one growled: "Ten minutes after ten o'clock!"

Jeff sighed and relaxed, his brain seemingly numb.

Suddenly attention was turned from him as a terrific racket came from outside. Shouts and yells and the tramp of feet and the sounds of struggle beat against the outer door. Louder and louder grew the racket until those inside the door rushed back, worried and fearful looking.

"The Italians are in our trenches!" they yelled.

THE WORDS were hardly out of their mouths when there came a deep-toned shout and a clump of boots. The doorway was filled with ten figures clad in the gray uniforms of the Italian colonial forces wearing the unfamiliar Italian trench helmets.

Accompanying a bearded Italian officer was another officer in the field gray of the German army, wearing a swastika arm band.

"Shoot down these swine!" said the German officer, speaking in German and then in French.

The Italian gave an order. The rifles of the men came up—they spread out, leveling their rifles at the startled inmates of the room.

The French officers stood as though carved in stone. There was silence for a space as though each soldier hesitated to be the first to pull the trigger. Suddenly a high pitched voice broke the silence.

"Stop! *Schweinhund!*" screamed the voice. The German officer and his Italian confrere stared at the man above Jeff Shannon.

"*Wehr sind sie?* Who are you?" asked the German officer brusquely.

"*Ich bin Erich, Graf von Drakenfels,*" returned the voice arrogantly.

The officers in the room stared uncomprehendingly at Major Desnot!

Jeff Shannon, tied to the chair, jerked his head toward Desnot.

The German officer at the door clumped across the room, his face shadowed within the coal scuttle helmet. Pausing before Major Desnot, who had just announced himself as Count von Drakenfels, the German officer did a surprising thing.

Suddenly he shoved an automatic pistol into the stomach of the psuedo Major Desnot.

"Hands up!" growled the German officer, and then spoke to Jeff Shannon out of the corner of his mouth: "Well, *mon ami*, we have our man!"

Under the coal-scuttle helmet showed the grim face of Captain Rene Martin, of the French Intelligence section!

The Italian officer turned out to be Sauvage and he quickly untied Jeff. Jeff heaved a sigh of relief. Thank God, the gang had carried out his orders!

It took the group a full minute to realize what had happened and it took them several minutes to realize that the whole thing was a put-up job. The adjutant of the Machine Gun Battalion was the most pleased, and rubbed his hands gleefully.

"Very excellent imitation of Italian soldiers and officers I turned out for you, *mon commandant*," he chuckled.

But the Eagle was busy watching von Drakenfels' face as he stood there, his wrists linked together with a pair of handcuffs.

"Well, *Herr* Graf," said the Eagle, "perhaps now you will stop writing me those sarcastic letters!"

"I admit to the mistake of having underrated your capabilities," von Drakenfels answered, bowing formally. "May I ask you how you came to conceive this plan?"

OLD COLONEL de Castex came blowing in then, in time to listen to Jeff Shannon's answer.

"Yes, I'd be glad to tell you. You probably remember a certain book of fiction you picked up in my quarters. It was, as you may recall, a collection of stories called the 'Justice of the Duke.' Had you read one of those stories instead of writing me a sarcastic letter, you would have found that one of Cesare Borgia's spies was captured in this exact manner several hundred years ago. Sometimes it pays to read fiction, eh *mon Colonel?*" This last question was addressed to de Castex.

"That may be so," said the old man stubbornly, "but what about the Senussi and their headquarters and all that wild stuff you were telling us of the attack from the Egele Plateau?"

Rene Martin spoke up.

"I can perhaps explain that to you, *mon Colonel*," he said politely. "My confrere here, alone and singlehanded, by ruse, caused blood to flow between the Ouled Delim, the Ouled Djerir and the Ait bu Reg, who were united with all the southern Sahara tribes and assembling upon the Egele plateau to join the forces of Mustapha ibn Hassen, the Senussi leader. By the efforts of Jeff Shannon, the tribes were diverted and returned to their homes."

"And Mustapha ibm Hassen?" Colonel de Castex leaned forward.

"Jeff Shannon made it appear that the tribesmen had revolted against the Senussi, went single-handed into the stronghold of that one, killed him and brought out Lieutenant de Krelis. With their leader, who was supposed to be charmed against bullets, dead, the followers gave up and scattered."

In the amazed silence that followed these words, two officers moved forward from the rear of the room. Captain Wagner and Lieutenant Mueller came to a stop before Colonel de Castex. It was Captain Wagner who spoke for both of them.

"We understand, *mon Colonel*, that we have been under suspicion, due to the Teutonic syllables of our names. Would it be too much to ask, *mon Colonel*, that as salve to our troubled feelings, I be allowed to command the firing squad that ends the life of this spy—with Lieutenant Mueller as second in command?"

"No, *messieurs*, it would not be too much to ask," returned the colonel absently, staring at the Eagle.

At last the old man cleared his throat and spoke, his voice sounding strangely humble:

"*Mon ami*," he addressed Jeff, "you have performed a wonderful service for France and for the world—and I have not always given you the cooperation you deserve. It may be that I am a little old fashioned, and do not read enough outside of regulations. Perhaps, *mon ami*, you would be so good sometime, as to loan me that book—what was it—The Justice of the Duke?"

III

THE MASTER
OF TREACHERY

CHAPTER I

SABOTAGE

IT **WAS** a dull, rumbling explosion that brought Captain Jeff Shannon out of bed in a hurry. Explosions to the average man may mean anything from just noise to a holocaust of destruction. But to Jeff Shannon it meant sheer catastrophe. This was a military arsenal, where explosives of the most violent type were manufactured, where huge guns and new type shells were tested and stored. Here men walked on rubber-soled shoes and took every precaution against fire or sparks.

There was a crimson glow to greet Shannon as he rushed out of his tiny cottage. Clad only in pajamas, he raced directly toward the blazing building. It was just a good-sized supply shed, containing nothing lethal at the moment. But there was grave danger from sparks.

Others were rushing out to fight the blaze. A warning siren began squealing. Sentries scurried about. Shannon cut across the spacious grounds between buildings and without the slightest hesitation he dived headlong into the flaming building. The door blocked him but a fraction of a second for it wasn't locked.

"Captain Shannon has gone into that blaze!" someone shouted.

Shannon most certainly had. Flames licked at his flimsy pajamas. He covered his face with a crooked arm and plunged on. There was a reason for this apparent madness. Old Solly Lynch, a retired private, had been hired to help test new guns. He had been busy until very late and Shannon had given him permission to sleep in this shack.

A groan attracted Shannon's attention. He could no longer see for the smoke was much too thick and acrid. Tears streamed down his face, but he battled his way toward the direction of that sound. Old Solly was there, a heavy beam lying across his chest and blood oozing from a wound across his forehead. He was still alive, but Shannon could see at a glance that it wouldn't be for long.

He bent down, hoisted the unconscious man over one shoulder and staggered toward the door. A sheet of hungry flame lashed out at him, singeing his eyebrows. It seemed to be literally shot from one of the long benches lining the walls. Shannon noticed it and emitted a curt cry. Eight years of intensive training told him a story.

This fire was not accidental. The color of the flame, the odor of the smoke and the rapidity and fierceness with which it burned indicated a chemical of high combustible qualities. But there was no chance to make any examination.

Shannon stumbled forward, challenging the blaze.

HIS PAJAMAS were in shreds. His body was covered with burns. Then he heard a hiss and a stream of water come crashing through the inferno. It sprayed him and gave him new strength. Someone spotted him. The hose was deflected and two men in helmets and rubber coats risked their lives surging through the flames. Shannon had to be helped out, but the fresh air revived him.

Just as the Eagle moved, the baron raised his clubbed automatic and brought it down on Shannon's head.

He knelt beside the stretcher on which Old Solly had been gently placed. He felt for a pulse, found it thready and weak. Solly opened his eyes, groaned and tried to talk, but no words would come. He gave a convulsive shudder and then relaxed in the limpness of death.

Someone put a hand on Shannon's shoulder. He looked up. It was Colonel Vane.

"How was it that the nearest sentry didn't give the alarm?" asked the colonel sternly.

A sergeant saluted. "Private Gorman is missing, sir."

"Find him!" ordered the colonel.

The sergeant drew his gun, took a flashlight and started on a swift search. He didn't have far to go. As he rounded the corner of the frame building just beyond the blazing structure he heard a groan. Sergeant Markley swung his light to reveal Private Gorman on his face beside the foundation, unconscious.

The sentry had been clubbed and hauled here out of the way. As soon as he was revived he reported that he had not seen his attacker. He had been walking his post when suddenly something crashed against the back of his head, and the world went black.

Captain Shannon turned to Colonel Vane.

"If the Colonel has time," he said in a low voice, "I would like to talk—privately. There's something about that blaze which requires an explanation."

Colonel Jerome Vane nodded grimly. "As soon as you are cleaned up, Captain, report to my quarters. You're not badly burned, are you?"

Shannon grimaced. "No, sir. Superficial burns I can treat myself. At your quarters then. Thank you, sir."

Shannon stumbled back to the little cottage assigned him. Corporal O'Toole, his runty, heavy-muscled orderly, helped him into a chair.

"'Twas a brave thing you did, sir. It's proud I am to be servin' a man like you, sir."

Shannon smiled and asked for a cigarette. Corporal O'Toole lit it and then began peeling off the remnants of the pajamas. The burns were very slight. A cool shower brought Shannon back to normal. He donned his uniform and O'Toole strapped the Sam Browne belt in place.

"Mike, you old horse thief," Shannon said with a laugh, "you've become almost indispensable to me. A word for your ears alone. That fire was set, and I think poor old Solly was murdered."

Mike O'Toole nodded grimly. "'Tis the work of spies, sir. There are more of them than locusts in China. It would do me heart good to wrap a couple of them together like pretzels."

"I'm going to see Colonel Vane," Shannon said. "You can go to bed if you like."

O'Toole touched his forehead in a mild excuse for a salute and opened the door. Shannon walked past the ruins of the shack. One beam stuck up into the night like a scorched finger. The rest of the building was in ashes. The excitement had died down. Sentries returned to pacing their posts. Fire apparatus was driven back to the garages.

As one man, the personnel of this vast arsenal gave a sigh of relief and tumbled back to bed. Two or three sparks to spread that blaze, and they'd all have been dead. Millions of pounds of ammunition lay stored in the long sheds nearby. Nobody in, or near, an arsenal enjoys watching a fire.

No one saw Jeff Shannon step into Colonel Vane's cottage. Shannon was a recent addition to the staff of the arsenal, and Vane wondered just why he had been transferred there. He had no chemical warfare experience and was not a scientist in the true sense of the word. Colonel Vane was brilliant, every ounce of him soldier through and through. He was in full uniform and he acknowledged Shannon's salute.

"Sit down, Captain," he said. "Brandy? I think you might enjoy a spot after that few moments. Too bad about Solly."

Shannon started forward in his chair. "Why, I didn't even think you'd heard of him, sir."

COLONEL VANE poured two inhalers of brandy and smiled. He was about fifty with iron gray hair and a closely clipped mustache. His bearing was as erect as Shannon's despite his additional years. For Shannon was young, not quite thirty. He had thick brown hair and blue eyes, eyes that could become very chill on occasion. His chin was clean-cut and aggressively typed. His uniform fitted him well, but did not hide the muscles that formed a good part of his shoulders and arms.

"I make it a point to know every man on these premises, Captain. That included Solly. Now, you wanted to see me. The feeling is quite mutual. After witnessing that act of yours, I realize you're not just a simple captain recently transferred here. Just what is your business?"

"Colonel," Shannon said softly, "that fire was incendiary. Solly was murdered. The gash across his forehead was made by a gun butt, one provided with a ring to which the lanyard is attached. I could tell by the wound. He was left there to die. And I'm somewhat responsible, sir. I gave him permission to sleep in that shack."

Shannon put down his glass slowly and leaned across the desk. "Colonel Vane, it may interest you to know that during the past five months there have been exactly eighteen fires on government property. Fires in old, nearly useless shacks like this one. They burned down a building where submarines are dry-docked in New London. They burned an office building at the Raritan arsenal last month. Important airplane factories have suffered similar fires. I've every one of them listed in my mind. That's why I was sent here—to prevent such incendiarism at this arsenal, and capture the spies responsible for such sabotage. I'm attached to the Military Intelligence. You won't find that information on my record. To all intents and purposes I am simply Captain Jeff Shannon, transferred from Washington."

Vane let a whistle escape his lips. "But why, Captain? Why on earth are they burning down small buildings when they could have blasted half of this arsenal to the moon? It doesn't make sense."

Shannon smiled grimly. "It does—to the people behind this. Colonel, we're up against a serious problem. During the last two or three years espionage has become a serious thing in this grand nation of ours. There are societies, enlisting half-witted fools who join because they are permitted to wear uniforms and to cheer the leaders, men—and women, too—who believe this nation needs a dictator, or whose Americanism is only superficial.

"There are spies in every munitions plant, in the navy yards, the army posts. They infest our airplane factories. We suspect them of some rather ghastly sabotage—all without proof, of course. Therefore, the government has decided to take measures. You are aware of all this, of course, but you are not aware that we suspect a man who is known to us only by the name of Baron Richter. I am after that man, and I need your aid."

The colonel looked grave.

"So you are really an undercover man from G-Two?" he asked.

"Yes, sir. I have no credentials to show you. To verify my authority and position I suggest that you send a wire, in code, to Washington and ask about—the Eagle."

"The Eagle?" exclaimed Vane, starting slightly. "So—you are the Eagle!"

"Yes, sir," admitted Shannon. "And this is in strictest confidence. I ask you to forget it. I am plain Captain Jeff Shannon."

"What do you want me to do—Captain Shannon?"

THE EAGLE leaned forward.

"I was sent here weeks ago to become established as an officer in the Chemical Warfare Service at this post. As such, the spies should now know me. I wish to get into their confidence, to join forces with them as a traitor who will accept their blood money and obey their commands. In the morning I want you to file advices that you suspect me of being in the pay of foreign spies. What sort of experimental work is particularly secret here? The new magnetic time bomb?"

"Exactly," agreed the colonel, shaking his head worriedly.

"Good," Shannon said, nodding. "We will prove that I stole and sold the plans of this bomb. Money will be found in my possession—far more than an army captain can account for. You will openly accuse me. I must be arrested, court-martialed, and thrown out of the service."

"But—but you will really be dishonored and detested," protested the colonel.

"Yes, sir. That is part of my job. And there will possibly be danger for you, although I hardly anticipate it on my account. However, I must warn you to take every precaution and to be careful. You are a valuable man yourself, and this Baron Richter may even put the pressure on you to glean any possible military secrets that he can."

Colonel Vane smiled grimly and held out his hand.

"You may depend on me thoroughly, Captain. You may expect arrest tomorrow or the next day. Not another soul will have any knowledge of our secret. Here's how we can do it. Tomorrow afternoon absent yourself without leave. Slip into my quarters and stay there. I will have had a report by then from Washington. I'll state in my own reports that I trailed you, saw you hand over the plans without knowing just what they were until later."

"Excellent," approved Shannon. "I'll carry on from there. You stick by your story, and we can clean up your spurious charges against me later. Good night, Colonel, and thank you for your cooperation."

They shook hands, and Shannon walked briskly to the door. He saluted in military fashion, pivoted, and walked calmly out into disgrace and false degradation for the sake of his country.

NEXT MORNING Captain Jeff Shannon reported to his laboratories and went to work. But his mind wasn't on chemical formulae or reactions. He was going to come to grips at last with Baron Richter. The Eagle of G-2, Military Intelligence, was going over to the camp of his enemies. He courted the danger involved. He was tired of laboratories, reagent bottles, retorts and armaments.

At noon he ate at the officers' mess, left early and made his way to Colonel Vane's cottage. He slipped inside, unseen by anyone. Colonel Vane was waiting.

"Good!" he greeted Shannon. "I'm expecting visitors in the next few minutes. After that, I'll drive into town so my testimony of trailing you will sound authentic. You will remain here until about midnight. Then return to your own quarters and wait until morning. You'd better go into the next room. I'll keep anyone out of there. You'll find cigarettes and brandy if you like."

"Thank you for your thoroughness, Colonel," said Shannon.

He went into the next room, pulling the door between the rooms almost closed. He divested himself of his jacket and relaxed. Half an hour later Vane's visitors appeared. Shannon took a quick glimpse of them through the partly open door.

One was major Nicholson of Army Engineers. The other man was stocky, had a florid complexion and wore civilian clothes. He was Manuel Otera, contractor. The introductions were made rapidly. Otera began talking.

"I'll take over the rebuilding of that shed," he said. "I've already done much of that work for you military chaps. I like it—it's patriotic, and heaven knows the country needs some patriotism these days. It will be of brick and fire proof, according to the latest regulations laid down by

Major Nicholson's department. We'll commence work on it within two days."

They went into details and costs for more than an hour. Finally the two men departed. Colonel Vane popped into Shannon's room, warned him to sit tight, and left immediately to play his own part in the drama.

At nine-thirty that night, Vane returned.

"Easiest job of trailing a traitor I've ever done," he laughed. "I saw two movies. We're about ready now, Captain. My report has already been filed. Heaven help you in the morning. I'll hurry the court-martial along. You're sure you'll be all right?"

Shannon nodded. "Do soldiers mind going over the top, facing bullets, flame and death? This job doesn't compare with that work, sir. I'm quite ready."

Shannon slipped back to his quarters and answered Corporal O'Toole's queries with grunts. Not even O'Toole could be told about this. Shannon wondered just how his striker would take it.

CHAPTER II

RUTHLESS MURDER

TWO HOURS after Shannon left his house, Colonel Vane closed his desk and sighed. He hated to send even the Eagle into such a mess, but it was necessary. Orders from Washington had been very clear on that point. There was something brewing, something that might boil over at any moment and mean the lives of hundreds. Europe was in its usual turmoil with dictators making demands and threats. War clouds were heavy.

And all the while spies slunk through every governmental division, ferreting out secrets, handing them over to superiors for a few hundred dollars. The societies flourished, and they were nothing but a mask for espionage. The most avid of the followers were selected and groomed for undercover work. It was as close to open war as anything could be without the grim actuality of flying bullets and screeching shells.

One thing the United States must do—stay out of war. No matter what happened, this nation must prepare. Preparedness comes with new inventions, new devices for wholesale slaughter. No dictator would be fool enough to attack a nation primed to deal swift, sudden death. This was what the spies sought to foil. If they knew the secrets as quickly as they were invented, enemy nations would quickly offset their value.

Colonel Vane began stripping off his uniform. His door bell buzzed. With an impatient gesture he answered it. A man stood on the front porch. A man shrouded in a heavy coat and a wide-brimmed hat.

"May I come in, Colonel Vane?" he asked politely. "It is very important."

"Ungodly hour," Vane grumbled, "but come on. First of all I'd like to know how you got through the gates? Are the sentries asleep?"

Vane dropped into his chair behind the desk once more. He was trying to discern the features of his visitor, but that was almost impossible. The heavy coat and the hat hid most of his face effectively.

"The sentries, *Herr* Colonel," the visitor said softly, "are fools. All of you are fools. Perhaps you would like to know who I am. Very well, I shall satisfy your curiosity. I am Baron Richter."

Vane was on his feet and tugging at a desk drawer. "Baron Richter?" he gasped. "Baron—the spy! I've heard of you. Well, you're the fool, to come here openly, and—"

"Do not reach for a gun," Baron Richter said quietly. "You have been covered for the last several seconds. Don't take my word for it. Either reach for your gun and die, or turn around and see for yourself."

VANE TURNED swiftly, suspecting a trick. There was none. Two men had climbed through the window while he went to answer the door. They stood now, dressed in somber black and reeking of menace. Each was short, stocky and held a foreign-made automatic.

"You see," Baron Richter bowed ironically. "I came prepared to cope with stupid violence. Now sit down, *Herr* Colonel, and listen to me. For the last six weeks you have been under observation. You blocked my getting a look at recent submarine plans. You are going to pay for that, *Herr* Colonel."

"You'll pay," Vane snapped. "It's a pity our positions aren't reversed. If you were an American spy, in your native land, you'd taste the kiss of an executioner's ax. We don't do things like that here, but I'll promise you a taste of prison. You won't like it."

Baron Richter began to pace the rug. He walked with a limp and when his heels struck the bare floor, they made a strange sound. The lame foot clumped while the healthy one clicked with military precision.

"What is the use in trying to fight me?" He whirled to face Vane. "Me—Baron Richter! No one has ever caught up with me and they never shall. I am inviolate! Perhaps it will interest you to know what I have done and intend to do. Already my men are safely placed in all of your industries. They are ready to strike at the moment I give the word. A flick of my little finger, and all your great machinery for producing arms will be nothing but dust and destruction. You and your kind shall not aid our potential enemies—not if we have to obliterate your entire nation to stop you."

Vane was slowly moving his right hand toward the desk drawer. He knew that death was grimacing over his shoulder. He wouldn't be permitted to live. Baron Richter was noted for his bloody acts. Human life was to him nothing more than a lump of clay. The fact that he talked openly spelled Vane's doom and he knew it.

Richter eyed Colonel Vane narrowly.

"Before you have the opportunity to get started," he said harshly, "I shall put a stop to it. Your counter-espionage plans will be done with before you can begin them—*Herr* Eagle. This is the end!"

"What?" ejaculated Vane in amazement. "What did you call me?"

"Ah, that surprised you, eh?" sneered his visitor. "Don't trouble to dissemble. I have suspected that you were really that accursed G-Two agent called the Eagle for some time. And now the time has come for you to be eliminated."

VANE REALIZED that Richter had made a bad mistake. The colonel knew he had been mistaken for the Eagle by this spy, and that his life was forfeit because of this. But the colonel was a soldier first of all. He never thought for an instant of denying Richter's accusation, even though it might save his life.

To deny the charge successfully, he would have to expose the real Eagle, and he had no such intention. But, if possible, he must live to put the finger on this man for the Eagle, perhaps saving Shannon many dangerous weeks of investigation.

Vane's hand darted into the drawer. Richter merely nodded. His two black-clad henchmen lunged forward simultaneously. One of them knocked the brave colonel back from the desk and pinioned his arms to his side in a gorillalike embrace. The second, with a malevolent sneer, placed the muzzle of his gun directly over Vane's heart. Baron Richter tossed over two pillows. The killer thrust them beside the gun.

But as his finger tightened against the trigger, Vane gave a convulsive leap. The pillows fell away. The gun blasted once and the sound of it roared through the rooms of the small house. Colonel Vane slumped forward, his forehead striking the desk with a thud. His own weight pushed the swivel chair back until he rolled off the desk and fell onto the floor. A trickle of blood oozed out over the rug.

Outside sentries, alarmed by the shot, began looking for the source of it. One of them glanced at his watch. It was exactly twelve-forty!

At that precise moment, Captain Jeff Shannon walked out of his cottage for a last look around the great arsenal grounds. A sentry saluted and walked by. Shannon turned back into his cottage and went to bed.

CHAPTER III

COURT-MARTIAL

CORPORAL O'TOOLE, his voice shaking badly, awakened Shannon at dawn. The Eagle sat up, rubbed his eyes and scowled. There were three other men in the room. Major Furnald was one of them. He stepped close to the bed.

"Shannon," he snapped, "keep your hands where we can see them. There are men posted at the windows of this room with orders to shoot to kill at the first signs of resistance."

"What's the big idea?" Shannon demanded hotly, acting out his part to perfection. "What the devil have I done?"

"Shut up," Furnald snapped. "I'm searching your possessions."

Furnald began pulling open drawers. O'Toole stepped forward as if to remonstrate. Furnald barked an order, and O'Toole snapped to attention. Furnald found a battered wallet in one drawer. He opened it and counted out twenty fifty-dollar bills. He sighed deeply and put the money into his tunic pocket.

"Get up, Shannon," he ordered. "You're under arrest. I couldn't force myself to believe this of you. Selling out your own country, your uniform, your honor for a rotten thousand dollars!"

Shannon got out of bed and stepped up to Furnald aggressively.

"Wait a minute," he rasped. "I know what this is about. It's that damned nosey Colonel Vane. I thought I saw him trailing me yesterday. Well, I'll punch his important nose into the back of his stiff neck for him. You've got nothing on me."

Furnald signaled two M.P.s outside the door. They seized the Eagle's arms.

"Shannon," Furnald said in a tired voice, "you aren't much afraid of what Colonel Vane might testify to, are you? But in spite of your desperate measures, he outwitted you. He filed a written report late yesterday afternoon. It will convict you, Shannon—without Vane's verbal testimony."

The Eagle frowned. "I don't get it."

"Colonel Vane is dead. He was murdered at twelve-forty this morning. You killed him so he couldn't expose you. It's not only treachery I accuse you of. It's murder! Take him away!"

The next few days were nightmares to Shannon. The murder of Colonel Vane was turned over to the F.B.I. and within forty-eight hours Shannon was cleared so far as the actual murder was concerned. Corporal O'Toole's testimony, coupled with that of the sentry who had observed Shannon in his quarters, alibied him firmly. The time of Colonel Vane's death was exactly set by the sound of the shot and the medical examiner's verdict.

It was almost two weeks after his arrest that Shannon had a visitor. The turnkey at the federal detention pen let Corporal O'Toole into the cell. But O'Toole was in mufti and he was nervously fidgeting with his hat.

"Thanks for coming," Shannon said simply. "And also for testifying that I was not at Colonel Vane's house when the murder was committed. You helped in saving my life. But, O'Toole, where's your uniform?"

O'Toole sat down on the edge of the bunk. He looked steadily at the floor. "My term was up, sir. I didn't enlist for another hitch. You see, it's like this. Bein' with you for those weeks—well, doggone it, I like you. I know you ain't mixed up in no spy business and in no murder either. It ain't the murder that worries me, you're clear of that one, but they do say that maybe some of your pals did the job for you."

SHANNON EXHALED deeply. "I thought they'd figure it that way. O'Toole, you gave up your chances of a pension on account of me? That was foolish. You see, I am guilty of helping a spy ring."

"You're not!" O'Toole roared. "'Tis a lie—even from your own lips. Me, who knows a man when I see one, I know it's a lie."

Shannon stroked his chin thoughtfully. He wondered how much he dared tell this loyal Irishman. O'Toole's act entitled him to some consideration. And Shannon was genuinely worried because of Colonel Vane's death. It had brought unexpected troubles on his shoulders. He dropped his voice to a whisper and pledged O'Toole to secrecy. Then he told him the story without revealing his true identity. O'Toole's eyes widened in horror.

"But with the colonel dead, there ain't nobody who can say it was all a plant, Cap'n. They'll railroad you sure."

"Unless I ask for special intervention from Washington," Shannon agreed. "And I can't do that, for it would ruin everything I've taken the trouble to build up. I have to go through with it as things are. Colonel Vane would want it this way. And when they free me, I'll find out who killed Colonel Vane—and why. Since you've thrown in with me, O'Toole, I'll accept your services with gratitude. Now you run along. I'll contact you as soon as possible. Just write down your address for me—and thanks for the faith you have."

At noon the next day Jeff Shannon in full uniform, stood in the center of the parade grounds at a fort not far from the federal pen. Hemming him on all sides were soldiers, their guns at parade rest. Brigadier-General Thorne stepped up to Shannon.

"You have been duly tried and found guilty of selling information to certain elements interested in stopping the military activities of this country. It was an act of a coward, of a man without a conscience. However, because the only witness against you was murdered, the court-martial has voted to give you a certain benefit of doubt. You remain guilty and it is my duty to deprive you of your sword, sir."

Shannon drew the sword and handed it over, hilt first. He saw it broken and hurled into the dust. Then his shoulder insignia were ruthlessly ripped off. The buttons of his tunic were torn away and thrown on the ground. Movie cameras clicked away, registering the whole sordid ceremony. Drums ruffled and it was over. Barked commands, and the soldiers marched away.

The Eagle was left alone, dejected, sweaty and more than a little worried over the whole thing. Things hadn't worked quite as he had planned. Why had Colonel Vane been killed? By whom?

Finally he shrugged and walked back to his old quarters. Sentries turned their heads the other way. There were no more salutes. The court-martialed traitor rated none of that now. He found O'Toole busily engaged in packing his few belongings.

"If it's money you need, Cap'n," the orderly said in a whisper, "I've got some saved up and I was pretty lucky in a crap game just before I quit, sir."

Jeff smiled slowly. "No, thanks. And don't feel sorry for me, Mike. It's working out well. Before long I'll swing into action. If the spy ring doesn't seek me out, I'll go looking for them. They're going to be unpleasantly surprised in the near future. I shall carry on exactly as the colonel and I planned. There's far more at stake than my army career—or even the death of Colonel Vane."

He hadn't let O'Toole in on the entire setup until he felt he could trust the Irishman implicitly. It looked as if now might be the time.

O'Toole looked a little dejected. "I thought, sir, seein' as how we've thrown together maybe I could—"

"Of course." Shannon put a friendly hand across O'Toole's broad shoulders. "You'll be in it as thickly as I, Mike. Together we'll see it through and I think I'll have need of your muscles before we're done. Let's see, I've got to adopt some personality. I'll have to disguise myself and I do know a little about dyes and such things."

HE BEGAN pacing the floor, pretending to think, as he covertly studied his companion. Satisfied, he took a half-dollar from his pocket and flipped it into the air. He caught it deftly and looked down at the coin. A slow smile crossed his face.

"Mike," he said softly, "I've got it. Take a look at the back of this half-dollar. See the emblem on it—an eagle with wings outspread and talons ready to close on its prey? That's me, the Eagle! And, Mike, I'm going to develop talons, too. They'll be sharp and deadly. From now on, when you hear from someone calling himself the Eagle—that'll be me."

"Sure and that's a swell idea, sir," exclaimed O'Toole with enthusiasm. "The Eagle, it is, Captain."

"But don't call me captain, anymore, Mike," cautioned Shannon. "Remember, I'm a disgraced army officer now."

"To me, sir, you'll always be Captain," said the ex-corporal stoutly.

Shannon was thoroughly satisfied. The simple soldier hadn't turned a hair at this subtle way Shannon had announced his real identity. In his lowly position as a corporal, O'Toole had never even heard of the counter-espionage ace called the Eagle. This was just a new name to him.

"Okay, Mike," he agreed. "Pack your own stuff and take up quarters in your new place. Take my stuff with you. I'll get in touch with you later. Right now I'm going to try to contact this sabotage spy ring."

He left O'Toole whistling cheerfully at his work. He knew that he had the same as put his life in the ex-corporal's hands, but he was unafraid. The Eagle, although he generally worked alone, was a good judge of men, and it looked as though O'Toole might be needed in this perplexing affair.

There was one other person not connected with the Counter-espionage Intelligence who knew the real identity of the Eagle. This was Joan Kirke, a lovely blond, who was Shannon's fiancée. But Joan was safely away at this time in Venezuela, the native country of her mother.

Shannon left the army post, walking slowly out through the gate, apparently lost in bitter thoughts. He had scarcely put the post out of sight behind him when a sleek sedan purred up behind him. There was a stolid-faced driver at the wheel, and another man was indistinguishable in the rear seat.

The door opened and a voice hissed for his attention. Shannon turned and put one foot on the running board. His heart was pounding faster than the pistons of that expensive car. It was coming then—as quickly as this.

"Get in, you fool," the man in the rear growled. "Do you want the whole post to see us?"

SHANNON CLIMBED in and sank back against the soft cushion. Such luxury, after two weeks in a cell, felt extremely good. He gave a sigh of intense satisfaction.

"Brother," he said, "I don't know who you are or what you want, but this certainly is some buggy. Must have set you back ten thousand dollars."

"Eleven," the man beamed. He was a fat, bald-headed individual, carefully dressed in expensive clothing. He wore glasses with thick lenses and his lips were full, cruel looking.

"You wonder perhaps why I have stopped to pick up a man so defamed by his own country. I have a reason. A good reason and one that will be profitable to you—if you cooperate."

He looked at the Eagle keenly and seemed satisfied. Shannon tapped a cigarette against his thumbnail, lit it and exhaled deeply.

"Keep talking, brother. I got a hunch there'll be musical words pretty soon, all nice and tinkling with gold."

"There will be money for you, yes. Plenty of it and"—the spy dropped his voice to a whisper—"a chance to teach those stupid dolts you worked for just how clever you can be. First of all, tell me, to whom did you sell the plans for that time bomb?"

Shannon turned angry eyes on the man. "I'm not talking. How do I know you're not another of those rotten lice of the F.B.I.? Anyway, I wouldn't tell if you were on the level with me. The damned government agents took the money I got. I'm broke! That's how I'm rewarded after five years of service in stinking laboratories where my life was in danger every second. A man can't live on an army captain's pay. Not the way I want to live."

"Good, good," the spy approved heartily. "You are a man after my own heart. Very well, we can forget that question. Had you answered it, I should have known you were not to be trusted. You would like to earn some money, *ja?* Lots of it? There is a way. A very simple way."

"Shoot the works," Shannon said grimly. "I'm ready for anything."

"Good. Now listen carefully. You will be watched by the F.B.I. You know too much and I think they purposely freed you so they might learn whom you contacted. That is why I came so quickly. Tonight, at eleven o'clock, you will be at number Two-o-three Western Boulevard. That address is a rooming house, but all the roomers are in my employ. There I shall give you precise instructions and discuss terms. It is agreed, *ja?*"

"Why not?" Shannon shrugged. "I said I was ready for anything."

The car turned into a public park, and Shannon got out. He sat down on a bench while he considered the sudden turn of events. Things were working out smoothly.

A patrolman sauntered by, glancing at him. Recognition dawned on him. He tapped the Eagle none too gently across the knees with his club.

"On your way, bum. Parks ain't for the likes o' you. Don't argue—I saw your ugly pan in the newsreels last night. Sellin' out to a bunch of spies. A fine man you are. Scram, or shall I give you a good taste of my nightstick."

Shannon got up and slouched away. Oh, it was working all right. Working too damned good. He had become a leper, a pariah. Decent people would have nothing to do with him. Grimly he realized just how easily cashiered men in his position could fall into the clutches of a spy ring. Ostracism can make a man go a long way for revenge.

Then he sighed as he thought about Colonel Vane's death. That the army officer had been killed because he had been suspected of being the Eagle, Shannon had no idea. All he knew about that was that he intended bringing the colonel's murderers to justice at the same time that he broke up the spy ring of the mysterious Baron Richter. He had a feeling that both cases were, somehow, entangled.

CHAPTER IV

THE EAGLE

BEFORE ANOTHER hour passed, Shannon knew something had to be done about disguising himself. The side glances of pedestrians, the harsh off-side remarks of men who recognized him instantly, all served to confirm this necessity.

He visited a clothing dealer, selecting one whose eyesight seemed to be none too good. He looked over several suits and shook his head. He wanted something outstanding, something to make a different personality of him. His own suit was now wrinkled and soiled.

With a wry smile he selected a natty outfit consisting of a short, formal coat and striped trousers. He tried them on in the fitting room and eyed himself in the mirror. Talk about fops! He'd gone the limit on this one.

"All you need," the tailor told him, "is a monocle. You look like a statesman in those clothes, a regular big shot guy."

Shannon grinned and paid him, but the idea of a monocle clung. It would serve to augment the disguise he had been planning. He stopped and bought one, stowed it into his pocket and looked around for a modest hotel. His new black felt hat had a wide brim, and he turned this down as he walked through the lobby and up to the desk clerk. He registered under a false name.

"I'd like a nice room, on a permanent rate," he said. "Not too high!"

He paid a week's rent in advance, but instead of going directly to his room, he visited a drugstore and bought various chemicals. Then he returned to his room.

He experimented with his purchases for an hour. Finally he rubbed his own dye concoction into his skin. It darkened him considerably. He dyed his hair, his eyebrows and his eyelashes. He knew that minute precautions were necessary. He could remove all trace of the disguise within a few minutes, but while it was on, he defied the keenest eye to detect its falseness.

He wadded bits of cotton in his jaws until his cheeks bulged slightly. With tiny pieces of aluminum, fitted cleverly into his nostrils, he flared out his nose. Then he looked at himself in a mirror and decided he'd do. The disguise had added about ten years to his appearance.

He had memorized the address given him by the spy. The Eagle had always maintained one policy—to get the jump on the other man as quickly as possible. He decided to pay that address an unofficial visit at once.

He used two taxi cabs to reach the vicinity of the address, dismissed the last one four blocks away and walked past the house. It was dark except for a weak light in the hallway. There was a dirty sign tacked to the door indicating that rooms were to let. The Eagle looked around, made sure he was unobserved, and darted into the alley between the building and its next door neighbor. This kind of work was familiar to him, and he moved as softly as a jungle cat on the prowl. He studied the back door a moment and decided against picking the lock. There was a cellar hatchway that intrigued him. He opened the slanting doors and let them drop over him.

The darkness made him grimace. He should have had a flashlight, but matches served the purpose this time. He found the door leading into the cellar a cheap affair. He leaned against it and pushed gently. A couple of hooks holding it shut gave way with a slight rasping sound. In a minute he had it open.

HE STEPPED into the cellar, lit another match and held it high. Above him he heard footsteps and gruff voices. One man was walking along the hallway toward the front door. He walked with a peculiar limp. There was a click of one heel and then a clump, as if one leg was deformed. Shannon made a mental note of this.

He crept up the stairway and tried the door at the top. It wasn't locked. He opened it a crack and peered into the hall. The roly-poly man who had met him at the army post was delivering curt orders to a brutal looking thug who towered over him.

"The French agent is no longer of any use to us. The baron has said he must die. Therefore, Schnell, I have a job to your liking. Use a knife and do it well. There must be no noise."

Schnell's mouth parted in an ugly grin. He drew a short bladed knife from his pocket and fondled the edge.

"His pig's throat—*ach*—it shall bleed slowly until he dies. *Ja*, that is the way all of them should die. I obey, *Herr Doktor!*"

The man stepped back and raised his hand in a salute popular in certain European countries. Then he ran up the stairs. Shannon found his body bathed in cold sweat. These men talked of murder as though it were nothing. He had to save that man upstairs—the French agent, whoever he was—and do it quick.

For the moment luck was with him. The man addressed as *Herr Doktor* ambled into a room far down the corridor. The Eagle slipped through the door, tiptoed up the staircase and reached the landing as a door opened somewhere down the hall. He ducked into the nearest room.

A huge woman with a harsh face and a slit for a mouth, almost brushed against him as she strode by. He waited until she was downstairs. Now he had to find the room in which murder was being committed. If he blundered into the wrong room and encountered more of these spies he'd be on a spot.

Sergeant Markley swung his light to reveal Private Gorman
on his face beside the foundation, unconscious.

A groan gave him the clue. He walked gently toward the door behind which it came. He grasped the knob firmly and turned it so that there was no noise. The man called Schnell was talking venomously and in a low voice.

"*Ach*, such stupid fools. You have no more brains than the Americans. In a moment you will begin to die, when my little knife cuts deep. Before that happens, I want in tell you something, *ja*. It will make your death harder. You are of the French *Sûrêté*. You came here to expose *Herr Doktor* and Baron Richter. But we knew you were coming before you got on the boat. One of us has taken your place. He will confuse the Americans and find out their best secrets. And for you, *Herr* LeBlang, there is death. Like this—ah-h-h."

An arm had suddenly curved around the thug's throat, blocking off the scream that rose to his lips. The knife hand moved fast and the blade swept back toward Shannon. He retained his grip on the man's neck, seized the spy with his other hand and deflected the direction of the blade. The spy, his muscles set to deliver the death thrust at this unseen menace, drove the knife into his own breast. Blood welled up and bubbled in a gory froth from his mouth. Shannon let him sag toward the floor and then hastily lowered him so there would be no sound.

The man was dead! It made the Eagle a bit squeamish, for he never liked to kill, even such rats as spies. He removed the knife from the spy's breast gingerly and cut the Frenchman free.

FOR A moment the French agent couldn't talk. A cruel gag inserted into his mouth had paralyzed his tongue. But speech soon returned.

"*Bien, mon ami,*" he said hoarsely. "You came in time for which I thank my patron saints. But we must get away from here. An impostor is in my place, with my identification papers. He will be taken into the submarine base at Newport News and permitted to wander about. He is dangerous."

The Eagle put his lips near LeBlang's ear and spoke in a whisper. "Not yet. The impostor may lead us to the real brains behind this spy business. You've got to cooperate with me."

"You are an American agent, *oui?*" LeBlang asked. "But of course."

"I'm on your side of the fence, no matter what," the Eagle answered. "Now we've got to get away from here. Go to Eleven-twenty-six White Street. A friend of mine named O'Toole lives there. Tell him the Eagle sent you. Here—over by the window. It isn't far to the ground. I'll drop you easy."

LeBlang nodded. They raised the window gently and the French agent slipped out. He hung from the Eagle's hands a moment and then dropped softly to the court behind the house. He was up instantly and streaking away. Shannon eyed the dead spy and frowned. Then, on inspiration, he went into the adjoining bathroom, found a bottle of iodine and returned to kneel beside the dead man. He had been something of an artist before he took up espionage as a career. Deftly he painted on the man's forehead the outlines of an eagle, wings outspread, talons closing on an invisible prey.

Those spies would know one thing from this moment on, that the Eagle was hovering nearby. He fervently hoped they'd worry themselves to death. How badly they would worry he had no idea. He glanced at his watch. It was ten-twenty—almost time for him to keep his appointment with *Herr Doktor*. He slipped out of the house, using the same means that had gained him entry.

Returning to his hotel was accomplished by devious routes and means. He checked into another room, near the one he had formerly rented. There he removed his disguise, quickly changed his clothing, donning the soiled and wrinkled suit he had worn when he was released from the federal jail.

As he passed through the lobby he saw a slender young man arise and follow him. The Eagle's pulse quickened. Baron Richter's spy ring was checking up then. Perhaps they knew he had left the hotel in disguise. If that was the case, he'd be greeted by death when he visited *Herr Doktor.*

Yet he had to go through with it. He had accepted this gamble, knowing that one part of the stakes was his own life. If he overplayed his hand, he'd be doomed.

He spent fifteen exciting minutes losing his shadow.

He grinned slightly as he climbed the steps to the front porch of the spy ring's headquarters. No matter what happened he had a certain satisfaction in having saved the life of a prisoner of the spies.

Herr Doktor answered the door himself, greeting the Eagle with outstretched hand. But there were worried wrinkles between his eyes and he closed the door hastily.

"You are late," the spy said suavely, "but no matter. We have been very busy. And there will be a new headquarters next time you report. Now to business. You worked in the laboratories of the U.S. army. You know many of the Chemical Warfare Service secrets. Oh, we have checked the record of Captain Shannon carefully. I want you to write down all the latest inventions in detail, being especially careful about the formulas."

SHANNON TWIRLED his hat and betrayed no interest. That record had been prepared for spies.

"We were to talk over money matters first," he said coolly. "How much do I get?"

The spy leaned forward. "One hundred dollars a month and bonuses. It may sound small, but the bonuses will bring your pay very high. For instance, after you have concentrated on some of the laboratory secrets, I shall assign you to a certain task. If you succeed in carrying it out, there will be two hundred dollars for you immediately."

"Not enough," Shannon snapped. "I'm risking a term in prison. If they catch me again, it will be curtains. With my record they'll throw me into Alcatraz to rot. Make it two hundred a month."

Herr Doktor shrugged. "Very well. We do not worry about minor details like that. Now, your first assignment. I shall give you an address. Also a key to the door of that house and the combination to the safe. At three o'clock this morning you will go there, open the safe and remove a leather zipper case. It contains documents essential for the success of our scheme. There will be no one at home. The house is closed up. You see, the owner is dead."

The Eagle nodded and made a mental note of both the address and the safe combination. *Herr Doktor* insisted that he carry around nothing written. All facts must be retained in his mind.

"There is another thing," he told Shannon. "You have entered the secret service of the country I represent. From this moment on your will is my will. Your actions are governed by my orders. I demand blind obedience. You will not question any orders. That is understood, eh?"

"I can take them," the Eagle answered. "If you had served in the army as long as I did, you grow used to taking orders. Give me a room where I can concentrate, and I'll hand you a few formulas that will make your eyes open wide."

He was promptly given a small study to work in. He closed the door and sat down behind the desk. This was one of the most difficult parts of his work. He had to give them something, and yet be certain his revelations wouldn't injure the Chemical Warfare Service. He noted down formulas of gases, powders and armament compositions. They were comparatively new, but in the rapid turn of events they had all been replaced with more efficient processes.

He worked until two-thirty, left his notations stacked in a neat pile and went into the hallway. Two men, with guns strapped to their middles, were on guard at the front door. They eyed him narrowly, but stepped back to allow his exit. He walked the distance to the address, found it to be a suburban bungalow without a light showing.

He walked boldly upon the front porch, shoved the key into the lock and opened the door. He had provided himself with a pencil flashlight and he sent the thin ray around the room. There was a low bookcase, apparently built into the wall at the farther corner. He swung this back and revealed the glistening door of a wall safe. He knelt beside it, spun the combination and had the door yawning wide within a minute.

THE LEATHER zipper case was the only thing in the safe. He removed it, pulled back the zipper and thumbed through the papers it contained. Most of them were concerned with the building up of a counterespionage system in the United States. But one document listed the names and addresses of a number of American agents operating on foreign soil. The Eagle whistled softly. With this list, the spy ring could quietly do away with those men. They'd simply vanish and without the slightest publicity.

"This must be what *Herr Doktor* wants," he told himself, "and he's not going to get it. The other stuff isn't important."

He rolled the list of agents' names into a spiral, struck a match and watched the document burn to ashes. He heaved a long sigh of relief.

Then his whole body grew tense. There was a gun muzzle resting against the back of his neck. He dropped the other papers and raised his hands quickly.

"I know how to use this gun," a soft, feminine voice said. "Stand up, and keep your hands just where they are."

Shannon arose. In the darkness he could only make out the shadowy form of the intruder. Then lights were turned on. He blinked for a moment to accustom his eyes to the light, and then he continued blinking as he studied the features of the girl who stood before him. She was young, blond and decidedly beautiful.

"So it's you," she said scornfully. "Ex-Captain Jefferson Shannon! You weren't satisfied to betray your country once. Don't move! I'm going to turn you over to the authorities as soon as I can."

The Eagle laughed harshly. "Don't be silly. You're after the same things I came for, otherwise you wouldn't be here. Let's get together on this and—"

"I live here," the girl retorted hotly. "Walk ahead of me over to that table where the telephone rests. I—I'll shoot if you try anything. Perhaps I—I might hesitate if you were someone else, but I think I'd enjoy killing you, ex-Captain Shannon."

The venom in her tone made him ponder. She sounded as though she really would shoot—and welcome the opportunity. Yet he had never seen this girl before. Why did she bear him this grim animosity?

Then the Eagle's eyes widened. The front door had opened and two of *Herr Doktor's* ruffians were sneaking in. Both had guns. One of them covered the girl while the other moved forward with his weapon raised for a skull-smashing blow. They were going to kill her!

The girl heard the slithering sound their feet made and gave a little cry of panic. She half-turned around, and Shannon made a swift lunge. He wrapped both arms around her, lifted her and carried her bodily toward a closed door. He opened it, kicking it wide with his toe.

"Wait," he called to the two men who watched. "I'll take care of this wench in my own way."

He closed the door, set the girl down gently and grinned at her. She was perfectly white, but there was no terror in her eyes. She expected brutal treatment, even death, and she didn't flinch.

The Eagle took away her gun, held her close and kissed her, full on the lips.

"That's a substitute for a nice healthy sock on the jaw or a bullet through your pretty head. Fall to the floor and make it a real fall. Then lay there, like you were dead. Glad to have met you."

He let her drop. The door opened and the two spies entered. Shannon swung to face the entrance as the girl threw up her arms and toppled backward to the floor to lay in a silent, crumpled heap.

"I broke her blasted jaw," the Eagle snarled. "You guys showed just in time. Why wasn't I told this house was occupied?"

"You have the case?" one of the men demanded. *"Ach,* but of course. Hurry, before there is an alarm. You are sure she will not awaken?"

The Eagle smiled. "When I sock 'em, they stay socked. Let's go!"

CHAPTER V

THE SPY DOUBLE

IT WAS dawn when Jeff Shannon opened his hotel door. He flung his hat on the bed, started to divest himself of his coat, and then he stopped dead. A high-backed chair faced the window. From its depths a spiral of smoke curled ceilingward. Shannon licked his lips, suddenly gone dry. He tensed and stepped forward. The man in the chair was the same one who had started to follow him earlier in the evening. He was neatly dressed, alert looking and his dark eyes burned through the Eagle.

"Sit down, Shannon," he said calmly. "I'm Hogan of the F.B.I. You gave me the slip rather neatly just a few hours ago. Don't bother to deny it. Where have you been?"

Shannon had an unpleasant part to play. He couldn't reveal his true mission to this operative. In the first place it wouldn't be believed, and secondly, all the work he had so far accomplished would be ruined by a quick raid on the spy headquarters. This man didn't know him by sight, and he could not admit that he was the Eagle of G-2.

"None of your business," he retorted tartly. "This is supposed to be a free country."

"Sure it is," Hogan replied. "You know, Shannon, I find it hard to believe the charges they filed against you. There was no background for such treason on your part. I used to feel sorry for you. That's all over with. You're playing a dangerous game, working with spies. If we don't land you, they'll kill you. Just a friendly warning and the only one I'll give. From now on I'll be gunning for you with both barrels. Thought I'd let you know. I'm still after the murderer of Colonel Vane."

Shannon sneered a reply. "Thanks—thanks very much. I bleed in appreciation of your kindness. Now get the hell out of here. I want to sleep."

Hogan snuffed out his cigarette, yawned and left. After he was gone, the Eagle sat down slowly. He felt as wilted as a rose cut ten days before. If he hadn't hidden the clothing and make-up he wore as the Eagle in another room, his whole game might have been up. Hogan was nobody's fool, and he was undoubtedly going to be difficult to handle.

So the regular F.B.I. was keeping an eye on him, watching that he didn't reveal any of the secrets he knew, and diligently seeking the murderer of the colonel. Well, the Eagle intended doing something about that himself. Then his thoughts turned back to the girl. Who was she? How could she be implicated in such a dangerous business? At least she was safe and unharmed.

Shannon reached for the phone and hesitated before he picked up the instrument. Likely Hogan would have that line tapped. Despite the long hours he had been awake, he felt no fatigue. The tenseness of the past day had been too gruelling to allow him to think of himself. He made his way unobtrusively to the floor below, opened the door of the room he rented under his anonymous identity as the Eagle, and quickly disguised himself. He donned the natty clothing, experimented with the monocle for a few moments and then strolled out. He took the elevator down, walked through the lobby and saw no sign of Hogan. But he wasn't deceived. Hogan would be as invisible as a wraith from now on.

A taxi whisked him to the address which O'Toole had given him. He tapped smartly on the door. O'Toole, his eyes heavy with sleep, glared out at him.

"You're in the wrong room," he said truculently. "Beat it!"

A tolerant smile crossed the Eagle's face. "But of course I'm not, Mr. O'Toole. I've important news for you. Let me in, and have you a pencil?"

THERE WAS a small clothes closet, overhung with cheap curtains. Shannon saw them move slightly. Someone was concealed behind them. He sat down.

"Monsieur LeBlang," he said softly, "you may put the gun away and come out."

LeBlang emerged quickly, but his gun was ready for action. He looked at the Eagle carefully, then threw the gun on the bed and embraced him.

"Mon ami," he said gleefully. "I was sure you would come." He turned to O'Toole. "This is the man who saved my life. He is to be trusted, *oui?*"

"Maybe," O'Toole compressed his lips. "I don't trust nobody. Who are you, Mister?"

The Eagle picked up a pencil, drew a pad of paper toward him and skillfully drew the outline of an eagle. O'Toole's jaw dropped, his eyes lighted up.

"Cap'n, sir! Why—what have you done to yourself? You're a dude, no less. Your own mother wouldn't be recognizin' you, sir."

Shannon grinned. "If I pass your inspection, Corporal, I'm safe. Now, don't mention names. *Monsieur* LeBlang is to be trusted, surely, but he accepts me as a friend without naming names."

"The impostor!" LeBlang cried excitedly. "We must get him, *tout de suite,* before be can steal the secrets of your navy."

"We'll get him," the Eagle promised. "That's why I'm here. Mike, this impostor, the fraudulent LeBlang, is probably staying at one of the hotels in town just outside the submarine base. Contact the hotels and ask for LeBlang. Locate that man and meet me in front of the city hall. Snap it up. I'll be there at three this afternoon. You can get a plane within thirty minutes."

O'Toole dressed quickly, eager for action. When he was gone, Shannon faced the French agent.

"You came here to help identify certain spies. Is a man called the Baron one of them?"

LeBlang ran his fingers through his hair. "One of them? But yes, he is the whole works, as you say. Baron Richter, the most brazen of all agents. He is here to foment trouble, to sabotage your armament industries, make trouble for you. And mark me well, *mon ami,* he is dangerous. Also he is a master at disguise. But one thing identifies him. His left leg is shorter than his right. We know him in Paris as *Monsieur* Clubfoot!"

The Eagle's mind flashed back to his first entry into *Herr Doktor's* spy nest when he had heard a lame man walking across the floor. He was close then. *Monsieur* Clubfoot considered *Herr Doktor* important enough to visit personally.

"And Clubfoot's plot?" he asked LeBlang. "You have definite news of his objectives?"

"No, not definite, *mon ami.* We trapped several of his men in Cherbourg last month and decoded certain letters which indicate he hopes to destroy all American armaments industry at a second's notice. How he is to accomplish this we do not know."

"Perhaps," Shannon said slowly, "the man who has adopted your identity may know. We'll see."

AT THREE o'clock the Eagle and LeBlang drove slowly by the city hall in the town that neighbored on the submarine base. O'Toole was leaning against a hydrant, puffing on a cigarette and looking hopefully at each car that passed. He spotted the Eagle, threw away his cigarette and ambled up the street. The car slid to the curb and he got in.

"The Hotel Forester," he reported breathlessly. "He's there right now. Said something about being tired from his trip. But listen to this—yesterday they took him through the navy yard. I'm bettin' that baby had a nice little camera hidden on him some place. What'll we do, sir—grab him and make him talk?"

The Eagle piloted the hired car to the imposing entrance of the hotel. "Phone the spy," he ordered O'Toole. "Tell him you were sent from the Commandant—that an important diving test of a new sub is to take place and that he is invited to attend. Get him into this car, and we'll take care of the rest."

O'Toole grinned, and lovingly caressed his knuckles. "Man, I'll be helpin' you take care of him, too. It'll be a pleasure."

Five minutes later O'Toole emerged with the impostor in tow. He looked amazingly like LeBlang and without the use of too much disguise. O'Toole opened the door of the car, set his right hand against the spy's back and gave him a mighty shove. He sprawled at LeBlang's feet and was instantly pulled onto the seat and a gun poked into his ribs.

"Ah, my precious twin," LeBlang said gleefully. "It is time we got together, *n'est-ce pas?*"

The spy growled an oath, but his voice trembled. He had been chosen more for his resemblance to LeBlang than his nerve. The Eagle parked the car far out of the city and got into the back seat.

"Now," he said, "we shall have a talk. Where can I find Baron Richter? No lies. We know far more than you think."

The spy shook his head stubbornly. O'Toole gave a derisive snort from the front seat. "Let me have him a minute, sir. I'll show him what his tongue's for."

The spy cowered against the cushions, but threats, pleas and promises couldn't make him utter a word. His silence indicated that he had knowledge of the entire plot. The Eagle tried every method of coercion that he knew short of torture. He might as well have been questioning the Sphinx. This man was just as terrified of the vengeance of his own people as he was of the consequences resulting from his capture.

"LeBlang," the Eagle said at length, "I give him into your keeping. Guard him well and keep him hidden. A small house on the outskirts will serve the purpose. O'Toole will stay with you until I need him. So far as you are concerned, it is best for your own protection that *Monsieur* LeBlang drop out of sight. It will confuse Baron Richter, worry him and he might overplay his hand. O'Toole, drop me off at the airport. As soon as you are established, notify me by wire of the new address and its phone number."

The spy suddenly gave a flying leap for the car door. Shannon hauled him back and rapped home a powerful blow to the jaw. The spy went limp and dropped to the floor. The Eagle left him there.

THREE HOURS later, in his foppish disguise, the Eagle sat in the office of the Army Engineer Corps, impatiently fussing with his monocle.

"Sorry," a uniformed colonel told him, "we're not especially interested in making any purchases right now. All our construction work is done by contract."

"May I look at the figures?" the Eagle insisted. "I feel it a patriotic duty to offer the services of my firm to the government. All those fires you have been experiencing—it makes a great deal of construction work necessary, doesn't it?"

"Yes, that's true, but the work is handled by three or four firms who usually underbid everyone else. Have a crack at it if you wish. I'll send a clerk into one of the conference rooms with the details."

The Eagle bowed and went out. He received the records in quick time and checked them. Four contracting firms seemed to be doing all the new construction work, and the figures they submitted made the Eagle's eyes blink. He knew enough about the building trade to realize that no contractor could break even at those terms. He noted the firms, glanced at his watch and decided the Eagle had best vanish for a few hours and let drummed-out ex-Captain Shannon present himself for services with the spy outfit.

Returning to the hotel, he removed his disguise and hurried to his own room. The moment he stepped inside, he knew that someone had been there. He didn't smoke cigars and the aroma of a cheap stogie was pungently prevalent. Then he saw the edge of a piece of paper sticking from beneath a scarf on the bureau.

Phone booth—Beekman Drug—eleven sharp tonight.

That was all. He burned the message and washed the ashes down the sink. He had a few hours left and the events of this night might require all his wits. He put in a call for ten-thirty and went to bed.

CHAPTER VI

THE BARON SUSPECTS

AT ELEVEN o'clock the Eagle walked out of the hotel in his ordinary identity. He proceeded briskly toward the drugstore to which he had been ordered, but on the way he felt a growing suspicion that he was being trailed. There was no time to throw a shadow off now. He had to risk it.

There was only one phone booth in the small drugstore. As Shannon entered, a thick-set man emerged from the phone booth, passed by him without a glance, and vanished. The Eagle stepped into the booth. He wondered if the phone would ring or if someone would come personally. Then he saw a folded slip of paper wedged under the receiver hook. It kept the connection open.

He worried it free and realized the clever method they used to contact him The man who had been in the booth planted those directions there and at the same time left the hook up. At the other end of the connection, a listening spy would hear the receiver go down and know that Shannon had the message.

The Eagle unfolded the paper, read the directions and gasped.

Tonight new address. 1298 Elmwood Road. You are to meet our leader. Midnight. Be prompt.

The paper was thin tissue and he wadded it into his month, chewed on it for a moment and gulped it down. He opened the door of the phone booth and ran into Hogan's arms.

"Stay right where you are," Hogan snapped. "I'm checking the call you made."

Shannon groaned inwardly. He couldn't be stopped now when actual contact with Baron Richter was at hand. Ideas were already spinning through his brain. Hogan stepped into the booth and significantly kept one hand deep in his side coat pocket. The Eagle edged toward a counter.

There were bottles of eau de cologne arranged neatly on it. His hand flicked out, seized one and he hurled it directly into the phone booth. Then he spun and began racing madly toward the exit.

A gun exploded and the bullet plowed into the wall beside the door. Then the Eagle was outside. He raced down the street, turned into the nearest alley and kept going at top speed. He vaulted fences, tripped over tin cans and finally reached an avenue parallel with the one on which Hogan was desperately trying to find him and at the same time explain to a patrolman the meaning of that single shot.

The Eagle looked around carefully for a second and then walked into another drugstore.

"Fifty cents worth of malachite," he ordered. "Just put it into a small box."

He glanced at the colorless powder, nodded in satisfaction and carefully placed it in his pocket. Then he turned east, heading in the direction of the new rendezvous. It proved to be a house of pretentious dimensions with a spacious estate surrounding it. The Eagle made certain that Hogan hadn't picked up his trail, and turned into the long path leading to the house.

The door opened as he stepped on the porch. One of *Herr Doktor's* scowling men let him in. The cherubic, spectacled vice-leader of the ring greeted him with a sour grimace.

"You have not done very well, *mein Herr.* There are necessary explanations. But first come into this room and meet our leader. You will treat him with all the respect he deserves. Is that clear?"

The Eagle nodded and followed the man into an ornate living room.

THE CURTAINS were all drawn and the room dimly illuminated. Standing at the far end, his bulky frame drawn up rigidly, was a man who wore a heavy coat and a turned-down hat. He began walking toward the Eagle, and his left leg dragged and clumped its way across the expensive rug.

Herr Doktor bowed from the waist and raised his hand in a salute the Eagle had grown to detest. He wondered why these men didn't have sore arms from all the kow-towing and saluting they did. But he thought it better to follow a good example. He raised his hand also.

"You may stand at ease," Baron Richter said pompously. "So you are Captain Shannon. Do you find our service more interesting and remunerative than fussing in your dingy laboratories, Captain?"

The Eagle drew himself erect. "Yes, sir. And I'm working for people who understand me. The money isn't so much—if I may say so, sir. I could use a little more."

"But, of course," the baron grunted. "When you do good work, you will be properly paid. Those formulas you gave *Herr Doktor*. They are worthless. All of them are old. We sent them abroad weeks ago. What I want are modern inventions, like the new time bomb that takes the place of the one whose plans you sold. Perhaps you know something new like this one, *ja?*"

The Eagle shook his head. "I'm sorry, sir. You see, I was arrested two weeks ago and thrown into a stinking cell. I don't know what's gone on since they took me, sir. I think I might find out something if you give me time and a little money. It takes cash to buy secrets."

"Later we shall talk of it," Baron Richter said. "Now one other thing. *Herr Doktor* sent you on an important mission not many hours ago. You were to get certain documents. You did, but the one I wanted especially was missing. Where is it?"

The Eagle shrugged. "How do I know? Your *Herr Doktor* sent me without telling me anything except I was to take a leather zipper case. I did, and that's all there is to it. Damned near got my head shot off for my pains, too."

Baron Richter swung around, and the Eagle had a glimpse of his face. It was heavy and ruddy. His nose, incongruously thin, was twitching. His eyes were piggish and were narrowed now.

"Then what were ashes doing on the floor in front of the safe? Something was burned there. What?"

The Eagle barely restrained his slight start. He'd forgotten about that. His mind sought an answer to the damaging question. One came— quickly.

"That damned girl, sir! She put a gun against the back of my head and took that document. She opened the zipper case, took one paper, and burned it right in front of me. I couldn't stop her. She was a human devil. She'd have shot me down. She claimed she lived there, and I hadn't been warned to look out for tenants. But I socked her on the jaw later and got even."

"Perhaps," Baron Richter wagged his head up and down slowly. "We shall see. Now, Captain, you are a chemist. If you wished to elicit information from a certain person, what chemicals would you use as a persuader? Especially if that person wished, above all things, to keep his good looks?"

Shannon faced the entrance
as the girl threw up her arms
and toppled backward.

SHANNON SHRUGGED. "Acid, I guess. It hurts like the very devil and it will make a mess of anyone's face. Hydrochloric acid—the fuming type, would be the best."

"At the rear of this house is a small laboratory. Find a bottle of that acid and then go upstairs. I have a patient who may respond to that kind of treatment."

"But burning a man's face," Shannon protested, "is not part of the work I was hired to—"

"Silence," *Herr Doktor* shrilled. "You would defy the baron's orders? If you wish to die, it is quicker to put a gun to your head. Off with you—get the acid—and hurry!"

Shannon sighed. This *was* a ticklish spot. He was expected to burn some helpless person—scar him for life. It was a horrible thing to do, yet his own life might hang in the balance and there was no telling how many others. War was war and certainly the atrocities of these scoundrels couldn't be classified under the word "peace." And the Eagle had gone to too many pains and spent too much time establishing himself as a disgraced army officer to back out now.

He followed one of the bulky thugs to a rear room and found a well-equipped laboratory. Then he had an inspiration. He purposely missed the bottle of fuming hydrochloric acid, depending on the inability of his guard to read the chemical symbols etched into the bottle.

"Have to make it up," he grumbled. "It will take a minute or two."

He secured an empty reagent bottle, picked up the hydrochloric acid and poured about half an ounce of the fuming stuff into the bottle. Then he filled it almost full of water, taken from a vat of distilled water. Next he dumped a small quantity of ammonia into the solution. The hydrochloric acid, even in dilute solution, reacted with the ammonia to produce wisps of smoke that were really ammonium chloride gas. It would do. To all appearances the stuff fumed like hydrochloric acid, yet it would produce only a very mild burn, hardly felt by even the most sensitive skin.

He marched after the burly thug, proceeded up the stairs and was escorted to a barren sort of living room containing a fireplace and a big table. The baron, *Herr Doktor* and several henchmen awaited him. As he turned into it, one hand found the box of malachite powder in his pocket. He deftly slipped off the cover and inserted the tip of his finger into the stuff. Then the Eagle almost forgot what he was doing.

He had his first glimpse of the victim he was supposed to torture. It was the mystery girl who had held him up when he was robbing the safe. She saw the Eagle, and for a scant instant her eyes possessed a gleam of hope which she instantly removed by lowering her eyelids. Baron Richter was bending over her where she was held in a chair at the far end of the table by a hulking thug.

Jeff Shannon took a long breath and stepped close. In an almost unconscious gesture, he let his right hand rest for an instant on Baron Richter's shoulder.

Instantly the baron drew himself erect, but as he did so, the Eagle's hand brushed across the back of the baron's neck.

"You dare to touch me?" the baron rasped. He raised his hand and struck the Eagle across the face. "Carrion—filthy American pig! I am not to be touched or approached closely, do you understand? *Herr Doktor,* why have you not given this man the proper instructions of respect?"

Herr Doktor lowered his gaze and fidgeted nervously. The baron limped away, growling oaths under his breath. Then the business at hand took his attention.

"You know this girl?" he demanded.

"Yes, Excellency," the Eagle answered. "It is the girl who burned that document."

"Very well. Now here is what you must do. We believe she has a copy of that same paper. I want it, no matter what you must do to get it, understand? Perhaps if you smear a little acid across her forehead she may decide to talk. Try it!"

THE GIRL, at the word acid, shuddered and raised imploring eyes to Shannon. He only glared at her and sneered. He removed the glass stopper from the reagent bottle and the white fumes spiraled out. Baron Richter nodded in high satisfaction.

"Go ahead," he rasped. "Burn her pretty face. That will make any woman talk."

The Eagle knew that beads of perspiration stood out on his forehead. If he failed now, it meant not only his life, but the girl's as well. She was, of course, doomed anyway, but the Eagle had a grim resolve to see her out of this perilous spot no matter if his whole plan of campaign toppled like a castle of blocks.

He took his handkerchief from his pocket and saturated one end of it. Then he bent close to the girl.

"You will be scarred for life, perhaps blinded," he warned her roughly. "It is better and easier to tell his excellency what he wishes to know."

The girl shook her head stubbornly, but there was terror in her eyes now. The Eagle spoke in a whisper that he could hardly hear himself.

"This won't hurt, but scream."

He wiped the moist edge of the handkerchief across her forehead. The fumes bit into his nostrils. Baron Richter coughed, but he watched the proceedings with narrowed eyes filled with the lust for torture. The girl wisely bided her time and then she gave a convulsive lurch in the grip of the man who held her and at the same time emitted a wild yell of pain.

"Going to talk?" the Eagle asked her, and in an undertone added, "Swell!"

"No," she half-screamed. "No, I haven't a copy of that listing. I don't know what was on it. I'm telling the truth."

"Her cheeks this time," Baron Richter suggested suavely. "And use more of the acid. Let her scream. The room is sound-proofed."

The Eagle saturated the cloth once more and daubed the stuff on her cheeks. She screamed again, and then slowly wilted in what seemed to be a dead faint.

"The stuff is too strong," the Eagle protested in a cracked voice. "Nobody can stand it for long. You can't imagine how this burns."

Baron Richter strode forward. "Give me that bottle," he snarled. "When she revives, I shall pour it on her. Perhaps there is no other listing, but she must die, anyway."

He yanked the bottle from the Eagle's hand, and some of the fake acid splashed over his fingers. He let out a howl of pain and terror, and then he gaped at Shannon. His piggish eyes blazed as he sniffed of the bottle. Angrily he hurled the flask into the dead fireplace.

"Fool!" he roared. "This is not acid. You—but are you such a fool? No! Traitor is the better word, perhaps. We shall see. Karl, use your gun and pistol the wench while Captain Shannon looks on."

EVERYBODY PROMPTLY fell back save for the agent who held the groaning and twisting girl helpless in her chair. The man called Karl drew his automatic and aimed it at the girl's white throat.

This was more than the Eagle could stand. He knew these ruthless men were not bluffing. And he was already suspected by the baron because of the acid trick. He tensed himself and drew a deep breath. Then he raised his hands waist-high and set himself to grab the side of the heavy table and hurl it over at Karl.

Just as the Eagle moved, the baron raised a clubbed automatic and brought it down on Shannon's head. The Eagle crumpled to his knees, things going black around him as pain lanced through his skull.

"Don't shoot, Karl!" he heard the baron's voice dimly. "Just as I suspected—this man is a spy. This was all a plant, *Herr Doktor*. If I hadn't killed Colonel Vane myself, I'd think that the accursed Eagle was still alive and directing activities. Tie up the girl. We'll get something out of them both later."

The Eagle tried to struggle erect, and the gun butt descended once more. With a slight groan he toppled forward on his face just as he heard the girl scream slightly. The last thing he remembered was that the baron himself had admitted killing Colonel Vane because he had suspected the colonel of being the Eagle. Then things went utterly black for him. He was unaware of it when Baron Richter limped around and kicked him brutally in the side of the face.

CHAPTER VII

EMBLEM OF THE EAGLE

L **ATER, THE** first thing that Jeff Shannon saw when he opened his eyes was the mystery girl's face. It was strained, deeply etched with worry, and her eyes were filled to overflowing, but she was still safe. When she saw that he was awake, she smiled.

The Eagle became aware that they were still in the room of the fireplace. The girl had been tied securely in her chair, and he lay on the floor where he had fallen. His face was stiff with dried blood and his head ached terribly, but he summoned a chuckle.

"Looks like were sailing a rough sea just now, but you're a good sailor."

"I—I thought they'd killed you, Captain Shannon," she said in a low voice. "You looked so pale and—and bloody. What are they going to do with us?"

The Eagle attempted to pass that one off with a laugh, but it didn't work. He tried to sit up and found that he was securely bound, with his hands lashed behind his back. He tugged at the ropes and gave up after a moment. There was no breaking them.

"There's no use kidding ourselves," he said grimly. "That Baron Richter is a man without a heart or a conscience. All I wonder is why they permitted us to live this long. You—haven't talked?"

She shook her head. "They tried to make me say that you burned that document at my house where we first met. I—I told them I burned it. Captain, isn't there anything we can do?"

The Eagle was thinking intently. He had an idea that before one of Richter's thug's would appear with his inevitable knife, there would be a certain amount of interrogation at the questionably tender hands of *Herr Doktor*. If the Eagle knew character analysis, *Herr Doktor* was just a stuffed shirt and as big a coward as the man who had impersonated LeBlang. If Shannon could shock him somehow, divert his attention for a brief moment, he might have a chance. One thing stood in the Eagle's favor—*Herr Doktor* was a fat little man and probably unable to take much punishment.

"I'm going to worm my way over to you," he told the girl. "In my breast pocket you'll find a piece of blue crayon. See if you can get it out and put it between my fingers."

She eyed the Eagle as if he had suddenly gone mad, but when he laughed at her dismay, she nodded eagerly. He inched across the floor, reached the chair and pulled himself up to his knees. Her arms were still strapped to the chair just above the wrists, but she could move her hands slightly. She located the piece of crayon.

Shannon turned himself around and she put it into his hands. He managed to draw himself to his feet and then, in what seemed to be a hobble race, he crossed the entire length of the room and turned his back on a huge expanse of bare wall, covered with a very light wall paper.

"I'm going to draw an eagle," he told the girl. "Don't ask me why. Just guide me so it will look like an eagle and not a cow. Here we go!"

"Don't ask you—I don't need to," she gasped. "I—go ahead."

It was slow, painful work, but when he was finished, Shannon looked at the drawing with some admiration. He hobbled back to where he had been lying when he recovered consciousness, sank to the floor as gently as possible and stuffed the piece of crayon into his shoe.

MINUTES CRAWLED by and he began to lose hope. He glanced at the girl and was somewhat encouraged by her smile.

"Just who are you?" he asked. "And what makes you so important to these spies?"

"They want a listing of American agents working in Europe—the one you burned," she said. "But you know that. I—I don't matter, but Colonel Vane was—was my father."

"What?" he exclaimed.

"Yes," she said simply. "And I know now you are neither a traitor nor a coward, Captain Shannon."

There was no time for further conversation. *Herr Doktor* opened the door and strolled into the room. He glanced at the girl and then kicked the Eagle in the ribs. His attentions were completely focused on his two prisoners and he didn't notice the crayoned eagle pictured on the farther wall.

"So," he snarled, when the Eagle groaned, "you are awake, *ja?* That is good, for we shall talk a little. You belong to G-Two. Colonel Vane arranged that court-martial so we would approach you. That is the truth, is it not?"

Shannon drew his bound legs up as far as he could and gauged the distance between himself and *Herr Doktor.*

"What's the use asking me questions?" he countered. "You wouldn't believe me anyway, and it doesn't matter now."

Herr Doktor seemed a little jolted by that one. "You will tell me what you mean by that!" he thundered. "You will talk or one of my men shall slowly slit your *schwein* throat. Do you hear me?"

"Sure I do," the Eagle retorted. "So does someone else. If you weren't so stupid and so near-sighted, you'd realize your number was up."

Herr Doktor raised his head and for the first time he saw the emblem of the Eagle. A strangled cry came from his throat. He reached toward his hip pocket as his frightened eyes darted about. Instantly the Eagle's legs shot out. He kicked the spy with all the strength he could muster and he heard his heels rap against the spy's skinny legs.

Herr Doktor tried to move away, but the kick had almost paralyzed his lower limbs. He staggered back a step and stumbled over Shannon's outstretched legs. Instantly the Eagle pulled himself up, dug his toes against the floor and hurled his body at the spy. He landed on top of the man, knocking the wind completely out of him and cutting off the scream that welled up from his throat.

The Eagle wormed himself into a better position and clasped both hands around the spy's neck. He squeezed with all the power he could summon. This was a battle to the death. Such things as mercy were unknown in fights of this kind. If he lost, there would be a slow, agonizing death and even more painful than that would be the murder of the girl. This served to lend added strength to his fingers and they clawed deeper into the fat throat of the spy.

He felt his opponent grow limp, but he retained his grip until he was sure *Herr Doktor* was unconscious. Then he rolled off him, hedged his body directly beside the spy's and began clumsily searching his pockets. In one he found a heavy automatic. This he placed on the floor and continued his search. At last his fingers closed around a knife. He got this out by tearing the pocket away. His fingers eagerly maneuvered the blade open and he began sawing at the ropes.

HIS WRISTS came free, but he had no time to attack the bonds around his thighs and ankles. Someone was approaching the room. The Eagle dragged himself across the floor, holding the automatic in his teeth. He raised himself and carefully set the gun down, balancing it on the arm of the girl's chair.

"Take it," he whispered hoarsely. "You can hold the gun. Shoot if you have to, but stall them until I get free."

Two of the thick-set spies came into the room expecting to find victims ready for their knives. Instead, they saw *Herr Doktor,* his face purple, his breathing labored, lying on the floor. They saw the emblem of the Eagle blazing blue at them from the farther wall. This manifestation of the presence of a man they thought dead was as unnerving to them as it had been to *Herr Doktor.*

"Don't move," the girl rapped out. "You are both covered."

They backed against the wall and raised their hands, but their eyes shifted from side to side. If each jumped aside, they'd be out of range of the gun, for both saw that the girl's bound hands couldn't turn the gun quickly enough to keep them covered.

One of the men took a chance and jumped. The gun barked, but its bullet only smashed into the wall. Both spies reached for their own weapons. At that split-second the Eagle sprang into action. He had freed himself of the ropes. He struck the nearest spy, slammed him with all his strength just over the heart. The spy turned white and gasped for breath. The Eagle rapped another blow to the chin.

The second spy was yelling for help, proof that there were others in the house. He turned his gun toward the Eagle, but he was too late. Shannon was gripping the first spy by the collar and the seat of the pants. He hurled him at his companion just as the second man fired. The bullet thudded into the spy's chest and he crashed lifelessly into his slayer. The killer staggered, shrieked in terror, and tried to run for the door. The Eagle stopped him with a well placed haymaker, and he toppled to the floor.

Shannon scooped up the gun and spun on his heels to meet the danger that was barging into the room from downstairs. The gun blasted twice. One of the three men on their way in collapsed. The other two ducked back to safety, one of them clutching his right shoulder.

They began shooting. The Eagle skidded across the floor and reached the wall beside the door. Then he realized what was going to happen. The girl was in direct line of fire from the doorway.

"Drop your gun," one of the spies shouted, or the girl we shall kill. You have one minute."

The Eagle sighed in despair. He didn't hesitate though. He flung the gun to the floor directly in front of the door. The unwounded spy, a shout of elation on his lips, blundered into the room. There were two quick explosions, but not from his weapon. He didn't even begin to pull the trigger. They had come from the girl's weapon.

The spy went down, and the Eagle was sailing through the door. The last of the spy ring was fleeing toward the stairway. He got halfway down before an avalanche of human flesh and bone came swooping down on him. He was on the bottom of a tangled mass of arms and legs when they reached the landing. The Eagle slugged him hard on the button, appropriated his gun and went racing back up the stairway.

Herr Doktor was sitting up, fondling his throat and trying to figure out what was going on. He saw the Eagle and gave a screech of fear. He arose and staggered toward the door. Shannon polished him off with a one-two punch to the face.

THEN HE rushed over to where the girl sat slumped in her chair. She raised her head.

"Captain Shannon!" she cried. "I—I thought they'd killed you."

"Except for you they would have," he complimented her shooting as he attacked the bonds with his knife. "All this shooting is bound to draw the cops. I've got to get out of here as soon as possible."

He helped her up and steadied her until circulation returned to her legs. "You can explain what happened. These men are to be placed under arrest. If the cops want to know who killed them, mention the name of the Eagle. But don't couple it with the name of ex-Captain Shannon. The murderer of your father doesn't know yet that the Eagle still lives, and I must trap Baron Richter."

"But *Herr Doktor*—he knows you. He'll talk," she protested.

"He doesn't know that I am the Eagle. Only you know that. And don't worry about *Herr Doktor;* he's going to take a little pig-a-back ride."

The Eagle hoisted the spy leader up, slung him over one shoulder and started down the steps. On inspiration he turned back.

"I want you to know that I deeply regret the death of your father, Miss Vane, and I shall avenge it. I didn't know until just now that he had been murdered because he was mistaken for me."

"I know that now," she answered quickly. "And I will follow your orders. I—"

Downstairs the front door crashed. Heavy feet trampled on the porch. The Eagle flashed her an encouraging smile.

"You're a staunch soldier yourself. Some man is going to be mighty lucky when he meets you. Good-by until later—and good luck."

He raced into one of the bedrooms, quietly raised the sash as he heard the girl stalling the police at the bottom of the steps. He shoved *Herr Doktor* out of the window, grasped him by one wrist and lowered him as far as possible. Then he let go and heard the spy leader hit the grass and soft earth in the backyard below. The Eagle thrust one leg over the sill, hung from the window a second and let go. He landed two inches away from *Herr Doktor.*

In a flash he was up again, hoisting the spy to his shoulder. The ray of a flashlight swept around the corner of the house. The Eagle dropped his burden, whipped out a handkerchief and quickly tied it around his face as a mask. Then he set his back against the side of the house and sidestepped to the corner.

A LONE patrolman, bent on investigating the thud, walked by two feet away. The Eagle shoved the muzzle of a gun into the officer's back.

"Don't move," he warned in a low voice. "I don't want to harm you, but I've got to get away from here without interference. It's all in the interests of peace."

"Yeah," the patrolman blurted. "Peace, is it—with a dozen stiffs inside this joint and at least one out here. Peace! You make mockery of the word."

"Just the same," the Eagle said softly, "I'm sorry I must do this."

He knocked off the patrolman's hat and brought the butt of his gun down in a smart blow, the full force of it held back, for he only wanted to knock the officer out.

A whistle shrilled somewhere. The Eagle rushed over to the spy, lifted him again and made his way to a garage at the rear of the house. There were two cars parked there and ready to travel. He threw *Herr Doktor* into the back seat of the nearer machine, slid behind the wheel and stepped on the starter.

It responded beautifully. He rolled out of the garage, but he didn't head down the driveway. With the sirens screaming, whistles blasting and excited voices and feet making a din of the night, he figured that the police in the house wouldn't hear the car if he got away from the driveway.

He turned the wheel sharply, headed across the spacious lawn and mowed down a hedge. He crossed another wide estate and saw that the driveway to this house led from street to street. There were no other buildings to bar the way. He turned sharply into the drive and sent the powerful sedan racing away. Until the police found that smashed hedge and saw the wheel marks of the tires they wouldn't even know an escape had been effected.

The Eagle glanced back at *Herr Doktor*, saw that he would give no trouble and thanked his lucky stars that it was early morning and that there was no traffic. His foot became heavy on the gas pedal.

CHAPTER VIII

THE SECRET POLICE

J EFF SHANNON knew that he couldn't drive far in this commandeered car, for once his escape was noted, the police would obtain the numbers of the marker plates and broadcast them. The Eagle wanted no trouble with the police at this stage.

Baron Richter didn't know yet that his local clique of spies had been effectively broken up. Once he found out, there was no telling what he would do. And Shannon wanted to apprehend him before the spy master took flight.

The Eagle parked the car a few blocks from his hotel, made sure *Herr Doktor* was still unconscious and well hidden and then hurried down the street. He turned into the hotel lobby with a prayer on his lips. If Hogan was there, he'd have another battle. The time element would give him no opportunity to take the F.B.I. man into his confidence. He had no proof of his real identity, and the job of making Jeff Shannon a bonafide army captain had been thorough.

But Hogan wasn't there. The Eagle secured a telegram from the desk clerk and shrewdly guessed that it had already been examined and a copy made. He ripped open the envelope, read O'Toole's brief message giving him his phone number and new address. Then he went to his rooms, gathered the clothing and make-up materials comprising his disguise and beat a hasty retreat back to the car. He sent it rolling across town until he reached O'Toole's quarters in a modest rooming house.

He had a key to the front door and he entered, listening to be certain everyone was asleep. He hauled *Herr Doktor* out of the car and carried him into the house, up the steps and finally dropped him on a bed in O'Toole's room. Only one more thing was necessary before he could relax. He spent twenty minutes getting rid of the commandeered car.

Herr Doktor was groaning behind his gag when the Eagle returned. Shannon drew a gun and snapped off the safety.

"I'm going to remove that gag," he warned, "but if you raise your voice above a whisper, I'll plug you."

Herr Doktor nodded his head violently in agreement. When the gag was removed, the Eagle helped him sip half a glass of water. *Herr Doktor* showed no appreciation of this favor. He began cursing his captor in three languages.

"You are the man who is using the insignia of the Eagle," he said hoarsely. "You are a fool! Baron Richter will soon know. Do you think he will take this without a fight? He has already killed the real Eagle. And he can wreak destruction from one end of this nation to the other. He has promised us to do so if we are caught. It is better that you let me go. I—I will not say anything about you."

The Eagle grinned broadly. "Of course, you wouldn't. In fact, you're completely a man of your word. Listen, you run-down heel, you'd have me knocked off ten minutes after you got out of here. You're going to find out what our prisons look like instead. That is, unless you want to talk and maybe find out this government repays those who try to help."

"I know nothing," *Herr Doktor* grated. "I am in this country on a passport. I am a student and practitioner of medicine. My word is better than yours. The laws of your country are favorable to one in my position."

"What does Baron Richter intend doing?" the Eagle asked. "And just who is he? Under what name does he live here and enjoy the freedom of this nation?"

"I will not talk," *Herr Doktor* reiterated. "You are a fool with a too vivid imagination."

THE EAGLE raised his eyebrows at that one and then he shoved the spy flat on the bed and began searching him. By the way *Herr Doktor* resisted the frisk, the Eagle became certain that he did possess something of value.

He found it, after twenty minutes, a two-foot square piece of fragile paper cleverly rolled up and inserted within a cigarette. The ends had been closed with tobacco and only the Eagle's extreme thoroughness uncovered it. He spread the paper on a table.

It was a map of the United States, but one devoted solely to the placing of armament factories, airplane plants, submarine bases, coast guard stations and arsenals. Through several of these had been drawn a cross in red ink. He noticed that the arsenal at which he had recently worked had been treated in that manner.

The Eagle picked up the phone and called long distance. He got O'Toole, several hundred miles south, and gave him precise instructions.

"I've got one of the bunch here in your room, Mike. You bring your prisoner here by plane. Do it so no one will suspect that you are holding him. If necessary, knock him stiff and pretend he is very sick. We'll get these two together and see how their stories check. I'll expect you tonight, so step on it."

"But I will not tell you anything," *Herr Doktor* insisted belligerently. "You cannot make me talk—not if you kill me."

The Eagle lit a cigarette, sat down and crossed his legs. "You know," he said thoughtfully, "I really believe that and I know the reason why. You're not afraid of us here, in the United States. You know only too damned well how lenient our laws are and how fair our courts can be. If this happened to be in your country, you'd soon loosen that stubborn tongue of yours. They'd do it by various methods—make you glad to spill everything you know."

Herr Doktor glared at him, but he lowered his head after a moment in a silent admission to the truth of the Eagle's statement.

The Eagle didn't question him further. He was tired, but anxiety kept him awake. It wouldn't be long before Baron Richter discovered that the Eagle was operating again and that the police had rounded up many of his own best men. When that happened, he might swing into action.

Yet the Eagle could do nothing without proof. Simply to accuse a man of being a spy ring leader was a serious business. Richter would have his steps well covered.

There had to be some way in which to make *Herr Doktor* talk; some method of frightening him into an open confession, one that would stick and expose Baron Richter. The Eagle glanced at the glowering spy. Something clicked in his mind. O'Toole, LeBlang and their prisoner would be here soon. He had to act now.

First of all he gagged *Herr Doktor* again and also blindfolded him. Then he opened his make-up box. He quickly dyed his skin and hair, used the rubber cushions to make his cheeks rounder and the aluminum inserts to widen his nostrils. This done, he donned the natty clothing, adjusted his monocle and looked in the mirror. He shook his head. The effect wasn't exactly what he wanted.

With a pair of scissors he began clipping his hair far upon his temples, until only a stiff bristle of hair remained. Now he was satisfied. He went out to watch for his men.

WHEN O'TOOLE finally drove up, he saw the Eagle approach. LeBlang, recognizing the disguise, greeted him enthusiastically.

"We've got to work fast," the Eagle said. "I've got *Herr Doktor* tied up in your room, Mike. You have the spy in this car who became LeBlang's double. Now here is the idea. LeBlang, you have good connections as a member of the French *Sûreté*. Get on a telephone, call someone you know and make the arrangements I'll outline now."

The Eagle noticed the impostor listening avidly. He signaled O'Toole. "Take our pal upstairs and let him join *Herr Doktor*. If they want to talk, that's okay. Maybe they'll get on one another's nerves until they are willing to confess. Guard them well, Mike. You see, despite the fact that we've broken up their spy ring, there are still a great number of their kind prevalent in this country. The baron may send some of his pets to make certain that neither this man nor *Herr Doktor* is able to talk."

The spy shivered as O'Toole gestured that he was to get out. O'Toole grasped his arm firmly and piloted him into the rooming house. After they were gone, the Eagle got into the car and talked to LeBlang for ten minutes.

O'Toole, in the security of his room, herded both prisoners into a corner and made them sit on the floor. He relaxed, but watched them narrowly. They were whispering in their native tongue of which O'Toole knew not a single word. But if they were hatching some surprise move against him, he'd be more than ready. He wondered what was keeping the Eagle and LeBlang. They had been gone for almost an hour and a half now.

Someone tapped on the door and O'Toole got up hastily. He opened it wide, expecting to find the Eagle there. Instead, a gun was poked directly under his nose. Two men forced him back into the room and closed the door.

They were husky men, with closely cropped hair and they wore black clothing, the same type affected by *Herr Doktor's* thugs. O'Toole was forced into a chair. A gag of adhesive was slapped across his lips and he was securely shackled.

"Ach!" Herr Doktor exclaimed in his own language. "It is about time you came. Baron Richter has sent you, of course. Release me, fools! I am his aide. Hurry, or you shall hear about this."

"Silence," one of the men snapped. "We do not come from the baron. Have you not heard of the Secret Police, *Herr Doktor?* Have you not heard how we take good care of those who fail our leader? We take orders from no one but him. The baron means nothing to us. You do, for you have failed in your mission and probably talked in the bargain. You are going back."

"Back?" both spies chorused, and *Herr Doktor* grew deathly pale.

"But—I—I do not want to go back. I—I am of great value here. My credentials are in order. They will not let you take me back. The United States government will prevent you from sending me back."

"You are going back," one of the two men snarled. "The puny government of this land cannot prevent us from taking you. One of our ships lies in the harbor. It is night. Both of you will be taken aboard there and locked up. No one will even know you are there."

"But Baron Richter—he will not permit it," *Herr Doktor* half screamed. "He is in charge of activities in this country. You must see him—"

ONE OF the two men stepped over to the spy and slapped him soundly across the mouth.

"Silence, pig. Have you no ears? Did you not hear me tell you the Secret Police take orders from no one but our leader! You are going back whether you like it or not."

He began cutting *Herr Doktor* loose while his companion freed LeBlang's double. Guns covered both men, foreign-made weapons that made *Herr Doktor* tremble. Handcuffs were produced and each was cuffed to one of the agents.

LeBlang's double was led out first. The other Secret Police member stopped beside O'Toole, growled something and tweaked his nose. Then they were gone. O'Toole struggled and fought his shackles, but it was hopeless. Maybe in three or four hours someone would hear him, but he had selected this rooming house purposely because it was all but empty and there was no maid service until it was called for.

"A fine mess I've made of things," he told himself with a groan. "What'll the cap'n think of me now, I wonder?"

CHAPTER IX

DEATH AND DESTRUCTION

DIRECTLY IN front of the rooming house a big car was parked. The two spies and their captors entered it and were quickly driven away. One of the secret police leaned forward and spoke to the driver.

"We go to the ship quickly. It sails at daybreak and we have two passengers."

"No," *Herr Doktor* whined. "You cannot do this to me. I do not want to go back, I tell you. They will throw me into a concentration camp. They will torture me—kill me. You must let me remain here, where I can work and accomplish great things. Baron Richter will tell you I am invaluable. What is there to be gained by sending me back? You must—"

One of the secret policemen slapped him hard across the mouth again and hissed a demand for complete silence. The car rolled north, turned east and crossed town toward the river. *Herr Doktor* began shivering violently. LeBlang's double seemed too frightened to care much what happened to him. When he tried to talk, his chin trembled so hard his words became only a meaningless jabber.

The car stopped near the entrance of a pier where a great liner was tied up. The two men from the secret police took adhesive from their pockets, plastered it across the mouths of their prisoners and applied more of it over their eyes.

"It is not fitting that you even see our glorious flag," one of them hissed in *Herr Doktor's* ear. "You—who had failed it and our great leader. We do not put up with failures, my friend. And we must also be sure you have not talked to the authorities. Now—out with you. March beside us and do not make a motion to escape for it is futile. You are handcuffed to us. There is no chance of escape."

Herr Doktor made animal noises behind his adhesive gag. He was all but dragged up the gangplank. He heard men whispering, the sound of many feet on the deck of the great liner. Once or twice he overheard muttered threats against his life; threats made in his own language. He knew that he was being led below decks and then his shoes clanked against metal flooring. He heard a key inserted in a lock and a bolt grate as it was drawn back. Then the adhesive was stripped from his mouth and eyes. LeBlang's double was similarly treated.

Herr Doktor gazed into the narrow confines of a cell, the ship's brig. Its door was of solid steel with only a few small openings for the admission of air. There was no window. A small, none too tidy bunk and a metal chair comprised the only furniture. Another of these cells was opened and LeBlang's double was hurled inside. He began screaming for mercy, adding shrill yells for help. One of the secret police scowled and walked into the cell.

There was the sound of a fist cracking against human flesh and bone. A thud told of the spy's hard fall to the floor of the cell. The agent came out, snapped orders and the door was slammed shut. Then he approached *Herr Doktor*.

"You will go inside quietly or suffer the same treatment I gave that other fool. March, pig!"

HERR DOKTOR'S shoulders sagged. Sweat ran down his face unheeded. His eyes were bulging in terror, his breath came in hoarse gasps. He walked into the cell and sat down on the edge of the bunk. One of the agents stepped in.

"On your feet," he roared. "Have you no respect for your betters? *Herr Doktor*, it is time we had a talk. You failed in your mission. You allowed the American counter-espionage agents to get the best of you. We do not tolerate failure, as you know, but there is another thing far more important. Did you talk? Did you tell them anything?"

"I swear I did not," *Herr Doktor* whined. "They beat me, tortured me, but I refused to tell. Even when they promised I would go free, I refused."

The agent sneered. "Perhaps you do not know anything. I do not think Baron Richter would be fool enough to confide in you."

"But he did," *Herr Doktor* cried eagerly. "I was his closest aide, I tell you. I know all his plans. He has been very successful and I have helped him. We have burned down over twenty buildings in arsenals, ammunition factories and navy yards.

"We have erected new buildings to replace them, and in their walls are enough explosives to blow each factory or munitions dump into little pieces. The baron has sworn that if his work is interrupted he will blow them up anyway, even though his orders are to wait until there is a military necessity for such actions."

"You mean," the secret police agent leaned closer to the spy, "that those new brick buildings are lined with explosives? That all this was prepared in case the United States helped our enemies in Europe? That the explosions of these buildings would destroy entire factories and arsenals? Kill thousands of people?"

"Ja, ja," the spy cried eagerly. He hadn't hoped that the secret police agents would be so taken aback by his news. Now they would realize his importance. "You must let me go. Only *Herr* Baron and myself know the men assigned to blow the buildings up. The walls contain radio sets, tuned to a frequency never used by any stations. But *Herr* Baron and I have devised transmitters that will send impulses to set the explosives off. It is a great plan—it cannot fail."

The agent who stood closest to him suddenly galvanized into action.

"LeBlang," he said crisply and in English, "I leave these men in your tender care. Thanks for helping me. We fooled them completely. Now that they are on a French ship, I suggest you transport them to some nice quiet island about ten thousand miles from here. They won't dare return to their native land—not after spilling all this."

"Mein Gott!" *Herr Doktor* exploded. "You—you are not of the Secret Police. I have been tricked! *Ach*—you will die for this. The baron will blow up every one of your factories. He will wreak destruction such as your nation has never known. It will prove to his superiors what he can do. They will reward him."

LeBlang stepped forward and gripped the spy by the throat. "And you, my fine little parrot, where will you be? If this happens, we shall see how bravely you face the guillotine—or the American electric chair."

"But—but I do not understand," the spy quavered. "This must be a ship from my own country. I heard my language being spoken. You are trying to trick me."

The agent who had quizzed the spy so closely, swept off his hat and turned down his coat collar. *Herr Doktor* only glared at him without recognition.

"You have heard of me before," the agent said quietly. "I am the Eagle! Take care of him, LeBlang. I'm on my way."

Herr Doktor didn't know or care much what happened after that. He had collapsed in a dead faint.

Shannon swept off the heavy, encompassing coat he had used in his guise of a foreign agent. He returned the salutes of French officers aboard the French liner. They cleared a path for him. The same fast car was waiting at the pier.

"The offices of the Army Engineers—quickly," he said. "Never mind lights or policemen."

"*Oui, monsieur,*" the chauffeur grinned and stepped on it.

CHAPTER X

CLOSED TALONS

MANUEL ORTERA, his fat face flushed in pleasure, arose and shook hands with the commanding officer of the Engineering Corps' eastern headquarters.

"These fires are really quite suspicious," he said. "But they haven't done a great deal of damage. Sometimes I think they look like sabotage, other times I believe it is only coincidence. The losses are so small that I can't reason out why spies would wish to destroy them."

Brigadier-General Thorne nodded. "Quite right, Ortera. We've had our men working on those fires and they've gotten nowhere. It's too strong to be coincidence, but we are prepared to believe it is the work of cranks, persons who want to exhibit their power without causing any great amount of damage or loss of life. You will take over the building of this new storage house at the navy yard at your usual terms?"

"Within forty-eight hours I shall lay the foundation." Ortera bowed. "It is little enough, this small way I have of serving my adopted country. Good evening, General. You will not be disappointed in the building I shall construct."

Ortera turned toward the door and stopped dead. A man, brawny, tall and nattily dressed, blocked his way. One hand brought a monocle to his right eye. The other gripped a gun.

"I am quite certain, Mr. Ortera, that we are gravely disappointed in those buildings you have already erected. Please sit down. And you,

General—I'm extremely sorry to force my way in here at the point of a gun, but it is necessary, believe me, sir."

"What's the meaning of it?" General Thorne demanded. "Who are you?"

The man with the monocle bowed slightly. "I'm known as the Eagle. Ask the head of G-Two about me. Ask Mr. Ortera. He has heard of me before—or am I mistaken?"

Ortera started violently and stared with popping eyes. He recovered himself, although the color receded from his heavy face. Then he growled something under his breath, but he obeyed a nudge from the gun and dropped into a chair close by the general's desk.

"I don't know what you're talking about," he said thickly. "I've never heard of anyone called the Eagle."

"Liar," the Eagle said in a grim tone. "Now, Mr. Ortera, it has struck me with considerable force that you have gone to extremes to get contracting jobs with the U.S. government. You underbid any other contractor and during the past few months you have erected new buildings over the ruins of others destroyed by fire."

"I work only in the East," Ortera snapped. "Out of twenty structures I have erected only eight."

"But those other companies that work in different sections of the country—I find that you dominate them. Under various names of course, but you slipped up, Ortera, when you signed the incorporation papers of each. You used different names, but your handwriting is exactly the same. You have erected these buildings with a purpose in mind. For a long time I didn't know why, but I did know that spies were sent to burn down those old structures so you could replace them."

Ortera mopped his face with a handkerchief. He turned to General Thorne. "This man is mad. Why don't you have him arrested? Why don't you call in the police?"

THORNE LEANED forward across in his desk.

"Because I'm interested in his story. We rounded up several spies a few hours ago and all they talk about is the man called the Eagle. I thought he was a myth until now. I find him extremely interesting. You see, Mr. Ortera, I've been wondering about you, too. You haven't made a cent of profit in any of those jobs you've done for us."

Ortera slid his chair around. "You wish confirmation of my patriotism—of the reason why I did not wish to make money out of the government? Allow me to use your telephone. I shall call someone so important that even you will be amazed."

The Eagle signaled that Ortera was to be allowed to do this. The construction company owner picked up the phone and began dialing. The Eagle moved closer, very quietly. He watched the numbers dialed. Then just before the connection was completed, he wrenched the phone out of Ortera's grasp.

"Baron Richter," he snapped, "you are under arrest! General, I have the number this spy called. He was about to issue orders that all those buildings he has erected were to be blown up, and the entire area around them would be blasted to ruins, too. That's why he undertook to erect them at no profit. He makes enough—from a foreign nation—to repay him. His intentions were to stop this country from joining any aggression against his nation in the event of war—or even helping nations attacked by his armies. This man is Baron Richter."

The Eagle pulled down Ortera's collar and exposed a bright green streak on the back of his neck which he showed to General Thorne.

"I put that there," he said. "When you cursed me for touching you, Baron, you really had a good reason. My finger was coated with malachite, a colorless chemical that turns green when moistened by sweat. You didn't notice it on the back of your neck, but no further proof is necessary now. You're Richter, and you're under arrest for the murder of Colonel Vane, whom you killed because you thought he was the Eagle. Miss Vane, the colonel's daughter, is a witness also to your confession."

Ortera dropped his mask. He was on his feet, face crimson with rage, lips trembling with hatred. He made a move for the telephone, and the Eagle's gun roared once. Baron Richter cried out as his hand dropped to his side and oozed blood. He limped back a few steps.

"Here is the number he called, General Thorne," went on the Eagle grimly, repeating the number he had watched the spy master dial. "He was calling his private headquarters to give instructions to blow up all of those mined buildings. Trace it. Get in touch with Hogan of the F.B.I. and send men to round up anyone there.

"Then you must have each one of the new Ortera buildings demolished at once—carefully, because they are all loaded with high explosives. Make haste."

The unmasked Baron Richter was staring in horrified fascination at this monocled man he could not remember ever having seen before.

"Who—who are you?" he demanded hoarsely.

"Look carefully, Baron," suggested the Eagle. "You are a master of disguise yourself. You adopted the identity of Manuel Ortera, pretending to be a South American who loves this country. True, you are limping just now. You have forgotten for the moment that Ortera doesn't limp.

By glancing at your left leg I can see that the shoe has been cleverly built up from the inside. It helps you walk straight—when you remember to be careful about it.

"Look through my disguise, Baron. I will help you. To whom did you admit that you killed Colonel Vane? His daughter, whom you had captive, and another. You thought them dead by now, but they escaped."

AN INSTANT of terrible silence. Then:

"Captain Jeff Shannon!" exclaimed Richter, his face a study of passionate rage and frustration. "So I was right about you being a spy in the accursed G-Two."

"With a slight error," added the Eagle grimly. "You mistook Colonel Vane for the Eagle instead of suspecting me. And you killed him. For that one deed alone you will go to the chair."

It was General Thorne's turn to be surprised.

"Shannon?" he said incredulously. "You are Jeff Shannon?"

"Yes, sir," admitted the Eagle, saluting respectfully. "Some days ago, General, you took my sword from me and broke it. You stripped me of my insignia and drummed me out of the army."

"But—but—" spluttered the general.

"It was all for this purpose," went on the Eagle, indicating the figure of Baron Richter, "to apprehend this dangerous spy. Don't feel too badly about it, sir. You can restore Captain Shannon's untarnished name and record, but it is only a faked record which fooled even the astute Baron Richter. I am not a regular member of the army staff. I am attached to G-Two as a special agent, and I will be returning to Washington at once, now that my job here is—"

Baron Richter could stand no more. He let out a mad scream, took three swift steps, and dived headlong through the nearest window. Too late the general and the Eagle rushed forward.

"My God!" whispered the general, "it's sixteen stories to the ground."

"I know," agreed the Eagle, nodding soberly. "Perhaps it is best this way. He might have got out of the extreme penalty for the killing of Colonel Vane, but he knew he couldn't face the punishment to be meted out to him in his own country for failure. That's why he jumped. Will you convey my respects to Miss Vane, sir, and say that—"

"Why not say it for yourself?" asked General Thorne, smiling slightly for the first time. "She is at present in one of the outer offices. She was waiting to see me when you came in."

The general went out to give orders about the final apprehension of the spies at Richter's headquarters and to send the girl in. The Eagle waited.

In a moment the door opened and Colonel Vane's daughter entered. At sight of the Eagle she came forward swiftly.

"Captain Shannon," she cried, "I want to thank you with all my heart for what you have done. I shall never forget you. You have been so kind and noble and courageous."

"Please," he protested. "I feel that in a way I am responsible for the death of your father, even though unwittingly, and I want to tell you how badly I feel about it."

The girl's eyes filled with tears, but she straightened her shoulders and raised her chin proudly. "He died for his country," she said. "Nobody could ask for more than that."

The Eagle took her hand and bowed deeply, pressing it to his lips.

"As I said before," he murmured, "you are a gallant soldier, and you're going to make some man mighty happy."

"Thank you, Captain Shannon," she said simply. "Or should I say, Captain Eagle? And may I return the compliment? What is your sweetheart's name?"

The Eagle colored slightly. Then he laughed.

"Her name," he answered soberly, "is Joan Kirke."

Valerie Vane looked at him for a smiling moment. Then she impulsively kissed him.

"I'm returning what you gave me," she murmured. "Give them both to her, with my love."

And she turned and was gone.

IV

THE STOLEN
GAS GUN

CHAPTER I

OFFICIAL TRIAL

THE SLIGHT breeze that blew across the proving grounds where a group of civilians and U.S. Army officers waited was damp and chill. In the middle of the field about fifty yards from the scattered groups was, of all things, a large wire cage filled with live rabbits, and with a regulation bull's-eye target tacked to the middle panel.

Off to one side, talking to a gray-haired man in a colonel's uniform, stood a vigorous young man in neat brown suit, snap-brim hat and belted topcoat. His fine blue eyes, wide-set and piercing, had an alert look that fitted his lean jaw and wide, humorless full lips.

"So this is the spectacular setup for the famous Scheck gun trial, Colonel Ormsby?" he commented.

"And why are you here at this early hour, eh, Captain Shannon," countered the colonel, his eyes twinkling.

Jeff Shannon smiled. Captain Jeff Shannon, to give him his military title, was more than simply an officer in the U.S. Army. He was also the ace counter-espionage agent of G-2, feared by all spy enemies of America. Known as the "Eagle" he was the relentless Nemesis of all espionage rats who gnawed away from within at the bulwarks of the United States. Fearless, intrepid, keenly intelligent, and splendidly trained in his particular field, he was really answerable only to the Director of the fairly new Secret Service Corps known rather vaguely as G-2.

"My job is to keep an eye on any and everything that might interest the agents of foreign nations, Colonel," Shannon answered. "This Professor Otto Scheck, an Austrian I understand, has Ralph Mortimer all in a flutter over this new invention of his, and Mortimer is some research chemist himself." He laughed a little. "Rather odd hobby for a governmental undersecretary."

"Yes," admitted Ormsby. "Mortimer swears Scheck's gas gun will supersede even the new Garand rifle."

A BIG black sedan was turning into the grounds, having passed the sentry challenge at the gate. The two men strolled closer to the main group as the sedan stopped. The tonneau door was opened, and Ralph Mortimer carrying a heavy, oblong package descended. He turned to help a slender, slight little man out of the car. Mortimer, big, hearty, and affable, introduced his companion briefly to General Bridge, in command, and to several others in the group.

Professor Scheck blinked his mild eyes, looked a bit bewildered, and then set about opening the package and assembling what seemed to be a hand-gun with a rifle stock attachment.

"This gun, General Bridge," Mortimer started to explain, "fires a projectile containing a charge of highly compressed gas of Professor Scheck's own invention. The bullet bursts like shrapnel, upon impact, and releases this gas to kill everything within a radius of six feet. If you hit a wall beside a man—or even the ground—six feet away from him,

The Eagle stepped out seddenly from behind a tree, his
pistol raised. "Stay where you are!" he ordered.

you kill him as surely as if you had scored a direct hit. Even ordinary
gas masks are no protection against the penetrative powers of the gas."

"So the correspondence on the matter claimed," said the general
dryly. "We are here, Mr. Mortimer, for a demonstration, not a lecture
on the theory."

Mortimer colored slightly. "But I must tell you, sir, that I have tried
the weapon myself—Scheck is staying with me and working in my
laboratory—and I killed a couple of rabbits upon which I had previously placed special gas masks. First, the professor will demonstrate the
power of the gun under ordinary circumstances. Then he will show you
how it works with gas masks. We can't waste any bullets, because there
are only six of them in the gun. It is highly dangerous to manufacture
them, and Scheck hasn't the proper equipment for the job. It will be

easy in regular firearm and munition factories, of course. Are you ready, Professor Scheck?"

"*Ja.*" The inventor nodded.

The spectators fell back as the little man raised the gun to his shoulder, aiming at the rabbit cage. Ormsby spoke softly to Shannon.

"If this thing is that good, and we can fit it to rifles and machine guns, the results will be devastating. A machine gun firing along a line of trench, with every bullet killing everything within six feet of where it hits, could wipe out a couple of battalions of infantry in one burst of firing."

"Ghastly," agreed Jeff Shannon, his face grim. "No wonder this demonstration is being kept quiet and private."

Professor Scheck located the target on the rabbit cage and pulled the trigger. The gun roared, and the bullet kicked up a little geyser of dust squarely in front of the cage.

"Watch the rabbits!" cried Mortimer.

They did, and the animals went right ahead eating carrots or hopping around. Professor Scheck goggled his astonishment and fired again. This time the bullet didn't even hit the ground.

"Here, Professor!" cried Mortimer, as ripples of amused laughter arose. "Give me that gun. You're a rotten shot."

He snatched the weapon from the mild little inventor, slammed it to his shoulder and fired two rapid shots which distinctly hit the target. And still the rabbits lived, though disturbed by the impact of the missiles against the central panel.

"*Herr* Mortimer!" cried the inventor in bewilderment. "*Der* rabbits, they don't die!"

"Major Kelly," snapped General Bridge, "you are a sharpshooter. Will you accommodate us by firing the round from this gun into the bull's-eye?"

THE OFFICER stepped forward and took the gun from the patently astounded Mortimer's lax hands. He slapped the weapon briskly to his shoulder and snapped one shot at the target—a perfect bull's-eye. And the rabbits became friskier than ever.

Laughter became derisive. The inventor and his sponsor became the center of a group, vehemently protesting and gesticulating. Jeff Shannon grasped his companion by the arm.

"Colonel, get hold of that gun—quick! Mortimer said there were six rounds in it. Get that last unfired shell for me."

Colonel Ormsby pushed forward and joined Major Kelly who obligingly handed him the gun for examination. Shannon bent his keen gaze to the ground, searching for the spent shells. He quickly picked up three of them, dropping them into his topcoat pocket carelessly as Colonel Ormsby rejoined him. The colonel unobtrusively slipped a heavy cartridge into the Eagle's hand.

"Quite a fiasco, wasn't it?" he murmured.

"Apparently," agreed Shannon, frowning. "But I know that three foreign powers are interested in Scheck's claims. Something smells fishy about this test."

General Bridge had only one thought. The test was a failure. He said so in no uncertain terms as he crisply dismissed the inventor and Ralph Mortimer. As their sedan drove away Shannon climbed into his own coupé and drove thoughtfully back to Washington. Then, temporarily, he dismissed the matter from his mind, for he had a breakfast date with lovely blonde Joan Kirke, his fiancée.

Joan was the tonic for him she always was, but before they had finished breakfast Shannon could see that the girl was not her usual happy self. She seemed restless and dissatisfied. And suddenly she came out with what was troubling her.

"Jeff," she said firmly, "I simply can't go on doing nothing, except worrying about you, while you are risking your life constantly in this espionage work that apparently is your whole life. You've got to get into something safer, or—"

He set down his cup in amazement, his eyes wide as he saw her lovely face clouded with anxiety.

"Why, darling, you know that's impossible—at least for the present. I thought we had a thorough understanding about my work."

"We have," she said. "But not about mine. That's what I mean. You've simply got to let me help you—somewhere, somehow! I can't bear the useless life I'm leading—have been leading ever since I was left an orphan, with no relatives I know of, and enough money so that I don't have to work. Oh, I know G-Two has no place for an untrained woman but surely there are times that I can help you in small ways. Darling, I—I just can't stand being kept out of your life except for rare little stolen intervals such as this."

"Why, Joan, I wouldn't dare endanger your life by dragging you into any such messes," Shannon declared. "Besides, if I could find little jobs for you to do, you wouldn't be with me any more than you are now."

"At least I'd be working on something for you!" she persisted. "I'd have something to do, too, and I'd see you oftener than I do now."

An idea struck Jeff Shannon as he studied her eager face.

"All right," he agreed suddenly. "Think you'd make a good secretary?"

"I can type and take dictation, and I have normal intelligence," she said spiritedly.

"Okay. I'll try you out. There may be nothing at all to this matter I have in mind—I hope there isn't—and then again there may be a lot. But there'll be no particular danger in what I'm telling you to do. Here's the setup. Ralph Mortimer, an under-secretary for the government, and an amateur research chemist, has a Professor Otto Scheck living in his home. Scheck is the inventor of a new gas gun—or he's the perpetrator of a swell hoax."

Shannon told her what had happened that morning. "Now, what I want you to do is to get a job as secretary in Mortimer's home. I don't know how—that's up to you. But get in and start checking up on everybody in the household. I'll keep in touch with you."

"I'll do it!" cried Joan, her eyes shining. "But what do you suspect, Jeff!"

The Eagle's eyes grew suddenly thoughtful.

"I may be all wet," he said slowly, "but I think somebody switched cartridges on the little professor. And it could have been anybody from Mortimer to Hitler."

CHAPTER II

RUTHLESS RAID

THE LARGE, rambling colonial home of Ralph Mortimer set back in wide grounds, surrounded by a high grille fence. Out beyond Chevy Chase, it was a landmark of antebellum days. Mortimer, whose private income far exceeded his salary as an under-secretary, had fitted up the third floor of the house as a private laboratory for the pursuit of his hobby—research.

Just now, seated comfortably in his library before the crackling logs in the wide fireplace, he had just finished dictating a letter to his secretary.

"That's all for tonight, Miss Kirke," he said. "You might show the typed answer to Professor Scheck for his approval before you bring it to me for signing in the morning." He sighed. "Well, I guess that washes us up here in America. Professor Scheck will have to consider foreign offers for his gas gun after all, I fear. Confound that hardheaded General Bridge for not giving us a new trial because of that failure ten days ago!"

"I'm sorry," said Joan, and she meant it.

In ten days' time she had become fond of the mild little professor who could not understand how his gas gun had failed in the crucial test. Mortimer, she hadn't made out yet, but he seemed to be heartily interested in the invention for the sake of the United States. He believed in the efficacy of the thing, anyway.

"Don't you think—" Joan had begun to say when a sudden, terrible explosion in some part of the building shook the house to its foundations.

Books toppled from the shelves, window panes shattered, pictures dropped from the walls, and both occupants of the library were flung to their knees.

Mortimer staggered to his feet.

"Scheck!" he shouted. "He's had an accident in the laboratory!"

He had started for the door, with Joan after him when suddenly the door was flung open, and three men burst into the room. The leader, a tall, incredibly thin man with the coldest eyes Joan had ever seen, came straight on, while his two companions, vicious-looking thugs carrying sub-machine guns, deployed to right and left of him.

"Don't be alarmed," he said in precise tones. "Where is Otto Scheck?"

"Who—what—how—" spluttered Mortimer helplessly.

"Shut up and sit down!" ordered the menacing stranger. "Merely my way of creating a distraction so I could enter without trouble—and dispose of your servants at the same time. I asked you where is Otto Scheck."

"What do you men by making an armed entry into my house?" Mortimer shouted angrily.

The tall man leveled his gun squarely upon Mortimer's face and pulled the trigger. Joan screamed. But there was no sound of gunfire. A fine stream shot from the gun, splattering over Mortimer's face. With a choking cry, he clawed at his throat, and pitched forward on his face.

Without the slightest compunction the stranger shifted the muzzle of his gun and fired a stream at the girl. Her cry was cut off as though he had used a knife, and she fell to the floor, senseless.

"Come on, boys," the tall man ordered crisply. "Get busy and find the professor."

They raced out of the room and headed for the stairs, taking them three at a time. Another pair of armed thugs came from the rear depths of the bombed house. The quartet of gunners moved quickly, as though they knew exactly what they were doing.

SWIFTLY SEARCHING the second floor, they followed their leader to the third. As they reached the third-floor landing a door opened, and the startled face of the inventor appeared. With a yelp of alarm at sight of the armed men, he leaped back, and tried to close the door. But the ruthless leader was on him before he could get it shut.

"Scheck!" he grated as he barged through the door, knocking the little man backward.

His quick, cold eyes took in the laboratory in one sweeping glance. On a bench lay the assembled model of the gas gun. In a vise was a cartridge shell, surrounded by a litter of shell-loading paraphernalia. On another bench were glass retorts in which a gaseous chemical mixture was bubbling.

"So you're still at it, eh?" snapped the tall man, with a hard laugh. "Your failure at the proving grounds wasn't enough for you? Now—what is the formula for that gas? Where…. Ah, there is your notebook!"

He shot a glance at one of his men. "There's the gun on that bench, Sawyer. Get it!"

The professor uttered a cry of protest and turned to run over to protect his property. The tall man cruelly slapped him alongside the head with his gun. Blood spurted from the scalp wound.

"Not so fast, squarehead! I asked you what the hell's in that fiendish gas of yours? Tell me, before I beat your head to a pulp!"

Scheck groaned and stared at his tall captor pathetically.

"It is a special compound of cyanogen," he gasped. "But it is more deadly than cyanogen because it penetrates right through the skin and stops the heart instantly. I have to be very careful when I make it. I—"

The tall man leaped to the bench to snatch up the formula book. Rapidly he riffled through the pages until he came to a sheet with the heading "Death Gas." Below was a list of chemical equations and detailed processes in the professor's crabbed handwriting.

"Your precious formula!" he exulted. "The whole thing—here in this book!" He glowered at the inventor. "How many other people know this formula? Quick. I want to know."

"Nobody," groaned the professor. "That is, nobody who is aware of it. I kept the formula in my head until—"

"Until you wrote it down here. Well it's too late for you to tell it to anybody now. Blast him, Mike!"

One of the criminals nodded and swung the barrel of his chopper around. At last aware of their cold-blooded intentions, the professor started screaming and scrambling to his feet. Mike coolly waited until the little inventor had raised himself in line with the ugly snout of his machine gun, and then callously released a short burst of slugs that ripped into Scheck's chest and literally cut him to pieces. With his blood spurting like water from a sieve, the little Austrian's body jerked and shuddered and dropped back to flop on the floor like a rag doll.

"Okay, Mr. Machin?" asked the executioner indifferently.

"Good work." The ruthless leader nodded. "Get out of here now, all of you. Give me your chopper, Sawyer."

THE THUG called Sawyer handed over his sub-machine gun and started out, cradling the stolen gas gun in his arms. The man who had answered to the name Machin stuffed the black formula book into his coat pocket and ran to the door. At the threshold he turned and, leveling the tommy gun at the banked mass of flasks and retorts, he cut loose with a burst of slugs that smashed the equipment into hopeless ruins.

He slammed the door behind him and leaped for the stairs.

"The neighbors will have reported the explosion to the police by now," he snapped to his men. "Let's get out of here!"

Leaving wreckage behind them, they raced outside. On a level stretch of meadow beyond a row of poplar trees, a huge monoplane stood waiting with idling ticking motor. The ruthless killers piled into the giant bird of the skies. The pilot opened the throttle, the motor roared in full-throated song of power, the huge propeller disappeared in a shimmering circle in the moonlight, and the plane headed bumpily down the field.

At the far end it lifted sluggishly and took to the air like a huge bat, droning off into the night. At the same moment, with sirens howling, two police cars came roaring into the grounds.

CHAPTER III

THE FIRST LEAD

PEMBROKE, OF the War Department, was worried as he stood in front of the mantelpiece in the living room of his apartment, clad in dressing gown, and talked to his nocturnal visitor.

"I called you over because it's urgent, I'm afraid, Jeffrey," he said. "About that gas gun trial of that little inventor, Scheck, ten days ago. General Bridge is a grumpy sort, and he's generally right, but there may be more to this invention than meets the eye."

Jeff Shannon, who had been busy the past few days on another matter, pricked up his ears.

"What do you mean, sir?" he asked quickly.

"Today I received reports confirming the fact that Italy wants Scheck to bring his gas gun over there and demonstrate it—at Italy's expense. And I know that two or three groups of espionage spies of other countries are snooping around."

"In spite of the fact that you had those empty shells and the loaded one I gave you analyzed and found nothing but ordinary ammunition?" asked Shannon.

"Yes. But you haven't heard the worst, Jeffrey—why I got in touch with you as soon as I was notified by an F.B.I. man. About ten o'clock tonight the Mortimer home was bombed and several people murdered. The killers escaped in a monoplane, wrecked the laboratory, destroyed or carried off the professor's notes, took the gas gun, and left the inventor riddled with machine gun bullets."

"Good God!" Shannon leaped to his feet in horror.

His face drained of color. Then he exerted his iron control. "Have you a list of the dead, sir?" he asked in a strained voice.

"No. But since this is now a matter of grave importance, I think you'd better get out to Mortimer's place and see if there's anything there for us."

"There is for me," groaned Shannon. "My fiancée has been working there as Mortimer's secretary since that day of the gas gun test. She must have been one of the victims—or she'd have got in touch with me by now."

"Good Lord!" exclaimed Pembroke. "I'm terribly sorry, Jeffrey. What—I mean, why was she—"

"A fool stunt of mine," said Shannon tersely. "I had her there as a sort of checker-up because I suspected spy work and cartridge switching. She—she insisted on helping me, and I figured that the real secret of this Scheck gas gun was the gas bullet. Therefore, if the spies had already switched ammunition and were in possession of the gas bullets, there'd be no reason for them to come back, and no danger for Joan."

"Did she communicate with you at all while she was there?" asked Pembroke quickly.

"Twice," said Shannon. "She was learning about Mortimer and Scheck getting the cold shoulder from government and private concerns alike in this country. I haven't seen her for several days, and—" He broke off and choked.

"Better get out there," said Pembroke. "Let me know as soon as you can. And—good luck, Jeffrey."

They shook hands firmly, and Jeff Shannon hurried from the apartment. And his face now was only the keen, cold and alert face of—the Eagle, America's ace of counter-espionage. He now had a personal motive for taking the trail of Otto Scheck's murderers and despoilers, perhaps vengeance to exact for the life of his own loved one.

THE MORTIMER home blazed with lights, and there were fully a dozen cars in the front drive when the Eagle reached the place. A police ambulance was backed up to the front porch, and a dead wagon was just rolling away. Police and Federal men overran the house and grounds. An impromptu interrogation bureau had been set up in a room off the front hall.

"Where the devil d'you think you're going?" a uniformed policeman accosted Shannon as he ran up the steps.

SHANNON THRUST his identification card at the man. It told everything except that Jeff Shannon was really the Eagle.

"Yes, sir, Captain Shannon." The uniformed man snapped to salute. "You will find Lieutenant Gorram inside, first door to your left."

Shannon burst into the room, his face white, his heart in his mouth, braced to receive bad news. He saw the ambulance surgeon administering to two people lying on couches at the far side of the room. One was the corpulent figure of Ralph Mortimer. The other one was—Joan Kirke!

Shannon sprang forward, barely speaking to the harried police lieutenant, and dropped on his knees beside the couch.

"Joan! Joan!" he whispered. "Is she…. Will she live, Doctor?"

Joan answered for herself. She opened her eyes, stared at Shannon, then smiled slightly.

"Jeff!" she murmured as he caught her hands. "I knew you'd come. I'm all right. And I've something to tell you."

"What happened to her, Doctor?" Shannon asked the police surgeon.

"Gas," was the answer. "Fired in liquid form. Mortimer got quite a heavy dose of it. Miss Kirke has practically recovered."

"Thank God!" murmured the Eagle fervently.

While the surgeon and police lieutenant listened, Joan described the sudden and brutal attack in the library.

"We found Miss Kirke and Mr. Mortimer in the library, Captain Shannon," corroborated Lieutenant Gorram. "Three servants at the back of the house were killed, and the bullet-riddled body of a man identified as that of Otto Scheck, an inventor, was found in the wreckage of a laboratory on the third floor. A couple of F.B.I. agents are up there now."

"No one else found alive?"

"Yes, the cook, butler, and the housemaid. They were upstairs at the time of the explosion. Two gardeners and a chauffeur were killed in the kitchen by the bomb. They were having a late snack before going to bed."

"You question them?"

"Only hastily. I've been pretty busy straightening out things since I reported to Headquarters. It's espionage activity, of course—with the inventor's papers and plans and weapon model stolen."

"No," said Joan Kirke positively. "I saw the leader of the gang that raided us, and I recognized him—from seeing his picture in the papers recently, when he was released from prison. I remembered the name, too—John Machin."

"Machin!" exclaimed the lieutenant incredulously. "That big-shot crook is in Chicago. What would he be doing here in Washington, fooling around with an invention that doesn't work? Why, that's ridicu—"

"Is it?" interrupted the Eagle sharply. "Are you absolutely certain Joan?"

"Positive," the girl insisted firmly. "When Mr. Mortimer is able to talk, he may be able to back up what I say. Perhaps he also recognized that crook Machin."

"John Machin!" murmured the Eagle, swiftly recalling what he knew about the criminal. "If John Machin is mixed up in this mess, it is big. But we don't know which foreign crowd is interested enough to have Machin stage a raid. And suppose Machin is working on his own, intending to offer the gas gun to the highest bidder! That would fit in with killing the inventor to prevent him from supplying a duplicate set of plans to anybody else. But what good would it do him if somebody else had already stolen a set of the gas cartridges ten days before?"

The Eagle went up to the small laboratory where he found the two F.B.I. men checking the wreckage and the body of the victim carefully. Shannon was considering what he knew about John Machin. Internationally known crook and jewel thief, he had been convicted of subversive activities, spreading propaganda for a European power that sought to get its dictatorial hooks into America. For lack of sufficient evidence, Machin had drawn only a year, when he had warranted life.

There were three people in Machin's private mob, himself and two of his accomplices, about whom the police of half a dozen countries knew little, though they had roamed the world, preying on anything that offered lucrative returns. And now it seemed they had entered the profitable realm of espionage. Or had they? If no big foreign spy ring was backing them, what had made Machin so bold in his attack on Mortimer and Scheck? Had he wanted to leave no witness behind him to talk? Or didn't he care? Or—queer thought, but tenable—was Ralph Mortimer mixed up in the game?

After half an hour spent in careful investigation of the premises and in checking with the F.B.I. agents, Shannon returned to the improvised office. Mortimer had fully recovered and was making a statement. Nothing he said threw any light on the mystery. He seemed genuinely grief-stricken over the death of the little Austrian inventor.

"I can't understand it," he mourned. "We were dickering with the Italian government—among others—it is true, but I had the secret hope that we would convince our own military experts before it was too late that Scheck's invention was all that he claimed. The professor was hard at work manufacturing a new batch of gas to make new shells when—when we were attacked."

"The laboratory was wrecked," pointed out Shannon. "Not even a scientist would be able to tell what Scheck was doing. Have you a duplicate set of plans and formulas filed away anywhere, Mr. Mortimer?"

Mortimer sadly shook his head. "Scheck wouldn't trust anybody with his precious formula. He said it was safer kept in his own head."

"You mean he didn't have it written down?"

"Not so far as I know. Of course, he had several sets of formulae written down in the black notebook he kept in the laboratory. But the formula for the death gas was not in it."

The Eagle's eyes narrowed. "If what you tell me is true," he said, "somebody made a bad mistake when they bumped off Scheck. Well, I guess that's all around here for the present, Lieutenant Gorram."

He drew Joan aside.

"Get your bag packed, darling," he said. "I'll take you back home."

"Are you dropping this case, Jeff?" she demanded sharply.

"On the contrary," he said grimly. "I'm just beginning, but the trail is cold here."

"That's where I think you are wrong," she told him. "I know there is something here, and I'm going to stay on."

"Oh, you are? And me worrying all the time what might be happening to you? Not on your life, young lady. You're going to fade out of this picture."

JOAN LAID a finger against his lips.

"Ah!" she murmured. "So now you begin to realize how I feel about you. But seriously, Jeff, I think I can learn something here. And surely there can be no further danger—now that poor Professor Scheck has been murdered and all of his invention plans stolen."

"You suspect Mortimer?"

"Not necessarily, but somebody had to switch those bullets in the first place, didn't they? And nobody has been on the place except the people who are here now. Professor Scheck was such a mild and good little man, Jeff. We learned to like each other a lot. I talked to him often in the laboratory when I would confer with him about the correspondence Mr. Mortimer dictated to me.

"And he was so thoughtful and considerate. One morning I tripped and tore the heel from my slipper. He made me sit down and read the letters to him while he repaired my slipper as well as any cobbler could have done it."

"He struck me as being that type," agreed Shannon soberly.

"And that's why I've got to help you solve this case, Jeff. I—I feel like I owe it to Professor Scheck."

"You would," the Eagle said thoughtfully. "All right, here's what we'll do. I'll make a show of carrying away important notes of the professor's—say they were overlooked by the killers. Then you watch everybody and everything that happens after I've gone and get in touch with me at noon at my place and give me any dope you've unearthed."

"Done!" she exclaimed, and kissed him.

When Shannon took his departure from the house of tragedy one pocket of his coat was bulging with blank paper from the laboratory. He drove rapidly back to town to G-2 Headquarters where he sent out calls to the police departments of the surrounding cities up and down the Atlantic seaboard. The search for John Machin was on.

Promptly at twelve o'clock Shannon was back at his apartment. The imperious ringing of his phone brought him on the jump. Joan was on the wire.

"Jeff," she said breathlessly, "I'm calling from the extension phone in the laboratory. Just about daybreak Jenner—he's the butler—put in a long-distance call. I waited until he finished talking, then called the operator on this extension and asked her how much the charges were on that call we had just made. I managed to get the information that Jenner called a Mr. Sutliff at the Hotel Plymouth in Baltimore. I don't know what their conversation was about, but I'll bet it concerned the notes you took away with you."

"Good girl, Joan!" Shannon murmured in swift approbation. "I'll let you know the minute we have anything."

CHAPTER IV

BATTLE IN BALTIMORE

A SECOND-RATE HOTEL, close to the waterfront, was the Hotel Plymouth. It had a heterogeneous patronage. Mr. Sutliff, for example, was a seafaring man by the cut of his jib, one who drank rum by himself and smoked Turkish tobacco. He was a broken-nosed man with a dour face and a blue eagle tattooed on the back of one hairy hand.

This afternoon, however, Sutliff was neither drinking nor smoking. He was busily writing in his room on the third floor, the window of which overlooked the bay. An unusual occupation for a sailor and an unusually fine hand for anybody. He paused to listen as the sound of a chantey, roared by a drunken sailor, floated into the room through the open transom.

Without warning the song stopped in mid-verse, and a body lurched heavily against the door. The flimsy lock gave, and a rowdy-looking man with ragged red hair and in typical longshoreman's garb staggered into the room. With one swift move Sutliff shoved his unfinished letter under a pile of papers and started angrily to his feet.

"Get out of here!" he grated in a savage voice that didn't sound at all like a sailor's. Then he covered himself quickly. "Ye're scuppers under, me hearty, but ye're in the wrong berth. Avast there!"

The intruder straightened up and grinned foolishly as he clumsily sought to get out through the door. Instead, he managed to shut the barrier in his own face. Sutliff started forward to boot him, then halted abruptly in the center of the room, in surprise. For the drunken longshoreman had whirled with his broad back to the door, and an ugly automatic was gripped in his right fist.

"Sit down, Sutliff," he said firmly. "We're going to have a quiet little chat."

"Who the hell are you?" snarled Sutliff, his eyes darting rapidly about the tawdry quarters.

"Not so loud." The gun was waggled suggestively. "You can call me Mr. Neptune, and if you don't talk straight, hard, and fast you'll likely find yourself in Davy Jones' locker."

"What do you want?" Sutliff demanded.

"Information," said Mr. Neptune grimly. "You received a long distance telephone call at dawn this morning from Washington. Within fifteen minutes you left this hotel and were gone for half an hour. Then you returned, and you've been hanging around your room closely ever since except for forty minutes you spent downstairs in the dining room for lunch."

"A copper, eh?" sneered Sutliff, recovering his aplomb. "So wot? I've done nothing you can pinch me for."

"Where did you go and what did you do during that half-hour this morning?" demanded Mr. Neptune. "Talk, if you want to save your skin."

Rushing to Baltimore from Washington right after receiving Joan's tip, the Eagle had canvassed the hotel and Sutliff thoroughly. But that one half-hour, that one vital space of time, he was unable to account for, though Sutliff could not have gone far.

"I had a breakfast date with a mermaid down the harbor," said Sutliff. "Now, scram outa here."

"You went to use a telephone or to send a telegram or a message somewhere," stated the disguised Eagle. "And I haven't any time to waste on you. Where did you send it, or to whom did you talk? And what did you say? Don't lie! I know who called you from Washington this morning and what about."

"If you're so good," jeered Sutliff, "figure out where I went."

"All right," said the Eagle curtly.

WITH ONE bound he leaped past the defiant Sutliff. With his left hand he swept the pile of papers from the desk, revealing the letter on which Sutliff had been working.

The broken nosed Sutliff let out a startled cry and, despite the menacing automatic, dived headlong for the Eagle's knees. His heavy shoulders crashed into Shannon with the force of a battering ram. Wrapping his mighty arms about the Eagle's legs he bore him to the floor in a terrific shuddering thud as the gun blasted just once and slapped a streak of livid fire along his back.

But this only served to galvanize the man, and the Eagle found himself fighting for his very life. The letter was forgotten as they threshed around on the dirty floor. The Eagle didn't want to fire another shot for fear of arousing the house. Also, he wanted to subdue this man and force him to talk.

"*Schwein!*" panted Sutliff as he pawed and clawed his way up along his adversary's body to reach the throat. "I'll teach you!"

"Oh, German?" gasped the Eagle as he fought.

Sutliff took a numbing blow on the shoulder before he could grasp Shannon's gun wrist, and then they locked in a bearlike embrace and rolled desperately over and over across the floor until they brought up against the wall. Sutliff was on top and, still gripping the Eagle's gun hand, he reached into his trouser seam at the hip and whipped up a keen and glittering stiletto.

Only by moving his head with the desperation of a doomed man did the Eagle avoid that needlelike, hungrily licking blade. The point burned past his neck, bringing the blood, and went half an inch into the splintery floor. With a sobbing grunt Sutliff tugged it free and tried for a short jab at the throat.

There wasn't anything else to do. The Eagle's gun was pressing now against the chest of his antagonist as he fought to lever him off. He squeezed the trigger twice.

Sutliff jerked convulsively, and he went limp. Panting from his terrible exertions, the Eagle rolled the dead man aside and scrambled to his feet.

There was no time to lose. He had to get out of here. But he snatched up the crumpled paper which had precipitated the fight and glanced at it. In a fine copperplate handwriting he read:

—immediately. Jenner's call indicated that the detective called Shannon must have found certain data overlooked by Machin in his haste. Careless fools, these cursed American criminals. I went to the *Amsterdam Koenig* and radioed you at once. Your Excellency's reply that the formula was a dummy confirms my suspicion that Scheck was too shrewd to put all his eggs in one basket. Again that haste of M. in liquidating S. makes matters difficult. For the weapon and shells are worthless without the formula. Any fair engineer can design and construct a serviceable gun and projectile. What we must have is the gas formula. Until he produces it, I instruct you to pay M. not one pfennig, but keep the gun, and I am allowing just forty-eight hours for him—and you—to produce results. It is dangerous for me to delay sailing any longer. And after that purge by M. the American Intelligence will be hot on the trail. This letter is official confirmation of my orders, via wireless—

"Sit down, Mr. Sutliff," said the intruder in perfectly somber tones.

That was all. There must have been more ahead of this, but the Eagle didn't have the chance to find out. Still he could visualize the general setup. The *Amsterdam Koenig* was a Dutch freighter—ostensibly—tied up at the docks. Sutliff undoubtedly had been a high-ranking person in the espionage system of his native country. He had been waiting here at this cheap hotel for the hired crook, Machin, to steal Otto Scheck's gas gun and turn it over to someone he called "Your Excellency" who in turn was to check the genuineness of the invention, pay off Machin, and deliver the gun and formula to Sutliff to be taken to Europe.

This line of swift reasoning definitely pointed to Jenner, Mortimer's butler, as likely the man who had switched the bullets on the inventor so his official gun test would fail. It likewise cleared Mortimer of suspicion. The use of Machin in the steal was to throw all suspicion upon an internationally known criminal and leave Sutliff and his country free of taint or provable guilt.

His face set grimly, the Eagle stuffed the note into his coat pocket and was on the verge of searching further, when he heard people running in the hall. Swift as thought, he placed the dead man's right hand, the one with the tattooed blue eagle, upon the man's chest. With a red pencil, he drew a heavy circle around the emblem. Then he silently rolled under the bed.

The unlocked door shuddered open, and three men came tramping in. The Eagle could not make out any of them but their hurried conversation told him plenty.

"I smell gunsmoke," said a cold, hard voice.

"Hell—look!" gurgled a coarser tone. "Sutliff—dead!"

Two pairs of feet ran over to the corpse.

"Look, Mr. Machin!" exclaimed one. "His hand! A red circle about this tattoo mark."

"The Eagle!" snarled the cold voice of the first speaker, but there was a note of fear in it. "Damn that government spy! Leaving that sign of his everybody knows, too!"

"Boss, let's drop this gas gun business," begged one henchman. "It's gettin' too hot for us now."

"Drop hell!" growled Machin. "We've got everything now except the formula. What if this kraut is dead? Schmidt is still living to pay us. All we need is the formula."

"But—but how can we get a formula out of a dead man?"

"You heard Sutliff talking to Schmidt by radio phone this morning," said Machin. "And we all read Scheck's notation in the back of his formula book that if anything happened to him that girl, Joan Kirke, had a right understanding."

"Boy! Was Schmidt mad when those chemists tested out the formula in that black book and got nothing!"

"They only tested one," reminded Machin acidly. "They just read the others and bawled hell out of me for being stupid. And how was I to know? I'm no chemist. But I took the bawling out—for two hundred grand. And Jenner's tip ties in with the inventor's note. That girl knows plenty. She gave the dope to that Shannon guy. I'll bet Mortimer knows plenty, too. So what do we do? We can't talk to this big shot Sutliff now. We go right back to Washington and grab Mortimer and the girl—that Federal dick, too—if we need him. We'll burn the feet off of them to make 'em talk!"

"Go back to Washington? Hell, Machin, that town's red-hot for us now."

Machin laughed curtly. "That's exactly the place for us to be—right under their noses. They won't be expecting us back for a thousand years. And with this squarehead croaked, that changes the setup. We'll make Schmidt come down here to meet us and make the pay-off. Come on, let's get out of here before some dumb Baltimore bull comes stumbling in."

The Eagle would have liked to see and identify the two thugs with Machin, but didn't dare take the risk. It was lucky they hadn't searched the room. But now he had to get back to Washington—quick!

CHAPTER V

THE EAGLE STRIKES

IT WAS nine o'clock that night Ralph Mortimer impatiently rang from the library for his butler.

"That's the second time I've had to summon Jenner," he said in annoyance to Joan who was busily typing away. "There is no reason for him taking so long in coming."

"Jenner!" exclaimed Joan, startled. "Why, Mr. Mortimer, didn't you send him to Robert Pembroke with an urgent message right after dinner?"

"I did not!" exclaimed Mortimer.

"He said you did," the girl said. "I was out in the garden for a breath of fresh air, and he told me you were sending him into Washington with a message for Pembroke. He took the motorcycle."

Mortimer was about to speak when the sound of a car rolling along the driveway made him pause to listen. The door bell pealed hurriedly, and Mortimer went to answer it. An insignificant looking little man stood there.

"Good evening," he said hastily. "My name is Walters. I live just a few miles along the highway. I—well, I'm afraid there's been a bad accident. A man named Jennings or Jenkins skidded off the road on his motorcycle near my house. I heard the crash and went out to bring him in. His skull's fractured and I think he's dying. I called the nearest doctor, but this man has been calling for you. Your name's Mortimer, isn't it?"

"Yes, yes," exclaimed Mortimer.

"I volunteered to come for you," went on the visitor.

"Come in, come in," interrupted Mortimer hastily. "I'll get my things on and go with you at once. Take care of things, Miss Kirke. Jenner! No wonder he didn't answer the bell."

For some reason she couldn't name, Joan Kirke grew suspicious. Replying to Mortimer, she casually went to the rear of the house, leaving the two men alone. From the partially demolished provision room she procured a fresh bag of rice and quietly slipped out the back door. Making her way to where the visitor's car was parked, she hurriedly but securely fastened the bag of grain to the rear spring. Then she punched a small hole in the bottom of the sack and returned to the house.

She walked back into the hall in time to respond tardily to Mortimer's excited farewell. Then she returned to the library and thoughtfully sat down before her typewriter. She was still sitting there when another car came roaring into the driveway, and Jeff Shannon rang for admittance.

"Why, Jeff!" she greeted, somewhat startled at his manner. "Was my tip any good?"

"You'd be surprised how good," he assured her. "Are you all right? Where's Mortimer? Protection is on the way. Thank God, I got here first."

"What on earth are you talking about?"

He told her swiftly. "We're going to trap Machin and his killers," he concluded. "Where's Jenner? I was afraid I'd be too late."

"You are," said Joan sadly. And then she told him.

The Eagle was startled himself then.

"Well, there's nothing else for it," he said. "Machin's beat me again. They won't come here again tonight, though, now that they've snatched Mortimer. But you're next on the list, honey. So sit tight and when the police come, send them after me. I'll take your bicycle and set out on that rice trail. Keep the house locked, and send the police hot-footing it after me." He hastily kissed her and was gone.

The Eagle quickly found the thin trail of rice and set off in pursuit of Walters' car. It was slow business in the moonlight. He had to stop at every cross-roads and search carefully for the trail. But finally the chase led him into Maryland.

THE TRAIL of rice petered out at the driveway of a large, old-fashioned house. Had the roadster gone on, or had Walters turned in here? Since there was no trail to follow now, the Eagle promptly decided to investigate this place.

The old house sat well back from the road and was half-obscured behind trees and shrubbery. Cautiously every sense alert, the Eagle hid the bicycle in some bushes and climbed the heavy iron gate. Moving off into the shadow of the trees he studied the faint chink of light escaping from a shuttered window of the house. He was still speculating on just what course to pursue when from the side of the house came the sound of a motor engine starting. The next minute a blaze of powerful headlights swept down the drive.

Crouched behind a tree trunk, the Eagle waited. A big limousine came slowly down the drive and halted, its engine still running, while the driver got out to open the gate.

In the back of the car were two men. Jeff could see that one was Ralph Mortimer, and that he was sitting in a stiff, unnatural attitude, his hands behind him. The other was a tall, thin man with a long, pale face, cold blue eyes, and a thin slit of a mouth. He was talking, and on his lips was a sly, sneering smile of infinite craftiness and malice.

The Eagle, looking at him, recognizing him as John Machin, felt that he had never before disliked anyone so much at first sight. The man reminded him of a big pale slug.

The driver of the car got the gate open, and thrust a stone under it to keep it open. Then the Eagle acted!

As the driver turned to step back into the car, Shannon sprang from behind the tree, raised his clubbed gun, and brought it down with a dull, vicious thud on the back of the man's head. The driver pitched forward to his knees, then fell on his face.

The man in the car beside Mortimer uttered a startled exclamation. He flung himself toward the door of the car, gun in hand. His finger pulled back the trigger.

Shannon fired, too, from the hip. The two reports rang out almost simultaneously, startlingly loud in the silence of the night. Shannon felt something twitch at his left sleeve. The tall man gave a sharp gasp, twisted suddenly, and collapsed to the floor in the back of the car.

Shannon jerked the car door open, seized Machin by the collar and heaved him bodily into the drive. He lay quite still. From the house, fifty yards away, came a sudden sound of shouting. Mortimer was looking slightly dazed by the suddenness of it all. His hands and feet were tightly bound.

Thrusting his gun into his pocket, the Eagle produced a penknife. With lightning rapidity, he cut the binding cords. Then he seized Mortimer by the arm and thrust him toward the front seat of the car.

"Drive away—fast," he ordered curtly. "Go back to your place and wait there!"

"What about you—" began Mortimer.

But Shannon slammed the door and jumped back into the shelter of the door just as there came a rush of feet down the drive, and hoarse shouting.

The engine of the car accelerated; the car slid forward.

"Shoot!" bawled a harsh voice. "Don't let them make their getaway!"

A fusillade of shots rang out, but the car turned out of the gate and roared away into the night.

The Eagle waited. He could see that there were four men in the drive, blurred figures whose features it was impossible to distinguish in the darkness. Two of them ran out of the gate and looked down the road after the departing car. The other two bent over the two men whom Shannon had laid out.

THE TALL crook the Eagle had shot groaned and stirred. The bullet had merely creased the side of his head, knocking him out for a few minutes.

"What happened, Mr. Machin?" the man bending over him asked. "We heard a couple of shots and came running!" Machin groaned again, and swore venomously.

"What happened to the car?" he asked, in a curious soft, even voice. "Has he escaped?"

The two men who had gone out of the gate returned hurriedly, one of them wheeling a bicycle.

"We found this outside," he interrupted excitedly. "But the car's got clean away!"

Machin rose a little unsteadily, and looked at the bicycle.

"So there was only one of them," he said. "And he's snatched Mortimer from under our noses, and taken our best car." He did not raise his voice, but it became suddenly charged with a chill menace. "What were you fellows doing to let him get away with it? You had plenty of time to shoot!"

"We did shoot," protested one of the burly gunmen in injured tones. "We—"

"Then why the devil didn't you shoot straight?" demanded Machin in the same chilly voice. "You profess to be gunmen, and that's what you're paid for."

He made a gesture toward the unconscious driver.

"Bring him along," he ordered. "And you, Dokel, get the other car to the front door. We must get away from here at once. The chances are that that fellow, whoever he is, will have the police on us before an hour's out."

But it did not suit the Eagle's purpose for Machin and his gang to get away at once. He stepped out suddenly from behind a tree, his gun raised.

"Stay right where you are," he said.

One of the gunmen made a sudden snatch at his pocket. But before that snatch was half completed, the Eagle had pressed the trigger of his automatic. His luck, for the moment, though was out. The hammer came down with a faint click upon the cartridge—a dud.

The gunman's hand jumped from his pocket, and Shannon did a lightning duck sideward. The gunman's weapon roared. The bullet hit a tree with a sharp *phut,* a foot from Shannon's head.

With his own gun useless, the Eagle could do nothing. He made one tremendous spring for the shelter of the woods. Again the gunman's automatic roared. But, moving swiftly between the tree trunks in the dark woods, Shannon was a difficult target.

"After him!" shouted Machin's voice. "Get him!"

The small band broke into quick, purposeful action.

Machin and one of the gunmen began to make their way swiftly along the drive toward the house. The other three men, thirsting for blood, plunged into the woods after the Eagle.

CHAPTER VI

DISASTER!

SUPPOSED TO be expert gunmen, these crooks were by no means expert woodsmen. They proved that as they crashed about in the dark, swearing ferociously, daring Jeff Shannon to show himself and get his head blown off. Then they separated, each intent on searching for himself, but by that time Shannon seemed to have vanished utterly.

Then one of the gunmen heard a slight rustle in the undergrowth. He turned swiftly, his gun ready, but could see nothing. He took a couple of paces forward, and a silent figure stepped behind him from the shelter of a tree. There was a dull, soft thud and the gunman collapsed like a limp sack. The silent figure slipped away behind another tree.

"Whitey!" bawled one of the gunmen.

There was no answer.

"Whitey!" he bawled again. Again there was no answer. Then he shouted: "Mike!"

"Hello!" replied a voice. "Where are you, Sawyer?"

"Where's Whitey?"

"I dunno. I—"

The voice tailed off suddenly into silence.

"What the—" began the first gunman, then called anxiously: "Whitey! Mike! Mike!"

There was a moment's silence. Then a soft, low laugh sounded near him.

With a furious imprecation, the gunman sprang in the direction from which the laugh had come, his gun blazing. Something kicked his legs from under him, he felt a sudden crashing pain in the back of his head, and a thousand stars danced before his eyes the instant before everything went blank.

"And that's that!" Jeff Shannon muttered softly.

Those gunmen would not be taking any interest in what was going on for an hour or so. To make sure that at least one of them would be there when wanted for questioning later, the Eagle paused long enough to truss up one of his victims before he made his way swiftly through the woods toward the house. The important thing now was to see that Machin, if he should happen to be in that house, did not escape before the police arrived. With his freshly loaded gun in hand the Eagle took up his vigil.

For an hour he circled the house, watching for the least sign of movement. But the place remained silent, and the faint gleam of light continued steadily through a chink in the shutter of one of the rooms on the ground floor.

Dawn was already lightening the eastern sky when he heard a couple of big cars entering the drive. That would be the police. He went to meet them at a run, hoping desperately that the occupants of the house would not try to sneak out the back way. The cars stopped in the drive, two big cars full of armed police, with Williams of the F.B.I. at their head.

"Surround the house at once!" directed the Eagle curtly. "Shoot anyone trying to make a getaway."

The Eagle briefly recounted what had been happening during the last hour and a half.

"You've been pretty busy," Williams said admiringly. "Even the mysterious Eagle himself couldn't have done better."

Jeff Shannon grinned. "No," he said. "I'll sprint across the lawn and blow the lock off the front door. You and your men come after me hell-for-leather."

"Let's go!" said Williams.

"Going!" said Shannon.

CROUCHING, HE sped swiftly across the lawn, zigzagging, to make as little a target of himself as possible, but no shots had blasted a greeting when he reached the front door and two heavy bullets from his gun went smashing into the lock. He hurled himself forward, and with a loud crash of rending wood the door burst open.

The Eagle leaped into the hall, gun in hand, ready for instant action. But nothing happened. No one fired at him, no one was there to oppose him. Behind him there was a thudding of heavy feet as Williams and the police came through the doorway.

"You, Williams," Shannon ordered crisply, "follow me upstairs. The rest of you search this floor."

Not a possible hiding place was left unsearched, but in short order the Eagle was forced to admit that the house was empty. The raiding party were in the main hall again, with Jeff Shannon thoroughly disgusted, when one of the local policemen in the group stepped forward.

"Folks in these parts," he said, "talk a lot about some secret passage or other somewheres in this house. They say it was used during the Revolutionary War by the Continentals—"

"That's the answer," snapped Jeff. "Take hammers or spanners or anything fairly solid, but not too heavy, and tap all over the walls. If you find a wall that sounds suspiciously hollow, let me know."

"I'll get on the phone," said Williams, "and order all surrounding police stations to keep a sharp lookout for Mr. Rattray or any of his servants."

"Mr. Rattray?" queried Shannon.

"Yes. One of the local police told me this house was let furnished about three months ago to a man named Rattray."

"I see," said Shannon. "All right. Send out an alarm for John Machin, too—his description is well known. And"—the Eagle's eyes narrowed—"he's hiding out right in Washington, unless I miss my guess. I think—"

The telephone ringing sharply cut him off. He reached out his hand and lifted the receiver.

"Good morning," said a silky voice at the other end of the wire. "This is Mr. Machin speaking."

"Yes," said the Eagle coolly. "What can I do for you?"

Outwardly calm, he was inwardly excited. Now why was Machin phoning?

"You are the police, aren't you?" the smooth voice asked, and went on quickly: "Would—ah—Jeffrey Shannon be there with you by any chance?"

"He would," snapped the Eagle. "And intending to gather you in shortly."

"Really?" said that smooth, soft voice. "That's interesting. But somehow I doubt that."

Over the wire came the sound of a low laugh. Tough though the Eagle was, there was something in the sound of that laugh that momentarily chilled his blood. Cold, inhuman cruelty was in it.

"Good-by," said the mocking, triumphant voice. "I only called to make quite sure that you were there."

The Eagle slowly replaced the receiver. Inwardly he was boiling with rage because of that taunting call. He had been listening to the voice of the man he would give a year's pay to lay his hands on, and Machin's whereabouts were as uncertain as ever. No use to try to trace that call. It had come from a pay station unquestionably, and Machin was far away from it now, as he was from this house. For the Eagle was certain the man had been here and escaped.

But there was something more to that call—something that for only a moment escaped the Eagle. Why had Machin been so anxious to know whether Jeff Shannon was in the house? Why....

LIKE MANY other men who live in constant danger, Shannon's sixth sense was keen. He could depend on it to warn him when deadly peril threatened. It was warning him now. That cold, inhuman chuckle, the note of triumph in that soft, mocking voice, had surely meant something—but what? Then he had it! In one illuminating flash!

"Get out of here at once—all of you!" he shouted. "Quick! There's no time to lose!"

The F.B.I. inspector stared, and started to speak, but the stony look on Jeff Shannon's face checked him. He shouted to the police who were tapping the walls in the next room, and instantly the whole raiding party was piling out of the house.

"What's the big idea?" asked Williams, when they had gained the shelter of the woods.

"I don't know," Shannon confessed. "But something's going to happen in that house! I *know* it! I—"

Even as he spoke, it happened. With an ear-shattering roar, and a burst of smoke and lurid flame, the whole house seemed to rise bodily into the air and fly to pieces. A tremendous blast of hot air swept through the trees, whirling the police off their feet and flinging them to the ground. Bricks and masonry fell like rain. And then silence—dead silence in the explosion's aftermath.

Shannon scrambled shakily to his feet. His ears were ringing and he was dizzy, but otherwise unhurt. Williams and the police officers were also getting up from the ground, most of them trembling from the sheer nerve shock of that tremendous explosion. But one bluecoat did not rise. His head had been smashed to a pulp by a huge piece of falling brickwork. It was gruesome.

And the house, which a few seconds before had been a splendid old Colonial home, was now a blazing ruin from which a thick cloud of acrid yellow fumes was rising slowly to the sky.

No man among them spoke. But their jaws were hard and their eyes blazing with wrath as they looked down at their dead comrade. Jeff Shannon finally turned away.

"Take charge here, Matthews," he said crisply. "Somehow or other, I've *got* to trace that call!"

CHAPTER VII

ENTER MR. RATTRAY

O **NLY AN** hour later the Eagle was in the home of George Lewis, a neighbor of Ralph Mortimer. It was there that F.B.I. Inspector Williams had left Joan Kirke when he had set out to follow the trail of rice. Mortimer also had dropped over.

"I've been talking to Robert Pembroke on the phone," said Shannon. "He's coming out himself as quickly as a car can get him here. He'll probably be at Mortimer's by the time we get back there. Incidentally, he knows Rattray—they were at Harvard together. From what Pembroke says, Rattray is not a man to be mixed up with criminals. He's an archaeologist, quite well known, too. For seven years he's been in the East, excavating at Ur. Only returned to America about three months ago. Pembroke described him as a shy little man, totally uninterested in anything except his excavations."

Inspector Williams entered. Jeff turned to him.

"Have you found out where that call came from?"

"Yes. And it was a bit of luck, too, that it didn't come from a pay station. Machin was so sure we would all be dead in a few moments that he didn't bother. So I was able to trace the call. It came from Hill View, a small bungalow outside the village of Fairmount about two miles from here."

"Do you think that it will be safe now for my secretary and I to go back home?" asked Mortimer anxiously.

Shannon nodded. "You've got a strong police guard, and you'll be as safe there as anywhere else. Williams will join you there later. I'm off to Hill View."

A couple of minutes later Jeff Shannon and half a dozen officers set out for Hill View. Shannon's plans had all been formed. The men with him needed no instructions, so when the car stopped before the bungalow, Shannon and three of the policemen made for the front door. Three others made for the back door. Shannon did not stand on ceremony. With his gun he blew in the lock and hurled himself into the house.

From a room off the hall came a startled shout. Shannon barged through the door of the room as two men sprang to their feet. One of the men darted his hand toward his pocket, but before he could reach it, Shannon's gun butt crashed on his head. A couple of bluecoats hurled themselves upon the other man, and bore him, struggling fiercely, to the floor. In half a minute both men were securely handcuffed.

No one else was in the bungalow, but the door of one room was locked, so Shannon and a hefty policeman put their shoulders to it and burst it open. The room they entered was small, with little furniture in it except a large table, on which were laid out a couple of gold drinking cups of exquisite design and workmanship, a jeweled head-dress, and a number of jeweled bangles and ornaments. Shannon gave a low whistle.

"Say, this is old stuff!" he exclaimed. "About four thousand years old, I should say. Probably some of the stuff that Rattray brought back from Assyria."

"Is it valuable?" asked a policeman.

"Valuable? It's priceless! It's so valuable that it's impossible to say quite what it's worth. Pack it up carefully, take it to the car and guard it. Don't leave it for a second. And keep your gun handy."

Shannon stalked back to the two prisoners. They were sitting in sullen silence, guarded by two officers. Shannon glowered at them.

"Where's Machin?" he demanded curtly.

One of the prisoners gave a short, ugly laugh.

"Maybe you think you were smart to raid this place," he sneered. "Well, maybe you were. But you won't be feeling so damn happy when the gang gets busy on you. Now scram, big boy. You'll get no squeal out of us."

THE FACES of both men were set and stubborn. Shannon nodded to the bluecoats.

"Take them to the car!" he ordered.

Then, swiftly but efficiently, he searched the bungalow. Probably he would find nothing here to indicate Machin's whereabouts, but he hoped he might find papers or letters giving him some clue to the identity of the man called Schmidt. But there was nothing—only tradesmen's bills made out to "Sydney Curtis"—in all likelihood the alias of one of the gangsters.

Leaving four officers in charge of the bungalow, Shannon returned to Mortimer's home, taking the captured crooks with him.

During his absence, Inspector Williams had kept in constant telephone communication with F.B.I. Headquarters. As a result, an alarm had been broadcast for Machin. The description of the big time crook was known from one end of the country to the other, but it was also broadcast in the hope that someone might see the man and report to the police. An alarm was out for Rattray, also, and the archaeologist's description was being radioed.

Grilling had brought no information from the crook who had been captured in the grounds of the burned Colonial house, but he had been identified as Eddie Jason, an underworld character with a string of convictions to his credit. The secret passage by which Machin—probably—and his henchmen had escaped from the scene of the explosion had also been uncovered. It led into the woods not far from the house.

"I'm turning Jason over to the police," said Williams. "They'll set the wheels moving on that angle."

"Make it a trio with the two gangsters I captured this morning," said Shannon. "Now I'll have a talk with Pembroke before I make another move. I see he's just arriving."

Robert Pembroke, of the War Department, listened with strained attention to Shannon's account of all that had happened. At its conclusion he struck the table in front of him with his clenched fist.

"Those fellows have got to be caught—and quickly!" he firmly announced. "Heaven only knows what they're up to right now! What are your plans, Shannon?"

"For the present our business is to safeguard Mr. Mortimer and Miss Kirke. Machin has vanished, but he's sure to make an attempt to get at Miss Kirke and the formula sooner or later. We ought to be able to grab him and his men then."

Pembroke frowned.

"Do you mean to tell me, Shannon, that you expect to catch those rats—who *must* be caught—by sitting here and waiting for them to show up?"

Jeff Shannon glanced curiously at Pembroke. He had never heard him speak in that angry, sarcastic tone before. But Shannon could afford to be patient. Robert Pembroke was Jeff Shannon's superior, but Jeff Shannon was also the Eagle—who took orders from no man, but was the Nemesis of criminal spies through his own courage and ability.

"What do you suggest I do?" he asked Pembroke.

"I suggest you work with Williams," replied Pembroke curtly. "No harm can come to Miss Kirke here. She's strongly guarded. And it's not enough for you to wait for these spies to move. It's up to you to get after them."

"Okay," said Shannon, smiling to himself.

There was a knock on the door, and a servant entered.

"There's a big packing-case come for Mr. Pembroke, sir," she said. "It's in the hall."

"For me?" said Pembroke, frowning.

SHANNON WAS already at the door. Pembroke hurried after him. In the hall a group of bewildered servants were standing around a big heavy square packing-case.

"Stand back, everybody!" Shannon curtly ordered. "I'll open it."

With a heavy screwdriver he began to force it open. There was a creak of protesting nails as one of the boards across the top came away.

"There's a man inside!" Shannon shouted.

Hastily, the top of the packing-case was wrenched off. Huddled inside, tightly bound and gagged, was a thin, elderly man. His eyes were moving, and he was fully conscious. Quickly, Shannon's strong arms lifted him out of the case. Across his chest was pinned a paper on which was written:

TO MR. ROBERT PEMBROKE
WITH THE COMPLIMENTS OF JOHN MACHIN.

"Rattray!" Pembroke cried.

"Bring some brandy," Shannon ordered, and when a servant hurried forward with it Rattray took a glass in trembling fingers and drank. He sighed, and blinked a little dazedly at the group around him.

"Why—!" he said slowly, bewildered. "I—I—"

"Are you hurt?" asked Pembroke.

Rattray shook his head. He seemed not to know whether he was awake or dreaming.

"I—I don't think so," he said. Then suddenly he sat bolt upright. "My cups, my ornaments!" he cried shrilly. "They've got them! That man's got them!"

"No, he hasn't," interrupted Shannon comfortingly. "Don't worry, about them. They're safe."

"We got them back this morning," chimed in Pembroke. "But for God's sake how did you come to be inside that packing-case?"

It was an extraordinary story that Rattray told haltingly, but excitedly. He had met Machin in Paris on his way home from the East, he said. They had met again in New York, and lunched together. He had found Machin a pleasant companion, and had invited him down to his country place for the week-end. On the second day of Machin's stay, Machin had kidnaped him and taken him to a small house somewhere. There another man who had been skilfully made up to resemble Rattray, had gone away with Machin in the car. Rattray had been kept prisoner for nearly ten days. When Machin had come back to the little house he had brought the gold cups and ornaments with him.

Early that morning Rattray had been tied and gagged and placed in a packing-case, and taken away in a car. After a time the packing-case had been transferred to another car, and he had been brought to this estate of Mortimer's. That was all he knew.

"They simply took you to Fairmount, handed you over to an expressman, and had you brought here," said Mortimer. "The small house must have been the bungalow that Captain Shannon raided later. Now, this fellow Machin seems to be on the job, all right, even to knowing you were coming here, Pembroke."

"He is," snapped the War Department official acidly. "And we've got to be, too." He glanced at the bewildered archaeologist. "You'd better rest for a few hours, Rattray. This evening I'll take you and your ornaments back to the city with me. And you, Captain Shannon—get after Machin!"

"Right," said the Eagle, and stalked out to order a police car to take him to the nearest railroad station.

But he did not take a train for Washington. Instead, as soon as the police car disappeared, he headed for a drug store and called F.B.I. Headquarters. In a few moments he had F.B.I. Inspector Williams on the wire.

"Any news yet?" he asked.

"Hardly," said Williams. "I've only been here a few minutes. Did Pembroke show up out there?"

"I've just left him," said Shannon. "Why?"

"Pembroke's been on the necks of the Department. He's used his influence with the director to distribute some of our men on espionage cases that I think of trifling importance. I want to take them off and get them busy tracing the movements of Eddie Jason and company."

Shannon hesitated for a moment. Then he said: "Listen! Pembroke's sent me to join you. But I'm not going to. I'm going to stay here. Say, are you willing to take a chance?"

"What is it?" said the inspector cautiously.

"Call Pembroke and ask permission to take those men off the jobs he's sent them on. If he refuses, take them off on your own responsibility. Pembroke is too worried to know what he's doing. He may kick up a fuss at first, when he finds out, but he'll probably be grateful to you afterward. One more thing. If he asks about me, say you haven't seen me, but you've had a message from me. I don't want him to know I'm not following his orders."

"I take it that you've a good reason for making that request?"

"The strongest one I can think of," said the Eagle emphatically. "I believe that if I can stay down here under cover that I'll stand a good chance of putting a spoke in the wheel of the smart Mr. Machin and his confederates."

"All right, then. But if I lose my job over this, I hope you've got another one for me."

In a roundabout way Jeff Shannon left the station, made his way on foot back to the Mortimer estate. It took all his skill to make the woods, at that, for time and again he had to dodge the police guards that surrounded the place. He smiled with satisfaction. In one way, at least, Joan and the formula secret she held were well guarded. But that prodding sixth sense of his was telling him even these sharp-eyed police would not be enough.

At last, however, he reached the woods. Once inside them he swerved aside from the path into a thicket which would be an excellent hiding place. He settled down to wait—indefinitely, if need be. But if what his instinct told him was going to occur did happen—it would not be long now!

CHAPTER VIII

THE SIEGE

BENEATH THE porte cochère of the Mortimer home the engine of Pembroke's big car was turning over silently, its headlights burning brightly. In the back of the car were Rattray's carefully packed gold cups and ornaments. Pembroke, Rattray, Mortimer, and Joan were standing on the steps as Pembroke and Rattray were saying good-by.

"Look!" shouted Rattray suddenly, and pointed.

As everyone turned, startled, Rattray made a lightning spring forward and gave Pembroke a tremendous push in the back. Pembroke collided violently with Mortimer, and both fell to the ground. Instantly Rattray sprang at Joan, and his hand, holding a short, thick sandbag, whirled.

As she collapsed he grabbed her, flung her into the car, and jumped for the driver's seat. The car shot away. Pembroke rose shakily to his feet—but Mortimer did not rise. His head had struck violently against the edge of a stone step, and blood was pouring from a deep cut in his temple.

As the car gathered speed, a man darted swiftly from behind a tree at the edge of the drive, and hurled himself at the car. Clutching fingers grasped a portion of the luggage bracket at the rear. For two or three seconds the Eagle was pulled along behind the car. Then, grasping the bracket firmly, he gave a tremendous pull and jumped.

One foot obtained a precarious footing on the large gas tank which projected well beyond the back of the car. For a moment he balanced there, then with his other hand he got a grip on the spare tire.

The car tore on. The Eagle could not move. It was as much as he could do to hang on.

Mile after mile the car swept on at high speed along the country roads. Shannon's arms began to ache unbearably. He felt as if they were being almost wrenched from their sockets, but still he clung on grimly. Not only was the life of the girl he loved at stake, but devils in human form meant to force from her the secret of a weapon of war that was capable of spreading incalculable carnage.

Before long, however, the car slowed slightly, and the driver sounded two long blasts and one short one on the siren. The car turned through the iron gates of a long drive. The gates clanged to behind it.

Once more the driver sounded a long blast as he drew up in front of a large house. The Eagle dropped from the back of the car, the door of the house opened, and men came running out.

"I've got the girl!" the driver shouted.

There was only one thing to do, and Jeff Shannon did it. He made a tigerish spring at the two men dragging Joan up the steps, and his clubbed gun rose and fell in two lightning motions. The two men dropped without even time to cry out. Keenly realizing that he had only the advantage of surprise, Shannon grabbed up Joan and darted into the house.

Across the hall he saw a wide flight of stairs. And between him and the staircase was the arch-criminal, Machin! His rush did not slacken, though. Again his gun rose and fell. With surprising quickness, Machin flung up his arm and managed to shield his head, but the force of the blow was sufficient to send him staggering across the hall. Shannon sprang for the stairs.

Behind him came a rush of feet and angry shouts. A shot rang out, then another.

"Don't shoot!" Machin shouted shrilly. "You'll hit the girl! I want her alive!"

SHANNON SPED up the stairs a bare breath ahead of his pursuers. At the top was a hall with doors on either side. He flung open the first door, barged through it, and dropped Joan unceremoniously. Then he flung his weight against the door from the inside just as his foremost pursuer flung his weight against it from the outside. But the door closed and the key grated in the lock. From outside came loud cursing as blows thudded on the door.

Shannon pressed the electric light switch beside the door and saw that he was in a large bedroom, luxuriously furnished in old-fashioned style. Joan had risen. Her face was pale and her hands were trembling, but there was a light of determination in her eyes.

"Keep out of the way," warned Shannon. "They might start shooting through the door."

Even as he spoke he seized the big four-poster bed. One tremendous heave and the great bed turned over sideward, one end against the door. Without pausing, a heavy washstand, a wardrobe, and a dressing-table were piled in a heap on the four-poster.

"That ought to hold them temporarily," Shannon panted.

Almost instantly there came another thunderous assault on the door. With a tremendous crash of rending timber a panel in the upper part caved in. There was a howl of exultation from the attackers outside, which changed to one of rage when they saw the barrier Shannon had erected. But four of them, having procured a huge log capable of being used as a battering-ram, prepared for an assault on what remained of the door.

That smashed panel was an advantage to Shannon. He could see his attackers. Crouched behind the thick marble slab of the washstand, he waited till they swung the big log back. Then his gun roared—twice. Two of the attackers sprawled in a heap as the log crashed to the floor.

In spite of Machin's orders, one of the attackers emptied his gun at the barrier. The air was vibrant with the ear-shattering crack of the explosions and the vicious hum of bullets. Puffs of smoke drifted upward in lazy whirls as the room was charged with the acrid smell of burst cordite. Then silence for a space. The attackers had drawn off.

"Are you hurt?" Joan came forward anxiously.

"Not a scratch," said Shannon, and added admiringly, "You don't seem very frightened."

"I'm not—with you," she said. "How long do you think we can hold out?" Then suddenly she cried out sharply:

"Look out!"

He whirled as be heard a tinkle of breaking glass behind him. The end of a ladder poked suddenly, through the window at the other side of the room. Then came the real attack on the door, and the battering-ram crashed into the barricade.

Jeff Shannon sprang quickly across the room. He reached the window as a man's head and shoulders appeared above the top of the ladder. As Shannon leaped, the man fired. His bullet grazed Shannon's arm. Then the Eagle reached the window, and his fist shot through the hole in the glass, full into the man's face.

As the man fell he struck another man who was mounting behind him. Both thudded to the ground, as with a mighty heave Shannon hauled the ladder up into the room.

The attackers at the door were making the most of their opportunity. The battering-ram crashed into the barricade, and the side of a wardrobe suddenly caved in. A gap appeared in the top of the barricade. Shannon turned from the window just as a gun arm appeared in the gap, the gun leveled at him.

For a second death stared him in the face. Joan saved him. With a lightning movement she picked up a water bottle that had fallen from the washstand and flung it. As it crashed into the man's face, his arm jerked upward, and the shot went wide.

"Thanks," said Shannon briefly. "You're a honey."

GUN IN hand, he sprang to the barricade. His automatic spoke and there was a howl of pain from the hall. The attack died away abruptly. The footsteps of the attackers receded.

"End of Round Two," Shannon said cheerfully. "And so far I think we're well ahead on points."

Hastily he busied himself strengthening the barricade. It was again built up when a voice outside the door said:

"We want to discuss terms."

"Go ahead and discuss," said Jeff.

"You can't hold out in there forever," went on the voice outside. "We're bound to get you in the end, and you probably can guess what will happen to—both of you then. We'll have that formula before we've finished with you."

"Think so?" drawled Shannon.

"There are ways of getting information from people who won't talk," snarled the man outside. "Give us the formula, and we'll let you both go, and make it worth your while into the bargain—if fifty grand is any good to you. You've got nothing to gain by holding out, and everything to lose. What's your answer?"

"We can't make up our minds about a thing like that off-hand," Shannon snapped. "You'll have to give us time to think it over."

"We'll give you ten minutes. But if you've got any sense, there's only one answer for you to make. Think it over."

The sound of footsteps receded.

"You're not really thinking we—we ought to give in to them?" Joan quavered.

He shook his head, his jaws tightening. Ten minutes passed quickly. The voice sounded outside the door again.

"Have you decided?"

"Yes," rapped Shannon, and grinned at Joan. "You can go out and boil yourselves, stew yourselves, or hang yourselves, and save the hangman a job."

No answer. Again the footsteps faded away.

"Third Round," said Shannon.

Nothing happened then for so long that the Eagle began to feel uneasy. If the gangsters had stopped attacking the barrier, it was not because they had abandoned hope of capturing him and Joan, it was because they were up to some new devilment.

It was nearly an hour before the gangsters made a move. Then they moved suddenly and effectively.

"Well, you had your chance," snarled a voice in the hall. "Now you're going to get what's coming to you!"

The end of a rubber pipe was flung over the barrier. There came a faint hissing sound, and from the end of the rubber pipe emerged a thin stream of bluish vapor.

Shannon sprang toward the pipe and snatched at it, to fling it back over the barrier. But instantly something seemed to grip him tightly by the throat. Desperately he flung himself forward. But a gray mist came before his eyes as everything whirled around him. His fingers touched the pipe, but there was no strength in them. Slowly he fell to his knees, then onto his face, and lay still....

CHAPTER IX

THIRD DEGREE

JEFF SHANNON opened his eyes and blinked. His hands and feet were securely tied, and he was sitting in an armchair in a small, comfortably furnished room.

His head ached slightly, but otherwise he felt no ill effects from the gas he had inhaled.

Opposite him, in another armchair, sat Joan. She had not yet regained consciousness. Three men were in the room with them. One was Machin. The other two bore the unmistakable gangster stamp. Seeing Shannon's eyes open, Machin stepped forward, smiling slightly, a wicked, ugly smile.

"So you're feeling better," he observed. "That's good. And I see that Miss Kirke's feeling better, too. That's excellent. Now we must have a little chat."

Joan had opened her eyes and was looking around her. Machin bowed elaborately.

"Allow me to introduce myself," he said. "My name is John Machin. My friends here are Doker Nash and Mike Morrison. My colleagues,

Herr Schmidt, and a certain charming lady, are unavoidably prevented from being here at the moment, but *Herr* Schmidt will join us later. For the present I must try to entertain you."

He sat down.

"I think it would help to establish a more friendly atmosphere, Miss Kirke, if you were to start off by telling me the formula for the Scheck gas," he said.

Joan looked him straight in the face, with eyes that did not waver.

"I'll never tell you that," she said steadily.

"You must allow me to differ," said Machin genially.

The smile left his lips. His eyes narrowed, became terrifying in their fixed intensity. His mouth hardened into a thin, cruel line. Deliberately he produced a small automatic pistol. Deliberately he aimed it at Joan.

"You're going to tell me that formula," he said in a slow, soft voice that was infinitely more menacing than bluster. "I shall count five. If you haven't started before I finish counting, I shall fire."

His eyes, cold and pitiless, did not leave her face. The small gun, held steady as a rock in front of him, pointed at her. She saw the round O of the muzzle, saw his finger crooked around the trigger, and knew that a slight pressure of that finger meant that she would die.

"One," he counted.

"Why, bother to count?" she said contemptuously. "I shan't tell you."

"Two!" counted Machin deliberately. "Three!"

Jeff strained at his bonds. This business of pretending knowledge of the dead inventor's gas formula was having a blow-back.

"Four!" counted Machin slowly.

Joan turned her head slightly, and looked at Shannon.

"So long, Jeff," she said calmly. "It's been swell knowing you."

"Five!" said Machin.

His finger tightened on the trigger and there came a sharp, vicious crack. A portion of the chair, not half an inch from Joan's head, detached itself and flew with a smart click into the wall. She blinked. Was she still alive? Then she saw Machin's face, the lips set in a slightly sneering smile, and she knew that she was.

"That was just a friendly warning," said Machin softly. "The next one won't miss. Now will you tell me the formula?"

"No," said Joan steadily, but her face was pale and drawn.

"She doesn't know the formula, you fool!" ground out the Eagle. "You killed the only person who could tell you."

"I suppose you guessed that I was bluffing," Machin said to Joan, ignoring Shannon. "That I should never shoot you so long as you knew the formula and I didn't. It occurs to me that no such objection applies to our friend in the other chair."

HIS HAND made a slight movement; again the gun spoke viciously. The bullet grazed Shannon's ear. A thin trickle of blood ran down his cheek.

"You'll notice that I'm rather a good shot," said Machin blandly. "Next time I shall just graze his eyes. I'm afraid that it will blind him. I'll count five again."

Joan drew in her breath in a sobbing gasp. Her dark eyes looked at Jeff Shannon with agonized fear in their clear depths. Machin was counting— "One two, three, four—"

"Stop!" Joan cried suddenly. "I'll tell you!"

"Ah!" said Machin in a tone of satisfaction, and lowered his gun.

"No you won't, Joan," Shannon said coldly. "This isn't a question of your safety or mine. It's a question of the national safety. We're weighing our lives against the lives of thousands, perhaps millions. There can be no doubt of what our answer should be. Silence. I won't have you speak to save me."

Nash struck Shannon brutally across the face. Blood ran from his lips, but Shannon did not heed it. Joan nodded at him.

"The formula," demanded Machin curtly.

Joan sat tight-lipped.

Machin slowly raised the pistol, and the girl closed her eyes.

Then there was a sound of voices outside the door, and a man abruptly entered.

"*Herr* Schmidt has arrived," he stated.

"Ah!" purred Machin. "*Herr* Schmidt is most anxious to have that formula. He will probably like to have a few words with you heroic people himself. Pardon me, while I go to greet him."

As he closed the door after him, Shannon looked at Joan and grinned feebly.

"Don't tell 'em anything, whatever happens."

"Shut up," snarled Doker Nash, and again his heavy fist struck Shannon's face.

Apparently *Herr* Schmidt was in no hurry to interview the prisoners, for there was a long-drawn-out wait. Then suddenly, from downstairs, there came startled shouts and a fusillade of shots rang out. There was a tremendous crash down below, then Machin burst into the room, a smoking gun in his hand.

"Come on, you two!" he shouted to his two henchmen. "The place is being attacked!"

Doker and Mike reached for their guns and made swiftly for the door. Machin followed, slamming the door after him. The noise of fierce fighting below continued.

"Well," said Shannon grimly, when he and the girl were alone, "at least we are still alive."

Joan began to cry softly.

"Don't break down now, honey," Shannon begged. "Your courage has made me ashamed of myself. And I feel like a dog for having let you in for all this. But, damn it, Joan, there is something crazy as the devil about this setup! Why should Scheck have written that note in the back of his black formula book which implied that you knew the formula? Are you sure you don't know anything about it?"

"Cross my heart," she said solemnly. "I don't know the first thing about it. Professor Scheck never told anybody!"

"But he must have meant something," Shannon said tightly. "If I can just figure it out...."

The noise of fighting below swelled to a climax, then abruptly died down. Footsteps sounded in the passage outside. The door burst open and Robert Pembroke entered, followed by two plainclothes men.

"Thank heaven I came in time!" he shouted breathlessly.

CHAPTER X

FLIGHT!

QUICKLY PEMBROKE crossed the room to Joan's side and cut the cords that bound her.

"Are you hurt?" he asked solicitously.

"No, I'm all right," she answered quickly, "but Jeff is wounded."

Pembroke cut Shannon loose.

"Are you hurt badly," he asked anxiously.

"A slight graze on my arm, another on my ear, and a cut lip. That's all. You showed up at the right time. Where's Machin?"

"Dead," answered Pembroke. "You take it easy for a few minutes. We've got everything well in hand. There'll be plenty for you to do shortly. I've got to get back to Washington at once, and I'm going to leave you in charge here."

"How did you get here to rescue us?" asked Joan.

"Sheer luck," answered Pembroke. "A state trooper spotted a car with a man hanging on to the back of it. It was out of sight before he could reach it, but he reported it, and when the report reached me I took a chance on the man on the back of the car being Captain Shannon. Thank heaven someone else saw that car turn in here. I've no time to go into details now—got to get back to Washington at once, as I said, and I want to take the formula with me."

"The formula?" echoed Joan blankly.

"Yes. The War Department wants it. We want to make sure of having it ourselves. Just dictate it to me quickly, and I'll write it down."

He produced a notebook and a fountain pen, as he sat down at the table. Shannon stared at him intently.

"But—but I haven't the formula," protested Joan. "I thought you understood that—that it was all just a—"

"Don't tell him anything, Joan!" cried Shannon suddenly, sharply.

Both Pembroke and the girl looked at the Eagle in surprise.

"You're overstepping yourself, Captain Shannon," said the War Department man brusquely.

"On the contrary, you are."

Joan looked uncertainly from one to the other, then tried to play up to Shannon's perplexing lead.

"I'll go back to Washington with you, Mr. Pembroke, and tell the formula to General Bridge," she said.

"Of course, if you wish," he said easily. "But I imagine you'd rather not go to Washington until you've had a chance to straighten up a bit—and I have no time to wait Give me the formula, Miss Kirke, and I'll see that you and Captain Shannon get full credit for breaking this case."

At this moment there came a murmur of voices from the hall outside. Shannon strode across the room and flung the door open. Six men were posted in the hall, with Machin and Mike Morrison at their head.

Pembroke leaped up with a furious oath.

"Grab this wise guy!" he snarled in a changed voice.

The Eagle sprang, and his fist, with all his weight behind it, took Pembroke fairly under the chin, knocking him flying into a corner. From the doorway came hoarse shouts and a rush of men. Shannon turned swiftly. He had the satisfaction of feeling his fist go home once, hard into Machin's face. Then the rush overwhelmed him, and he went down, struggling, hitting out with all his force in a mêlée of fiercely fighting men. The something hit him on the head with stunning force, and he suddenly went limp.

DAZED, HALF-CONSCIOUS, he was aware that cords were being tied around his wrists and ankles. A couple of the men had seized Joan and bound her also. Machin was mopping at a bleeding nose with a silk handkerchief. In a corner of the room one of the gangsters was helping the pseudo Pembroke to rise. He walked groggily to a chair, and sat down.

"Clear out—all of you!" he said harshly. "Machin and I will talk to these people."

The man who had called himself Pembroke recovered his air of bland assurance when the gangsters left the room.

"So our little ruse failed," he said in a tone of polite regret. "I think you made a mistake, Machin, in leaving them together. If I'd had the girl by herself, I'd have got the formula."

"I—I don't understand," said Joan, bewildered. "Mr. Pembroke—"

"He's not Pembroke," snapped Shannon. "I suspected it this morning, but I wasn't sure."

The false Pembroke shook his head sadly.

"And I thought I was so well made up," he observed.

"You are," Shannon said shortly. "But there were a few things you didn't know—how to act, for instance. And you kept calling me Shannon. Pembroke always calls me Jeffery. Added to that, you seemed a little too anxious to get Williams and me out of the way. I assume you're really the spy known as *Herr* Schmidt."

"Your perspicacity is remarkable," said the bogus Pembroke. "As you know, our friend Machin is anxious to conclude a little deal with me, and it requires your cooperation. And now to business. We still have to get that formula."

"Suppose we try a few experiments on Shannon," suggested Machin. "Miss Kirke seemed quite indifferent to anything that we might do to her, but seemed rather upset when I threatened to blind her boy friend. If we devote our attention to him, we probably will be able to persuade her to come across with, the formula in short order."

He crossed the room to the fireplace, where a fire was laid, and put a match to it. Joan watched him with horrified eyes. What were they going to do to Jeff Shannon?

Machin waited till the fire was blazing brightly, then thrust a poker into it.

He had turned to speak when the door burst open and a man barged in breathlessly. Jenner—the missing Mortimer butler!

He spoke hurriedly to *Herr* Schmidt, paying the others no attention.

"There's something I must tell you, Karl!" he said urgently. "The police are onto us! I had all I could do to throw them off my trail to get here to warn you! Somebody's been careless and the Feds are likely to swoop down on this place any moment! You've got to get away at once!" He swung on Machin, glowering. "This ruthless idiot Machin has ruined all our plans!"

"You fool!" Schmidt snapped to Machin, his voice rising angrily. He mastered his temper with an effort.

"Well, I suppose there's nothing for it but to get away at once. We can't afford to take any chances. Get the monoplane out of the hangar quickly, Jenner, and get the engines started. We'll fly to my place in the Azores Islands, and stay there till we've got the formula and manufactured a good supply of the gas. We can make it non-stop, and we shan't be so liable to interruption there. As soon as I have the right process, I will pay you, Machin."

"But after what happened last night," pointed out Machin, "every plane on the coast will be on the lookout for strange aircraft. Suppose they try to intercept us?"

"They'll have their work cut out. We'll be flying high, and we have our machine guns. Come on, we've got to get these two into the plane at once!"

IN ONE corner of the small landing field to which Shannon and Joan were carried, stood the dark, widespreading mass of a large monoplane, capable of carrying five or six passengers.

Joan and Shannon were thrust roughly into the back cockpit behind the pilot's seat where Jenner, as pilot, was already installed. *Herr* Schmidt climbed into the front cockpit, and Machin into the rear cockpit with Shannon and Joan.

Two men drew away the big wooden blocks from under the wheels of the undercarriage. Again the engines roared and the machine trembled and moved forward slowly. It gathered speed, lifted off the ground, and started to climb steadily.

Black, clammy darkness surrounded them as they passed through the clouds. But Jeff Shannon was not thinking of the cold and dark. For he had discovered that the cords which bound his wrists were a trifle loose, and he was struggling with them silently and desperately.

They were above the clouds, with the starry sky over them, when Machin suddenly uttered an alarmed shout. He leaned forward, touched the pilot on the shoulder, and pointed. Approaching them was a small cluster of swiftly moving lights—the lights of three small, single-seater aircraft.

Instantly Machin and Schmidt leaped to man the machine guns, Machin in the rear cockpit, the German in the cockpit projecting in front of the pilot's seat. The pilot pushed forward the control lever. The nose of the big machine dropped dizzily as it dived steeply at top speed for the nearest layer of clouds.

But the single-seater fighters, built for speed, came hurtling after the big machine, almost standing on their noses, diving in close formation. Then came the rattle of machine gun shots.

That burst was not armed at the big machine—it was merely fired as a warning for the big plane to glide down to land. The men in the pursuit planes had no idea that the big plane was provided with machine guns. They discovered their mistake a moment later, and the discovery cost the life of the foremost flyer.

At a range of twenty feet Schmidt took aim coolly, and fired. The single-seater seemed to stagger in mid-air as the bullets crashed into its fuselage. A small, bright flame flickered behind the pilot's seat The machine fell into a spinning nose dive, burst suddenly into flames, and spun downward in a whirl of death.

As Schmidt fired, Machin also fired. But the man in the plane that was Machin's target kicked on full left rudder and pushed his control stick well forward. Machin's burst only flicked a piece of canvas from the tail-plane of his vanishing machine.

The pursuit pilot was immediately underneath his big, twin-engined enemy, out of range of its machine guns, and his own guns, firing forward through the propeller, raked the forepart of the big machine. *Herr* Schmidt flung up his arms and collapsed, his head and shoulders hanging over the side of the machine.

Black darkness suddenly enveloped the whirling combatants as Jenner dived into a thick layer of clouds, hoping to shake off his pursuers.

CHAPTER XI

FIGHT IN THE AIR

DURING THE fighting the Eagle had been struggling with a strength born of desperation. As the machine dived into the clouds he managed, with a tremendous effort, to drag one hand free from the loosened cords that bound his wrists. Flinging the cord from his other wrist, it took but an instant to free his feet.

He flexed his arms and legs to restore the circulation, then he moved forward slowly. His outstretched hand touched something in the darkness—Machin's knee. Machin, alert behind the mounting of the machine gun, half-turned to look downward as he felt something gently touch his knee.

But before he could move, strong arms closed suddenly around his legs and he was heaved up suddenly off the floor of the cockpit A yell of terror burst from his lips as he made a desperate clutch at the gun mounting. Then he was hurled over the side of the machine into the black darkness.

The plane was swaying and side-slipping terrifyingly.

The Eagle moved back through the darkness and unbound Joan.

"Hold on—tightly!" he told her, his lips close to her ear. "I'm going to try something dangerous!"

His most ticklish job was still before him. With some difficulty he removed the heavy bolt of the machine gun. That made a good weapon. Clinging on to the front of the cockpit, he brought the heavy piece of metal down with all his force upon the pilot's head.

Jenner slumped forward unconscious in his seat, and his body pushed the control stick forward. The nose of the machine dropped swiftly. It began to turn, plunging downward, both engines full on.

Clinging desperately to the sides of the fuselage, the Eagle thrust one knee over the front of the cockpit, made a swift grab for the back of the pilot's seat. For a few seconds he hung there while the air swirled past him in a terrific blast, as if trying to snatch him from his precarious perch. Then he gave a tremendous pull and landed on top of the pilot.

Swiftly he pulled the unconscious pilot off the controls, shut off the engines, and gently eased the machine out of that terrifying spin. Then he thrust Jenner's body over the edge of the fuselage. He could not afford to take any chances of a fight in mid-air.

He put the machine into a steady dive. He had to land before the two remaining pursuit machines spotted him and renewed their attack. But when he came out of the thick cloud bank the two pursuit planes had also come out of the clouds, were only a few hundred feet away. They swung around in a sharp turn in his direction. Shannon knew that he could expect no mercy from those two machines. Their comrade had been shot down in flames and they were out for blood. Once more he sent his plane into a sharp dive.

In a flash the two pursuers were streaking down after him, their guns spitting a hail of bullets. Shannon put the plane into a spin, for a spinning machine is far more difficult to hit than a machine in a straight dive. Down he went in a mad, dizzy swirl, with the earth leaping up to meet him. Then suddenly he felt a searing pain across his right arm. At the same moment his starboard engine coughed and spluttered, and was silent. Almost instinctively, he throttled down the other engine. And still those two small fighters were streaking after him like avenging furies.

AND THEN the luck turned. Apparently the men in the pursuit planes believed Shannon was spinning out of control, and there was no point in pursuing him down any farther. The bursts of machine gun fire died away.

The Eagle looked anxiously down, seeking a place to land. With only one engine working he had to land at once. Below him was hilly country, but a car headlights showed him one fairly long, flat field. At five hundred feet he could not turn into the field, so he tilted the plane over in a steep sideslip, aiming at the field. A dark line at the end of the field became discernible as trees. There was no way of avoiding them. He was bound to crash! One wing struck a tree and splintered inward, breaking the force of the crash. There was a sound of rending, and the plane came to rest The force of the crash flung the Eagle against the dashboard. His eyes closed and he knew no more....

The Eagle came to his senses in a small hospital. He was lying on an operating table, and Joan Kirke was holding his hand while a doctor was stitching up a gash in his head. All around were blue uniforms, big feet, and loud voices.

Joan uttered a cry of thankfulness as Shannon stirred and blinked his eyes.

"Take it easy," advised the surgeon. "Lie still until I take a couple more stitches."

"Joan!" the Eagle murmured anxiously. "Are you hurt?"

"Just a few bruises, darling. Everything's all right, Jeff."

The real Robert Pembroke thrust his way forward.

"Jeffrey!" he exclaimed. "What kind of a show were you putting on up there in the air? State troopers picked up the badly smashed body of John Machin. And at the front gunpit we found a dead man who at first was mistaken for me."

"That was *Herr* Schmidt," said the Eagle. "Head of the spy ring dealing with Machin for Professor Scheck's gas gun. I got the big guy in Baltimore. What's the report on that end of the business?"

"All cleaned up," said Pembroke. "Police and F.B.I. lads bagged the lot of them. We're interning the *Amsterdam Koenig*. We netted a number of spies who have been operating from that ship as a base. We—er—persuaded one of them to talk, and traced back and found where you had been taken off by plane. Calling a few army planes into the chase was simple. Too bad they didn't catch up soon enough to let those pursuits know who you were. My boy, you've cleaned up another nasty business for Uncle Sam. We've even unearthed my old friend Rattray where those crooks had him a prisoner. Now if we only had the formula—"

Shannon bounced up on the operating table. A startling idea had suddenly come to him.

"Joan!" he exclaimed. "Your slipper—the one that Scheck repaired for you—where is it?"

"I'm wearing it," she said. "Why?"

"Which heel did he fix? Get a hammer, somebody, or a chisel. Quick! Take off that slipper, Joan!"

The Eagle ruthlessly removed the heel of the slipper. And in a neat cylindrical cavity bored in the heel was a tiny scroll of paper. As the Eagle carefully removed it and unrolled it, it was seen to be covered with chemical symbols and figures.

"There is your deadly gas formula, Mr. Pembroke," Shannon said. "I should have thought of that before, but I got tangled up running around after Machin."

"Jeff!" cried Joan, laughing hysterically. "And I really had the formula all the time! If I had known it when Machin and Schmidt were torturing you, I—oh, I don't know what I'd have done."

"Which makes it just as well that neither of us knew it then. The future Mrs. Jeff Shannon should never have to make such choices. And if you gentlemen will kindly clear the hell out of here, I've a few things to discuss—privately."

Marriage was not for the Eagle yet, though, and both Jeff and Joan knew it, but for a little while they were content.

V

GOLD OF
THE GESTAPO

CHAPTER I

MISSION IN BUDAPEST

THE MAN who entered the beer garden on one of the narrow, ancient streets of Budapest, was clearly not a Hungarian nor were his clothes Continental. A glance at his lean, tanned face would give positive proof that here was a man unaffected by a *Blitzkrieg*, a war of nerves or the constant threat of hunger and death. Then closer observation would have shown a small American flag pinned to the lapel of the man's coat, and this tiny emblem would have answered all questions.

He sat down at one of the tables in a far corner and ordered beer. He glanced at his wrist-watch, then gazed thoughtfully at the door of the beer garden.

Jeff Shannon was the name on his passport and the occupation was listed as "correspondent." But in fact Jeff Shannon was the ace agent of the G-2 branch of the United States Army Intelligence Service, assigned temporarily to the State Department.

Jeff Shannon also had another identity, one known to few people and those only among the more highly trusted officials of the government. He was the Eagle, America's master counter-espionage agent. Not even the men who had issued his passport knew this.

Precisely at eight o'clock another man, indisputably an American, entered the beer garden, took a table across the room and sipped beer for several minutes. A waiter whispered something in his ear and looked meaningly at Jeff Shannon. The man arose quickly, strode across the room and stretched out his hand.

"Welcome to Budapest, countryman," he said heartily. "Americans are as rare as smiles in Budapest these days. What in the world are you doing here?"

Shannon shook hands and grinned. "Looking for news. My name is Marvin—correspondent for the A.P. News Service. Sit down!" Shannon had calculatingly given the name of Marvin.

Shannon launched into a violent, unexpected attack squarely in the middle of the group.

In case of certain eventualities he did not even want the American consulate to be able to tie up Jeff Shannon with the Eagle.

The man pulled up a chair and had his beer brought from his own table.

"I'm Tom Craig," he said. "Attached to the American consulate here."

THEY KEPT on talking in generalities for half an hour and other patrons only glanced at them with interest engendered by their smiling faces and their neat clothes.

Finally Craig dropped his voice when a quick look around showed that the novelty of their presence had worn off.

"Now listen carefully, Marvin, because I won't have time to repeat this. We asked for a crack operative and I certainly hope you're one. Why didn't they send the Eagle?"

Shannon, answering now to the name of Marvin, shrugged. "I can't answer that, Craig. I don't even know who the Eagle is except that he's

They were determined to
murder the American.

an accredited agent of the service. That guy travels by himself. We never come into contact with him. But don't worry. I'm capable of handling your problem. Let's have it."

Craig ordered more beer, maintained silence until the waiter had served and departed, then he spoke earnestly, although the cheerful expression on his face belied the seriousness of his words. Any casual observer would have thought these two Americans were merely trading news.

"You are here unofficially," Craig said. "You have absolutely no connection with the consulate or the United States State Department. If you get into trouble, we won't even be able to recognize you. Is that clear?"

Shannon nodded. "Very. From what I gather the marines won't show up at the crucial moment. Go ahead."

"I just wanted to warn you, Marvin. Budapest is an international clearing house for spies. Agents of every nation in Europe—and Asia too—are here to keep an eye on which way the wind blows and, incidentally, on one another. They suspect everyone with more than two dollars, American money. The Hungarian police watch them closely, but they can't do much because Hungary is in a tough spot. Germany wants her meat and grain. England demands that Hungary sell only to her.

"Now to the point. For several months we've been bothered with spurious United States currency showing up. It's clever counterfeit and practically undetectable. Nazi agents and trade missions bring it in, buy Hungarian money for it, then laugh up their sleeves when the deception is discovered."

Shannon whistled softly. "The same trick Russia used to pull. But Craig, if none of that currency reached the United States, we have no great interest in it. Counterfeits won't upset the bookkeeping of the mint unless they are passed around in the United States."

"We know all about that," Craig said. "But the Gestapo agents aren't just passing it in Hungary. They peddle the stuff to all the Balkan states, and even to Italy with whom they profess eternal friendship. It's caused by desperation alone. Germany has no gold to back up her own currency and needs good money with which to make foreign purchases.

"Recently we've learned that some of this counterfeit has reached South America and even Mexico. There is where the trouble starts. Our money is A-One in those countries. We can't afford to allow anything to spoil that. Do you grasp what I mean? It creates a bad situation in the United States too, for all money coming from abroad must be carefully scrutinized."

SHANNON COUNTED on his fingers as he replied.

"Three definite objectives to keep me busy. I've got to locate the men who pass the money, prove the stuff is phony, and get all the evidence to back up that proof. Once we can make these countries suspicious of the currency which Germany is passing and show them how to detect the phony from the real, we'll have won our battle. Any idea where I can start?"

Craig nodded. "We know that a *Herr* Karl Wunderlich, presumably a trader, passed the last lot. You'll have to work from there. Now, I can't risk staying here any longer, but just another warning, Marvin. Gestapo agents are selected for their shrewdness and cruelty. They'll stop at nothing to put you away if they have the remotest suspicion as to why you are here.

"They use two methods—outright murder here, which the police can never solve, or a quick shanghai into German territory, and that's even worse than quick death. You can't come to us for help or even show your face around the consulate. In the event that you need information, phone a number listed under the name of Hans Lustig."

Craig arose, shook hands with Shannon, alias Marvin, again and left.

Shannon sat down, sipped his beer and considered the problem. He was essentially a solo agent, but this particular job placed him in the most dangerous surroundings in which he had ever worked.

Here he could trust no one, and he must maintain an outward attitude to raise him above the suspicion of the Gestapo agents in Budapest. If he mixed with them and was caught, the Hungarian police would throw him into the same prison with his enemies. The American consulate could try to help, but they would not be able to save him from a prison term.

Shannon's eyes glittered. This was what he liked. Tremendous odds made the fight all the more interesting, and sharpened all his faculties.

He paid his bill and wandered out into the street. It had grown dark, but there was no blackout in Budapest. Half the street lamps were not burning, but that was merely to conserve on power and the coal necessary to produce it. Night clubs and other amusement centers were running full blast, to give the jittery public some degree of solace.

Shannon stepped off a curb, walked across the dimly lighted street and kept his eyes open. He had small hope that his presence and real mission were not known. The Gestapo maintain an elaborate spy system in the United States. It was highly possible that they were already engaged in baiting some kind of a deadly trap.

Four men were walking toward him. Two of them seemed to be arguing volubly about something and when Shannon was within a dozen paces of them, the argument reached the stage where fists were used. Shannon's eyes narrowed. He deliberately turned and tried to make a wide circle of the two fighting men, but they moved also, and cleverly intercepted him.

A wild swing caught Shannon hard on the cheek. It rocked him back on his heels and brought a flush of anger to his cheeks. Still, he only tried to move out of the way. There were shouts behind him and three more men rushed up to join in the battle. Shannon caught the glimpse of a sleeve-shielded knife and knew this fight was staged for only one purpose—to accidentally murder an American.

NOW HE had to fight. Shannon backed up against a wall. Two of the men kept on tussling, but the others were closing in on Shannon. One of them made a rush toward him. Shannon moved aside so swiftly that the man could not slow up in time and he hit the brick wall of the building with a thump that sent him into an awkward sitting position.

He growled a Teutonic oath, rasped orders and the others approached. Shannon did not believe in the theory that defense is the best offense. Not when he had to face seven men bent on slaughtering him. He moved forward a few steps, weaved, and upset that concerted charge by flanking the killers and sending one of them ten feet away by a long, powerful punch to the face.

It was impossible to fight them all with any hope of victory. Shannon had to find some refuge. There was an inn about a hundred yards down the street. If he could reach that, perhaps the police would arrive before the agents could get at him.

Shannon ducked a slashing thrust with a knife. Somewhere up the street a man began yammering for the police in shrill tones. Shannon saw the look of indecision on the faces of the agents. They had no more desire to meet the police than had Shannon. Suddenly Shannon launched into a violent, unexpected attack squarely into the middle of the group. His surprise tactics and the way he swung two good fists created a beautiful hole in their ranks. He darted through and kept on going like the wind. They pounded after him. Then a police whistle shrilled.

Shannon headed for the inn, and as he approached it, the door opened. He darted inside and the door was hastily closed again. A burly man with tremendous mustaches quickly shot a heavy bolt into its socket, grabbed Shannon's arm and piloted him up a flight of steps.

"You are an American, eh?" he asked in fairly good English. "I once lived in Detroit. Americans are my friends, yes. I saw those cursed thieves try to kill you. But they will not find you here—*ach* no. You are permitted to remain as long as you wish, *Herr*—"

"Shannon. Thanks for the help. They nearly finished me off, and I didn't want to encounter the police either. I'm a newspaper man. One spot of trouble and the gendarmes would kick me out of the country. Nice place you have here. Perhaps I'll stay."

"Good." The innkeeper rubbed his hands. "Business being what it is since this accursed war, you are more than welcome and we can talk about America often, eh? What a fool I was to leave your country. But I have not told you my name. It is Hatvan. In Detroit they made fun of my name and called me Hattie. I liked it."

Shannon walked over to a window and looked out. Two policemen were scouring the neighborhood, but there were no signs of the agents who had attacked the American agent. Shannon let the curtain drop back in place and turned to the innkeeper.

"Then I'll call you Hattie too," he said, "and thanks again. My luggage is still at the railroad station. Will you send for it? I'm going out again. I'm paid to write stories about Budapest and the only way I can do that is to look around."

"But keep off the dark streets," Hatvan warned. "Budapest was once as peaceful as a village on the Great Plains but now, with the war, one does not know a friend from an enemy. I shall have your baggage brought here."

SHANNON LEFT the inn warily. Gestapo agents are noted for their persistency and one or two might have remained, either to trail him or use one of their knives.

No one moved to intercept him and he saw no signs of a shadow on his trail. Shannon walked to the center of the city and for two hours worked hard, gathering any news he could get, openly questioning officials, storekeepers and pedestrians.

If he was under observation, no one could believe him anything but a reporter. He could fool the Budapest authorities easily enough, but not the Gestapo. Somehow they knew why he was here and even knew his identity—as Jeff Shannon.

One thing he was sure they were not aware of was that other identity he possessed—the Eagle. And Shannon had a hunch they would feel the grip of the Eagle's talons before he was finished.

Craig had indicated that one Karl Wunderlich had passed some of the spurious currency. Shannon had to begin his work with that one meager clue. Through Wunderlich he must uncover the entire counterfeiting agency of the Gestapo and warn every merchant and trader in Hungary to watch out for fake American money.

The only possible way to do that was through publicity, and that required absolute proof. Shannon had no false ideas as to what he was up against.

CHAPTER II

THE EAGLE'S TRICK

BUDAPEST'S FINEST hostelry was the Dunatalota. Shannon had intended to check in there, but Hatvan's little inn seemed better suited after mature consideration.

He decided to let *Herr* Wunderlich wait, temporarily. A scheme was fomenting in his mind, a method by which he might uncover some of the more important Gestapo agents. There was no use in trying to bluff it out so far as they were concerned. They knew he was an American agent. But Shannon didn't know them, and he had to see whom he fought. Besides, they had landed the first blow. This was the Eagle's round now.

He stopped a ragged little urchin, took him into a doorway and spoke in a brand of Hungarian that made the boy's eyes light up with humor. But when Shannon produced a few coins, avarice shone in those eyes instead.

"You can earn these and more," Shannon told him. "I am going into the hotel restaurant. Wait for twenty minutes. Then you slip past the doorman and the employees, run across the dining room, and do it as if you didn't want to be seen. Hand me a note I shall give you, and in return there will be more coins. Then leave quickly, reach a telephone, and call the hotel. Ask for Shannon."

Shannon ripped a page out of his notebook, scrawled something on it and folded it. Five minutes later he was shown to a small table by a bowing waiter. He ordered and sipped a drink while his eyes roved over the room, watching all the guests. A party of four men was directly across from him. By their studious avoidance of his deliberate stare, they gave away the fact that they had him under observation. One thing about Gestapo agents—they were rarely subtle.

There was some confusion near the entrance. Then the ragged little boy, hotly pursued by a uniformed hotel employee, came dashing into the dining room. He looked around, spotted Shannon and evaded his pursuers with some uncanny dexterity.

He reached Shannon's side and planked the folded piece of paper on the table. Shannon gravely handed him a few more coins and the boy vanished. Shannon opened the note, pretended to study it for a moment, then pulled a small black book from his pocket. He used a pencil and the back of his menu card. Anyone suspicious of him would believe he was decoding a message.

Finally he stuffed the note carelessly into his pocket, ripped the menu card into shreds and allowed the waiter to serve his meal. Nothing happened, but Shannon was patient. Another waiter came to fill his water glass. He brushed against Shannon as he did so, apologized profusely, and went away.

Shannon watched him covertly. The man was a clever pickpocket, but the Eagle had expected that note to be stolen. He had felt those quick, agile fingers scoop it up.

The waiter moved around the dining room with his carafe of water. He reached the table where the four men sat. Shannon did not see it but he was positive that the note had been passed. After a few moments one of the men arose, bowed to his companions and walked out.

A waiter approached Shannon's table and informed him that he was wanted on the phone. Shannon followed the man out of the dining room, but instead of approaching the phone booths, he got his hat from the check room and darted out the door, just in time to see the departing member of that foursome, hurrying up the street.

SHANNON KEPT close to the shadows of the buildings. His movements were sure, and not for one instant did the man he trailed realize that someone was watching him.

The American looked around every few steps to be sure that he, in turn, was not being followed. Now he was no longer Jeff Shannon, but the Eagle. He seemed to blend with the gloom and made no more noise than the swoop of the great bird from which he had taken his name.

The man he trailed passed by an ornate residence, slowed up and then stood at a corner for a moment or two. Then he doubled back, ran up the steps of the big house and the door opened for him at once. The Eagle sighed in relief that he had not continued on the trail. Someone observed everyone who passed that house, and was prepared to admit authorized callers instantly.

The Eagle considered his problem. In order to rout the Gestapo agents completely, he must first determine their leader and expose him. True, the moment that one group of agents was arrested, others would slip into the country from Austria, but they would be new and without the contacts of regularly established men.

The ace American agent could deal the spy ring a serious blow in this way and before the others became organized, could reveal their entire cheating plot to the proper people. The resultant publicity would travel around the world, and when American money was given in trade by a Nazi agent, that currency would be scrutinized most carefully.

Shannon ducked into the narrow yard of the adjoining house, reached the rear of the spy nest and studied the place intently. Approach looked too easy, and he guessed that any intruder would be spotted fast.

Drawing up the lapels of his coat to conceal his white shirt, Shannon crouched and began moving forward cautiously. He stopped and listened as he reached the boundaries of the next yard. He heard the crunch of dirt under heavy feet, and a husky man—a guard—strolled idly by, two feet from where the Eagle was hidden.

The American agent leaped with his arms outthrust. He clapped a hand across the guard's mouth, bent him backward with the other hand and then rammed home a short, neat blow to the chin. The guard slumped, but he was not unconscious. Shannon let him drop, bent over him and as he opened his mouth to yell a warning, Shannon let him have a real blow. The cry was choked off and the guard went limp.

The Eagle searched him, appropriated a long muzzled automatic and made sure a bullet was ready in the firing chamber. He crept closer to the house, kept away from the back door and selected a likely looking window instead.

It was locked but quick manipulation of a knife blade slid the catch back. He raised it slowly and quietly, hauled himself up and climbed into a darkened room.

He scraped a match, held the small torch high and then walked quickly to the door and opened it a crack. Someone was talking excitedly in German and Jeff Shannon, the Eagle, understood every word. He guessed that the speaker was the man he had followed.

"Ach, ja! The note was delivered by a dirty little boy. Whoever sent it was afraid to be seen. It is in code. I saw the stupid American decode it."

There was silence for a moment, or two. Shannon slipped into the hall and crept toward the doorway of a lighted room from which the conversation emanated. He heard a grunt of baffled fury and then a gruff voice began cursing the man who brought the note.

"You stupid *Schweine!"* he thundered. "This message is in code—the simplest international code. Do you know what it says?"

"Perhaps I can answer that," a voice broke in.

He transferred his grip
to the killer's throat.

Four men in the room turned quickly and four pairs of arms shot straight up. The Eagle walked in, gun at a ready angle.

"It's just a well known excerpt from a song—one whose meaning you men wouldn't understand. It simply says, 'My country 'tis of thee, sweet land of liberty.' Strange word, isn't it? Liberty, I mean. Well gentlemen, our cards are on the table. You know why I am here. I know what you have been doing.

"If any one of you were in my position, this gun would speak, for that is the only language you understand. Don't get me wrong—I wouldn't hesitate to pull the trigger if you showed the slightest inclination to trick me. Now, one at a time, each of you empty your pockets. Thoroughly too, because after you are finished, I shall search you. Go on—start!"

The leader of the group was a tall, slim man with a hideous duelling scar across his cheek. That scar was deathly white while the rest of his face was flushed as if he were near apoplexy.

He looked at the Eagle and there was no fear in his eyes, only cold logical reasoning. This American meant what he said about shooting. It was plainly visible. The slim man barked a command, he and his men rapidly dumped the contents of their pockets on the table.

Shannon lined them up against the wall, facing it. He had no time to sort the valuable papers from the ones useless to him, so he stuffed everything into his pocket. Then he stepped quietly toward the door.

There was a sudden movement behind him. Instead of turning as any ordinary man might have done, the Eagle ducked. A blow, intended to break his skull wide open, landed on his shoulder instead and he rolled with the blow, breaking its full force.

A huge man, with murder written all over his wide face, tried to reverse the gun for quick shooting. Shannon drove a hard right to the chin, connected and whirled to face the four inside the room who were now heading his way and shouting to their companion that the intruder was to be killed.

The Eagle fired two shots. They stopped the four in their tracks, for none was armed now. Shannon swerved slightly. His gun spouted flame again and the heavy slug tore into a light switch. The shattered wires shorted and lights went out all over the house.

Beating what apparently was a noisy retreat toward the back door, Shannon slipped into a room and heard the others rush past him. He doubled back, calmly opened the front door, stepped on the porch and with a grin punched the door bell. Then he raced away into the night.

He entered a small restaurant, ordered a meal and began examining his loot. He whistled in surprise at the sight of a series of small photographs depicting some intensely interesting military scenes in and around the fortified line at the Raba River, thirty-five kilometers from the Austrian border. Nazi agents were not idle in Hungary.

Certain other documents linked this Karl Wunderlich—Shannon was certain the tall, slim leader was Wunderlich—with both the possession of these photos and the elaborate plot that had been made to get them.

One other paper interested Shannon greatly. It was a brown card with a diagonal red streak across it, signed by the head of the Nazi Secret Police. This document would enable the bearer to travel freely throughout any part of Germany or the nations it had thrust its rule upon.

"VERY USEFUL," The Eagle told himself, "if I had to enter Austria or Germany, but Wunderlich won't let much time elapse before he notifies his superiors of the loss of this card. Unless Wunderlich might be in danger of being purged because of his failures. I'd better do something about this."

He stowed the all-important card in his pocket, together with an intriguing bit of thin paper covered with code, carefully stacked the other papers and the photos and left the restaurant. He found a rusty, but still sharp nail sticking out of a discarded board. In the shelter of a doorway he pierced the papers with the nail and proceeded directly to the headquarters of the local police.

The door of the building was closed and the Eagle smiled as he contemplated his method of putting Wunderlich and his men into custody. He picked up a good-sized rock, stepped up to the door and quickly tacked onto it the nail with the revealing papers.

He darted away before anyone arrived to answer the banging he made. From a place across the street, Shannon saw the police examine the papers and go into swift action. Thirty minutes later he witnessed Wunderlich and his men being led into police headquarters. They would be locked up and held without bail or the right to communicate with anyone else.

If he worked fast now, the Gestapo card would be of invaluable aid. At any rate, an important cog in the machinery used to distribute the counterfeit American money had been effectively broken up and with no visible direct pressure from the United States Government.

CHAPTER III

INTO THE MOUTH OF DANGER

O NE PIECE of thin, onion-skin paper covered with code words had not been turned over to the police by Shannon. On a hunch that it might contain some important information he decided to go back to Hatvan's inn and decode it at his leisure.

Hatvan, excited and considerably worried, waddled down the steps as Shannon walked into the hotel. He wrung his hands and began apologizing. Shannon noticed an ugly bruise on his cheek.

"It has happened as I feared," he explained. "Your baggage was brought here at once. Two men registered soon after. I heard them moving about and went up to investigate. They were searching your baggage, *Herr* Shannon. One of them struck me—so!" He touched the bruise gently. "I could do nothing. They were those accursed Gestapo agents. No one enters Budapest without their trying to find out his mission. I am very sorry."

Shannon brought Hatvan over to the bar and ordered two drinks.

"Forget it, Hattie. There was nothing of importance in my luggage. I've nothing to hide, so if they come back let them search away."

He went to his room, locked the door and began studying the piece of onion-skin paper. It had a tendency to curl. The Eagle knew what that indicated. The message had been packed into a cylinder and delivered by carrier pigeon.

He opened his bags, pulled down the window shade and then slipped the back off an ebony hair brush. A thin code book lay in a specially created slot. He compared the code on the message to other sample codes in the book, found that it was not a difficult one and set to work translating it.

Gradually his pencil created the message in English. It read:

> Contact *Fraulein* Ethel Landreth at Wiener Neustadt on the western shore of lake. Absolutely reliable. Prepare to transport ten millions in usual currency for quick disposal. *Heil!*

"So," the Eagle contemplated, "the beautiful female operative is in it. We'll have a look at her."

Through this woman Shannon knew he could contact the messengers from Gestapo headquarters in Austria. They, in turn, would lead him to the agency through which this counterfeit money was being manufactured.

There was a bold, typically American scheme up Shannon's sleeve. If it worked, the Balkans would immediately cease granting credits or exchanging their own sound currency for the spurious American money.

If it didn't work, there would be a concentration camp at the very best, with his much more probable finish before a firing squad. So far as the United States was concerned, Operative Jeff Shannon would simply have vanished and only discreet inquiries would be made by the State Department.

He studied maps then, and realized just how dangerous his journey would be to this lake near Wiener Neustadt. First he must slip out of Budapest without arousing any suspicion. Then his apparent destination must seem to be Bratislava in what had once been Czechoslovakia.

At a certain point along the route he could get off the train, and from there it was a matter of only a few kilometers to the Austrian town, but each kilometer would be full of peril. Every moment which he spent on German soil would tax his ingenuity to the utmost, and if Karl Wunderlich ever managed to send out word of the theft of his card, Shannon would have to run for his life.

HE COULD not risk taking a gun with him, but he did have a camera—a peculiar little mechanism camouflaged to look like a watch. It did tell time, but through the winding mechanism a shutter could be operated and almost microscopic pictures could be taken. This watch-camera never left his pocket.

Only one thing bothered Shannon. The mysterious leader of the Gestapo now established in Budapest was unknown to him. The man was bound to be crafty, and brilliant too, or he would never have been entrusted with the supervision of the secret police in a foreign land.

Yet Shannon had neither the time nor the opportunity of ferreting him out. He had broken up only one of the sources of distribution of the money, but to break them all down would be both difficult and useless, for the Gestapo would simply create other agencies as fast as the Eagle smashed them.

He had to get at the source of the money—the place where it was being printed, even if that meant a one-man invasion of Berlin itself. The thing had to be dried up at its source if American money was to remain trusted.

Shannon remembered what Craig had told him. In the event that he needed help or information he was to phone one Hans Lustig. Unable to contact Craig, the Eagle decided to call this man and have him forward word of his departure to Austria.

Someone tapped on the door. Shannon hastily swept all incriminating evidence out of sight and let Hatvan in. The burly Hungarian sat on the edge of the bed and fingered his flowing mustaches.

"It has occurred to me," he said, "that perhaps the Gestapo had more than a casual interest in your possessions, *Herr* Shannon. I want to help, even though it is in but a small way. I have no reason to love these men. They cannot be trusted and they have taken over a good part of Europe. Hungary will be next, mark my words. We have too much fine wheat, too much fertile land and fat cattle for those pigs to pass up. If you are a reporter, let me help in getting information that will show the world what these men are like."

Shannon lit a cigarette and leaned back in his chair. "Sorry, Hattie," he said. "The world knows what they are like already. But there may be one thing you could do. What are the chances of my getting to Bratislava without a passport?"

Hatvan shrugged. "It is like walking into the path of a machine-gun, my friend. It has been done, yes, but of those who have tried, more have failed than have succeeded. Why do you wish to go there?"

"News. I want to see for myself just how these Czechs are being treated. I want stories from their own lips. Facts, concrete evidence, verbatim stories. We can't use unverified items any more. It's been overdone. I thought you might have some friends—"

Hatvan shook his head. "None I would trust with your life, *Herr* Shannon. Yet I could reach the Border without suspicion, for I have relatives there. Perhaps I could help if it became necessary. Do not hesitate to call on me. I consider myself as much American as Hungarian. I was a fool to ever leave Detroit. Now I cannot get back. You are leaving at once—yes?"

"It's still early evening," Shannon explained. "It will be easier by night, especially at the Border, in case I have to cut and run for it. Keep my things here. I'll pay you a month's rent in advance."

The American took out his wallet, pulling from it several American bills. Hatvan took them with a deep bow. When he was ready to move. Shannon stowed only bare necessities in his pockets, made sure the Gestapo card was intact, and hurried downstairs. Hatvan was nowhere in sight. The tiny lobby of the inn was deserted. Even the barmaid had vanished. The Eagle stepped up to a phone in one corner, looked up the number of Hans Lustig and called it.

A deep, resonant voice answered him and acknowledged his identity at once.

"Listen carefully," Shannon said in a low tone. "I'm ready to leave for Bratislava and thence to Wiener Neustadt and the lake. Tell Craig that's where to send for the body of one Marvin—if I trip. That's all."

"But *Herr* Marvin," Lustig's deep voice protested, "you are mad to undertake such a mission. It cannot be done."

The Eagle frowned slightly and turned his head. It seemed as though that booming voice almost filled the room.

"Then I'll show you it can be done," he said, and hung up.

He hurried out of the inn and went straight to the railroad station. He purchased his ticket, boarded a train that rolled in ten minutes later and settled back, wondering just what would happen once the Border guards demanded his papers. If he passed those guards, the first hurdle would be over, but to get back on neutral soil from then on it would be like breaking out of Alcatraz.

Somewhere just over the Border he had to leave the train without being seen. If he went all the way into Brastislava, as he had indicated to Lustig and Hatvan, it would become necessary to enter Vienna and then double back to the lake region. A highly difficult task if the Eagle knew his Gestapo agents.

An hour crawled by while the train whizzed across the level lowlands of Hungary. Looking out at the terrain, Shannon realized just what the Hungarians were up against in case of an invasion. There wasn't a hill or a gully where defenders might establish their lines. Here the Nazi *Blitzkrieg* would work to a remarkable success for the topography was ideal for the use of tanks and fast armored car brigades.

Then he felt the train jerk and slow down. It stopped at the Border and a score of uniformed Nazi passport inspectors came aboard. Shannon felt his first twinge of uneasiness. Now he was in for it. The next few moments would tell the story. He mopped his forehead with a handkerchief.

The door of his compartment was opened and a stolid-looking officer merely stretched out his hand for passports. The Eagle took the Gestapo card from his pocket, arose and glared at the officer.

"Stupid *Schweine*," he thundered. "Is it not customary for a superior to be saluted, or have you become weak and spineless like these people we have conquered?"

The officer glanced at the card, stiffened and raised one hand in the Nazi salute.

"I am sorry. I did not know. Excuse my stupidity, Excellency. I am new here."

The Eagle growled something under his breath and sat down. But he was worried. Despite the kowtowing of this Border guard, he had undoubtedly noted the number on the stolen identification card. He was bound to report that.

The ponderous German machinery would work slowly, but efficiently. Sooner or later someone would wonder just what Karl Wunderlich was up to, traveling without orders. The merest investigation in Budapest would reveal that Wunderlich had vanished, and the rest would be quickly guessed at. Speed was now essential if the Eagle hoped to put his scheme through.

The passport inspectors got off, signaled the all clear, and the train began moving. Shannon studied maps intently until he determined just where he should slip off the train. He decided on a small, sleepy village, untouched by the ravages of war, for when the Nazi invaders finally had reached this portion of the country all resistance had become nil.

Magyarovar was no more than twenty kilometers from the lake. He could hire a car or cart, reach the lake and bribe the owner of some boat to take him the rest of the way.

The Eagle began making preparations for a quick exit from the train as it slowed up to enter Magyarovar. The door of his compartment opened suddenly and a man with clipped hair, wide face and an ingratiating smile, stepped in. He saluted stiffly and sat down without invitation.

"Your card," he said quietly. "All agents are examined in due course of a journey. Your presence has just been reported to me."

Shannon found his throat dry, his nerves on edge. Here was an intelligent man, no stupid guard. This man would ask questions, trap him probably and then—the Eagle knew the answer to that one.

Yet, with the train whizzing along at high speed, how could he hope to escape? He reached into his pocket for the card, presented it with a flourish and saw the secret policeman's eyes narrow. The Eagle did not wait any longer, he doubled his fist, brought it up suddenly and smashed a healthy haymaker straight to the point of that square jaw. The agent sagged back limply.

The Eagle pulled the unconscious man's hat well down to mask the glazed eyes and the sagging mouth.

He took back his card, wondering just how much value it would have now, and headed for the compartment door. He opened it and drew in a quick breath.

There were two uniformed men just outside!

CHAPTER IV

ESCAPE FROM DOOM

S HANNON'S MIND worked at a mile a minute clip, he stepped into the corridor boldly, turned and bowed in the direction of the unconscious agent.

"You will not be disturbed, *mein Herr.* I shall awaken you when we reach the next stop," he said.

The two guards peered into the compartment and saw their superior apparently sleeping somewhat ungracefully. They glanced at Shannon, raised their hands in salutes, and resumed their posts.

The Eagle forced himself to amble slowly away even though the urge to cut and run for it was overwhelming. At any moment the agent would awaken, give the alarm, and then merry hell would break loose.

The American stepped into the next car, eyed the passengers suspiciously, and kept on walking. He wondered if the appearance of that secret agent was just a coincidence or if they already knew he was traveling with stolen credentials, and were merely toying with him until the train reached a larger city where the invaders ruled with steel fists. If the news had preceded him into this territory, he would have a handicap to overcome which would prove gigantic.

Approaching the end of the train, Shannon pushed open the door of the second to the last coach. A brawny arm barred his way and a member of the police frowned at him.

"Get out of here," he snapped. "Go back to your second-class carriage, or is it your wish to go among the refugees?"

Shannon grabbed the man by his shirt and shook him until the guard reached for his holstered gun. He started to draw it, but the brown card with the diagonal red stripe across it acted like a powerful brake. His hand shot up stiffly and he seemed to be swallowing with some difficulty.

"Open the door," Shannon ground out. "If it is my wish to go among the refugees, I shall not be stopped. Open it!"

The guard obeyed with an alacrity that would have been amusing under any other circumstances.

The Eagle was heading for the rear platform of the train to make his jump for freedom from that point. The presence of these refugees, packed like cattle in the dirty coach, aided him. It would require several minutes of violent shoving for the guards to get through.

Sullen glances were shot Shannon's way. None of the poorly clad, drawn-faced refugees had missed the salute of the guard, and they would not budge until he actually elbowed them aside.

Then the Eagle caught sight of a uniformed guard lying on the platform. At the same moment someone wound an arm around his own throat and some kind of a club crashed against his head. He sank to the floor and was quickly stuffed under one of the seats.

He was not unconscious and knew that the train was slowing up for one of its regular stops. These refugees—some of them anyway—had rebelled and overpowered the guard. They would make an attempt to bolt for freedom at any second. The Eagle grimly crawled into a spot from which he could jump quickly.

There was a crashing of glass, shouts, and then the shooting started. The train came to a stop with a jerk. Shannon plowed through the refugees who were not taking part in the escape plot. They let him go now, as if they recognized the futility of all this.

As the Eagle came out on the rear platform, he saw a dozen of them racing away, separating, and each man choosing his own method of escape. Guns cracked. He saw two of the fleeing men buckle and fall heavily.

A NUMBER of guards jumped off the train and went in pursuit, others headed toward the refugee coach to keep the rest of them from breaking out. Shannon vaulted off the back of the train, but he didn't make the mistake of running for it. They would have stopped him before he had covered a dozen feet.

But there was a culvert just beneath the last car. A small earthenware pipe ran through it, and some muddy water trickled out. The Eagle, protected some by the darkness, dropped over the edge of the culvert and crawled into the blackness of the pipe.

He lay there, in the chilly water, wondering if they would find it, and put a few experimental bullets through it just for luck. He curled himself up in as tight a ball as possible and got braced for the impact of any slugs that might come his way.

He could hear the guards returning, dragging some of the escaped men with them. He heard the gruff voice of the secret agent he had knocked cold.

"The American *Schweine*—he went with them," the agent growled. "Because of the stupidity of these so-called guards, an important foreigner escaped. Why were these cattle not more carefully watched? There will be a report—mark you—and it won't look good for you either. Now get on with you. Have the train continue. I must reach the next town to send out an alarm."

Car platforms banged and the train rolled across the culvert. Shannon did not move. It might have been just a trick to lure him from his hiding place. Then he was sure that that hunch was right, for as the noise of the train died away he heard hoarse breathing, and then the sound of someone moving about—within the culvert itself.

Whoever it was crawled toward him. The Eagle waited until he was close, then he threw himself forward. His outstretched hands encountered a man's throat and he brought the unknown intruder flat in the muddy water. Shannon crawled beside him, found a dry match and lit it. He relaxed his grip, blew out the match and helped the man up. He was just one of the refugees.

"You're safe," Shannon told him. "The train has gone. I'm on the run too. Maybe we can go together."

"Of course," the refugee answered in German, a horse whisper. "The cursed Gestapo—they are gone?"

They crawled out of the culvert, peered around cautiously and decided they were in the clear. Shannon had lost his sense of direction, but this refugee knew the territory well.

"My name is Gherla," he explained. "I am an Austrian, but I spent many years in Germany where I discovered what this Nazi regime is like. I returned to Vienna and preached against them, so with *Anschluss*—well, you can imagine for yourself what happened. They were taking me to a concentration camp—and death within six months."

"But why the break for freedom?" the Eagle asked as they trudged along the dark shoulders of an automobile highway which ran near the railroad tracks. "What did it get you? It's impossible to slip over the Border."

Gherla looked wise. "It was prepared. Of course we knew that some of us would not be so lucky, but we were desperate—those of us who chose to run for it. Death there would be easier than that which they dole out in the camps. Now—you will tell me about yourself."

SHANNON SHRUGGED, ducked under the low-hanging branches of a tree, then both of them darted behind that same tree as headlights of a car broke the darkness. After the car passed, Shannon answered Gherla's question.

"I'm an American reporter traveling without passport or papers. A pug-faced Gestapo agent on the train started asking me questions, so I slugged him."

Gherla whistled. "That must have been Fritz Pommer, one of the higher-ups. It will go hard with you if you are caught. I suppose it is safe to explain other things to you now. There is a way of getting out of Austria. For those who can furnish money or jewels, that is. A band of Hungarians help us. We proceed to the lake and under cover of night we take a small boat which lands us in Hungary. We can arrange it for you too, if that is what you wish."

The Eagle shook his head. "Maybe later, but I haven't completed my work here yet. Tell me—do you know a woman named *Fraulein* Ethel Landreth?"

Gherla's eyes flashed. He half turned toward Shannon and then seemed to regain possession of his startled nerves. He merely shook his head and plodded on. The Eagle caught Gherla's surprised hesitation and wondered about it. He was not sure of this man.

The Gestapo frequently operated by placing their own men among refugees. Gherla could easily be one of these. His astonishment at the mention of Ethel Landreth's name indicated that he must know she was a spy, working for the Gestapo.

His mind filled with these thoughts, Shannon did not hear the approach of the three-man patrol until it was too late. He and Gherla had taken to the road again because they could progress much faster there. A sharp bend in the road concealed the patrol until they were almost face to face.

Bayoneted rifles came up just as the Eagle charged toward the men. He hit the first one, sent him sprawling, and saw that his rifle went flying a good ten feet away. Another of the patrol made a lunge with his bayonet, slit a gash in Shannon's coat and then went back on his heels under the driving impact of a terrific right. The third man had hastily backed away as the flight progressed. Now he held his rifle against his shoulder and sighted along the barrel.

"You will not move," he said nervously. "You are covered."

Shannon let loose a groan, raised his hands and watched the other two members of the patrol scramble to their feet. Their rifles were concealed in the darkness and they began searching for them, muttering curses against this man who dared to attack.

A bulky shadow pointed a gun at the Eagle's heart.

The Eagle saw no signs of Gherla and whatever faith he had in the man was gone now. He still had the Gestapo identification card, though, and determined to use it as a last resort. It was more than probable that this patrol already had been warned to look out for the man who carried it, for Fritz Pommer would certainly have lost no time in broadcasting the alarm.

"Wait!" the Eagle barked authoritatively in German. "You blundering idiots! Why didn't you challenge me first? Attention—do you hear?"

The soldier with the rifle pointed Shannon's way looked blank. The other two, still trying to locate their guns, straightened up and gaped at the Eagle. Then, before he could produce the card, a shadowy form flitted from behind a tree and stated running noisily and crazily away in the night.

THE SOLDIER who held the only rifle swiveled to protect himself from possible attack. Shannon waited no longer. He charged forward in a crouched attack. One of the unarmed men shouted a warning, but the armed soldier hesitated a fraction of a second too long before he wheeled back.

As his rifle came around, the Eagle's hand seized it by the barrel, pointed the muzzle skyward and started a small offensive of his own, aimed directly at the soldier's ample paunch. The man groaned in pain, let go of the rifle and tried to defend himself with his fists. Shannon measured him with a long, looping right, heard bone crack as the blow hammered against his jaw.

Like a flash the Eagle faced in the other direction, rifle poised at his hip. The other two men hastily elevated both hands. Then Gherla came cautiously out of his hiding place. He gripped two rifles, and Shannon grinned. No wonder the other members of the patrol had not been able to find their guns.

"Line up!" the Eagle snapped. "Both of you!"

The soldiers obeyed promptly, their hands stretched as high up as they could get them. The third man was no longer dangerous. Not after that powerful swing Shannon had rapped against his jaw.

"Good man," Shannon told Gherla. "We'll get out of this."

He forced the two German soldiers to about face and with Gherla at his side they slowly backed away into the gloom. When the shrubbery closed about them, they turned and ran. After half a mile of this, they threw the rifles away.

Now the utmost in speed was essential. The patrol would spread the alarm quickly. The next time the Eagle and his new-found friend would not be able to duck out of trouble quite so easily.

"We should have shot the pigs," Gherla grumbled. "That is what they'd have done to us."

"Oh, no," Shannon said, and then grinned. "Not me. I'm an American citizen. If I killed one of their men, I wouldn't have a defense in case I was caught. Now I still have a chance of getting nothing worse than a prison sentence. Anyway, reporters don't go around killing men."

"You startled them back there," Gherla said slowly. "You had a trick up your sleeve, eh?"

The Eagle did not answer. If he told Gherla about the stolen Gestapo card, the refugee might doublecross him. Shannon could not afford to take a chance now because he needed Gherla for a guide. Without him he would stumble around blindly until another patrol caught up with him.

Neither man spoke, but Gherla assumed the lead and they dog-trotted across some rough, marshy ground. Shannon had an idea they were not far from the lake. Suddenly his foot struck a low bog and he pitched forward on his face. Gherla came back, helped him up and while the Eagle brushed mud off his clothing, Gherla bent down and picked up several papers which had dropped out of Shannon's pocket. The top one was the brown, red-striped Gestapo card.

Gherla apparently had not noticed it for he handed the papers back without a word. Shannon stuffed them into his pocket and they started away again. It would be dawn in a couple of hours. Unless they reached some refuge by then, they would have to wallow in this swamp for hours and never dare to sleep in case patrols were sent out.

THEN THE marsh gave way to firmer ground, the dense underbrush thinned and finally the Eagle caught sight of a huge building, closely resembling a medieval castle. Gherla pointed to it.

"That is our destination. We can hide there until night comes again. Then a boat across the lake to safety and freedom…. The castle? Yes, it really is one. It has been in the Landreth family for—"

Gherla stopped abruptly and seemed to bite his lower lip in exasperation. Shannon's eyebrows shot upward. So this was the home of Ethel Landreth, through whom the counterfeit money was being smuggled into Hungary and thence to all the other Balkan states! And Gherla knew the family.

Shannon's suspicions about this man grew firmer in his mind. Perhaps this was all a trap. Perhaps Fritz Pommer would be waiting in that castle with a firing squad primed for quick action.

The American agent keenly felt his lack of a weapon, but he dared not carry one. Whatever went on in this land of *Blitzkrieg* was none of his business. He had no right to interfere and above all, must not commit murder to insure his own safety. Such an act would give the Gestapo something to squawk about, and they were more than ready to make trouble for the American embassies in the Balkans.

Gherla crouched for a moment before they reached the clearing around the castle. He peered through the darkness intently and then signaled Shannon to remain quiet.

"Two of its cannot go at the same time," he whispered. "We would make too much noise. I will go first. When you see me admitted, then you run for the same door. Good luck!"

CHAPTER V

INTRIGUE

G **HERLA WENT** streaking across the cleared space, heading directly for the huge front door. He reached it, flattened himself in a nook so that Shannon could no longer see him, and a moment later the door opened, casting yellow light into the darkness. Gherla slipped inside.

The Eagle took a long breath and went racing toward the castle himself. This time the door opened just as he reached it and he went straight through. The door closed softly behind him.

Gherla had vanished. A girl, dressed in colorful Bohemian clothes and looking for all the world like something out of a Viennese musical play, slid heavy chains in place. When she turned around, Shannon actually blinked at the blond beauty of her. Automatically he removed his hat and bowed.

Her features were frozen and betrayed no signs of welcome. She did not speak—merely indicated that he was to follow her. Shannon knew then that Gherla had already warned her of the Gestapo card he carried. And yet, if she was a Gestapo operative herself, why should she resent the coming of a man who was, to all intents and purposes, one of her own kind?

She led him through a kitchen, where the cooking was done over a huge fireplace. Shannon, trained to notice details, saw that a number of pots and pans were dirty and that dishes enough for a dozen men littered the sink.

Then he found himself in a beautifully furnished room. The girl closed the door, put her back against it, and spoke for the first time.

"You have come too early," she said. "First may I see your identification card?"

Shannon gulped. He was in a tight spot now. If this girl was faithful to the Gestapo, she might recognize his card as being stolen. If she wasn't, he would be in a bad predicament by showing the card.

It all hinged on Gherla. If he was really a refugee and had come to this castle so openly, then the girl must he aiding and abetting escaping men, and at the same time acting as a Gestapo agent. This sounded both illogical and impossible to the Eagle, for the Gestapo were extremely careful in their selection of agents.

"Now don't get me wrong," Shannon began, but she broke in coldly.

"If you have identification, I must see it at once."

Shannon sighed and brought out the card. She merely glanced at it, dropped it on a table and sat down. The Eagle noticed that her face had turned pale, and that she was unconsciously tearing a small lace handkerchief into strips.

"About the man who led you here," she said. "Of course you know who and what he is. You let him bring you here for the usual reason, I suppose. Well—there is money. Gold, and enough to silence your tongue. Is it agreed that you will accept pay for keeping his presence a secret? He is—my—brother."

Shannon blinked and wondered what on earth this intrigue was all about. He merely nodded, and wished he had a cigarette. The girl arose and the Eagle jumped to his feet. She seemed a little startled at this courtesy, but her expressionless face did not change—only her eyes. They were a liquid blue and Shannon found himself admiring her almost unconsciously.

"Then we understand one another," she said. "I shall take you to your room where you are to wait for the arrival of the messenger."

"With the money?" Shannon asked on a hunch.

She nodded. "With the money. What else do you expect?"

SHE LED him out of the room, across a huge corridor and up a flight of stairs to a neatly furnished bedroom. Shannon stepped in, felt the breeze of the closing door and heard a key turn in the lock.

"This is quite customary," the girl said from the other side of the door. "I am only ordered to give you the shelter—not the privilege of wandering about my home."

The Eagle sat down on the edge of the bed. The thick goosefeather-stuffed blankets invited rest and he was tired enough to sleep on the bare ground.

Everything was still a puzzle to him. Gherla, this girl, how the Gestapo had learned so swiftly of his presence on the train to Bratislava.

He decided not to remove his clothes while he slept. There might be a necessity for some haste in getting clear of this place once the girl discovered he was not a Gestapo agent.

But Shannon took no chances. He placed two chairs about eight feet apart, directly in the path of anyone who might slip through the door in the darkness. He tied a piece of string, which he found in a drawer, to the legs of the chairs. It was a crude but effective alarm system.

Then Shannon threw himself across the bed and went to sleep wondering about the girl with golden hair and liquid blue eyes. His last thoughts concerned themselves with the motive behind her membership in the dread Gestapo.

He couldn't have been asleep long, for it was still dark when the two chairs efficiently tripped the intruder. Shannon was on his feet in a flash. The dark form of a man was busy untangling himself from the string. There was a knife in his hand and he used it to sever the cord. Then he glanced up, saw Shannon on his feet and without a word, charged toward him, the blade upraised.

The Eagle moved aside dexterously, but the descending blade swept uncomfortably close to his cheek. He thrust out a foot. The killer tripped and toppled forward.

Instantly the Eagle's hand grabbed the wrist of the killer, twisted it, and he heard the knife clatter to the floor. He transferred his grip from the wrist to the killer's throat and then pinned him against the wall.

Then he turned on a small lamp beside the bed and gave vent to a gasp of astonishment. The man who struggled in his grasp was—Gherla!

The Eagle let him go, but watched the man warily. Gherla rubbed his throat, but hatred still shone in his eyes.

"Now what's the idea?" Shannon demanded. "First you bring me to this house, and then you try to kill me. I want the truth, Gherla. I owe you something for saving me from that patrol, but you seem to have wiped out that debt by your actions tonight."

"Because you are a damned Gestapo spy!" Gherla found his voice and the words tumbled over one another. "I led you here because if I hadn't, you'd have killed me on the spot. Well, now you know. Yes—you know everything. Ethel has told me you have accepted money for your silence, but I know that dogs of Gestapo agents can never be trusted.

You and your kind have my death already listed to take place soon. What else can you expect when a man fights for his life?"

The Eagle pushed the refugee onto the bed, pulled up a chair and then straddled it. He decided to tell this man the truth. Perhaps all this was nothing more than a trick to make him reveal why he had invaded Austrian territory but if so, then Gherla was a superb actor, for bitter hatred had been shining in his eyes when he held the knife.

"IT'S TIME for a showdown," he told Gherla. "I am not a Gestapo agent. You must have spotted that card when it fell from my pocket. I stole that card. I told you I am an American war correspondent—which is the truth—and I've landed myself into a miserable mess before I've even had a chance to look for news. Whatever goes on in this castle is none of my affair. I'm strictly neutral until my own life is threatened. Then I'm primitive and not responsible for what happens."

Gherla seemed convinced.

"Yes—yes, that must be the truth, even though it sounds so incredible. You would never have permitted me to escape if you were a member of the Gestapo. You would have persuaded me to lead you here, found a patrol and arrested everyone in the place. I—I'm sorry about the knife, but I…. Well, I thought I had to do something. There is the girl to think about. Her safety must come even above mine."

The Eagle wondered what Gherla would think if he told him that the girl had active Gestapo connections. But he mentioned nothing of this and accompanied Gherla to the door. The refugee smiled sheepishly as Shannon let him out.

"I stole the key. That is how I got in so quietly. Again—I am sorry and if I can do anything to repay…."

Shannon grinned good-naturedly and shoved the man out. He closed the door and locked it from the inside, using the key Gherla had left in the lock. Now he felt a little safer. It would require a battering ram to break down the thick oak paneling of that door.

He sat down on the bed again, but was not sleepy now. There were too many confusing angles running through his brain and also the bitter knowledge that so far his mission had been marked by some important failures.

He was here, though, and on the verge of picking up the trail to wherever the spurious money was being manufactured. But was the girl to be trusted?

Was she just pulling the wool over Gherla's eyes, or was the Eagle's luck really becoming so amazing that here he might find someone to aid him, someone who might tell him everything necessary to put an end to this business of passing phony United States currency and blackening the reputation of good, sound money backed by real gold?

The whole world knew that there was nothing *ersatz* about the bullion buried deep in the ground in Kentucky, and that the United States met its obligations promptly. Yet, if the Gestapo continued to flood the Balkans with phony currency, that reputation would be blasted to the skies. As a great neutral the United States had to maintain it integrity and permit nothing to impeach it.

There was a light tap on the door. Shannon arose quickly and his heart skipped a beat. Was this it? Would a horde of surly Gestapo agents stream into the room and take him?

The rapping was repeated. Shannon picked up a chair and carried it over to the door. He took a firm grip on it with one hand, determined to fight bitterly if this were an arrest.

He turned the key and the door opened. Ethel Landreth entered and she was alone.

"I merely came to apologize," she said. "Gherla is too impetuous. You fulfilled your word to me better than I expected, and I am grateful. Gherla will not molest you again and the gold will be ready for you soon."

THE EAGLE took the girl's arm and gently eased her into a chair.

"Now look here," he said firmly. "I told Gherla I was not a Gestapo agent and that is the truth. However, I know that you are and yet, for some reason, you permit men like Gherla to take refuge here. I don't pretend to understand your motives, but you must understand mine. I am a newspaper correspondent. My mission here is to gather news."

"The Gestapo card," the girl said softly. "You cannot explain that away, and stealing one of those is impossible. But I do understand you somewhat. You are a foreigner and even though a member of the Gestapo, you have shown that you do not possess the cruelty of most of them. I am grateful, but I do not trust you. Let it remain as things stand now. I am here to act as an intermediary between certain parties and yourself. When the money comes, you must leave at once. Now may I go?"

Shannon groaned. "But how can I convince you—"

She walked to the door, turned around and for a moment he caught the semblance of a smile on her face.

"You can't convince me. If you are a newspaper man, then why did you mention the money to me? No one but the most trusted of the Gestapo knows about that. No, you are a strange man, a kind man, but you are also a Gestapo."

She closed the door and the Eagle slowly shook his head. This Old World intrigue baffled him completely. Again he sat down on the bed, convinced himself that he must not sleep, and three minutes later he was sleeping soundly.

CHAPTER VI

GESTAPO TACTICS

WHEN JEFF SHANNON awoke, it was dusk. He started up, angry with himself for having slept all day. The messenger with the spurious money might have arrived and left. He hurriedly washed up, combed his hair and ran downstairs. The girl was seated in the vast living room in front of a glowing fireplace. She looked up and nodded.

"No," she answered his silent question, "he has not yet arrived. There is food. Wait here."

She served him and Shannon had never tasted food that was better. For the final touch there was an inhaler of brandy. He rotated the glass and looked at the girl inquiringly.

"Yes," she answered, "I still have some left. You know almost everything about me and my home, so hiding a little thing like the possession of brandy from you isn't necessary. Your man is due to arrive in exactly ten minutes and he will be neither late nor early. The Gestapo is like that—as if you didn't know."

Shannon was finishing his cigarette when the great brass knocker on the front door thumped. He signaled the girl for caution, hurried into the corridor and selected a darkened room in which to hide. She opened the door and a man in an ink-stained apron came in. He clutched a huge package which he placed on a table.

"A million American dollars," he gloated at the girl. "We are printing one more batch—twenty millions this time—so be ready to accept that for shipment into Hungary. It is a profitable business, eh, *Fraulein?*"

She said nothing, merely held the door open. He grimaced at her and left. The Eagle came out of his hiding place swiftly.

"I've got to trust you," he said, "even if you have no faith in me. Keep that money here until I get back. I'm going after that messenger. This is your chance to repay me for anything I've done for you."

He opened the door, stepped out and looked around. The village was quiet and peaceful. The man he was to trail walked leisurely along the street but Shannon noticed that none of the inhabitants greeted him, so he knew this man must be from Germany.

The trail was easy to follow, for the messenger had not the vaguest idea that he was under observation. But the Eagle had to watch out for military patrols, Gestapo agents and the regular police set up by the Nazis. There was no question in his mind but that every accredited officer everywhere had been instructed to look out for him.

The American kept well into the shadows of the modest dwellings. By seeking the shelter of doorways on the better lighted streets, he kept the messenger in sight at all times.

Then his heart sank. The messenger boarded a trolley car destined for the city three miles away—a city in which the Gestapo maintained a divisional headquarters. Still the Eagle kept doggedly on the trail, and even boarded the same trolley with the man he was after.

Pulling his hat low, he pretended to be sleepy. He paid his fare and thanked his lucky stars that he had provided himself with the prevailing currency of this nation.

The messenger got off in the heart of the big city, ambled two blocks north and turned into the entrance of an imposing building. Two uniformed, rifle armed guards were at the door.

Shannon, concealed in a doorway across the street, saw a military car pull up. The two guards became rigid and raised their rifles to present. One man climbed out of the car, shot his hand upward in the characteristic Nazi salute and passed under a light set in the arched doorway. Shannon gulped. The man was Fritz Pommer, the Gestapo agent he had slugged on the train to Bratislava.

"GESTAPO HEADQUARTERS," he told himself. "They probably do the printing of the money under their own roof. What a set-up for me to tackle."

Yet it never occurred to him that the danger involved would warrant some careful consideration as to whether or not he should risk exposing himself to all this peril. The Eagle studied the building intently. It was four stories high. Adjoining it, with an alley no more than three feet wide, was a building of similar height. That structure was darkened and apparently not in use.

Shannon smiled grimly. He walked on up the street, turned to look in a store window when a gendarme approached and passed him by. Then he darted across the street and straight down an alley almost a full block from Gestapo headquarters. Like a ghost he flitted from one rear courtyard to another, climbing intervening fences agilely and making very little noise.

He reached the rear of the building next door to the Gestapo head-quarters and found the door boarded up. The windows were unguarded, although locked. He used a small penknife to slide back the lock, as he had done at Karl Wunderlich's house in Budapest—something that seemed to him to have happened months ago, though a matter of hardly more than forty-eight hours had since elapsed.

He climbed into the building, stifled a sneeze brought on as the dust of weeks stirred up. Closing the window, he locked it again, and by sense of touch found his way to the stairway leading to the floors above. Finally he reached the roof, opened a skylight an inch and peered out across the roof and over to the roof of the building he wanted to enter. He breathed deeply in relief when he saw no guards posted there.

Examining the distance between buildings, he walked back and started a run. He jumped, cleared the alley easily and landed with a thud. He was up in a flash and running for the protection of a chimney. Nothing happened, and he guessed that the thump had not been heard.

He approached the skylight, forced the lock with a minimum of noise and as he opened the door, he heard the rumbling of machinery. His eyes narrowed. He had struck it right. The spurious currency was being printed here, probably along with a lot of propaganda literature.

As he slipped down the stairs he drew back just in time, for a uni-formed guard with holstered pistol came strolling along. Shannon had selected a wash-room as his refuge. The guard ambled by and the Eagle went into action. He moved silently up from behind, seized the man in a grip that stopped any attempts to cry out and at the same time yanked the man's gun free of its holster.

He brought the butt of the weapon down effectively, caught the man as he slumped to the floor and carried him into the washroom. There were several lockers there. He opened one, stuffed the man inside and closed the door. Air vents would prevent suffocation.

Now the Eagle had to work fast, for when that guard recovered, he would set up a devil's din.

The presses stopped suddenly. The Eagle heard several men moving about. Four of them, including the messenger Shannon had trailed, had finished their work and were headed toward the washroom.

Jeff Shannon held his breath, for they were removing overalls as they walked along. If that locker belonged to one of them, he was done for. His heart pounded while he waited for any reaction. Then two of the men came out, conversing affably. Shannon breathed normally for the first time in minutes.

HE SLIPPED into the room from which the men had originally emerged and discovered that it contained a complete printing plant. One weak light had been left burning. Over in one corner was a bench and cabinets filled with chemicals. In the center of the floor were three big presses.

The Eagle examined them and grunted in admiration for the work done here. Two of the presses were set up with plates to manufacture United States currency. This was a peculiar situation. In most cases of counterfeiting United States money the destruction or confiscation of the plates meant virtual cessation of the work, but here, in a mint maintained and abetted by a complete government, such action would only result in the engraving of new plates. There were plenty of capable engravers.

Shannon made sure that he did not touch any part of the machinery. He examined the ink reservoir which fed the two machines. They were half full.

He tiptoed over to the bench and miniature laboratory and saw that some trained chemist had been experimenting with colors in order to get the exact shade used by the United States mint. He studied the bottles of chemicals and selected two of them, hurriedly mixing a portion of their contents in a beaker, glad that he had majored in chemistry. Half of this resultant liquid he poured into the ink reservoirs of the printing machines. Next he located more of the ink, in huge metal drums. He opened these and poured in some of the chemicals he had mixed. Then he carefully rinsed out the beaker, replaced everything and started in on the more dangerous part of his work.

His ears were attuned for the first sounds of trouble emanating from the washroom and the guard imprisoned there. So far Shannon had spent only fifteen minutes in this printing plant and he reasoned that the blow which the guard had suffered would keep him quiet about another half hour.

He turned on all lights, hoping that if this were noticed from the street that no one would inquire as to the reason. Then he brought out his tiny watch camera and began taking pictures, registering about twenty shots before he was satisfied.

Then he doused the lights again, walked into the corridor and listened. He could hear voices from the floor below. Just in front of him was a window overlooking the street. He peered out and then drew back hastily. Another of those official cars—the only automobiles that still operated in Austria—had pulled up. One of the guards opened the door, and Ethel Landreth stepped out!

The Eagle's hopes, which had soared high during the last few moments, dropped into his shoes. She could be here for only one reason—to relate how he had trailed the messenger. Fritz Pommer would not need three guesses to know why this had been done, and from that moment on, the building would be searched and guarded.

He watched her enter the building. She had removed her peasant dress, and wore smartly modern clothing now. Then he heard her high heels clicking against the steps, accompanied by the tread of military boots. Someone knocked on a door.

"*Fraulein* Landreth, Excellency," a man's voice announced, and then the gruff, uncompromising tones of the Gestapo leader requested her to enter.

The Eagle gauged the location of the room into which she had gone. It must be directly below the printing plant. He ran back into the big room, opened a window and looked out. It faced the rear of the building and was not under observation.

Prowling around until he found a coil of sturdy looking rope, he tied one end of it to the machinery and let it drop out the window. He hauled himself up on the sill, took a hitch in the rope by coiling it loosely around his middle, then gently lowered himself. If he were spotted now, he would be riddled on sight, but the Eagle was used to taking chances.

He discovered that there was a two-inch ledge running around the building and on a level with the window through which he wanted to peer. Also, that window was raised an inch or two and he could hear Pommer's voice. Shannon held on and listened.

"So, *Fraulein,* you did not know this American pig was a spy, eh? Perhaps! He tricked me for a moment or two. And he did have that cursed identification card. I sent for you because I wanted to warn you. There are grave consequences if you fail to obey me, you know that."

"I know," the girl answered sternly. "There is no need to remind me."

"Ah—good. Then here is what you must do. You say the American is still at your castle, or was when you left. That is well. I think I know why he risked his life to come over here, but I am not sure. He may even be a British spy and we must take no chances with him. Therefore, you will return to your castle at once. Make him comfortable, make him trust you, and find out why he has come. Tell him you hate the Gestapo. That will not be so hard, will it, *Fraulein?* At midnight be certain he is within his room and asleep. I shall come for him myself and awaken him—by thrusting a gun into his face. You understand what you are to do now?"

"I understand," she said calmly, "and I refuse. That man is an American. A newspaper man who is only trying to earn his living by getting the truth about conditions here. Why should I be instrumental in planning his death? No, *Herr* Pommer, you can force me to do many things, but not to aid in the murder of an innocent man!"

CHAPTER VII

OLD AMERICAN CUSTOM

JEFF SHANNON silently applauded Ethel Landreth, but realized that for his sake she was placing herself in a dangerous position. He braced one foot up against the ledge and moved quietly until he could look through the window.

Pommer was smiling suavely and reaching for the phone.

"Get me the concentration camp at Luntz," he ordered harshly. "I wish to talk to the commandant."

There was a moment of silence. The girl stepped forward a pace and then reached out one hand in a plea. Pommer sneered at her, got his connection and began talking in a loud voice.

"The prisoner Landreth—he is to be given sixty lashes immediately, then thrown into an unheated cell for ten days. He is to be fed nothing but black bread and only enough of that to maintain life. Each morning sixty more lashes in the presence of the other prisoners as an example to them."

"No!" the girl cried. "No—please! I—I will do it. My father, he is old. He cannot stand that punishment."

"The orders are countermanded for the time being," Pommer said into the phone. "But perhaps you shall have the pleasure of fulfilling them later on."

He hung up, clasped his hands together and leaned across his desk looking up into the frantic eyes of the girl.

"You are wise, *Fraulein*, for undoubtedly your father would die of that punishment and then I should have no hold on you. That would mean an end to your usefulness—and a concentration camp for you.

Neither of us would like that, I am sure. Go back now. Set your little trap for the American.

"If it were not for the fact that I desire his arrest to be kept a strict secret, I would send around a patrol. But if news leaked out, there would be reverberations from the American consulate. They can become a great nuisance when they have a mind to. You see, *Fraulein*, this affair is between the American and myself. I do not care if he is but a newsman. He struck me—and those who strike Fritz Pommer must be punished.

"That is all. But wait—you are absolutely certain he did not mention the money we ship to you? I have knowledge that this man, in fact, is an American agent trying to upset our little scheme of things."

"He did not mention the money," the girl said. "Why should he? He does not know I have any connection with the Gestapo."

She turned and walked out. For a moment Shannon felt like swinging himself back, kicking in the window and confronting Pommer without further delay. His fists ached to pound home some of the same punishment Pommer so casually ordered done to an old, inoffensive prisoner.

Instead he silently climbed back up the rope, into the printing rooms, then carefully replaced the rope, then moved toward the door.

At that moment the guard locked in the washroom apparently regained his wits enough to begin kicking. The Eagle streaked down the corridor toward the exit to the roof, hearing Pommer's voice bellowing for help. He reached the roof-top, but this time the outside guards were prepared for such an escape and their numbers had been augmented.

A rifle cracked and the bullet twanged against a metal rain gutter. Shannon darted for the chimney and wondered what he should do next. The men posted outside knew he was on the roof. Below, the building more than likely swarmed with agents, and Pommer would certainly have his suspicions as to the identity of the intruder.

IT CAME to him in a flash, while his mind still tried to find a way out, that Pommer knew he was at the Landreth castle. How had he obtained that information? Through Gherla? Who else?

Then Pommer's bellow sent all thoughts except those concerned with escape, out of the Eagle's mind. Pommer was determined to finish this matter effectively.

"It is an accursed *Englander* spy! He is to be shot on sight. If he gets away, your own heads will roll! Go up—get him! Shoot him for the dirty swine that he is."

The Eagle could not remain there, trusting to the protection of the chimney. He crouched low, ran like the wind and leaped across the alley to the adjoining roof. Rifles exploded again, but he could only be seen when he was near the edge of the roof.

He glanced over his shoulder. Half a dozen men, with Lugers in their fists, had popped out of the skylight door of Gestapo headquarters, but as yet they were not sure in which direction his flight had taken him.

He rushed to the exit from this roof. The door he had opened hung from one hinge and the other was loose. He wrenched it free, propped it against the doorway and then deliberately exposed himself to the men on the adjoining roof. They saw him and raised shouts for the outside guards to cover the abandoned building.

The Eagle, in partial view of his pursuers, apparently ducked through the door, but instead he gave that old door a push and it clattered noisily down the steps, hit the floor below with a resounding crash and the men who were now leaping across the alley believed Shannon had lost his footing and plunged down the steps. They were screaming this information as they sped toward the exit.

Flat on his stomach behind a skylight, the Eagle saw them stream past not a dozen feet away. The intense darkness protected him to a great extent. They all plunged through the doorway. The Eagle arose, ran like a deer across the roof and jumped back to the Gestapo building.

The guards below did not see him. They were busy closing in on the adjoining building. He scurried toward the skylight, slipped down the steep stairway and paused halfway. Pommer was berating the guard whom the Eagle had knocked cold.

"How long were you unconscious, fool?" Pommer yelled. "How long? I must know whether or not he had time to find the printing presses."

"Not more than a minute, Excellency," the guard lied. Pommer's ruthlessness was defeating his own purposes. The guard did not dare tell the truth. "I swear it was no more than that, and I was only stunned, Excellency. He did not reach the printing room."

"Report yourself to the barracks under arrest!" Pommer screamed. "Get out with you before I forget myself and use a gun on you."

The guard hurried away and clattered down the steps. The Eagle grinned tightly. Pommer was heading his way, making sure he was the last man to reach the roof and therefore certain not to expose himself in case the American decided to fight.

He did not look up as he started along the stairs. That is, not until he heard a swishing noise, and then it was much too late. All he saw was a giant form swooping down on him. He tried to scream, tried to raise the gun he held, but the utter surprise of the attack stunned him.

SHANNON CARRIED the Gestapo agent to the floor, pinned him there by the throat and wrested his gun free. He put the muzzle of it under Pommer's nose.

"Now, my fine friend," he said, "you'll take the orders for a change. Your car is out front. We're going to it and you won't tell a soul who I am. They're searching the next building for me and no one will suspect."

Pommer said, *"Glug-glug,"* a few times and the Eagle relaxed his grip around the man's throat.

"You understand," the American went on in perfect German, "one trick and you'll die—instantly. Also you will understand that it would be bad for your prestige if your men discovered you actually helped a spy escape. You would be stood against the wall and shot yourself. Get me out of here and they'll never know."

Pommer, blustering, cruel and domineering to those who served under him, was now a blubbering, quivering, terror-stricken man. His eyes implored the Eagle not to shoot. Curt nods of his head indicated that he agreed to the terms. Pommer seemed to have lost the power of speech through fear.

The Eagle raised him, jammed the gun against his back and they walked along the corridor, down two flights of stairs and out the front door. They met no one during this part of their trip. As they stepped out on the stone steps leading to the walk, four privates hastily came to attention and saluted.

Shannon prodded Pommer with the gun and he returned the salute. They climbed into Pommer's car and the Gestapo agent slid behind the wheel. His driver had disappeared, probably to aid in the search for the spy.

"Drive," the Eagle ordered. "Do it nice and easy or I'll handle the wheel myself and I couldn't very well do that unless you were dead. You're going for a ride, *Herr* Pommer. Just an old American custom."

Pommer gulped, started the motor and rolled away. The four privates still stood at attention, wondering just how it so happened that Pommer passed them by without berating them. Pommer, under the combined influence of the Eagle's soft voice and the uncompromising prods of the gun, drove out of the city in a northerly direction, away from the castle where *Fraulein* Ethel Landreth lived. The speedometer clicked off the miles until they were far into the country.

"You can stop now," Shannon ordered. "Then get out!"

"You are going to kill me!" Pommer howled dismally. "You are going to shoot me as I run away. I kept my word. You cannot do this to me."

"I could," the Eagle said, "if circumstances were different—and actually enjoy it—but I won't. Just get out. We part company here and I wish I had a fumigator in the car."

"But it is miles to anywhere," Pommer groaned. "What shall I do?"

Shannon gave him a violent push and threw him out of the car. The Gestapo leader arose and crouched in terror. The Eagle climbed out, searched the back of the car and found a tow rope. He forced Pommer deep in the forest that lined the road, put him against a tree and tied him firmly.

"Maybe I will put a bullet in you at that," he said coolly. "One thing can save your miserable skin. Tell me who passes the fake American money that is being spread all over Europe. Where is it made?"

"I don't know," Pommer lied. "I swear it! The Gestapo have nothing to do with it. Yes—it is being passed, but that is all I know. You cannot shoot me because I am unable to answer your questions. And you cannot leave me here. So far from anywhere. I will starve! How shall I get back?"

"Walk," the Eagle grinned. "The privates in your army do plenty of it and don't seem to suffer. Walk, and work off some of that fat, good, yellow butter which you deny the ordinary man and which you fill your stomach full of. Walk, Pommer! It's a nice night and I hope you stumble and break your thick neck. You can get free of those ropes in an hour or two, then you can yell your head off for help."

CHAPTER VIII

THE DOUBLECROSS

RETURNING TO the car, Jeff Shannon ground gears and shot away. He was headed straight for the Hungarian border, but many miles above the point near *Fraulein* Ethel Landreth's castle. He wanted to give the illusion that he was fleeing for his own safety and was apparently satisfied with the meager information he had wormed out of Pommer.

The Gestapo agent did not know he had invaded the printing plant. He had put the Eagle down as a poor fool with more mercy than brains. Yet Shannon realized that his next encounter with Pommer might be far different. The Gestapo sub-chief would gladly give a year's pay to get his hands on the intrepid American again.

At a crossroads the Eagle turned back, heading down a highway parallel with the one along which Pommer was tied. The chances of Pommer being picked up were meager, for only military and official cars were permitted to operate in this part of Austria, and they usually chose the best and shortest route from city to city. The road where Pommer had been abandoned was little used and not too smooth. The Gestapo agent could worry his ropes loose, but that would take time.

Suddenly Shannon's breath ceased. There was a barrier across the highway and soldiers with rifles barred his way. A powerful searchlight was trained on the car. Then, to his amazement, the barriers were hastily drawn back and the soldiers snapped to attention.

Then the Eagle discovered the significance of the two little flags fluttering from the fenders of the car. They saved him some embarrassing moments and possible capture, but also would serve notice on Pommer that he had doubled back. Hours might elapse before that information reached the Gestapo agent, but it would, in due course of time.

The Eagle's mission in Austria was done. He had foolproof evidence that the Gestapo were printing the money and he had played one other little trick which would surprise the Gestapo some day in the near future. Theoretically he should have fled to the Border and made his way into neutral country and the haven that it offered. But it rankled in his mind that Ethel Landreth had risked her life and her father's to save him.

He had to repay that favor and the best way was by rescuing both Ethel and her father. That this attempt might cost him his own life hardly occurred to the Eagle. One other reason motivated his apparently rash act. Through Ethel he might discover the identity of the real leader of the Gestapo in Budapest. Such knowledge could break up the league of money passers, at this source at least.

A full hour later he sent Pommer's car rolling up to the castle, but he did not stop there. Instead, he drove on by until he came to the lake. He opened the door of the car, climbed to the running board, then pulled the hand throttle all the way out. The powerful motor responded and the car seemed to leap forward.

He guided it skilfully until it was in a direct line with a small wharf. Then he jumped. He rolled over a couple of times and when he got back on his feet, the car had vanished and the lake surface was growing calm again.

He began walking back toward the castle, using a narrow, dark path. He had covered half the distance when a bulky shadow stepped squarely into the middle of the path and a gun was pointed straight at the Eagle's heart.

"Up!" the shadow grated.

SHANNON TENSED. His mind was made up to jump that gun though it meant a serious wound or even death, for certain doom awaited him if he should be turned over to Pommer.

Then he paused. There was something vaguely familiar about the squatness of the man. The Eagle raised his hands and moved forward. Recognition dawned on him.

"Hattie!" he exclaimed.

It was Hatvan, the owner of the inn where the Eagle had taken refuge in Budapest. The innkeeper lowered his weapon, came closer and suddenly threw both arms around Shannon.

"*Herr* Shannon!" he cried. "*Ach*, I came so close to shooting you. Come—we must get inside the castle at once. There are Gestapo agents everywhere. I have been waiting for you. That car—it went into the lake. Was it not an official car?"

The Eagle explained as they hurried hack toward the castle.

"But you, Hattie," he asked. "What on earth are you doing here?"

Hatvan looked a little sheepish.

"You will know anyhow, so I might as well tell you. Gherla has informed me of what happened on the train. He says you are to be trusted. It is like this—I operate a little smuggling business. Yes, I take Austrian refugees across the lake in my boat. Naturally I charge for it, because it is expensive. They must be hidden here, guards bribed to let them escape. Then in Budapest they must be well hidden until I can get them out of the country."

"And the girl—Ethel Landreth?" Shannon queried.

"Let her answer for herself," Hatvan said.

The back door of the big house had opened and she stood there in the dim light.

She took Shannon's arm and they walked to the main floor and into the living room. Hatvan had disappeared.

"He has gone into the cellars where the refugees are hidden," Ethel explained. "Where have you been? Oh, I was a fool not to have believed you! Now I know that you spoke the truth, for a Gestapo summoned me and demanded that I set a trap for you."

"Or your father would be lashed sixty times each day," the Eagle put in. "I know all about it, *Fraulein*. When he spoke to you, I was hanging outside the window of his office. But there is no time to lose. I kidnaped the estimable *Herr* Pommer and then dropped him twenty miles out in the country. He'll get help sooner or later and when he does, he'll come here first. We're in a bad trap—you, I, Gherla, Hatvan and all those poor refugees hidden in your cellar. There are things I must know. The money sent here tonight—how is it collected? How is it smuggled across the Border?"

"I'm not sure. My orders are to place it on a wharf jutting out over the lake. A boat must pick it up. I can tell you just how the thing is worked. Nazi traders cross the Hungarian border and they are searched. Plenty of good American money is found in their luggage and it is passed. Then the tradesmen contact the Gestapo in Budapest, exchange the good money for the false and peddle it. If Hungarian merchants become suspicious and phone their government officials, they are told it is genuine because they believe it is the same money that was taken across the Border by those very tradesmen."

"Clever," the Eagle acknowledged. "No wonder so much of it is being spread all over Europe. Now about Hatvan? He is reliable enough, I suppose?"

"Oh yes," she told him. "He has been taking refugees across the lake ever since *Anchluss*. You can go with him tonight. Gherla is going."

SHANNON SHOOK his head soberly.

"Unless you go, then I stay, too. Isn't there some way to get your father out of that prison camp? And you, *Fraulein*, you look more American than Austrian. That alone influences me."

"I am all American," she answered quietly. "I was born in New York where Father had his business. He never became a citizen and just before the trouble started, we returned to Vienna to see his people. The Germans came before we could get away. They seized Father and threatened him with death if I made any complaint to the United States embassy. Father was, at one time, a burgomaster just outside Vienna and his three brothers were high in the government. They are—dead now. No matter what happens, I will not leave unless my father comes with me or"—she looked down at the floor—"he is killed."

"Exactly how I feel," the Eagle told her.

She arose, stood beside him and put both hands on his shoulders.

"No, that must not be. I shall not permit you to lose your life, for it would be in vain. If Pommer connected you with my father, or even with me, he would take steps. I will not have the blood of two men on my hands."

"We'll call a council of war right now," Shannon said, disregarding her words entirely. "Hattie can make two trips if he can negotiate one. We'll see if we can't get your father out—tonight. Nothing is impossible when your heart is in it. And I have another confession to make. I am not a reporter. I am an American secret agent. As such, it is my duty to see that you reach safety and if you refuse to go without your father, well, he goes, too. Now can you understand?"

She was crying softly when Gherla and Hatvan entered. The Eagle explained the situation to them in briefly put words.

"You can either take your load of refugees to Hungarian soil and come back for us, or wait here, Hattie. Gherla, you can't help because you're a marked man."

"And you," Gherla put in sourly, "walk about as invisible as a ghost. If Pommer suspects you are here—and he knows you were—he'll tear this castle apart. This will be the first place he'll come."

"Then it's up to you, Hattie." The Eagle turned to the walrus-mustached innkeeper. "Put the refugees on your boat, shove off, but wait just out of sight. I'll hail you when we come back."

"You mean 'if'," Gherla said again. "I will have nothing to do with it. You are risking Ethel's life. Hatvan, I go with you. When you are ready, call me. I am going to my room."

The Eagle watched Gherla walk out the door and his eyes narrowed slightly. Was this man really going to his room or was he planning to slip away and warn Pommer of the plot? Shannon shrugged. It didn't matter—not with the plan he had in mind. Pommer could search all of Austria for him if he cared to, because by the time Pommer got into action, the Eagle hoped to be out of his jurisdiction.

"I'm going to take a chance," he told Ethel and Hatvan. "I still have this Gestapo card and I'm banking on the fact that Pommer hasn't bothered to notify the garrison at the Lutz prison that it is a fake. With it I can reach your father, *Fraulein*, and from there on things will fly. Pommer may come here. If he does, say I was gone when you got back and that you haven't seen me since. Wish me luck!"

HALF AN hour later Shannon got off the trolley in the city three miles from the lake. Pommer could not have returned yet and the Eagle was comparatively safe, for no one else knew his identity.

He started to walk up the sidewalk and had covered a block before he became aware that he was being followed. Two men were behind him. He looked for a chance to escape. Two more were coming toward him from the front. Four others were crossing the street. Guns flashed. Jeff Shannon groaned and surrendered.

He had never been trapped quite so neatly. Pommer must have returned. His captors seized his arms and without a word escorted him to the police station. He was whisked past the officer at the desk and thrown into a cell. The door clanged with a grim finality that tore into the Eagle's heart. He had failed miserably.

He glanced at his watch which he still had, for they had not troubled to search him, and had not taken anything away from him. It was little more than an hour since he had dumped Pommer out. The man could not have reached the city even if he had been lucky enough to thumb a ride. Therefore, someone else had tipped the police as to his arrival and appearance.

The Eagle's eyes blazed. Gherla? Hatvan? A refugee who was supposed to be hidden in the cellar? Or—Ethel Landreth? Women had been known to go to all extremes to save the lives of those they loved. Was she trying to obtain clemency for her father at Shannon's expense? He put the thought aside as absurd.

Forty-five minutes crawled by. Then the tramp of feet aroused Jeff Shannon. He looked between the bars and gulped. Two Gestapo agents were approaching, and between them walked—*Fraulein* Ethel Landreth!

CHAPTER IX

THE EAGLE'S PLAN

FRAULEIN ETHEL LANDRETH stood before the cell and gestured.

"It is too dark," she murmured. "How can I identify him?"

They opened the door for her, but both men held exposed revolvers. She looked up at Shannon, gave a derisive sneer and struck him across the face.

"Yes, it is he. There is no question about it. I.... Be careful—the cell door is closing. We'll be locked—"

Both men turned around. The cell door had been slowly closing. They snickered at the girl's alarm, led her out and the door slammed shut again. One of them paused long enough to taunt the Eagle.

"At daybreak you will face a firing squad. Your name will be German. You will be listed as a traitor. Sleep well, my friend."

To the Eagle, the whole world seemed awry. The girl he trusted and risked his life to save had betrayed him.

He turned away and something sagged in his pocket. He brought out a Luger pistol, fully loaded and he felt like giving vent to a whoop of pleasure. Thank heaven they *hadn't* searched him, feeling so sure of themselves, or they would never have overlooked that!

There was no time to lose. He picked up a tin cup and rattled it across the bars. A guard, sleepy and slow, bellowed that he was coming. He reached out his hand for the cup assuming that Jeff Shannon wanted water. Instead he looked into the wrong end of a gun.

"Open the door!" the Eagle snarled. "Open it, or I'll plaster you against the wall!"

The guard obeyed promptly. The Eagle took his keys away, used the gun butt effectively, and locked the guard in his own cell. He walked cautiously back to the main door and listened. Everyone was out in front discussing the prisoner.

He unlocked the door and started up the narrow corridor. Now he would shoot his way clear if necessary.

"Shannon!"

The voice brought him around with a jerk. He saw a short hallway to his left. At the end of it a door was invitingly open and *Fraulein* Ethel Landreth beckoned him. He hurried out.

"Pommer has just returned," she whispered hastily. "They will discover that I have not played fair. Not long after you left, two of the Gestapo came to see me, asked me to identify you. Hatvan and Gherla had already gone on their boat. I came because I knew I must do something. When they tell Pommer I visited you, he will know I came to help you. Now do you realize why you must go—quickly? The boat is waiting, and—"

"I go when your father goes with me," the Eagle whispered. "Let's get out of here and then I'll tell you exactly what to do."

They faded into the darkness, reached a small, deserted beer parlor and went inside. They took a corner table, near a side door and Shannon talked swiftly. The girl's eyes lit up at the sheer audacity of the plan he proposed.

"I will do it because I know it is the only way to save your life and my father's," she said. "Give me fifteen minutes."

She eased out the side door and vanished. The Eagle had given her his gun. He drank a stein of beer, enjoyed it to the last drop and then arose. He stretched his arms and sauntered out onto the street.

GESTAPO HEADQUARTERS was about four blocks north, and he headed in that direction. Everything was calm now and he had no trouble in reaching the rear of the abandoned building next door. He went to the roof, leaped across the alley and then moved softly toward the skylight door.

Then he paused. One uniformed soldier stood guard. Pommer's underlings were taking no chances of anyone using this entrance again.

The Eagle picked up a small pebble from among those with which the roof was coated, snapped it with his thumb nail and heard it land twenty feet away from the guard. Instantly the Nazi's rifle came up and he advanced threateningly.

Shannon sprang forward silently and he required no more than two minutes to put this man out of action. Then he brushed off his clothes, smiled a little and walked sedately down the steps. He could hear the presses rumbling. Apparently a night shift had been put to work in order that the spurious money could be shipped quickly, before anyone could expose the plot to the neutral countries for whom it was destined.

There were no guards around and he proceeded to the third floor. An orderly hurried toward the exit and the Eagle gave him time to disappear. Then he walked straight to Pommer's office. Someone was talking harshly as he opened the door.

Pommer sat behind his desk. Two men faced him, both at stiff attention. The Gestapo agent was giving the orders for a raid on Ethel Landreth's castle and instructions to guard every means of exit over the Border.

"This man must he captured at all costs!" he raged. "And he is not to be killed unless it becomes a question of escape on his part. I want him, do you understand?"

The Eagle stepped into the office and closed the door gently. He moved forward a pace. Pommer looked up, blinked twice and then catapulted out of his chair. The two men whirled. They saw Shannon and reached for their guns. The Eagle promptly raised both hands. Pommer came up to him, drew back his fist and his thick lips parted in a smile of genuine pleasure.

"I wouldn't," Shannon said softly. "Before I came here, I notified the United States Embassy as to my whereabouts. They know I am here and unless they hear from me within one hour, every agency of my government will be put to work for my release."

"Your government!" Pommer just sniffed contemptuously. "A soft democracy that will hesitate for months before they do anything. And what do I care if they act? You are guilty of assault on a high official—me!"

The Eagle grinned broadly.

"Sure—that was fun. But Pommer, do you forget that your own government punishes men who fail in their work? Now, if you were to arrest me, everyone would know that you aided in my escape, and—"

"Silence!" Pommer roared. He turned to the other men who were staring in awe at the audacity of this American. "Get out! Out with you, and if you so much as whisper what you heard here, I shall take steps. Out!"

The two men filed through the door. Pommer closed it, turned the lock and drew a gun. He walked over to his desk and sat down. The Eagle pulled up a chair and started to sit also.

"On your feet—pig," Pommer roared. "You are in the presence of a high official."

Shannon just grinned and sat down. "Not me, Pommer. You're just a bad natured tub of lard. Now let's talk terms."

POMMER'S PHONE rang. He barked into it. Then he listened carefully and asked the caller to come at once. The Eagle began to feel uneasy. Pommer seemed very sure of himself now.

About three minutes later someone tapped on the door. Pommer unlocked it and a tall, hatchet-faced man strode in. Pommer saluted and stood at attention while the new arrival strode up to where the Eagle sat and stared at him.

Now Shannon's heart really sank. This man was one of the most important international spies which the Nazi government employed. The Eagle had run into him before, in Central America, many months before when a spy ring had attempted to set up a base for operations against the Panama Canal.

"Yes," this man nodded curtly. "You have captured a most important person, *Herr* Pommer. My congratulations. This man is—the Eagle!"

Pommer's eyes popped wide open and a cruel smile played around the corners of his mouth.

"Thank you, *Herr* Baron," he said, and bowed. "I suspected as much when I broadcast a description of him. So he is the Eagle! Which means he operates alone and that his own government probably has no knowledge of his whereabouts."

"I am sure of that," the man called baron said. "I questioned certain people discreetly, and I know he has not contacted the American representative here. He is a valuable man. He knows more about international affairs than anyone. Talk to him, Pommer. Give him his life for information that will be valuable to us. Especially the defenses around the Panama Canal. I leave him in your hands and if he does not talk— then there will be a little accident, eh?"

The Eagle said nothing. He recognized the cold murder gleaming in Pommer's eyes and wondered if he had bitten off more than he could digest. Pommer let the baron out, locked the door once more and faced Shannon.

"You will talk, of course. I promise that for the information I require, your life will be granted to you. First draw me a comprehensive map and be quick about it. I am in no mood to dicker."

Shannon shrugged, picked up a pencil and arose. He walked over to the wall beside a closet. With a long sweep of the pencil he created lines to represent the canal. Pommer moved over beside him, breathlessly waiting for the work to he completed. The Eagle turned his head toward Pommer.

"How'd you like to die?" he asked blandly.

Pommer gulped and started to raise his gun. Then he felt the cold, round muzzle of another weapon gently touch his neck. He slowly lowered his gun. The Eagle took it out of his hand.

"Beautifully done, *Fraulein,*" he said. "Pommer, get back of your desk and sit down. If you've heard of the Eagle, as you intimated a moment ago that you had, then you know I do not compromise. Either you do exactly what I tell you—or they'll find what's left of you with a slug through your head."

Pommer looked from Shannon to *Fraulein* Landreth. His face was covered with sweat. A vein in his forehead throbbed and his eyes were crammed with fear. He nodded at him weakly.

"Pick up the phone, call the prison camp at Lutz and have them send this girl's father here at once," ordered the Eagle. "Say that you wish to question him alone. They are to use all speed. Get going!"

He tickled Pommer's nose with the muzzle of the Luger pistol and the Gestapo agent shivered violently. Pommer called the prison, gave his orders and then all three sat in grim silence for three quarters of an hour.

Someone tapped on the door then. The Eagle took the gun from Ethel Landreth, ejected the bullets, and then handed the empty weapon to Pommer.

"Keep me covered while you let him in—but remember, you're covered too, and my gun has fangs!"

CHAPTER X

THE EAGLE'S MARK

TWO SECONDS later an elderly, and white-haired man whose face was lined from hunger and worry, held his daughter close. The Eagle grinned. All this was worthwhile just to see the expression on her face.

Shannon gestured with his gun. Pommer sat down.

"Write a pass for the girl and her father," he ordered. "Have a car ready at the front door. You've been sensible so far, *Herr* Pommer. Don't get foolish now."

Pommer wrote the pass, phoned to have the car waiting. The Eagle whispered to the girl, let her and her father out, then he calmly put the gun into his pocket. He walked up to Pommer, grabbed him by the necktie and hauled him out of the chair.

"Now we'll have a little argument," he said smoothly. "Without guns or knives."

The Eagle would have admitted that Pommer fought, and fought furiously, because he thought his life hung in the balance. It lasted about three minutes and when it was over, Pommer lay stretched out on the floor, blissfully unaware of animate things. Shannon mopped blood from a cut over one eye, drew his gun, went to the door, and opened it a crack.

No one was outside. He stepped into the hallway. It was early morning and apparently no strong guard was maintained after midnight. He reached the first floor without being intercepted, but outside the door were the two soldiers on duty.

Pulling his hat down, he stalked out, and the guards instantly brought their guns to present. The Eagle raised his hand in a return salute and acknowledged fervent thanks that in this battered, humbled country new officials wandered about, and that mere soldiers had no way of telling an enemy from a man high up in party circles.

Shannon opened the front door of the car parked at the curb, got in and shoved his gun against the driver's side. He snapped an order. The car rolled away. Along a quiet street he used his pistol butt on the driver, appropriated the man's own pistol, laid him out in a dark alley, and then drove furiously toward the castle.

As he rolled to a stop near the water's edge he tooted the horn and blinked the lights. The ray of a flash answered him and a motor broke into life. A good-sized launch pulled up to the wharf.

The Eagle helped the girl and her father out of the car, hurried to the boat and saw Hatvan grinning in good humor. Gherla merely gaped in astonishment at the sight of the white-haired owner of the castle.

"There's a spy among you," Shannon told Hatvan. "Order everyone out. Line them up and search them. This includes your own men, Hattie, hurry! The Gestapo will be on our necks at any minute."

HATVAN GOGGLED at the Eagle, but obeyed the orders. The men were lined up, Shannon stepped aboard the launch. Finally he called to Hatvan and the burly innkeeper reported that he had found nothing on any of the men.

"We can't wait any longer," the Eagle snapped. "Let's get out of here."

They piled aboard again and the launch shoved off. Nobody spoke while the minutes flew by. The craft traveled without lights and complete silence was necessary, for fast Nazi boats were patrolling the lake.

They were halfway across before anyone said a word. Then Hatvan yawned and stretched. That seemed to be some kind of a signal, for all his men suddenly reached deep into the craft, tossed aside a tarpaulin and raised the submachine-guns. Hatvan smiled complacently.

"The time has come for us to part, my friends," he talked rapidly. "I thank all of you for the money and jewels you have paid me, for the information you have given about your relatives, who still reside in German territory. Now you have your choice. Get out and swim, since it is only five miles to the nearest land—or die by gunfire.

"You have three minutes. All except my good and stupid friend, *Herr* Shannon, who thinks he pulled the wool over my eyes. *Herr* Shannon, it may gratify your interest to know that I am head of the Gestapo in Budapest, that I knew your identity from the beginning and merely bided my time.

"You will not swim ashore or be shot—yet. Nor will the girl and her father. All of you are going back. I think Fritz Pommer may enjoy inflicting whatever punishment he wishes upon all three of you."

The Eagle did not stir. Ethel Landreth gave a despairing cry, and her father held her closely. Bitter defeat shone on the faces of the refugees. Four submachine-guns were covering them.

"So you're the mysterious gentleman," Shannon said quietly. "I walked into a neat trap. And Hattie, you take money to carry these poor people to what they believe to be safety. Instead you dump them out. They trust you and willingly talk, so that you get valuable information besides money. No one could possibly catch onto your little game. You betrayed me, sent word that I was in the city and had me arrested. You directed every move that imperiled my life. Hattie, in plain Detroit language, you're a heel."

Hatvan chuckled. "So? I am complimented, *Herr* Shannon—or shall I say, the Eagle? Oh yes, Pommer got in touch with me. There is a telephone hidden in the woods near the castle. I knew you were coming. Now it seems that our refugee passengers wish to die by the gun instead of drowning. I shall accommodate them. Attention! Aim your guns. Fire!"

The refugees threw themselves down. There was a series of clicking sounds. The Gestapo spies gaped and examined their weapons. Hatvan started to reach for his pocket.

The Eagle's gun covered the lot of them. Gherla had another, and he was smiling triumphantly. Shannon pushed Hatvan into one of the rail seats of the launch.

"You didn't fool me long, Hattie. I unloaded those guns and slipped Gherla a Luger. The moment you told me you spent four years in Detroit, you put a great big foot in your month. No alien could learn to speak such good English in four years. Not in Detroit where the aliens congregate in one group and speak their own language all the time. But you did spend plenty of time in the United States—as a spy.

"You searched my baggage and cooked up a phony story about being assaulted by two Gestapo agents. You exhibited a bruise on your face. But you hit yourself and that ring on your third finger marked your face with its own pattern.

"You wormed your way into the confidence of the American consulate under the name of Hans Lustig. I phoned you from your own inn. You answered that private wire in your office, used a disguised voice and gave yourself completely away, because I didn't have to listen at the receiver to hear you talk. Your voice came right out of that little office in the lobby.

"You knew I was taking the train to Bratislava and nobody else knew it, therefore you alone could have tipped off the Gestapo to look out for me. You knew that Karl Wunderlich and his men had been arrested and that I might have a Gestapo card, but you didn't know that I had also found a code message, flown by carrier pigeon to Wunderlich. It gave me the lead which I followed straight to Ethel Landreth's home.

"Hatvan, you're a rat! So it's five miles to shore, eh? Want to try swimming it—you and your band of human vultures?"

Hatvan cringed and shuddered. The Eagle made a wry face.

"It's too bad I'm not your breed, Hattie, because then I could go through with it. The best I can do is turn you over to the Budapest authorities and hope to thunder they have a murder rap hanging over your head. Now let's all just take things easy and watch out for patrols. Gherla, you pilot this tub."

DRESSED IN clean clothing, completely rested and fresh, Shannon walked into the American consulate in Budapest the next day. He shook hands with Craig and accepted a chair.

"It's all finished," he reported. "Twenty million dollars in phony currency will be smuggled over the Border soon. Your job is to publicize its presence here and tell all traders that if they wet that phony dough, the ink will run. I diluted the ink with a chemical that makes it anything but color fast. Even a wet finger-tip will smear it.

"Then here are films—pictures of the counterfeiting plant in operation. Have 'em published. Whenever Nazi agents try to pass United States currency from now on, I'm betting the Hungarians will test every bill. The Gestapo won't try this trick again—not after it's been made public all through Europe."

Craig whistled in admiration.

"I can't ask you how it was done, Marvin, because you're not exactly an official representative of the United States. But I will say you handled it well. Why, the Eagle couldn't have done a better job! Now can I help you in any way, John Marvin?"

Shannon, accepting the name of Marvin, which he earlier had given to Craig, nodded.

"There's a citizen of the United States in the waiting room. Issue her a passport and give her father an entry permit. I'll take care of their tickets back to the United States. That's the only reward I ask."

While Shannon talked, he was idly tracing something on a piece of paper. Craig started things rolling for the passport and entry permit. He shook hands with Shannon again, and watched him walk out, then sat down.

He saw the piece of paper on which Shannon had been tracing something. Craig's eyes grew wide and round. Shannon had drawn a neat picture of an Eagle, with talons outspread, beak and wings wide in flight.

Craig leaned back, folded the piece of paper and tore it into shreds.

"Imagine that," he said to the empty room. "He *was* the Eagle!"

VI

THE BLACK
DRAGON

CHAPTER I

SHADOWS OF UNREST

THE LEAN American officer watching in the shadow of the balcony window, stiffened slightly and stared more intently down into the courtyard.

The quietness of the courtyard was intensified by contrast with the noise and clamor in the city. It was carnival time in Manila and the echoes of blaring horns and the faint shouts of pleasure seeking multitudes broke in faint waves of sound over the high walls. The carnival spirit possessed the crowds. Gaily costumed, joyous and elated, they filled the highways and byways, the Luneta and the Escolta were jammed with masked revelers and the streets were already ankle deep with confetti and bright-hued paper.

And yet the American knew the spirit of this year's carnival was unlike that of any other carnival. The gaiety was there but it was brittle. The joyous spirits of the crowd were evident but there was something semi-hysterical in its clamor. The multitudes sought for pleasure but there was a strange feverishness about their search, as though they were weaving above a volcano, or dancing the wild dance of the Tarantula, dancing to deaden the rumble of thunder on the horizon, gyrating in frenzied effort to still the fears that were in men's hearts.

It was in effort to determine the source of that strange fear that Captain Travis Gordon stood in the shadows of the balcony window, watching the dark doorway on the opposite side. Behind that door, if his reasoning was correct, was a thread that might lead to the focal point of that strange cancer of evil that was blighting men's minds in Manila.

Gordon had watched that shadowed doorway for two hours and it had not yet opened. From his own quarters, darkened against the afternoon heat, he could see the fountain, most of the intervening courtyard and that doorway, its panels of darkened wood looking somber in the shade, its brass knocker green with neglect. There was no sound, as he

stared, unseen and motionless, except the gurgle of the fountain splash-ing away gently.

Above its plaintive murmur came wave on wave of distant sound, a clamor compounded of men's voices and the blaring of horns, beating ceaselessly against the walls of the house. So intense was the tropical heat that the *patio* and the house which surrounded it were alike drenched into a dazed and stricken silence. But silence does not necessarily mean lack of life. Silence will sometimes cover the most active and malignant type of life.

The courtyard gave no sign. It was quiet except for the fountain which lisped and whispered, discoursing after the fashion of running waters. There was a musical rise and fall of liquid melody which sounded sometimes like the faint ringing of innumerable silver bells, again like the distant confusion of the roar of vast crowds in a beleaguered city and softened anon into the voice of a woman murmuring happily to her lover.

"Gecko! Gecko! Gecko!" The silence was shattered by the monotonous, unhurried call of the "gecko" lizard coming from somewhere in the courtyard. The cry of the lizard seemed part of a hot Philippine afternoon.

Something glittering
flashed through the air.

Gordon wondered idly if the gecko lizard ever called at night. He could
not remember ever having heard one.

Suddenly he stiffened into sudden alertness, and withdrew more deeply into the shadows of his own room. For the door across the courtyard was opening slowly.

A MAN came out, holding his head low, his Panama hat well down over his eyes.

Gordon gave one quick glance at that slightly sagging left shoulder, that slightly dragging left leg and the slackness of that left arm in its sleeve to engrave the picture of the man on his brain for future reference and then concentrated his attention upon the doorway behind him to see who would follow.

If the half-caste was there he would undoubtedly come out. The door opened to its full width, this time to allow the passage of a bloated, yellow-featured, waddling man in creased and stained linen.

"So!" Gordon's lips moved soundlessly as the two men disappeared into the street. "We have our old friend José Toribio, alleged head of the Katipunan, holding secret conferences with an unknown semi-paralytic. Now who in the devil is that fellow with the crippled left side?"

Old timers, officers and soldiers who sweated and bled in the Philippine Insurrection of the late '90s, would have remembered the Katipunan, the dread Filipino secret society with its hand raised against all Americans. But only three white met in the entire Philippine Archipelago knew that the ancient society had come to life again under the leadership of José Toribio, the ex-Bilibid convict, the enemy of the Philippine Commonwealth and the American Government.

And Travis Gordon was one of these three men.

He had taken this apartment because of its proximity to Toribio's dwelling simply on a hunch, one of those hunches that are the necessary equipment of a good intelligence officer. And now Toribio was justifying his following of that hunch.

"Is the crippled one a Filipino?" he whispered over his shoulder.

"No, *Capitan*," came a slow and measured voice from the shadows behind him, and like some formless white-coated wraith, Sing, the Chino servant, detached himself from the darkness. "Him come from Shanghai, six seven days. Sing no catchem his name yet. Him not Chinee fellow!"

Shanghai? That was getting closer! Gordon went swiftly to the telephone, called a number and spoke low voiced.

"Captain Gordon speaking. Yes, cable immediately—the Sports editor of the Shanghai paper—yes. Message—

"'Shanghai bush leaguer with crippled south paw joining local team from what club and what is batting average query.'"

He had the message repeated and then hung up. There was a glint of amusement in his eyes, for he loved to put one over on the little bespectacled slant-eyed Japanese who solemnly read every cable that came into China. There was one infallible way of throwing them into a tail-spin and that was to send a message in sports slang, over which they would spend weeks of fruitless endeavor and be driven close to the verge of committing *hari-kari*.

Then his face grew serious again. There was little time to gather in all the separate threads of the thing that was causing this strange unrest in Manila. He had nothing to work upon. A hint here, a hunch there. He needed more data.

The telephone rang. It was the cheerful voice of Rogers, the Nth Field Artillery, who, in addition to his many other activities, was captain of the polo team at Pasay.

"Hi, old horse!" greeted Rogers. "We need you at Number Two today. I'll mount you on Betty and my Highball horse…"

"Call that thing a horse!" interjected Gordon.

"…and Timons is giving you his Kitty mare and Peroxide," Rogers went on, ignoring the insult.

Gordon waited for the real message.

"By the way, there's a whale of a good looking girl going to be here. White Russian, from Shanghai, in tow of a male relative. Father or uncle or something. One of the busted Russian aristocrats. She's an eyeful! Also there's a nice little Dutchman up from the Dutch East Indies, rubber or something. He'll call on you at home tonight. Boy, can he put away sloe gin fizzes! Thought you might like to meet him. I'm counting on you for Number Two. So long!"

In such casual fashion did Rogers relay important orders.

Gordon quietly hung up the telephone with a new lift to his shoulders.

Here was something definite to tackle. The Dutch sending him a man from their rich island possessions to the southward, those island possessions so coveted by Tokio. It gave him a sudden thrill there in the shadows, the realization that they were all pulling together here in the Far East, Dutch, French, British and Americans. United quietly against the menace of Hitler in Europe and the cynical opportunism of Japan in Asia.

But the White Russians? Where did they fit into the picture? The answer came to him instantly. Of course, Japanese! The pieces of the puzzle were beginning slowly to fit into place, nebulous as yet and only partially discernible.

But the Pasay Polo Club was his information center and the gathering place of his aides.

Sing waited before him patiently.

"Maybe you likem cocktail?" suggested Sing gently, whereby Gordon knew that the Chino had other things than cocktails to discuss.

"Not now. What's on your mind, Sing?"

"Me findem Pedro making *habla* with José Toribio's *muchacho.*"

Pedro was his Number Two boy, Sing's assistant, a Tagalog. Pedro was whispering with Toribio's servant! It might mean anything or nothing.

"Keep an eye on him, Sing," grunted Gordon and strode to his bedroom.

Sing looked out across the courtyard to the dark doorway that led into Toribio's quarters. Staring at this non-committally, he folded his hands into his capacious sleeves and faded silently out of the picture.

Gordon turned to his bed where his polo clothes, the white breeches, the boots and spurs, the soft linen shirt and the gloves were all laid out in shining spotlessness.

It was when he was slipping the tongue of the boot straps into the buckle that he heard the row from the kitchen.

Deeming it to be no more than the regular daily rows between the three native house boys and the Chino, he paid little heed.

But suddenly his ears were assaulted by a howl of agony. Hurrying through the dining room and thrusting aside the kitchen doors, he stood startled at the scene which presented itself.

Pedro, the Number Two boy, was armed with a long and vicious Malay *kris,* one of Gordon's own collection as he saw at a glance. The other two "boys" were variously accoutered with a Jolo spear and a *bolo,* one of those heavy bladed, razor sharp weapons, equally good at slicing away sections of tangled jungle or men's heads.

They were advancing upon Sing, who was armed with nothing but a coffee pot. It had been filled with scalding hot coffee. Brown stains and a look of dire pain upon the face of Pedro showed that Sing had defended himself with the nearest weapon at hand.

Gordon wasted no words. Riding-crop in hand, he struck one boy, knocked another one against the wall and slapped the third so that they all ran howling from the kitchen.

Sing, belligerently waving the now empty coffee pot, looked after them angrily.

"I wish to God, Sing, you'd stop fighting with the house boys. Why in blazes can't you keep them under discipline?" asked Gordon impatiently.

CHINO COOKS and native house boys were always a hard problem in any Philippine menage.

"Sing fight?" the Chino replied with an outraged squeak, his voice shrill. "Sing, he no fight, Pedro he fight, José he fight, Juan he fight. Sing no fight. Sing tell 'em house very dirty, clean 'em up house. *Muchachoes* say, clean 'em up house hell, bimeby house all belong Filipino! Bimeby kill 'em all white man and Chino, bimeby no more white man. All dead, white women all killed, white children all killed, Sing no likem that kinda talk—"

Gordon stopped and glanced narrowly at the Chino.

"When," he asked in a voice that he strove to make sound casual, "when did they say all this was going to happen?"

The Chinese shrugged his shoulders.

"Sing no hear. Sing too mad. Maybe two three days, maybe longer. Sing no savvy."

The Chinese turned to the cleaning up of the pool of coffee on the floor, just as unconcerned as though his life had not been endangered five minutes before by three nasty weapons in the hands of three determined and savage looking natives.

CHAPTER II

THE MYSTERIOUS LADY

COLONEL FOSTER had looked serious.

"The main thing," Colonel Foster had said, "is to appear to be totally uninterested in anything having faintly to do with Intelligence work. That's why I called you in from Stotsenburg. That's why I want you to stick around playing polo and drinking drinks. That's why I picked you because I think you pack around a brain cell or two under a blasé exterior."

"In other words I can be depended upon to look sufficiently dumb at all times and places," Gordon had retorted.

"No, no, not at all. But you are to look as though you thought a good looking girl, a cocktail and a polo pony were the most important things in the world."

"Which they are!" admitted Gordon frankly.

"Yes, yes," the colonel was a little testy. "I know all that, but I tell you here and now that this situation is damn serious."

And before the colonel was finished with his little preamble, Gordon himself was looking grave and serious, looking as though there might be more important things in the world than girls, cocktails and polo ponies.

"And you really believe, Colonel," he asked tensely, "that these *muchachoes,* these houseboys, these *lavenderos* and *cocheros* are stirred up as much as that?"

"I was here during the Insurrection," said the colonel crisply. "They are good people, most of them. But they can fight like wild cats, if they are sufficiently urged. And something or someone is working on them now. They are capable of mass murders and massacres if they are aroused. You've got to find out what it's all about. Find out what is going to happen and when!"

It was a big order. Gordon at the polo club was looking over his borrowed ponies, testing borrowed sticks and acting as though polo ponies and sticks were the most important thing in the world, while his mind was seething with unanswered questions.

He was fingering bits and curb chains, girths and stirrup leathers, but not with the full attention that one should pay to such serious rites. But so long had he played polo that his subconscious mind attended to most of the details for him.

Such part of his brain as might be called the conscious section was turning over some startling things as he looked over his string of horses, waiting for the gong to ring up the first chukkar.

First of all, there was that large handbill posted over the walls of a *tienda* near the Pasay Club.

It was in Spanish and Tagalog.

FILIPINOS YOU ARE THE SLAVES OF THE AMERICANS! WHY WAIT FOR A PROMISED INDEPENDENCE THAT MAY NEVER COME? THE PHILIPPINE ISLANDS PRODUCED MANY MILLIONS OF PESOS OF WEALTH FOR THE LAST YEAR. HOW MUCH OF THAT WEALTH DID YOU RECEIVE?

A crowd of muttering natives had been gathered around it as Gordon drove by and stopped to see what it was all about. It was the first time that he had seen a native crowd looking sullen.

The natives stared at him and from him to the billboard. Muttering there among themselves, they looked none too friendly, more like a pack of wolves ready to act in concert than like the usual kindly natives.

A quick surge of anger came over Gordon, not at the natives but at the sinister organization that would try to appeal to them by such means as the crude propaganda here on the billboard before him.

Stepping forward quickly, he jerked the offensive poster down, tore it into pieces and ground the scattered fragments into the dust with his heel.

THE CROWD looked startled at his boldness. Many of them, the older, saner elements, nodded an approval. They had seen the Islands advance from a condition bordering upon chaos under Spain's harsh rule to an orderly civilization under the kindly rule of the United States.

But some of the younger hot-heads of the mob before him muttered together angrily. It only needed a spark to start something.

Gordon alone, armed with nothing but his silver mounted polo whip, faced the sullen ones in silence, looking at them sternly until the muttering gradually died down.

He walked to his car through a lane which the crowd made quickly to aid his progress. Turning as he reached the car, he was just in time to see one of the white clad Filipinos behind him make a significant gesture.

The man had drawn his hand across his own throat as with a knife and was pointing to Gordon meanwhile. It was not a pleasant thing to see. The officer in his polo breeches and boots studied the fellow closely until the native grew embarrassed and slid back into the crowd.

One native looks very much like another to the casual eye of the white man, but there was something about the face of this specimen which stirred some dim chord of memory in Gordon's brain. Broad face, slanting eyes, high cheek bones, it was a typical Malay face.

He drove on to the club, wondering vaguely where he had seen that face before, He was still puzzled over it as he mounted up his pony for the first chukkar and cantered out into the field.

There was a loose ball resting near the sideboards. The first bell had not rung as yet, but it was almost time. For the sake of warming up, he put his pony into a gallop and drove at the ball. As he leaned outward and forward to make a back stroke, he felt his saddle give suddenly. It was only by throwing out his arm and grasping his pony's neck in a firm

Masked figures closed in.

grip that he was able to keep from turning with the now loosened saddle and falling to the ground.

Tightening his grip of knee and thigh, he managed to hold the saddle in place until he brought the animal down to a halt. Leaping to the ground, he examined the girth which was hanging loose from the near side. He went around to the offside and looked at the place where the girth had given way. Then he dropped the loose end of the girth and walked soberly back to the horse lines, a puzzled frown on his face.

The girth, a broad band of leather, was held in place by three buckles which fastened to straps on the saddle. Two of these three straps had been cut through entirely. The third had been cut almost three quarters through so that the first strain would break it and precipitate the rider on to the ground.

From the look of outraged anger on the face of his own horseboy when he saw the ruined straps, Gordon was instantly convinced that the damage had not been done in that quarter.

Saddles were changed. He dashed into the game and threw himself into it so heartily that he nearly forgot the incident. It was a good game, six practice chukkars against a pick-up team of cavalry and artillery officers from the *Cuartel,* who finally were beaten by Gordon's team to the tune of seven goals to two.

With polo coat thrown over his sweat-stained silks, Gordon walked across the polo field to the clubhouse. The grandstand was being emptied of people, and from the commanding general's box a laughing party of civilian and military aides descended.

Several of them hailed him but he was absentminded in his replies.

The general had descended from the box and was chatting with a civilian dressed in white serge.

"Good game, Captain Gordon," complimented the general, exceedingly pleasant voiced and courteous. "That was a beautiful near-side backstroke you made in the third chukkar." Then turning to his guest he introduced the civilian as the Baron Feodor Draskendorf.

WHEN THE stranger spoke it was a smooth and polished English, so well and correctly enunciated that it might have been learned in the confines of Oxford itself.

"You played quite marvelously," he said, bowing with that chill and unsmiling courtesy so typical of the European man of a certain type.

His eyes were very cold, cold and gray. Here was a man,

He whirled toward the house.

thought Gordon swiftly, whom one might respect but whom one never could like.

This was the White Russian from Shanghai. Rogers, in the background, glanced significantly at the man and went on into the bar.

"It is very interesting to me, the polo and the horses," the baron went on. "I was in the cavalry during the war. I commanded the Grodno Hussars for his Majesty the Tsar."

"That must indeed have been interesting," returned Gordon politely.

He thought to himself meanwhile that here was a cavalry officer before him, a man who should understand certain things.

"I almost had an accident," Gordon stated quietly, "someone cut through the straps of my cinch. Might have been serious if I hadn't discovered it before the game started."

The Russian looked up, his face full of anger and concern.

"What a rotten thing to do," he exclaimed vehemently. "A person who would do a thing like that should be knouted. You were lucky to discover it in time."

The man's concern was genuine. There was no doubt in Gordon's mind that the Russian had been a cavalry officer. The general expressed his concern. The three were slowly moving toward the club house.

"It's a very good thing that nothing did happen to you," said the general, "otherwise you might have missed meeting the Baroness Helene, and that would have been a tragedy in your young life. Come along with us and meet her and see if you don't agree with me that the baron is extremely fortunate in his choice of a niece."

As the three came up on the club porch there was much rising and bowing and many greetings to the general.

The three men made their way toward the far end of the porch where a gathering of many white-clad officers surrounded a table.

As the group opened out respectfully to admit the newcomers, Gordon felt a thrill go through him. In fact, everything else faded out of the picture, leaving nothing visible but a picture of startling beauty.

His first impression was of lazy-lidded, golden flecked eyes, eyes that seemed to open and widen invitingly, so that one was tempted to lose himself in their depths. The eyes burned and closed and enfolded him momentarily. It was some time later that he remarked the face, a face pale as clear-cut ivory, of ivory that still gave an impression of inward fire. The lips were perfectly modeled. Half opened as they were they seemed quite inviting, so that a man might grasp with the sudden shock of the beauty of this woman and feel his pulses throb intoxicatingly.

"Good Lord! What a knockout!" he whispered to himself. "Watch your step, old boy!"

But with man's persistent recklessness, he reasoned that it wouldn't do any harm to warm his soul a little at the shrine of this blazing beauty.

Through a mist of uncertainty and strange confusion he heard the voice of the baron. He was saying something that sounded like "my niece Helene."

CHAPTER III

CARNIVAL MADNESS

GORDON'S BRAIN, such part of it as was not taken up with the sudden sight of this girl, caught at the name Helene. Of course her name was Helene and he thought immediately of that other Helene, the wonder of whose beauty has echoed in men's minds, persistently down through the ages.

Something, some instinct, warned him that there was danger here, there was a subtle emanation of peril from this girl before him, but it was peril tinged with delight.

But it was high time he said something. The girl was watching him with those great eyes of hers, her lips half parted like the petals of a scarlet flower.

"Most appropriate name, Helene," the voice sounded strange in his own ears. "It's the first time that I have succeeded in understanding how one face could launch a thousand ships."

And of a sudden the golden-flecked eyes were smiling deeply into his. A white hand went out, inviting him to a seat by her side. She leaned toward him. To fight the unconscious allure of this girl was like fighting an impalpable fog of strange, heady, Eastern incense.

Instinctively he realized that this was an unusual type of woman beside him. She was a tigresslike flame of a woman who could sear and burn, a woman who was as fiercely lithe as a snake or a naked sword, and therefore, it followed, a woman who could be infinitely lovely in surrender.

Her voice fell on his ears, a voice with a low, musical throb which disturbed him to the roots of his being. "You officers," she murmured, "have absolutely no conscience about turning a poor girl's head with your flattery."

She spoke without a trace of accent.

"I would be conscienceless if I could keep your head turned in my direction."

The patter of small talk came to him, subconsciously directed, and without effort. Behind it, he was trying to solve the riddle of this girl and her startling effect on him.

Of course, she was deliberately exerting every weapon in her armory against him. That in itself was delightfully flattering and dangerous. He tried to discount its effect. But he had been so secure and serene heretofore. There was no doubt about it, he was a little troubled and uncertain.

"I have been so thrilled by your game," she admitted. "I followed every goal you made, five of them. It is really wonderful to watch a man who handles his horse and his stick as you do. It is like watching a perfect craftsman. You must have been playing for years. Every move you made counted for something."

To his credit it must be said that he was embarrassed.

"I've been playing polo long enough to play a better game than I do," he answered, "and I've been riding horses all my life. But I am going to practice on a wooden horse hereafter."

"A wooden horse?" Plainly, she was puzzled.

"Yes, wasn't Helen of Troy finally captured by means of a wooden horse?" he retorted, his face very grave and unsmiling.

She laughed a rich, contralto laugh, well content, then casting a quick glance at the general and the baron engrossed in their own conversation, she leaned toward him swiftly and whispered:

"Don't delay too long with the wooden horse. Troy is half captured already."

Then to make his confusion worse confounded, the native orchestra struck up the haunting melody of some wistful Spanish waltz. Those two found themselves rising without a word being said. Somehow she was in his arms. They floated out on the floor, oblivious of the crowd, oblivious of the world, their bodies swaying to the poignant appeal of the waltz, an old air which carried them on wings of throbbing harmony.

LIKE MOST good dancers, he danced indifferent to the femininity of the woman in his arms. But here was a girl who radiated so overpowering an aura of bewilderment that he could not forget her for an instant. They danced in silence for several minutes. Then he felt her stir in his arms and knew that she was going to speak. He looked down at the face tilted upward so dangerously near to him.

"You don't know how interested I am in the wooden horse," she whispered, her eyes dreamy. "You must start on him at once."

The music stopped. They were near her table. Before he had opportunity to reply, Rogers, the artillery man, grinning wickedly, claimed the girl for the next dance.

Before she left she flashed Gordon a look which said as plainly as though she had pronounced the words:

"Wait for me."

And he waited, listening to the chatter around him, watching the colorful crowd of polo players in crimson and golden silks, of officers in white and gold and of women in all colors of the rainbow. The music, a stringed native orchestra, tinkled and chimed with the wash of the surf against the beach below them. White clad *muchachos* in loose, flowing shirts worn outside their trousers and moving silently, shod in loose native *chenilas*, deftly filled glasses and served tea.

One of these *muchachos* was carrying a tray of cocktails toward the table at which Gordon sat. Raising his head suddenly, Gordon found himself looking full into the face of the servant. His glance passed casually enough across the face of the Filipino as one's glance would travel, unconsciously impersonal, over the face of a waiter.

As he turned away, however, something had suddenly clicked in Gordon's brain. Now he knew where he had seen the native before. He was one of the mob who stood before the incendiary billboard with its fiery and seditious exhortations. The native who had suggestively drawn his hand across his throat was the same man he had seen many times at the Polo Club, whose face he had remembered vaguely.

Gordon flashed a glance at the China barboy, jerking his head imperceptibly toward the strange Filipino. The barboy gave no sign, but after a moment or two he called his assistant to take his place and went quietly out to confer with one of the soldier chauffeurs. The soldier chauffeur thereafter had occasion to pass along the wide veranda, letting his glance rest on the face of the strange Filipino for a fleeting second.

At this proof that his organization was working, Gordon chuckled with satisfaction.

Helene returned, aglow from her dance. Giving but small return to the painstaking attention that Rogers lavished upon her, she turned again to Gordon. Rogers was trying to work up a party for the Carnival that night.

Gordon found himself drawn toward her again as though she were a magnet, found himself bathed in the aura of excitement and happiness and charm that she radiated.

They had scarcely time to whisper a word or two before the party broke up.

"I will be at the Army and Navy Club dance later."

Once gone, it seemed in truth as though the light of the sun had departed with her.

He shook off his preoccupation and his mind went to work on the problem before him as he walked the road into Manila. More pieces were fitted into the puzzle, but the motive behind the disturbances in the Islands was not clear. Who were the active agents and what were their plans? It was certain that they intended to create some sort of trouble, but what form would it take? He shook his head, his mind more confused than ever.

Suddenly Travis Gordon's heart skipped a beat.

One of those lightning hunches had come to him. What more suitable time than the night of the Carnival? The crowds would be in black and red dominoes, loose gowns under which weapons could be concealed. Everyone, all white men of note, would be at the Carnival. It was a perfectly ideal set-up.

His face grim, he leaped to the telephone and put through a call to the *Cuartel España*, the military headquarters. There was some argument at the other end until finally, impatient, Gordon asked for Colonel Foster. The two conferred together for several minutes.

"Very well," said the Colonel at last, "I think you are crazy, but I'll do as you say."

Hanging up the phone, Gordon plotted his next step. It was clear before him. It involved the Army and Navy Club and the beautiful Helene. It was only through her that he could find the principals in this ghastly plot. He drove rapidly to his quarters in the city.

Once there he asked Sing about Pedro. The Chino shook his head.

"Him gone. I think he go to the *barrio* of San Jacinto," said Sing.

The *barrio* of San Jacinto. That was out toward the Polo Club. His eyes grave and his bearing thoughtful, Gordon hurried to the Army and Navy Club.

Once there he called on the telephone, directing one Collins and one Bliss to head out toward the *barrio* of San Jacinto.

He telephoned to another individual and then went out to the great entrance hall of the club.

CHAPTER IV

NIGHT AND THE GIRL

AUTOMOBILES AND *Calesas* were discharging their passengers at its great white portals. Infantry and staff officers were arriving from the *Cuartel España* and from Fort McKinley. From Corregidor came Coast Artillerymen, from Cavite and Olongapo came Navy and Marines. These last were hilarious and singing joyfully, their voices booming out over the Luneta in that arrogant song, "The Armored Cruiser Squadron."

White coated *muchachos* took caps and swagger sticks, and men turned toward the enormous, high-vaulted barroom where even now the dice were crashing across marble top tables amid great bursts of shouted laughter.

Perspiring bar boys, balancing great trays of cocktails and highballs, teetered in and out among the thirsty officers. Enigmatic Chinese bartenders poured and mixed, rattled ice and filled rows of shiny glasses with pale amber and tawny yellow and ruby red concoctions while the cheerful din of men in from work and ready to play rose higher and higher.

In one corner a group of West Pointers, not very long out of the Academy and therefore a little sentimental, were singing "Benny Haven's, Oh!" with much feeling and little harmony. In the center the losers at several of the tables had foregathered to shoot dice for all the "chits" and the semi-finals of this event were causing great excitement.

From the direction of the ballroom came the first crashing notes of the infantry band playing, of all things, "Anchors Aweigh!" so that there were many shouts from the Army and loud cheers from the Navy while men began to drift toward the music and their women and respectability.

Gordon, strolling toward the club entrance to inquire for messages, looked out over the Luneta and saw the lights of the Carnival gleaming across the way. The streets were filled with hooded and masked crowds and the air full of confetti and laughter. Turning, he made his way toward the ballroom and looked in on the scene.

It was brilliant enough! The men a blur of white and gold, the women in soft pastel shades of old rose and amber or faint lavender and lustrous silver, of pale apricot and creamy ivory, swaying and turning, checking and balancing to the surge and flow of the music.

Gordon, lounging there in the doorway, nodded and smiled as this one and that one greeted him, his mind working in characteristic bachelor fashion after each greeting, classifying this one as one with whom he should dance and that one as one with whom he would like to dance. But the one whom he really sought was not there. Search as he might among that sea of flushed and happy faces, he could not find the girl of the afternoon, Helene, the vivid.

Her absence lessened the lustre of the gold and silver, dimmed the throb of the music and faded the colors of the ballroom into a vague and indeterminate gray.

Lounging there, tall and handsome, more than one woman looked at Gordon appreciatively, and noted the well knit figure, the bronzed face and clear eyes, the breadth of shoulder, and the trim lines of the white mess jacket tapering to snugness over the slim waist.

Oblivious to the glances, Gordon raised his head suddenly as some small commotion at the opposite entrance attracted his attention. He divested himself of his languor as one swiftly divests himself of a cloak.

The crowd opened out and she stood there. Gordon gazed at her amazed.

It was as though her beauty had become articulate. One could not analyze it, compounded as it was of ivory and ebony, the ebony of her lacy black dress, revealing the perfect long-limbed grace of her, the smooth, cream-ivory perfection of neck and shoulders and head and chin daintily poised and red lips faintly parted. The eyes were searching, searching until at last they came to rest.

A little unsteadily, Gordon started toward those eyes. Of the officers who fluttered around her, he saw nothing, but went directly to her.

Then the music started afresh. Without a word he led her out, felt her tremble into his arms and started to dance.

BLISSFULLY OBLIVIOUS of aught else in the world, these two danced. It was as though his feet spurned the clouds, and as though they danced alone on that great, crowded floor.

At last she moved slightly in his arms and spoke:

"You are very silent tonight."

Then it came to him very suddenly that there was something requiring explanation, that all was not clear between them. He pushed the thought away, determined to enjoy the present, let come what may.

"Is there any need of speech between us?" he asked simply.

So perfect was the harmony of their nearness that there was little necessity of replying. Without a word he felt that she agreed. After a pause she spoke again.

"No," she replied, her voice very faint and low, "there is no need."

But there was need of stopping the dancing, seeing that the music had stopped. They both smiled swiftly and understandingly at each other as they suddenly found themselves dancing alone on the floor.

To Gordon's way of thinking this was no time to be mixed up in the chattering party of inane people with whom she had come.

"No," he commanded assuredly, "we are going out on the balcony!"

The girl looked up at him quickly, then over to where the party was waiting for her, then back again at his determined profile.

"Very well," she acquiesced, and allowed herself to be led back, toward the balcony and out on its cool spaciousness.

The moon did all that it could do to make things pleasant. It stood up over Manila Bay serene, kindly, flashing a track of molten silver across the face of the dark waters.

Behind them, in the ballroom, the band struck up the next dance. The two stood there, arm in arm, silently drinking in the beauty of the tropic night, listening to the faint wash of the waves against the sea wall below them. Gordon stared off silently, his gaze fixed on the moon track.

"It's like a silver ladder," he remarked. "Makes you feel as though you could climb right up to the moon itself. Wouldn't that be nice?"

Her eyes were somber.

"Yes," she answered, her voice low and carrying a note of sadness, "if one could only walk up there away from it all, the sadness and the rottenness, the pain and the brutality of life."

"My heavens!" he exclaimed, "but you sound as cheerful as a condemned prisoner."

"Yes, a condemned prisoner," she replied, her voice bitter, then her mood changed suddenly. "But I am not always so pessimistic," she exclaimed lightly.

She laughed with a sort of forced gayety that somehow held a false note.

He was silent. Doubt and distrust of this girl came again to plague him, to stretch out grisly hands, spoiling the perfect evening of sea and sky and molten moonlight.

Far out on the floor of the bay the bulk of Corregidor loomed its vast mass of solid rock. A light or two twinkled from its tip. All else was in shadow. It stood there, heavy, powerful, a mighty fortress that the touch of a single button would change into an inferno of screaming shells, with the grim muzzles of guns suddenly peering out from innocent looking expanses of cliff.

It was the embodiment of American power in the Orient, the strong fortress outpost of the mighty Republic. It was the great Gibraltar of the Far East, honeycombed with galleries and pits and bristling with long-barreled, disappearing guns.

Should it fall, American power in the Far East would fall with it, reflected Gordon.

HE LOOKED down at her as she stood beside him. He found tears welling in her eyes.

"What is it? What is troubling you?" he asked gently.

She shivered slightly, shaking her head, then drew forth a powder puff and began to use it with that supreme concentration of body and soul upon the process which only a woman can achieve in carrying out that important rite.

Gordon turned and looked into the ballroom.

"Oh, damn!" he swore, "here comes that idiot Rogers and half a dozen more to claim you."

Helene looked back as well and made a faint gesture of distaste, then looked up into Gordon's eyes as though waiting for him to find a solution of the problem.

"Listen," he whispered, "let's beat it! It's Carnival night. We can get a couple of masks and dominoes and mix with the crowd and no one will be the wiser. Hurry, before they come."

The girl started to demur, looking back at her party in the ballroom, then thought better of it and nodded. The two walked swiftly away, circled around through the building and came out at the club entrance.

"Captain Gordon," the clerk on duty called, "a man just left a message for you, said it was important." He handed over a thin Signal Corps message envelope.

Taking it, Gordon asked his companion's permission, and, swiftly breaking the seal, read the message through. The girl watched his face narrowly. It betrayed no sign of what he read. Returning the paper to its envelope he placed them both inside his mess-jacket and asked for paper and an envelope. Hastily he scribbled something, folded it into the envelope, sealed it and handed it to the clerk.

"Get it to him immediately," he ordered.

CHAPTER V

THE DRAGON STIRS

THE MESSAGE had been rather stark and rather terrible in its terse, laconic simplicity.

Midnight tonight said to be time set for uprising of natives.

His hunch was right! Swift and terrible pictures succeeded themselves in Gordon's mind—pictures of isolated posts, of silent, creeping footsteps, of screaming men and children, of fire, of blood, of horror indescribable. But why? For whom?

He looked at Helene. Her face was turned from him showing her profile, a delicately chiseled profile, pure and lovely. Surely there could be no evil behind that lovely mask!

Stepping out under the big porte cochère, Gordon called his car and followed the girl into it. He gave the man his directions in Tagalog and they drove away.

The Luneta was crowded. From the bandstand in its center, the constabulary band sighed forth its melodies. Around the great driveways went an endless procession of *calesas* and automobiles all filled with laughing, chattering people, Spanish, American, Filipino and *mestizo*. Across on the far side of the Luneta, music and brilliant lights proclaimed the presence of the riotous Carnival grounds.

The sidewalks were filled with crowds of masked and hooded people, men, women and children in dominoes of all shapes and colors. The air was filled with confetti. The very atmosphere seemed to vibrate to the Carnival spirit.

Stopping at a booth midway down the Luneta, Gordon bought red dominoes and red masks for his partner and himself. The masks were large, covering the entire face, and the two put them on and laughed at the total eclipse of personality which ensued.

There were many red dominoes abroad. Gordon, gazing down a side street, saw the way filled from curb to curb with a crowd of silent, red-garbed figures. He and Helene drove around toward the walls of Intramuras, the old Spanish city of Manila. Here, close to the great gates, Gordon saw another group of these red garbed and silent people. There was an air of expectancy about them, as though they waited for something, some word.

The entire city was stirring with life and laughter but underneath it all was some exciting, mysterious undercurrent which gave an added tang to the Carnival gayety.

With all the bizarre costumes, white man could not be told from native. Men, women and children of all races were concealed and disguised.

Gordon was thoughtful and preoccupied.

"I've got to go out toward the Polo Club a minute or two. Do you mind coming along?" he asked finally.

She nodded an acquiescence and the driver was given his directions.

"To the *barrio* of San Jacinto!" said Gordon.

The dank air of evening came across the rice paddies, smelling of the earth and humanity. Blended inextricably with it was the faint smell of wood smoke, and that ever present and not unpleasant odor of coconut oil. Occasionally their nostrils would be assailed with the powerfully sweet perfume of the *ylang-ylang* blossoms.

The faint voices of women and children floated to them, along with the cry of some night bird, the barking of *barrio* dogs and the shouts of the fishermen rolling in on the waves with the day's catch.

THERE WAS one sound that impinged upon Gordon's consciousness with persistent reiteration. Blended as it was with all the other sounds, for a long time he did not separate it from its background. As they came nearer the place, the sound bore into his musings. Frowning, he tried to throw it off and to follow undisturbed his train of tumultuous thoughts.

The sound was behind him now and had grown louder. Impatiently he devoted himself to the task of solving the irritating interruption.

"Gecko! Gecko! Gecko!" the cry was thrice repeated.

Then followed a pause. After a few seconds' interval, the cry went forth again, in the monotonous voice of the gecko lizard.

Beside him sat Helene and he could scarcely keep his eyes from her face. She had thrown back the domino and her satiny shoulders and breast rose from out the foamy mist of her dress with such startling beauty that it made him grow silent with worship.

"Simply looking at you is slowly but surely disintegrating me into a poet. No girl should be allowed to be so disturbing and unsettling as you."

Looking toward him, she answered in a whisper, glancing at him through half-averted eyes:

"You are not exactly a calming influence yourself," she flushed ever so slightly. There was an indefinable thrill to her voice, a half lingering caress in her tone, an air of delightful and secret intimacy in the way she whispered.

"This would be an ideal evening," he whispered, "if only you and I did not have to return to the mob again."

For a second he thought he had gone too far and too fast, for she turned her head away. But it was only for a second. Her eyes sought his and clung.

"I hope this will not be the only evening," she whispered, her voice low and faint. And if ever there was yearning and surrender and wistfulness in a woman's eyes it was in Helene's eyes at that moment. Like the trumpet blast that brought down the ancient walls, it tumbled Gordon's last defense.

"And this is not all of this evening," his voice was husky.

She nodded, her eyes warm and friendly.

Her right hand rested on the seat between them. As he studied its slim perfection, she gently moved it in his direction, palm upward, as though in mute agreement.

How it happened he did not know, but suddenly his arms were about her and their lips shuddered together in an ecstasy of swift happiness that was almost painful in its poignancy.

Suddenly, she shivered as though chilled through and went limp and passive in his arms and slowly pushed him away. All the light and the joy and the sparkle had ebbed away from her and it was as though the world had suddenly turned gray.

Leaning back in the seat, she stared straight ahead, a hopeless, dreary despondency in her eyes as though envisaging Heaven only knew what sort of horror.

"What is it, my dear? What is it?" asked Gordon, leaning above her.

She would not reply for a space. Her hands were clenched until the nails must have bitten into her tender flesh.

"Helene, dear love, what is troubling you?" his voice was husky with concern. "Can't you tell me what is making you unhappy? Won't you let me help?"

"Don't! Ah, don't!" she moaned, as if in pain and her head drooped onto her arms, her shoulders shook with her sobs. "I cannot, I cannot!" she repeated again and again.

SILENT AND troubled, he sat beside her until she at last raised her head, her tear-filled eyes looking into space with that stare as of one envisaging distant horrors.

"All that I can ask," she said in a low tone, not looking at him as he spoke, "is that you will, in time to come, not think of me too harshly. All that I can beg of you is to remember that all people are not free to do as they choose, that some lost souls struggle for what they hold near and dear—and sink into the abyss at times, in their struggles. You will try to think of me kindly?"

There was a pitiful catch in her voice, her eyes pled with him as the eyes of a wounded animal might plead with the hunter.

For answer he reached down and raised her hand to his lips.

At that second came the raucous cry of a gecko from close at hand in the shadows lining the road. Hastily he drew her domino up about her and fastened his own, throwing its hood over his face.

Then he told the chauffeur to drive up the road a few yards where there were shadows under the shade of a giant banyan tree. Here, excusing himself, he left her and strode down the road toward the *barrio* of San Jacinto.

The strange cry of that gecko followed him.

Well, it was nothing but a gecko lizard, why allow it to disturb him? he reflected angrily, and tried again to fix his mind on the task before him. The gecko's note obtruded itself.

Having an analytical sort of brain, he made up his mind to solve the strange persistence of this one call above all other evening sounds.

The gecko, why did the gecko particularly interrupt? Where had he last heard the gecko? That might furnish him with some explanation.

It was in the heat of that afternoon, in the courtyard. Again it suddenly occurred to him that he had never heard a gecko's voice at other times than in the heat of the day.

He stopped, puzzled. The sound of the gecko seemed to be now ahead, now behind. But what was a gecko doing calling at night?

It came over him all at once, that he had been a little foolish in walking toward the *barrio* alone. The memory returned to him of that saddle girth, cut deliberately and carefully so as to ensure his being thrown during the game.

Memory returned to him also, of the native in the crowd before the crude poster, the man who had drawn his hand so suggestively over his throat. Suddenly the night seemed to be filled with sinister movement.

"Gecko! Gecko! Gecko!"

The cry sounded so close to him that he started involuntarily. There was something eerie about that call, something disquieting.

He stopped in his tracks where a small road ran off the main highway, turning into the rice paddies and lagoons to the right of the Pasay road. He could hear low voiced conversation somewhere along this track, the sound of many people talking together. As he listened there in the darkness, he saw the lights of a big car come sweeping up the main road from the direction of Manila. The car began to slow up as it approached the side road.

Gordon had just one second to jump out of the way, when with a roar it turned in and went past him. There was only time to get one swift glance at the two passengers in the rear seat. That one glance was enough to show the heavy shouldered, heavy featured, black-bearded baron and the sunken frame of the man with the half paralyzed left side.

As the light of the car illumined the narrow way ahead, Gordon saw two figures in white stand at attention and salute as the machine swept by.

"Sentinels!" Gordon said to himself, and watched the two natives, standing ghostly white against the somber shade of the roadside. The baron, with that crippled man! What did it mean?

CHAPTER VI

SINISTER ARMS

MOURNFULLY THE cry of some night bird floated across the marshes where he stood. The low murmur of voices up the road continued. A thin fringe of trees bordered the bamboo fence near which Gordon stood. Looking through this fringe of trees he saw a large field in the uncertain light. He stiffened to alertness as he watched. Across this large field, by driblets of twos and threes, moved many white-clad natives, all centering on a common point, the place from which came the murmur of many voices.

Something sinister was in progress. A meeting was being held. That much was certain!

From far up the main road in the direction which he had come from the club, Gordon heard the rattle of *calesa* wheels and two voices raised in song, two voices bibulous, careless and joyous past all imagining:

> "There once was a Philippine *hombre*
> Who lived on rice, fish *y legumbre*
> His trousers were wide
> And his shirt hung outside
> But this, I must say, was *custombre!*
> A—a—o-o-ooo, A—a—o-ooo, A—a—o-ooo!"

Gordon, after hearing the words, moved forward a little from his hiding place. But he stepped back just as quickly, for two white shadows detached themselves from the gloom on the opposite side of the main road and came hurrying into the side road. The rattle of the *calesa* wheels grew ever louder and the song more noisy.

> "His village once gave a fiesta,
> *Su familia* tried hard to digest-a
> Mule that had died,
> With the glanders inside,
> And now *su familia no esta.*
> A—a—o-o-ooo, A—a—o-ooo, A—a—o-ooo!"

The white shadows were opposite him now, hurrying forward with every indication of alarm. As the two natives passed him, Gordon stared at them closely, a puzzled frown on his face.

One of them was Pedro, his Number One houseboy!

The *calesa* was now opposite the small road. The song had died down. Voices, American voices, were raised in argument.

"Judas Priest, if I had a disposition like yoursh, Collins, ole kid, I'd hire myself out to fight bulldogsh. Always beefin', always chewin' the fat, never see such a guy fur growlin'. You're worser'n a top kick, tha's wha' you are." After which deadly insult there was silence.

Gordon had to get a word to them. Not thirty paces away stood the two sentinels.

He cleared his throat and with a creditable imitation of their drunken rendition of the "Philippine Hombre" he sang another verse:

> "A big gang of Philippine *hombres*,
> Is filling the road in large *nombres*,
> About fifty yards west
> There's a great big talk fest
> Get some men and some guns and some sundries!
> I'll wait here-ooo, Hurry up-ooo, A-a-o-ooo!"

There was a grunt of surprise from the *calesa* and the song was immediately resumed, as the cart started in motion again.

> "*Su mujer* she kept a *tienda*,
> Underneath a big stone *hacienda*
> Chewed *bujo* and sold
> For jawbone and gold,
> To *soldados* who said *yo comprendo.*"

The *calesa* gathered up speed and went on down the road to the tune of many long drawn "A-a-o-ooo's" of the chorus and for the first time, Gordon relaxed. It was good to know that his men were so thoroughly on the job. Those last words, *yo comprendo,* I understand, told him that.

COLLINS AND Bliss had wonderful heads on them. Whether their drunkenness was simulated or whether it was the real thing was immaterial. They got the big idea very quickly, and he knew they'd return in very short order with enough men to police up the crowd which was so mysteriously holding forth in this deserted vicinity, on a carnival night of all nights.

Working his way quietly toward the place where he had seen the two sentinels, he approached within ten feet of them. Their backs were toward him, and they were evidently deeply interested in what was going on up ahead.

The two were speaking together in low tones. Finally one of them nodded and walked toward the place where the subdued murmur of the crowd could be heard. The other one remained where he was, alone.

It was the chance Gordon had been seeking. Without a second's pause, he leaped forward, catching the man around the throat and hurling him to the ground. It was done so quickly that the native had no time to cry out. In a second he was bound with Gordon's belt and then gagged.

In another few seconds Gordon had dragged him off to the side of the road, bound him, and then stepped back into the shadows.

Thus it was that when the other sentinel returned he saw nothing out of the way and walked past the hidden watcher. In his hand he held two short, dark objects. Gordon had just time to see that the two objects were bolos, the razor-edged chopping machete of the Philippines, a deadly weapon in skilled hands.

Gordon stepped forward, shot out his fist, catching the native a glancing blow on the point of the jaw. It dropped the startled man into oblivion before he knew what had hit him.

Examining the fallen man briefly, Gordon estimated that it would be some time before the fellow would regain consciousness.

Leaving him there, he went forward toward the crowd, carrying one of the bolos in his hand.

The presence of the weapons puzzled him. They were not supposed to be in the hands of casual natives. As he approached the crowd, enlightenment smote him.

He stood still, barely repressing a whistle of amazement. Certainly he was none too soon in his investigations.

The natives were being issued arms from a long shed bordering the road.

Stretched out in a patient line before it, stood nearly a hundred natives. At the head of the column each native was issued a weapon as his turn came, many of them receiving bolos, a few of them revolvers. Superintending the issue, standing behind the tables, was the man with the crippled left side.

The baron was seated in the car which was standing a few yards away with its motor running.

A sudden flurry of excitement stopped the proceedings. All eyes were turned toward the large field which lay before them. A native came across the field shouting something and waving. Looking in the direction of Manila, Gordon saw the lights of three cars advancing swiftly up the main road. Collins and Bliss had wasted no time!

From where Gordon stood, he could see the line of natives, could see the open shed, with its counter, across which other natives passed the weapons, and the car in which the baron and the crippled man had arrived on the scene.

The lights of the oncoming cars swept steadily nearer up the main road from Manila. Suddenly the crippled man leaped for the waiting machine, there was the roar of a quickly accelerated motor, the clash of gears, and the machine swept up the narrow road at high speed, disappearing into the night.

The three cars from Manila turned into the small road. There was great excitement among the natives, a running and shouting and much confusion. White-clad Filipinos were scattering in all directions. The cars were among them before half the crowd could get away.

FROM THE machines jumped many constabulary soldiers. Without orders, they leaped at the nearest natives, holding them and disarming them. A brisk lieutenant of constabulary, in red-tabbed khaki, found Gordon and saluted.

"Confiscate all weapons, arrest every armed native," Gordon directed. The orders were swiftly carried out. A car was sent up the small road in pursuit of the fleeing machine, but it was useless! They had fled safely.

The toll of prisoners revealed little. Sullen, frightened, Tagalogs for the most part, they disclaimed all knowledge of the heads of this organization which had so blithely provided them with arms.

Collins and Bliss, severe, military and correct as always, turned up, saluting gravely.

"Sure was glad to hear you singing out that song from the shadows 'long-side the road," confessed Collins.

"Sure was," echoed Bliss.

"But we drew a blank," stated Gordon.

The two men nodded.

"We've got to run down this crippled bird."

"He's a Jap," Collins stated.

"Do you know where he lives?"

"He lives in the same house with this Roosian guy and his niece," volunteered Bliss.

Gordon grew very still for a space.

"You two keep in touch with me at my quarters, or at the Army and Navy Club. Meanwhile try to run down José Toribio."

He turned on his heel and made his way back to where he had left the car.

He was heavy hearted and despondent. It was a horrible thing, he reflected, to have to use the girl you love to track down your enemies.

Helene's face, pale in the half light, stared at him out of the shadows of the car.

"What is happening?" she asked. "I heard all the noise—and I was afraid you had been hurt!"

"Oh, it was nothing," he said easily. "Just a little disorder among the natives. But I'm afraid I'll have to take you home. I seem to have to go on duty tonight."

She said nothing to this, but made room for him as he climbed in the car.

They drove toward Manila again, coming at last into the city streets.

CHAPTER VII

THE DRAGON
STRIKES

FROM FAR away could be heard the subdued murmur and hum as of a multitude of people gathered together. As they approached the Luneta again, Gordon heard the tramp of feet on side streets and heard the subdued hum and rustle of vast crowds in movement.

He looked again at her profile as she sat silently beside him.

Studying her in the flickering light from the street lamps, he saw that she looked pale and stricken and that her fingers clasped and unclasped themselves nervously in her lap.

"What is it, my dear? Can't you tell me what worries you?" he asked again, his voice gentle.

She said nothing for a space, then as though making up her mind to something, she turned to him, her whole attitude beseeching.

"I do not know," she whispered, "but there is fear in my heart tonight. I fear for you—" she hesitated, "and for your friends. There are many, many evil people in the world—many, many evil people." She shuddered as though at some memory.

"You are afraid of something happening to me? And to my friends?" Gordon's voice simulated an incredulous note. "And why, pray?"

There was a long silence as she stared straight to the front, a long silence interrupted by nothing except the sound of the motor in the deserted street. The high wall of a garden rose on their right, one of those mysterious Spanish gardens, set apart from the world. Above its height, a single tree raised its branches to the sky. Its limbs and foliage were brilliantly lighted by swarms of fireflies so that it was like some immense outdoor Christmas tree shining with tiny candles. A faint, languorous breath of flowers stole on the breeze, the cloying scent of *ylang-ylang*, its persuasive perfume loading the air with sweetness.

Above them, the tropic moon looked down benignly and tolerantly. Through the eyelets of her red mask he found her eyes upon him.

"My dear!" she whispered, and again, "My dear!" and suddenly her fingers had closed about his hand, she raised it and he felt the velvet lips against it and thrilled as she pressed it against the softness of her breast. The car moved along smoothly. Those two rode side by side, behind the indifferent chauffeur, close pressed to one another, their hearts full of pain so that they could find no words.

They were now in the Luneta again, its broad tree-lined avenues stretching before them, almost deserted. The constabulary band had left and the evening parade had ceased. There was a suggestion of thunder in the air and Gordon felt that he could sniff a storm coming in from far out at sea.

The moon became overcast. The lights of the hotels and clubs along the sea wall shone brightly, but the crowds were all flocking toward the Carnival grounds from the brilliantly lighted interior of which came the deep throbbing of music and the voices of a great multitude.

Suddenly Helene sat upright.

"Take me home, dear. I must go home at once," she whispered, a half frightened note in her voice.

From far out toward the ocean they heard a faint rumble of distant thunder. A spasmodic wind rose and fell, the sort of wind that blows on ahead, warning of the storm behind.

Nodding, he looked inquiringly at her for directions, nor did his face betray his anxiety to find out. It was she that gave the address to the chauffeur, leaning forward and instructing him. The man swung the car into a side street off the Luneta, a street of quiet houses and high-walled gardens, a street wherein the light of the moon as it shone fitfully through hurrying black clouds, made silvery patterns along the way.

The car stopped before a high iron gate sunk deep in a stone wall.

AS THE sound of the motor died down Gordon was certain that he heard a reiterated call from behind him.

"Gecko! Gecko! Gecko!" went the call.

Throwing his head up, listening, he heard it again, this time without any question. The gecko lizard was again calling after nightfall. He stiffened slightly, a faint crease of worry showed itself on his forehead.

Meanwhile he had stepped to the ground and, turning, received her in his arms as she followed. Feeling in her bag she drew forth a key and unlocked a small door set within the great gate. The door swung back noiselessly.

"Gecko! Gecko! Gecko!" came that call from somewhere down the street again.

The opened doorway framed an oblong of velvety blackness, so black that it was tangible. Gordon stood back as she stepped within and was lost in the Stygian darkness of the interior of the garden. As he stood there uncertain whether to follow, the small white shadow of her hand came out of the darkness and beckoned him.

Without further thought he followed, stepping into the heavy somberness of the doorway and into the garden. The door swung noiselessly shut behind him.

He could see nothing to the right or left and naught but the vast shadow of a house ahead. A very peculiar sensation went through his body. It was as though every nerve coiled and thrilled to some unknown danger. He heard the soft gasp of her voice far ahead.

It was then that he knew that the dark was alive with humanity and leaped swiftly and silently to one side. It was at that instant that he felt something swish by his head, something vicious and deadly and heard a metal object clang sharply against the iron gate.

Moving still farther away from the gate, he distinctly heard the hard, excited breathing of many men and the rustle of garments. The place seemed filled with people. Suddenly an odor assailed his nostrils, that indefinable odor of the native, compounded of coconut oil, the faint scent of sugar cane and the warm smell of poultry. It was with natives that he had to deal.

His eyes becoming more accustomed to the darkness, he could more plainly see the outlines of the house looming up vast and silent, its windows darkened and no sign of life coming from within.

Whether Helene had led him purposely into a trap or whether she herself had been led into this ambush, he did not know. The only tangible idea he could maintain a hold upon was the fact that he loved her. A cold fear suddenly came over him that harm was being done her.

Crouching like some cat animal, he moved forward into the darkness of the garden. He had scarcely gone two steps when he collided with someone and felt his arm grasped in a tight grip.

Shaking off the arm, he struck blindly into the darkness and felt one go down before him with a choking cry. There were sudden shouts on his right and left.

It was just then that a shaft of light fell from a quickly opened window into the garden. Standing outside its radiance, Gordon saw the stream of light fall on a group of weird figures, all clad in scarlet dominoes and masks as he was clad.

The light seemed to freeze them into immobility and they stood like bird dogs, motionless but looking for the quarry nevertheless.

The stream of light was suddenly blocked by a figure. Gordon looked up at the window.

THERE IN the broad opening stood Helene, staring down, her eyes full of horror and anxiety. It seemed only a second that she stood there, before someone roughly pulled her backwards and she disappeared, a faint scream breaking from her throat. The window was closed. The garden was in darkness once more.

It was all that was needed to fire Gordon to action. With swift, sure steps he moved toward the door of the house, listening carefully as he advanced. The men in the garden began to stir about him. He heard whispers on his right and sheered away to the left, bringing up at last against the wall of the house.

Flattening himself against this, he crept carefully toward the door. As he placed foot on the steps, he heard the faint sound of movement in the darkness under the portico. Evidently a sentinel was stationed there. As he stood listening he heard a whispered conversation near the door. From the sound he judged that at least three men were there, undoubtedly fully armed and undoubtedly a nasty handful.

He made up his mind very quickly. Turning away from the door, he stepped out into the garden a few paces, toward the place he had seen, a lone man standing when the light fell from the window.

The man was still there, as he determined after advancing several steps. Suddenly Gordon leaped upon the shadowy figure, grasping the fellow in a powerful grip. The man struggled and cried out. He was a native and wriggled and squirmed in Gordon's arms like a very active snake.

Lifting him high into the air, Gordon flung him far out into the garden so that the man fell heavily and set up a yell. There was a rush toward the sound. Gordon heard footsteps hurry past him in the darkness and he retraced his steps swiftly to the door.

As he had hoped, the man guarding it had left. The door gave to his touch.

CHAPTER VIII

AN IMPATIENT ANIMAL

S OFTLY CLOSING it behind him, he bolted it from the inside. A long hallway stretched before him. Some sort of a salon was on the right. On his left was another and smaller salon. Both of these rooms were in darkness. A dim light burned in the lower hallway. A broad staircase led to the second floor. From somewhere up there he heard the sound of voices.

The sharp ring of a telephone bell came from a room at the end of the lower hallway, evidently the library. A man's voice answered it, speaking in Spanish.

Treading cautiously toward the sound, Gordon could hear the man giving some directions. From the few words that he could hear Gordon gathered that he was saying something about the Carnival.

A curtain of reeds and glass, one of those Japanese reed curtains which admit the passage of air and obscure the view, covered the entrance to the small library. These reed curtains tinkle very loudly when brushed against, as Gordon well knew.

Taking painful precautions to avoid any noise, he pushed some of the reeds aside slowly and carefully. The library was well lighted. It contained only one figure, that of a man seated at a desk in the center of the room.

Gordon's heart beat when he saw the man. The fellow was unmistakable. The droop of the left shoulder and the slight listlessness of the left arm were more than enough to identify him.

It was the man whom he had seen in the *patio* that afternoon, the man who had been in the car with Helene's uncle out at the meeting near the Pasay Road that evening.

The fellow was still speaking in Spanish. Suddenly he switched into English.

"Yes," he said, "we've got him, the American. He's standing right behind me now. He has overheard too much and it becomes my painful duty to have him killed."

His voice was quite easy and familiar, as though chatting of inconsequentials. Not even as he spoke did he look up.

Gordon felt rather than heard a movement behind him. It was partially his long polo training that made him act, that training which accustoms a man to think at the gallop. Without a single backward glance, he leaped forward into the room.

Straight as an arrow at its mark he drove his fist at the man in the seat. The man half rose but he was too late to avoid the crash.

The blow staggered him, his body started to sag. Before it had dropped limp into the chair, Gordon had acted again, still without looking around.

Lifting the now limp body in his arms he turned swiftly, bearing the unconscious man as a shield before him. The whole act has been consummated in less than a few seconds.

At that he had been none too soon. Two glittering bolos in the hands of two figures clad in scarlet dominoes were raised as he turned. Swinging the limp form of his enemy before him, Gordon rushed the two men in the doorway, rushed them with such impetuosity that they fell back, frightened, losing for a second their wits and their advantage of numbers and weapons.

That second of indecision was enough. Before they had recovered their wits, he had swung into one with his elbow, knocking him aside and had struck the other with the body of the man in his arms so that the fellow staggered and dropped his weapon. Scarcely pausing in his flight, Gordon stooped and retrieved the bolo, shifting the burden he carried onto his shoulder as he did so.

The next few seconds were full of confusion. He heard a shouting behind him as he hurried down the hallway towards the door. As he reached the foot of the staircase, Helene appeared from somewhere, her face white, her eyes staring, but a look of great joy lighting up her features as she saw that he was unhurt.

IN THE swift excitement of the crowded moments it seemed quite natural that she should be there. It seemed equally natural that he should shout to her:

"Follow me, and keep close to my left side!"

Another figure came suddenly out of the darkness of the left hand salon. In the dim light Gordon recognized the broad shoulders and black beard of Helene's uncle. Strangely enough, his hands were tied behind him.

Gordon came to a quick stop at the sight of him. The baron shouted at Helene, looking upward in horror. Then the Russian nobleman leaped forward, knocking her aside with his shoulders.

The light flashed on something that hurtled through the air from above on the second floor landing, striking the Russian on the head and splitting his skull as though it had been laid open with an ax. He fell heavily in a horrible welter of brains and blood. The shaft of a broad bladed native spear quivered above his body.

Helene, whose life had been saved by the quick self-sacrifice of her uncle, screamed aloud and hid her face from the horror of the swift doom that had overtaken him.

There was no time to be lost. Half leading, half dragging Helene, Gordon hurried to the door, still carrying the unconscious form of the man who had been at the telephone.

With Helene stumbling behind him, Gordon broke suddenly into the garden.

A confused shouting noise greeted him. There was the sound of running footsteps. He felt his bolo bite into flesh once and again heard the scream of a wounded man. She pressed hard at his side until they had won to the gateway where he turned at bay while she unlocked the small door. Suddenly they were outside and he held the door while she stepped into the car. Fortunately, the native driver had his motor going.

Gordon dropped the body of the unconscious man at her feet in the car and leaped in.

Reaching forward, he gave swift orders to the chauffeur as the car gathered speed. Gordon directed the way to the nearest police station, where he turned over the man whom he had overpowered. He gave some instructions hurriedly in a low voice.

If he only had the time to question the man! There were so many things he needed to know, things that only this man could tell him if he were as important as Gordon suspected. But there wasn't time! He needed to use every minute left him.

Helene sat like a rigid statue beside him, then suddenly moaned and collapsed.

Holding the unconscious girl, he glanced at his watch and frowned with worry.

In a few minutes he had arrived at his quarters. Bearing the quiet form of Helene in his arms, he carried her into the living room and placed her tenderly on the couch.

Sing, the imperturbable, aided him. Again Gordon glanced at his watch. The time was getting short.

"Sing, guard her with your life. Don't let anything happen to her!"

SING NODDED gravely.

"Me fixem," he announced.

There was a knocking at the door. Sing went to answer it. Going along behind the servant, Gordon found a heavy-set solid person demanding to see him. He gave his name as Mynheer van der Donk.

Despite the pressing nature of events, Gordon knew he had to see this man. He almost literally dragged him into the living room. But while Gordon chaffed, the Dutchman refused to be rushed into what he had to say.

The rubber business, he commented, was very good indeed. So good as to cause envy. The Shanghai and Tsien-Tsin markets were uncertain since the Japanese had assumed so much power in the Orient.

"It is too bad that the British St. George is so busy in Europe that he cannot fight the Far-Eastern Dragon," sighed the Hollander.

Gordon stopped abruptly in his pacing. There were dragons and dragons in the Far-East. He flung a sudden question at the Hollander, on a sudden hunch.

"You mean the Black Dragon?" he asked, low voiced.

The stout Hollander looked about the room swiftly before replying.

"Exactly," he answered. "You know of it?"

Gordon recalled the shreds and bits of information and conjecture— of that powerful old man, Mitsuru Toyama, the eighty-four-year-old, modern-day Japanese equivalent of the ancient Master of the Assassins. For Mitsuru Toyama was supposed to be the most powerful private citizen in Japan. His Society of the Black Dragons had assassinated cabinet officers and ministers, high-ranking naval and military officers and any number of liberal politicians.

Gordon began to see things—the intolerant and reactionary Black Dragon Society forcing the hand of the Japanese Army in Manchuria, in Shanghai, in Tsien-Tsien, and now perhaps—

"It is an impatient animal, the Black Dragon," van der Donk said. "It cannot wait for 1946."

The year 1946 was the year when the Philippines would become independent of the United States.

"The Black Dragon would like to make his base secure for a leap farther south without waiting until 1946."

That was logical. The Philippines, in addition to their own vast riches in iron and gold and sugar, would be a wonderful base from which to attack the Dutch East Indies. It all tied in, the activities of the Katupinan, the half-caste Toribio, the strange man with the semi-paralyzed left side.

At that moment Sing came to the door and signaled him. Excusing himself, Gordon went out and received anxiously the slip of flimsy pink paper.

It was a cablegram from Shanghai he was waiting for.

It contained three words only:

BUSHLEAGUER DARK WORM

Dark worm—Gordon frowned, puzzled for a moment. Worm, that was the old Germanic and Anglo-Saxon word for dragon! Dark Worm—Black Dragon!

He went back and gave his information to Mynheer van der Donk. The Dutchman nodded, unperturbed.

"It is for that I come here," he said, while a light dawned on Gordon's previously befogged mind.

"The Japanese!" he exclaimed. "That's who's stirring up trouble here. And that paralytic, he's their agent who's provoking the trouble for them!"

"Exactly," the Dutchman nodded sagely.

THAT MADE things even graver, more portentous. Gordon looked at his watch. Now he had to go. He wondered if he weren't too late.

He excused himself to Mynheer van der Donk, hurried to the door and started to open it.

At that second he heard a movement on the opposite side of the courtyard and slipped out, waiting tense, in the shadows.

As he stood there silently in the darkness, he saw a man leave the opposite quarters, a man attired in a scarlet domino and mask. After him filed some six other men likewise attired. Gordon noticed that each of them had a rosette of some golden cloth on their left shoulders. The men filed out of the courtyard, followed by two shadowy figures who detached themselves from the opposite side of the courtyard. Gordon was relieved, knowing that Bliss and Collins were on the job. He got into his own car after the strangers had left.

Sing, back in the living room of the quarters, looked down upon Helene as she lay there pale and lifeless.

"Tchk, tchk," he clucked commisseratingly, and went to his kitchen, moving silently in his loose felt slippers. Out in his own domain he found a Chinese earthenware jar filled with some grayish powder. This he mixed in water in a glass and carried back to the still unconscious girl. Raising her head, he forced some of the mixture between her lips.

Whether it was the real potency of the mixture or simply its vile taste could not be told but it had the effect of bringing her back to consciousness once more.

She sat up suddenly, her eyes wild with fright.

"Where am I?" she cried, then looking around, recognized the place again. "Where is Captain Gordon? Is he hurt?" Her voice was frantic.

"Allee lightee, allee lightee, Capitan Gordon he go to carnival mebbe so he come back soon," he tried to soothe her.

"Come back. From the carnival! Oh, my God, no! He will never come back alive!" and she dropped her head in her arms and moaned.

Sing studied her gravely for a moment, then went softly out.

Finally raising her head, she found herself alone in the room. Looking about her wildly, she sank back on the couch, staring into space, horror in her eyes. Minutes stretched into the quarter hour and then into the half hour, and still she sat there staring into the wall, as one half-demented.

A sudden thought came to her. She glanced down at her tiny jewelled wrist watch and drew in her breath sharply. The hand pointed at five minutes of twelve. Then as one thoroughly crushed she sat there, straining now and again to hear some sound that she waited for with expectant terror.

The house was silent. Out in the courtyard the fountain rustled and whispered and chuckled and wept by turns.

Again she looked at her wrist watch. It was exactly twelve o'clock. Half staggering, she rose and went to the outer door, listening, every sense directed at hearing what was taking place in Manila.

Nothing but a faint throb and hum came from the city streets. Suddenly a shot broke the stillness of the night. Another and another shot followed and then there was the sound as of many men shouting. The noise died down and all became silent as before.

The silence was ominous, it crept over her like some vast evil fog, vague and formless. Her heart beating so loudly that it seemed to shake her body, she listened. At the end of twenty minutes, she still stood there.

With a low moan she finally gave up, and stumbling made her way back into the quarters where she stood for a moment in the center of the living room as one paralyzed.

A dry sob shook her whole being as she came to a decision and fever-ishly set herself to seeking something. Through the living room she sought and finally in Gordon's bedroom she found what she had been looking for.

It was a small automatic pistol. For a moment she stared at it in a species of horrified fascination. As one in a dream she touched her head with her hand, then touched the pistol. Her eyes blank and staring, that horror still in them, she finally raised the pistol to her forehead and shuddered as the cold muzzle pressed against the warm flesh. Slowly she felt the trigger and began to tighten her finger upon it—

CHAPTER IX

THE CARNIVAL
UNMASKS

WHEN THE car arrived at a side street near the carnival grounds, Gordon left it. He turned into a nearby building and went to the telephone. For three or four minutes he held a low voiced conversa-tion with someone and then hung up. Going into the street again, he unobtrusively joined the colorful masked crowd which was swarming into the carnival entrance.

The masqueraders wore all sorts and types of costumes but scarlet dominoes seemed to predominate amongst them. The masqueraders clad in this vivid color moved in small groups of three or four, sticking closely together.

Brushing up against one of these scarlet clad figures purposely, Gordon felt the hard outlines of a bolo beneath the domino. His face set in grim lines beneath his mask. He looked at his watch. The hands pointed to a quarter past eleven. His heart beat a little more rapidly. The time was short.

There were many dominoes in the crowd, that being the cheapest and most effective form of costume, permissible to all, and easily made at home. Confetti flew thick and fast. Small boys with crude masks and cruder costumes ran in and out of the mass of people making a hideous din on horns and whistles.

Carried along with the crowd he approached the carnival entrance where he saw a group of black dominoed figures close to the gate. These stood there silently, their eyes incuriously shining through their black masks, watching the river of humanity passing them.

At these dark garbed revelers Gordon stared curiously.

Inside the gate he found another group of these black dominoes, looking somber and a little threatening in their black masks. They stood quietly around the great dance floor, not deigning to join the throng of dancers who whirled and turned to the cheerful notes of the band.

At the far end of the dancing floor was erected the throne on which sat the king and queen of the carnival, crowned and ermined and looking very stately and very warm in the heat of the tropical evening. Their glory of paste jewels shone forth bravely and their silks and velvets lent them an almost regal air.

Gordon threw up his head in sudden interest.

There to the right of the king and queen, unobtrusively mingling with the polyglot court, stood a group of scarlet dominoes, their masked and hooded forms making a sinister note in the brave tinsel show of the pseudo-royalty. What especially caught and held Gordon's eye was the fact that each wearer of the blood red costume in this group wore a golden rosette on the left shoulder of his disguise.

As though fascinated by this discovery, Gordon slowly began to make his way through the crowds of spectators at the edge of the dancing floor towards the platform. His own scarlet domino was not especially noteworthy in view of the large numbers of like costumes moving about in the crowds and concentrated especially at the foot of the platform on which stood the royal throne.

Another group of black dominoes stood to the left of the throne upon the raised platform as though they might be the reserve of the more brilliantly clad force upon the floor.

A worried frown appeared on Gordon's brow but he shook his head and continued to advance, pushing his way forward through the crowd.

Glancing at his wrist watch again he saw that the minute hand was inexorably creeping around towards twelve, it having taken him over half an hour to gain entrance to the carnival and to work his way through the press of masqueraders.

It was impossible not to be affected by the subtle undercurrent of excitement which held the mob in its grip. The masqueraders, unlike the usual happy, laughing, careless dancers, were tense and strangely silent, unconsciously affected by the throb of an expectant something in the air.

AT LAST he found himself at the edge of the platform occupied by the king and queen of the carnival and the ominous group of scarlet dominoes carrying the golden rosettes upon their shoulders. A small flight of steps led up to the platform. Forcing his way through the masqueraders occupying this vantage point, at last he stood upon the platform.

As he stood there, streaming with perspiration from his efforts at getting through the masses of people on this hot tropical night, he looked over the immense gathering and marvelled at the number of scarlet dominoes, marvelled with something akin to panic gripping him.

From where he stood he could see the entire dance floor with flowing, colorful groups of dancers. He watched the enormous crowds looking on from the sides, the group of black dominoes at the door.

The night was hot, too hot. There was a faint rumble of thunder on the far horizon and the electric tension which comes before a storm. Tropical storms came suddenly. Gordon hoped that this one would arrive before midnight. He glanced at his watch again and felt his heart almost stand still for a space. It only lacked ten minutes until twelve o'clock.

A flash of heat lightning tore aside the velvet curtain of the sky for a dazzling second. The hum and stir of the crowd died down and thousands of pairs of eyes stared aloft apprehensively.

As Gordon watched the crowd he saw a figure in a scarlet domino making its way slowly through the crowd. There was something sinister about the carriage of that head, something about the determined pose of that body that forced his wandering gaze to concentrate upon it.

Now the form was lost behind groups of masqueraders, now it appeared again, gaining little by little and slipping and sliding through the crowd with determination. It was coming on slowly and surely toward the platform.

Only an intensely vengeful or an utterly callous person could go through a crowd like that, with that supreme disregard of the feelings of others and without fear of resentment from those he pushed aside. Only someone fanatically determined could use elbows with the remorseless disregard of other people's ribs and general anatomy shown by this scarlet clad figure. Much more rapidly than Gordon had made the same trip, this figure made its way toward where he stood.

Now the scarlet domino was at the foot of the steps. Now it appeared in front of him, having fought its way up the narrow stairway to the platform. The new arrival shouted something to the other scarlet dominoes behind him.

Gordon glanced around. The group of scarlet dominoes in his rear had been watching him before this. When the newly arrived masquerader shouted they began to move forward. Nodding one to the other, they slowly and unobtrusively drifted toward Gordon, surrounding him like a fog of impalpable scarlet. Almost before he realized what had happened, he was hemmed about with a ring of silent forms who stared at him incuriously through scarlet masks.

Some cold hard object pressed against his left side. He did not show by any outward movement that he knew it was the muzzle of a revolver.

"Make a single move and you will be shot down instantly," a sibilant whisper grated on his ear.

"We unmask at midnight," the voice went on. "There are thousands of us all armed. We will kill all white men here at the carnival. We are waiting outside the Army and Navy Club to rush in and slay, we are waiting concealed at every army post and fort and camp in the Islands."

There was a short ugly laugh from one of the scarlet clad figures near Gordon.

"He speaks truly, the hour is almost here when the slaves arise against the white masters. You and your fellow white men have a few minutes left to look upon life," said the voice grimly.

Gordon could not tell which one of the men was speaking.

The voice went on.

"To drive the white man from Asia, that is the glorious task we are beginning here. And you have let us work and plot against you and uproot everything you have done, never knowing how powerful we are, how finely drawn our plans, how superb our leadership. It has been mere child's play. You do not deserve to hold these islands, you have not wit nor intelligence enough to guard them," and the voice laughed scornfully.

Around him Gordon heard the grim laughter echoed.

LOOKING UP at the sky, he gazed at it as a condemned man might gaze for the last time at the great arch above him. The muzzle of the revolver pressed close and ever closer against his ribs.

Glancing down at his wrist watch, he saw that it lacked five minutes until midnight. Evidently the outbreak was set for midnight as he had been warned by that message at the club. He wondered curiously how it felt to have a bullet go searing its way through one's body. Again Gordon glanced at the sky.

His glance dropped again to his watch.

The hands pointed at three minutes to midnight.

The nearest scarlet clad figure noticed the glance at the watch.

"Enjoy it while you may," he laughed easily. "You haven't got very long to go." Again that grim chuckle sounded from the others.

Saying nothing, Gordon looked again at the sky. As he watched, a faint curve of flame arched itself into the heavens and then exploded with a scattering of green light, green light that eddied and whirred toward earth again, scattering a faint luminosity as it fell.

"Well, you poor, half-baked revolutionists," Gordon's voice was surprisingly firm, "it's about time for the show to end!"

The men around him were vaguely puzzled by the tone, but one of them spoke up.

"Yes," he snarled, "just one minute left and you go where all white men belong!"

"Very kind of you, I'm sure," remarked Gordon easily. "But before you get careless with that pop gun of yours take a look behind you."

The man who was holding the revolver pressed to his side turned involuntarily and then gasped while the revolver fell from his nerveless fingers.

For there, not ten paces away, was a group of former black dominoes who were swiftly divesting themselves of their costumes. They were clad in olive drab, being very neat and fit looking men of a machine gun company of the Philippine Scouts. And to back up their claim as machine gunners, there, covering the scarlet group, was the vicious black muzzle of a machine gun, two men stoically at its breech, their fingers on the trigger.

And things were happening all over the great dance hall floor. Scarlet clad men were wriggling out of their dominoes and disclosing themselves as Constabulary soldiers and infantrymen. Very swiftly and very methodically they were tearing off the masks and taking away the bolos and revolvers of other scarlet clad men whose signal to unmask was unaccountably delayed. At the entrance to the carnival another black clad group had appeared suddenly with rifles and bayonets.

The whole thing was done so quietly that the dancers were scarce cognizant of what was going on. The band kept up its cheerful refrain. Slowly the unmasked ones were hurried out through the crowds, each little group of onlookers perfectly certain that this was a local event having to do with some disorderly and fractious masquerader.

The group about Gordon was swiftly disarmed and as swiftly handcuffed together.

Gordon looked at the man who had been pressing the pistol against his side.

It was the greasy half-caste, José Toribio, whom Gordon had seen leaving the *patio*. The others of the group were all Japanese, fanatic members of the Black Dragon Society.

"You poor, amateur trouble makers!" remarked Gordon. "Do you suppose that we didn't know what you intended doing? Do you suppose that we did not receive a complete cabled history of your man Takahashi from Shanghai? Don't you think we knew that Takahashi was a leader of the Black Dragon Society? I had the pleasure of knocking him out early in the evening and personally turning him over to the police. He has preceded you to jail by nearly an hour. When you get to jail you'll find a few of your friends there, who have been picked up at odd hours all during the night.

"Don't you realize you have been letting yourselves be used for the purposes of others, who would not, if they succeeded, give you independence at all?"

The fat and greasy face of the half-caste, José Toribio loomed up malevolently in the group of prisoners.

"Poor Philippine *hombre!*" Gordon said staring at the half-caste sadly.

Toribio shook his manacled fist at the American officer.

"That's all right for Manila, my friend!" he snarled, "but what about the provinces?"

"Out in the provinces they've had instructions for a week to watch out for you and your crew. They are all safely in jail by now."

THE SULLEN and scowling prisoners were led out and bundled into several patrol wagons which had been quietly waiting for hours in the side street near the carnival. The entire plot which was to have made a bloodstained shambles of this peaceful archipelago was scotched before the spectre of massacre had time to raise its head. With the exception of a few shots fired by an over-nervous police patrol at some skulkers near the sea wall, the entire job had been noiselessly and almost bloodlessly accomplished.

The voice of Gordon's chief, the colonel of Intelligence, sounded quietly jubilant over the telephone.

"Neat! Damn neat, Gordon," he complimented.

Gordon was intent upon gaining some particular information.

"Yes," answered the colonel, "we questioned your prisoner Takahashi. Yes, the whole story. He has already sent a cable to his chiefs. No, they will do anything now to avoid being exposed."

Gordon asked another question.

"The baron?" Colonel Foster's voice was regretful. "They forced him and his niece to act as front for Takahashi. The baron being a white man could mix with officers without suspicion, and his niece was ordered to keep you out of action. The baron grew rebellious when he found out how rotten the plot was and refused to play ball. The niece, I don't know what's happened to the niece!"

"She's safe and sound," Gordon said and started back to his quarters.

As he strode through the courtyard he could see the light from the living room of his apartment. The place seemed strangely silent and he could hear no sound as he set foot within the door.

The silence seemed brooding and eerie, it vaguely troubled him. Had he been less successful in preventing massacre here, in his home? He was surprised when he found the living room deserted. He thought however that he could detect a faint memory in the air of the exotic perfume which Helene used. It was as though she had just left the room. The place seemed still warm with her presence.

The silence suddenly broke into life. From somewhere in the rear, in the direction of his bedroom, he heard a voice—anxious, startled, concerned. The voice rose higher and higher. The ascending scale of it culminated finally in a single sharp crack, the explosion of a pistol. Then all was silent.

Almost paralyzed with fear of what the shot might mean, Gordon stood for a second, listening. Then he rushed swiftly towards his bedroom, flinging open the door, wondering what horror might greet his eyes.

Two figures were struggling silently, moving like people in a dream. The sharp odor of smokeless powder assailed Gordon's nostrils.

The two figures resolved themselves into Sing and Helene. The Chinese had Helene's arm in a firm grasp and was endeavoring to wrest the small automatic pistol from her. Just as Gordon arrived, Sing shook it loose from her weakening grip and it fell to the floor, where the Chinese picked it up with a worried shake of the head.

"Now Missy, now Missy," he soothed, "bimeby Capitan come back and Capitan no want find Missy all same dead!"

"Helene!" Gordon's voice rang out through the room. The two, so engaged with their own struggle that they had not noticed him, turned sharply as his voice fell on their ears.

Helene, staring at him as at one newly returned from the dead, had all the air of a person suddenly awakened from a nightmare, still uncertain as to which was dream and which reality.

"Why—you are not hurt?" her voice came at last incredulous and startled.

For reply, Gordon stepped up to her and took her hands. The touch of him reassured her slowly, so that color began to come back into her cheeks and a swift mounting look of happiness to appear in her eyes.

"I feared you were dead. Oh, my dear, my dear!"

She sank back leaning against the table as though too weak to stand.

"Then they did not succeed?" she asked, tremulously.

GORDON SHOOK his head. A great joy sprang into her eyes.

"Thank God!" she exclaimed, and stood silent as though trying hard to collect her thoughts.

Her face and eyes showed plainly the effect of the strain she had been through. A great surge of pity welled up in Gordon. He opened his arms to her. Trembling, she gazed at him, shaking her head.

"No," she whispered, as if to herself, "you must know all, everything. You must know how I was ordered to win you over and render you harmless, how I deliberately started out with that intention"—her voice broke, she turned away—"but I weakened, I weakened...."

"It is all past and done with, Helene," Gordon broke in gently, "I know all about it."

"You knew about my uncle and Takahashi!" She looked up startled.

"Yes, about your uncle's wife being in prison with your mother in Manchukuo, both under sentence of death should you two fail to carry out Takahashi's orders. They are both safe now with the British in Hong Kong."

"Oh, thank God!" Helene exclaimed and then after a silence:

"You knew all the time that I was playing a role?" she asked quietly.

Gordon said nothing for a space. Then he looked at her steadily.

"Were you playing a role all the time, Helene?" he asked.

Slowly she shook her head, a faint flush coloring the pallor of her cheeks.

"No," she answered in a low voice, "I am afraid not."

Their hands went out to each other.

Sing, the silent spectator of all this, nodded his head and slid out noiselessly muttering:

"Catchem fat baby boy, Sing fixem good chow."

But even Sing could not resist a single backward look as they went out through the courtyard. The fountains lisped and whispered, discoursing after the fashion of running waters, with a musical rise and fall of liquid melody which sounded sometimes like the distant confused roar of vast crowds in a beleaguered city and anon softened into the voice of a woman murmuring happily to her lover.

VII

LAST TRAIN
TO FREEDOM

CHAPTER I

MURDER IN THE LION'S CAGE

THERE WAS a barrier across the road marking the boundaries between Occupied and Unoccupied France. It was dawn and a single cart lumbered toward the Nazi guards who eyed it sleepily.

The cart was driven by a white-whiskered old Frenchman who wore tattered trousers, shoes that were bound with pieces of cloth and a smock which had once been light blue, but now presented a bedraggled, washed-out appearance. In the rear of the cart was green truck, raised on French farms for the consumption of the invaders. The cart was piled high with it and the German guards approached with fixed bayonets.

"Bonjour!" The farmer waved a hand and smiled. "The lieutenant is awake, *oui?*"

One soldier went to the rear of the cart and methodically pawed through the produce. Those portions of the cart which he could not reach were investigated by means of his bayonet. He grunted, satisfied that the cart contained no hidden passenger.

The driver lifted a heavy basket, covered with cloth, got off the cart and winked at the German soldiers. They all entered the shack which was used as quarters for the men on guard duty. A lieutenant welcomed the old man with a shout.

The old man lifted the cloth from his basket and exposed five bottles of good wine. The lieutenant took up a collection from his men, paid the Frenchman in francs and ordered five more bottles his next trip around.

"We do not reach town often," the lieutenant explained. "Not once have we been able to buy the wine of France. Never—except from someone like you who does not mind dealing with Germans."

The old man clinked the coins in his hand.

Spencer turned the victim over—Fraser's
throat had been ripped from ear to ear!

Those present at the bloody
sight, set up yells.

"Why should I mind, *Messieurs?* Money is money, *Le bon Dieu* knows
we need it these days. Next week I come again, eh?"

He stepped out of the shack. There were two carts standing there
now, in front of the barrier. Two soldiers went to the second one and
began searching it also. The one thing those Germans did not notice

was that those two carts were identical in appearance and carried approximately the same kind of produce.

The old man clambered onto the cart nearest him, waved a farewell and clucked his horse into activity. The barrier was raised and the cart lumbered on.

TWENTY MINUTES later, the old man laid down the reins, turned in his seat and hammered against the side of the cart.

"Mon ami, it is now safe to come out."

Some of the produce was rolled aside and a red-headed, eager-eyed young man sat up. He slowly massaged his arm muscles.

"Thanks, Pierre," he said. "I still don't quite know how you did it, but the plan certainly worked."

Pierre shrugged. "It was simple, *mon ami.* These pigs of Boches see only what is directly before their eyes."

The young man climbed onto the seat. Pierre hauled out another smock and a battered old hat. When the young man had donned these he looked like a typical French peasant.

"Don't kid yourself," he said in French idiom approximating the American slang. "The Boche are smart. As clever as they are ruthless. That's why I know you pulled a fast one. What happened?"

Pierre grinned. "Always I bring wine to the Boche guards. They allow me to enter their shack, but only after I watch them search my cart. While I keep their attention inside, another cart draws up. One similar to mine, *comprenez?* The driver simply moves from his cart to mine. When the Boche search again, it is the same cart they have already searched, while I continue across the border with whatever I am bringing. Sometimes it is guns or bombs. Sometimes men who wish to return to Paris. Men like you, *Monsieur.* Though I cannot see why anyone in his right mind would want to go to Paris these days."

"I'm on a rather important mission," the young man said. "My name is Jack Spencer. I'm an American."

"Ah, *bien.* You go, perhaps, to pave the way for invasion?"

"No—not quite yet, Pierre, and it will take many more men than just me. I work for the United States Government as a consular clerk out of Vichy. We received a tip that all remaining Americans in Paris are to be arrested."

"But I thought they were all interned long ago," Pierre commented.

"No. There are nearly two thousand Americans loose in Paris. Men too old for active military duty. Women and children, too. Seems Brazil has been rounding up a lot of Nazi people and Germany wants to retaliate. There are few Brazilians so they're going to pick on Americans."

Pierre wagged his old head solemnly from side to side.

"War is a bad thing, *Monsieur.* An evil thing, for it hits not only men, but everyone. Those Americans—I feel sorry for them. They will be put in a concentration camp."

"Not if I reach them first," Jack Spencer said. "We'll arrange some way to get them over the border. Two miles ahead is a railroad station. I have a passport that doesn't identify me as a consular official, but I can get through with it. Drop me there, Pierre, and many thanks."

The train ride to Paris was monotonously long, with stops at every village on the way. The cars were packed with Nazi soldiers, but none paid any attention to Jack Spencer.

It was dark when the train puffed into the Paris station. Spencer got off and started walking toward one of the exits. Two men in Gestapo uniforms saw him. They held a brief conversation and then a shouted command brought Spencer to a halt.

"Your papers," one of the Gestapo men said curtly.

SPENCER HANDED over his passport. The Gestapo man glanced at it, shoved the passport into his pocket and took a firm grip on Jack Spencer's arm.

"American, eh? You are under arrest. All Americans in Paris are under arrest. Come with us."

Spencer groaned. He was too late, and even worse was the fact that he was under arrest, too. He was of military age and liable to be treated like any prisoner of war. In Occupied France or the concentration camps of Germany, such a prospect was not pleasing.

They bundled him into a military car and it was driven across Paris straight toward a big park which was noted for its large zoo. The car stopped in front of a concrete building and Jack Spencer was hauled out.

There were guards all around the building and from inside he could hear muffled voices. His eyes caught the concrete bas-relief of a lion.

"What is this?" he asked in German. "Why am I being forced into the lion house of a zoo?"

"Because the monkey house is already filled." One Gestapo man laughed harshly. "Therefore, we throw you to the lions. Get inside or shall I boot you?"

Spencer stepped through the door and it was instantly slammed shut. He stood there in complete darkness, yet aware that a large number of people were around him.

"Yank?" someone finally asked.

"You bet I'm a Yank!" Spencer said. "A doggone sore one, too. Will somebody tell me what this is all about?"

"Welcome, Daniel," the voice said.

"Daniel?" Spencer frowned. "My name is Jack Spencer. I—"

"We're all Daniels in here," several voices assured him, and there was laughter. "Daniels in a lion's den."

As if in answer, there was a mighty roar from the rear of the building. Spencer gulped.

"Don't tell me there are real lions in here?" he demanded. "We're not locked up like a few hundred pounds of hamburger?"

Two or three matches were scraped and Spencer saw where he was. About eighty people were packed in the rather narrow passageway between big cages. Typical American humor pervaded and the consular clerk succumbed to it also.

A man of about fifty stepped up with outstretched hand.

"I'm Ted Tannen," he said. "Perfumes are—were—my business. The Germans have pinched every American in Paris. Imagine them being afraid of old ducks like me? Or of women like those locked up here with us? That's not all, either. Another hundred are decorating the big monkey cage, but they don't have the entertainment we're provided with."

Darkness settled again. Jack Spencer moved forward.

"You mean that lion, I suppose. I notice he is penned up in another cage at the rear of this corridor. Are you sure the bars will keep him back?"

"Don't worry." Tannen grinned. "We were put in here while it was still daylight and I examined those bars—when the lion let me get close enough. Take it from me, he's a hungry lion."

Spencer grunted. "Except for the Boche, there isn't a man, woman, child or beast in all of France who isn't hungry."

Tannen lit another match, studying Spencer. He whistled softly.

"You're young. How in the world did you stay out of their clutches this long? My partner—Ed Fraser—is just past fifty-seven and they almost tossed him into one of their concentration camps. Wait—let's find Ed. He'll be glad to meet a stranger."

TANNEN YELLED the name of his partner. A voice came from far to the rear of the lion house. It was suddenly cut short by a wild scream that made everyone grow rigid with terror. On the heels of this scream came a savage snarl from the lion.

Spencer started elbowing his way through the packed crowd. Tannen stayed right behind him. They cleared the frightened prisoners. Spencer felt in his pocket and fished out a lighter. He snapped the little wheel and a small flame sprang up.

Holding this high, he and Tannen slowly approached the cage where a lion eyed them malevolently. On the floor, in front of that cage, lay a huddled heap. Blood was slowly forming a miniature river. The lion thrust a paw through the bars and made a pass at the figure and set up another series of snarls.

"That's Ed—Ed Fraser!" Tannen gasped. "The cursed lion killed him! No—it was the Nazis who did it, curse them! They killed him."

"Hold this lighter," Jack Spencer said. "He may not be dead. Watch the lion and yell if he starts anything."

He dropped prone and wriggled closer toward the sprawled-out figure. He stretched one arm, secured a grip on Fraser's ankle and gently pulled him away. The lion bellowed savagely and tried to reach its victim with a bloody paw.

Spencer turned the victim over and grimaced. Tannen instantly shut off the lighter. What they had seen was not pleasant to look upon. Fraser's throat had been ripped from ear to ear!

CHAPTER II

PRISON HOTEL

E NOUGH OF those present had had glimpses of the bloody corpse to set up yells. Doors opened, rifle-armed guards came in and lights were turned on. A cocky lieutenant swaggered into the midst of the group, demanding silence in English, which he understood.

He saw Ed Fraser's body and cried out sharply. He rushed over to the man on the floor.

Jack Spencer stood beside him. The German looked up.

"He is dead," he said to Spencer. "The lion did this, I suppose. Look—the lion's paw. It is bloody. This foolish American went too close to the cage. It was his fault, do you understand? You were warned to stay away from the cage. We Germans are not responsible."

"You locked us up here," Spencer accused. "You put out the lights. You left that lion close enough to do damage. Now you say this isn't your fault. More colossal Nazi nerve, if you ask me. You might as well have stood Fraser up against a wall and shot him."

The Nazi lieutenant arose, his face grim.

"It is best you are careful what you say!" he shouted at the top of his lungs. "Perhaps it will be a wall at sunrise for the lot of you. But we Germans do not want you killed by a lion. If you are so stupid as not to stay away from the cage, it is your fault. However, I shall arrange that all of you are taken to more comfortable quarters."

As quickly as it could be managed they were all on a military truck, rolling across peaceful-looking country that showed no scars of war. Jack Spencer was jammed between Ted Tannen and a woman of about thirty-eight who identified herself as Anita Clark.

"I think I know where they are taking us," Spencer said. "We just passed through Moisdon. That means we're still in Occupied France, but not far from the Border. There's a resort hotel a couple of miles ahead. I'll bet we'll be held there and when arrangements are made, we'll be shipped to Lisbon."

"For a return trip home?" Anita Clark asked without eagerness. "Mr. Spencer, do you think they'll exchange us for German prisoners being held in the United States and Brazil?"

"Exactly." Spencer nodded. "You'll notice they didn't even take me to a camp. That means they need every one of us to get their own people back. You don't seem to enjoy the prospect, Anita."

"I don't," she said softly. "You see, I'm married to a Frenchman. He was injured during the fighting and isn't arrested. I'd been hoping I could find some way to get him out of the country—and now I have to leave him. I may never see him again. He won't know what's happened to me. Here—I'll show you his picture."

She opened her purse and took out a pair of small photographs. Her husband was a nice-looking man. Anita was also in the picture.

"We had them taken for passport use," she explained. "In those days we had hope. Now it's all gone."

Ted Tannen put a friendly hand on her shoulder.

"We all have troubles these days, Anita," he said soberly. "Ed Fraser would have given his right arm for a chance to go back to civilization. We talked about what we'd do when we got to New York together. I'll be glad to get there, but it won't be the same without Ed."

The truck made a violent turn. It passed through gates and climbed a steep driveway toward a homey-looking hotel on top of a hill.

"I was right," Spencer said. "This is the hotel I referred to. The death of Fraser must have scared the Nazis into providing us with good quarters."

ALL THE trucks stopped and the Americans hopped off, stretching their legs with considerable gusto until guards swarmed up and they were brought into line. An infantry captain addressed them—also in English.

"You will be quite comfortable here," he said arrogantly. "In a short time, arrangements will have been made to exchange you for Germans being held in Brazil and the United States. While you are here, it is permitted to take walks along the paths, but do not leave them. The fence around these premises is charged with high voltage. I would not advise anyone to try to escape."

Tannen let out a laugh. "Imagine, telling us not to try to escape. Captain, if you offered me fifty thousand dollars, I'd still stay here and wait until we're sent to Lisbon."

"Silence!" the captain roared. "You will remain within doors after dinner. Anyone found outside will be shot immediately. No radios, of course, no newspapers, and no talk about the war."

"We get it," Jack Spencer said.

"That is good because from now on, you are under the control of the Gestapo. There is a new unit in Moisdon. I cannot guarantee how they will feel toward enemies of the Reich. Brandt, who will head this unit, is not noted for his kindness. That is my warning. Now select your own rooms."

The hotel was without heat and everyone pulled coats close as they went off in search of a place to sleep.

Dinner consisted of some soup that tasted on the dish-water side. There was a sausage apiece and none of the weenies suffered from obesity. Potatoes were black around the edges and matched the color of the bread.

After dinner, Jack Spencer sat down beside Anita Clark. He had four cigarettes, broke one in half and offered her this. He lit it and they puffed slowly.

"There is something rotten in France and it's Germans," he said in a low voice. "Ed Fraser wasn't killed by that lion. He was murdered—or had you guessed that?"

"No—no," she said tremulously. "I never gave it a thought. What makes you think it was murder?"

"Locking us up in a zoo was a typical German gesture, but there isn't a zoo in all France that has a single animal left. Lions, especially, were killed when the war began. In a bombing raid, lions might get loose and create panic. That lion was brought there from some remote zoo with the express purpose of fashioning an excuse for the murder of Ed Fraser."

Anita gasped. "But why should they murder him? The Boche usually kill those they don't like and call it military necessity."

"Because if they did that, Brazil might march one of their Nazi prisoners to a wall and do the same thing. Or the United States would call a halt to these exchange proceedings. No—it had to look like an accident. Trouble is, it does and I haven't a thing to go on."

Two Gestapo men sauntered by and Spencer and Anita stopped talking. They snuffed out the tiny cigarette butts that were left and Spencer moved his chair closer to the woman.

"I've got to get out of here," he whispered.

Anita stiffed a gasp. "They'll shoot you!" she objected. "They'll be within their rights, too."

"I know. Just the same I have to get out of here and I will. I.... Who the devil is this guy?"

The German soldier investigated the cart by means of his bayonet.

THE MAN who approached walked like a ballet dancer. He was elegantly dressed, even though his clothes were not new. He had a thin, black mustache, a swarthy face and black hair.

"He," Anita said, "is Armando. He's a Brazilian. One of the few caught here by the war. A little sticky, perhaps, but not a bad sort. We met yesterday—in the zoo."

Armando stopped, bowed low, and implanted a kiss on Anita's hand. He nodded affably to Jack Spencer and sat down. Spencer talked for a few moments, arose and walked around the lobby of the hotel. Gestapo men kept their eyes on him, but there were many prisoners to watch and Spencer finally found an opportunity to slip through a door leading to the cellar.

He ran lightly down the steps, used his lighter again, and peered around in the gloom. Through a cellar window, he saw the electrified fence no more than a dozen feet away. A sentry paced slowly back and forth. Spencer ducked until the man was out of sight.

Prowling silently, he located a wine cellar, long since looted of its precious contents. He crawled through a small door, lay prone, and snapped on his lighter.

The wine cellar was long, narrow, and no more than three feet high. It was filled with cobwebs and had a musty odor. The floor was dirt. Spencer crawled back to the cellar, risked a quick look out of the window, and noticed that the wine cellar extended well beyond the fence. Elation gripped him. He searched for digging tools and found an old shovel, so badly rusted that the Germans had not taken it for their scrap pile.

It was better than nothing and he set about digging frantically, at the far end of the wine cellar. Lying on his back, he chopped away at the dirt roof, careful not to make any noise. In a short time, the guards would call the roll. He had to finish this and get back within forty-five minutes.

A clod of earth dropped onto his chest. He moved it away, dug again and then felt cool night air streaming through the hole he had made in the ground above.

He prayed that no Nazi sentry would wander directly above this spot and have it cave in under him. He quickly dusted himself off, climbed the steps, opened the door a crack, and groaned softly. Every prisoner was lined up while an officer called out their names.

Between Jack Spencer and that lineup were at least five Gestapo men, all on the alert. Soon, his name would be called and when there was no answer, all Hades would break loose. Spencer wondered if he should make his escape now and take a chance on getting back to Unoccupied France where he had the protection of the United States Government.

Then someone called out. The Gestapo guards moved closer. Anita, standing in the front row, slowly buckled and fell to the floor. In the resulting confusion, Spencer slipped across the room and mingled with the others. He elbowed his way to Anita's side, knelt and raised her head.

"Hunger did this," he accused flatly. "Not an hour ago she was telling me she felt weak and faint."

"Carry her to her room," the officer in charge ordered. "She was given the same food as all the rest. But I will see to it she gets some milk."

Spencer lifted her in his arms, walked toward the steps, and then turned around.

"My name is Jack Spencer," he announced, "when you come to it on the roll call. Don't forget about the milk."

HE CLIMBED the steps. Anita was laughing silently. Spencer got around a corner and chuckled himself.

"For that little act, I owe you my freedom," he said softly. "If I can repay you—"

"It wasn't all pretense." Anita smiled. "When you opened that door and I saw how you were trapped, I actually felt woozy. It was nothing, Mr. Spencer. And I learned a few things from Señor Armando which may interest you. "

"For instance?" Spencer put her down and held the door of her room open.

She stopped in the doorway and turned around.

"A fellow named Don Leeds was arrested with the rest of us," she said. "He didn't live in Paris and none of us knew him, but he struck up a warm friendship with Ed Fraser. He was the last man with Fraser, in fact. Perhaps he may know something—if it was murder."

"Take it from me," Spencer said, "it was murder. I'll check on Leeds as soon as I get back—if I get back. What else did Armando say?"

"He asked a million questions about you, that's all. Questions I couldn't have answered if I wanted to. After all, you popped in just like Don Leeds. You may even be a Gestapo agent."

"If I were," Jack Spencer said seriously, "that husband of yours might find himself in a lot of trouble. Seriously though, if I can do anything to help, I will. Soon as the place settles down for the night, I'm taking a walk. Just on a hunch, let me have one of those pictures of your husband and yourself."

CHAPTER III

PASSWORD OF FREEDOM

JACK SPENCER met Ted Tannen and Armando in the corridor, said good-night to them, and went to his room. Fortunately, he was one of the few who had a single room. Most of the others had to double up.

He sat on the edge of his bed trying to puzzle out just why Ed Fraser had been murdered. It was not an accident, even though the affair had been cleverly pulled off. Fraser must have known something dangerous to the Nazis.

Shortly after midnight, Spencer folded a long letter which he'd written to his superiors in Vichy, stowed it away in a pocket and slipped out of the room. It took him thirty minutes to reach the cellar. Gestapo men patrolled the hotel thickly. He had to duck from one sheltering spot to another and reach his objective by short stages and long waits. Inside the wine cellar, he seized the shovel, crawled to the end of the tunnel and finished cutting a hole through to freedom. Even outside this fence, he knew, Gestapo guards were constantly on duty. He poked his head out, like a mole, saw the back of a guard, and worked fast. He forced the hole wider, wriggled through and then quickly recovered it with long strands of grass.

Two minutes after he emerged, he was lying prone behind a thick bush along a path that led all around the hotel, but outside of the electrified fence.

The cumbersome pacing of a guard who was tired, drew closer. Spencer held his breath. If he were found now, they would probably make short work of him and above all else, he wanted to get back to the United States and join the fight in a uniform.

The guard passed on and came to a sudden halt while Spencer's blood froze. He heard a harsh voice.

"Guard, why did you not challenge me? I purposely crept up on you to see if you were prepared for trouble."

"I—I recognized you, sir," the guard answered. "Besides, all the Americans are accounted for and locked behind the steel fence. You could be no one but a friend."

"Fool. Gross idiot. They may have friends on the outside. So you recognized me, eh? That is a lie. I have been in this town for no more than one hour. I have not yet even visited Headquarters of the Gestapo and I probably shall not go there until I am finished with my job concerning the prisoners."

"Herr Brandt!" The sentry's voice cracked with fear. "I—I knew you were coming. They told me what you looked like. That you do not wear a uniform. That you head all Gestapo agents in this part of France. That you are undoubtedly the cleverest man in the whole service. No one gets by you. British and French dogs have paid with their lives every time they came against you."

The Gestapo leader drew himself erect. Behind the bush, Jack Spencer watched this and grinned. That soldier may have been a fool in Brandt's opinion, but the American had the idea that the Gestapo leader was the bigger fool. He fell for the common soldier's compliments, forgot all about his failure to challenge him.

"Perhaps I have been too harsh," Brandt said. "So they have heard of me here, eh? I am gratified."

"Excellency"—the sentry breathed it like a prayer—"who in all of Europe has not heard of you and your prowess? I have heard them call you a—a human bloodhound."

Brandt laughed and whacked the soldier on the back.

"Very good. Very, very good. Just be careful to challenge anyone else who may appear. Perhaps I will test your vigilance again, eh?"

"As you wish, Excellency," the soldier answered. "Be assured, all prisoners are well locked up."

BRANDT STROLLED away in the darkness and the sentry resumed his slow pacing. Behind that bush, Jack Spencer suddenly developed a daring idea. He knew all about Brandt. He was one of the Gestapo hangmen supreme, but always worked in Belgium and Holland. He was a brainy, trusted member of the New Order.

Why had he been sent here, to take over the imprisonment of a hundred odd Americans, mostly all of whom were too old for military service? It didn't make sense. There was something else behind it. Something big enough to attract Brandt's skill.

Spencer's idea came first though and now he had a double mission to perform before he slipped back into the hotel. He crept along the path and waited for that same sentry to return. As the man lumbered up the path, Spencer jumped out again.

Instantly, a rifle came to ready. Spencer threw up his hands and spoke in German.

"Much better, my dear fellow. I came back to test you again."

"Danke, Herr Brandt," the soldier said. "I am glad."

"At first," Spencer said, "I was tempted to have you sent to the Russian front. Now wait—do not start cringing. I believe you are too smart to waste your time here. Go to Gestapo Headquarters at once. How many men are on duty there?"

"Guards, Excellency? Only one, who paces up and down before the door. We have no trouble with the French here."

"Good. Then you will relieve the sentry on duty there and take the post yourself. I shall assign another man here in your place. And you failed in one respect. I told you I was Brandt, but you never asked for proof. You did not require that I show my face even. Remedy that at once."

The sentry nodded eagerly, lit a match and waved it in front of Jack Spencer's stern features. He blew it out and nodded happily.

"Never again will I forget your face, Excellency. Never."

Spencer walked quietly away. He had tricked this sentry, but if he ever met Brandt, he would be doomed. There were many things to do. Spencer began running as soon as he reached the road back to Moisden.

He saw the lights of a farmhouse and knew he had to take a chance with the occupants. Creeping up to a window, he peered inside. A middle-aged farmer was sitting in front of the fire. On the floor was a copy of a Nazi-controlled French newspaper. It had been crumpled and hurled to the floor. Spencer smiled. He was safe enough here.

He tapped on the door and it was opened half an inch. Jack Spencer spoke softly and in French.

"Liberty! Equality! Fraternity! Do you understand?"

The door was opened wide, bolted after he entered, and the farmer called out to his wife to bring food—the best. Then he looked more closely at Spencer and frowned.

"You are not French. British perhaps?"

"American—Yankee." Jack Spencer grinned. "But I know the password. It was taught to me by French patriots in Vichy. I was told that almost every farmer works for the Underground."

"We do," the farmer said. "The Boche never touch us because they need our crops. Is it your wish to be sent back to Vichy?"

"No—but I want a letter to go through. If the man who carries it is discovered, he will be shot and so will I. It must be someone you can trust."

"We have many such men. Give me the letter. Within two hours it will be on its way. Now eat. Good food such as even the Boche do not get."

THE AMERICAN tackled cold chicken with gusto. There was white bread, freshly baked. Cream and butter, even a bit of steak in lieu of dessert. He asked about *Herr* Brandt while he ate.

The farmer shrugged. "We know he is coming and that he is a dangerous man. What puzzles us, *Monsieur*, is why they should send such an important person to this little village. The brains of the Underground are in the big cities and the Gestapo knows this."

"I've been wondering too," the consular agent said. "Furthermore, I'm going to try and find out a few things. Be sure of the letter, my friend. It must not go astray. I am a diplomatic clerk, caught in a trap here. My superiors must know where I am and what I am up to. The letter explains."

He tried to pay for his food, but was roughly refused. Then he went out into the night again and headed straight for the center of Moisdon. He knew where Gestapo Headquarters was located—in the town jail. Handy when the Nazis had people they wished to question and whose screams they did not wish heard too loudly.

What Jack intended doing now had more chance of failure than success, but it had to be done. It was absolutely necessary to learn why a man like Brandt was in charge here, why Ed Fraser had been murdered. Why a lot of things, and the secrets might well lie inside Gestapo Headquarters.

Carefully peering around a corner, Spencer saw the sentry who had been on duty outside the hotel. He had already assumed his post and was pacing up and down in front of the place.

Jack Spencer drew himself erect, pulled his hat down to hide the red hair, and walked briskly up to the entrance. The sentry's rifle came to readiness, then he stiffened to attention.

"I recognize you this time, Excellency," he said.

"See that no one enters," Spencer told him. "I shall be busy with secret proceedings. If I am disturbed, you will be to blame. Is that clear?"

"*Ja*, Excellency. There is no one inside except for one prisoner."

Spencer walked up the four steps to the door, opened it and stepped into a receiving room. He passed through this and found a spacious office decorated with swastikas and the ever-present photograph of Schikelgruber. Spencer gave him a salute far more in style in Brooklyn than in the Reich.

He sat down behind the desk and the first thing he saw was a blank American passport. Spencer frowned. What was one of these doing here? He examined it briefly. It was the real thing all right, probably stolen from some conquered nation when the United States staff had fled in a hurry.

There was a seal on the desk too, a rather familiar-looking seal. Spencer thrust a piece of blank paper between the slots, brought down the handle, and got a perfect impression of a United States seal—the kind used on passports.

There was not time to figure this out. He searched the desk drawers and discovered what he wanted. A German passport. From his pocket he took the picture of Anita Clark and her husband. There was glue on the desk. He affixed the picture to the German passport, impressed the

Reich seal on it, then filled in the blanks. For good measure he also took a Gestapo pass and made this out for Anita and her husband.

CHAPTER IV

WOMEN MUST BE SAVED

FOR A few more minutes Jack Spencer searched files, trying to find the reason for Brandt's presence, but there was nothing. He couldn't afford to spend any more time here. Brandt might return at any moment and even that susceptible guard outside could not put off Brandt for long.

Spencer replaced everything, was tempted to ruin that United States seal, but decided to let it stay and see what developed. He walked across the room and then hesitated. There were two doors and he had forgotten which one led to the outer office. He shrugged, opened the nearest door and stepped into a small room with barred windows.

The only piece of furniture in the room was a low stool and on it sat a girl. A decidedly pretty girl, too, and she had been trying to check tears that came anyway. Her first glance was frightened, apprehensive.

"Good evening," Spencer said in German. "Excuse me. I am looking for someone."

"American," the girl said. "American. Help me! Please help me!"

She spoke with a faint British accent and Jack Spencer whirled around. She was coming toward him, one hand outstretched in silent pleading.

"How did you know I am an American," he asked. "Who the devil are you?"

"Never mind about me, except that I may be shot in the morning. I knew you were an American by the way you wear your clothes, the slant at your hat, your red hair. Don't let me down—please!"

Spencer hesitated. He didn't know what in the world he could do with this girl, but she obviously was sincere and needed help. He took her hand.

"Come on," he said quickly. "I'll get you past the guard outside. Then you're on your own. Is that clear?"

She nodded mutely and her hand felt cold in the young American's grasp. He took her arm when they reached the main door, drew himself up again, and altered the slant of his hat.

The sentry came to attention. Jack Spencer walked past him, still holding tightly to the girl's arm. He turned a corner and started to run. Minutes were as precious as life now.

They trotted along the dirt road leading to the hotel. The girl faltered several times and finally had to stop. Spencer led her off the road and they sat down beneath a tree.

"We can rest for three minutes," he said. "While you're catching your breath, how about some information? Maybe we can both leave this country?"

"My name is Valerie Cabot," she said wearily. "I'm British. I—I was a nursemaid in Paris before the war began. After Dunkirk I was trapped. I hid, but you can't hide forever. The Gestapo caught up with me at Moisdon. I was being held until some ranking Gestapo man arrived. That's all there is to it, except…. But how can you, how can anyone get out of this country?"

Spencer pursed his lips for a moment. Then he jumped up, pulled her to her feet and they began running again.

"Might be a way," he said. "In fact, I think there is one. You're coming with me to the hotel on top of the hill. It's full of Americans who are going to be repatriated. I think I can get you a passport. You'll wind up in New York if we're lucky. Is that satisfactory?"

"You ask if going to heaven is satisfactory?" she sighed. "I can't believe it. I'll do anything you ask. Just get me out of here, Mr.—Mr.—"

"Spencer. Jack Spencer. I'm one of the Americans. We'll start crossing this field now. I…. Duck! Get down, quickly!"

BOTH DROPPED flat. Two sentries came along the road carrying searchlights and drawn sidearms. They had been heard. Patrols were further away from the hotel than he had believed.

Spencer held his breath. It was tough to take it alone, but now he had this girl to think about which made matters even worse. Sweat oozed out of every pore. He felt Valerie's hand tight around his fingers. She knew what capture would mean.

The sentries talked in German and from a few words that drifted to the American's ears he knew they were certain that prowlers were about. Finally the pair separated. One of them came straight toward the spot where Spencer and Valerie were hidden.

Jack Spencer put his lips against the girl's ear.

"Crawl ten feet away and stand up. Don't make a sound when he throws the searchlight on you and don't move."

She didn't ask why, just crawled away. Spencer knew the German would hear her. A sharp command rang out. Valerie arose and stood quietly in the ray of the German's flash.

"Ach!" He walked toward her. "A girl. A pretty girl too. What luck!"

He stepped closer, gun ready. Valerie heard the second German soldier heading this way too, in answer to the commotion his mate had caused. The German reached out to seize her. Instead, an arm curled around his throat and he was yanked back. At the same time, Valerie sprang forward, seized his gun hand and brought strong, healthy teeth driving into the flesh of the Nazi's hand. The gun fell and she scooped it up.

There was a sinister crack. The German went limp. Jack Spencer let go and the man flopped to the ground.

Valerie handed the gun to Spencer. It was unfamiliar to him, but in one second he knew how it worked. The other sentry was calling out as he approached.

Spencer pushed Valerie behind a tree, bent down to pick up the flashlight, and a shot rang out. He actually felt the heat of that bullet as it zipped above his head. Without straightening, he fired back. The German was holding a flashlight of his own and was a perfect target. The flash dropped to the ground. So did the German. Spencer hurried over to him, took a quick look, then sped to where Valerie was waiting.

Hand in hand, they raced across the field, grateful for the tall grass that all but concealed them. He saw the rear of the hotel and that electrified fence. Sentries were running toward the sound of the shots. Twice, Spencer and Valerie Cabot had to duck down and let them pass.

Then he came to the hole leading into the long wine cellar and helped Valerie through it. He seized as much long grass as he could hold, slipped down himself and did a fair job of camouflaging the entrance.

Heavy feet pounded across the floor and more and more Germans rushed out to see what had happened.

"We must be inside the hotel," Valerie panted. "Those two sentries! They'll describe you—and me too."

"Not that pair," Spencer said grimly. "I don't think the population of Hades is interested in us and that's where those two are right now. I studied Commando tactics for a while. Come on—we must reach the upstairs rooms before they start checking."

There was no uproar at the hotel, but there was quiet activity. Guards hurried out to locate the source of those shots. As a result, there were only two sentries at the front door and Spencer could evade them easily because the stairway was hidden to their gaze.

WHEN HE and Valerie reached Anita's room he knocked softly and the door opened. Anita stared for a moment, then stepped aside so they could enter. Spencer explained quickly.

"Look at this." He laid out the passport he had fixed up at the Gestapo Headquarters. Beside it he placed the military pass. "The pass will get you through any lines because it's official even to the seal. The passport is made out to you and your husband. Reach him—proceed at once to Spain. You won't be refused admittance because this is a Gestapo passport and they have a certain amount of influence at the Border."

Anita could not speak for a moment or two.

"Don't start thanking me," Spencer said, "because if something happens and you don't make it, you're finished. Besides, I want your American passport for Valerie."

Anita excitedly fished it out of her bag. Spencer examined it and nodded.

"Good! The description fits both of you and the picture isn't so hot. There will be a check-up as soon as they find the two guards I killed, so Valerie will have to hide in your room, Anita. Remember she is British, may be classed as a spy, and by helping her you may forfeit your life."

Anita smiled happily. "For that passport, Jack Spencer, I'd risk anything."

"Later on, I'll show you a way out of here and give you instructions on how to reach Paris," he said. "Right now, I'd better get back to my room."

He was none to quick about it. Five minutes after he had undressed and slipped between the bedclothes, there was a knock at his door. He tousled his hair, blinked sleepily, and unlocked it. A Gestapo man, in civilian clothes, brushed the American aside, went over to the bed and thrust a hand between the covers. They were warm and he seemed satisfied. Without a word of explanation, he departed.

For more than an hour, this went on all through the hotel and then things quieted down. At two-forty in the morning Jack Spencer decided to risk a trip to Anita's room. He made it without detection, found Valerie safe, and said to Anita:

"Head north when you leave here. Stay off the road, but close enough to it to follow the route. There is a fork, a mile below the hotel. To the right, you'll see a farmhouse with a red-painted barn behind it. Go there.

Tell the farmer you're a friend of the American diplomat from Vichy. He'll see that you reach Paris."

"Diplomat from Vichy?" Anita asked, in a puzzled voice.

"That's me—but I'm only a consular clerk," Spencer said. "I was supposed to tip off people like you that arrests were expected. I failed, but I'm going to see that everyone gets back home safely. I'll be back an hour before dawn and show you how to escape."

Valerie came forward. "I don't know how to thank you—"

"Don't even try." He grinned. "You're British and we have to stick together in this mess. Learn all you can from Anita so if you are questioned, you'll have the answers. Good night."

Spencer slipped out of the room, tiptoed back toward his own quarters and heard someone running up the stairs. He ducked for shelter, heard the steps continue down the hall and took a quick look. He was too late to see who it was or what door closed with a loud click.

That person had entered the hotel as if he were a paying guest, not a prisoner. Jack Spencer frowned. This thing was getting more and more mysterious.

AGAIN, HE began the rest of a slow trip to his room. Just before he started to slip the key into the lock, he heard a strident yell from outside the hotel. An instant later the main door banged open and a man fled into the lobby. He was short, a little overweight, and looked as though he had crawled through thickets and swamps.

The most obvious thing about him was his terror and a determination to get something done. He was halfway across the lobby before the astounded guards pounced on him. The man started to screech something, but a hand was clapped across his mouth.

Four uniformed Gestapo men with drawn guns hurried into the lobby. Following them came a man of medium height, thin-faced and slender. He was dressed in civilian clothes, but exuded an air of authority. He stepped up to the prisoner, slapped him with the back of his hand, then whipped a gun from his hip pocket.

Slowly he reversed the weapon to be used as a club. He spoke, but in a voice so low that Spencer could hear nothing. He raised the gun and while the terrorized prisoner was firmly held, brought the gun down with murderous intent.

Jack Spencer did not forget his own position for one moment, but he couldn't stand by and watch a man's brains beaten out. He ran noisily down the steps. The man with the gun bellowed orders. This time his voice was loud enough to be recognized and Spencer knew who he was.

Brandt! The ace Gestapo agent! One of the deadliest men in that whole black service!

CHAPTER V

FRENCHMAN WITH GOOD SHOES

WITH A swift move Jack Spencer evaded one guard who tried to seize him, veered aside as another made a pass with a gun, but stopped long enough to smash home a haymaker to the jaw. The prisoner was slumped in the arms of the pair who held him, but he was still conscious.

Spencer ran straight toward Brandt and so quickly that the Gestapo man did not have time to turn his gun around and shoot. The American's fist thudded against the Nazi's stomach and Brandt gave a howl of pain as he doubled up. Spencer rapped him hard on the jaw, pushed him arm's length away and shot a right jab to the nose.

He saw blood spurt, saw the look of astonishment and pain on Brandt's face, and then everything turned red. Red, just like blood. Spencer felt himself slipping. The floor came up and he fell on it. There was another thump right beside him. That would be the mystery man they had chased into the hotel.

Vaguely, Jack Spencer heard mumbled words. They came from this man and never did make much sense, but he was trying desperately to say what was in his mind.

"Spy—America—danger—get him. Fraser mur—murd—murdered."

A shot punctuated the end of that sentence. Jack Spencer mentally braced himself for the next bullet. Mentally, because his muscles and nerves were completely paralyzed and limp....

It seemed that hours passed. He was being tossed around like a dummy and every time his eyes opened, he could still see that veil of blood and nothing else. His ears told him that confusion reigned. There were loud, protesting voices, sharp orders, and once in a while the sound of a blow.

Someone wiped blood out of the consular clerk's eyes. So that's what made him see nothing but red. As his vision cleared, he saw Valerie trying to help him, paying no attention to a Nazi who was doing his best to pull her away without actually lifting her up.

A sharp slap steadied Spencer's wits. His brain worked clearly now. Brandt stood before him, scowling.

"Why did you interfere?" he demanded. "The punishment for interfering with the Gestapo is death. You know that, American swine."

"I know I couldn't stand by and watch you beat a helpless man to death," Spencer retorted. "A man who was being held by your stooges while you hammered his brains out. If that makes me an American swine, I'm glad of it, but I hate to think what it makes you."

Brandt raised a clubbed fist, hesitated, then lowered his arm.

"That man is now dead. He was killed trying to escape. We arrested him, but he broke loose and ran in here, probably hoping some foolish American could help. I was forced to shoot him. He was a French spy."

"But he was still a human being!" Jack Spencer argued hotly. "Or maybe you wouldn't recognize a human after associating with faceless men so long."

Brandt smiled to cover up his anger. "Quite cocky, aren't you? May I remind you that you are an enemy of the Reich? That you are of military age and can be interned? That all of you here may be locked up for the duration?"

An American whom Spencer had not noticed before, went to his side. He was a husky individual with a slightly twisted nose that looked as if it were the result of a football game. Despite this, he was not ugly.

"He's right, Jack," this man said, calling Spencer by name. "Nobody blames you for trying to help that poor chap they just carried out. But consider all of us as a group. Relax, man. This is war. We got to take a lot of things."

"Who are you?" Spencer demanded.

"My name is Don Leeds. I'm going to be repatriated too. And believe me, it's like a dream for all of us. Don't turn it into a nightmare, Jack."

"All right," Spencer said. "I made a fool of myself, I guess."

TWO GESTAPO men led Jack Spencer to the hotel manager's office and shoved him into a chair. They mounted guard until Brandt bustled in. Brandt eyed the young American with open malevolence.

"You are an impulsive person, eh?" he growled. "So impulsive that you might have escaped from this hotel earlier tonight and murdered two of my men."

"I'd even risk a crazy thing like that if I knew I'd meet you somewhere outside," Spencer grunted. "Otherwise, I don't know what you're talking about."

Brandt sat down. "You will. Also, I promise that if you know anything about those murders tonight, I shall find out. You'll tell me because not until you do will the pain stop. You will be willing to talk. Wait and see."

Spencer digested that threat for a second and knew that desperate circumstances called for equally desperate measures.

"So I'm under arrest," he said slowly. "I won't be permitted to take that train to Lisbon, I suppose."

"That is correct. You are of military age."

"I suppose you know," Spencer went on, "that the nephew of one of your big shots in the Foreign Office is interned in Brazil. This whole transaction is mainly to get him back to Germany. Well, if I'm held here, he'll be held in Brazil. What do you think of that?"

"Nonsense," Brandt sneered. Then he looked at Spencer sharply. "Just how did you know this?"

"Because I'm connected with the United States legation in Vichy. They know I am here, under arrest. They will notify Brazil that if I am not returned with these others, then that pet nephew will also remain where he is. Go ahead and phone Vichy if you don't believe me."

Brandt tapped the end of his fingers a bit nervously. He arose.

"Very well. You shall go along with the others. But if you are not telling the truth, I shall personally remove you from the train before it passes into neutral territory. You cannot escape, because the train will be sealed and guarded. Now go back and prepare. You leave here within an hour."

When Jack Spencer emerged from the office, he saw Valerie at the foot of the steps. Her worried face relaxed somewhat. She took his arm and they both went to the second floor.

"Jack," she said, "that man who was shot. I saw them place him on a stretcher. He was no Frenchman. His clothes were old and rugged, but his shoes—they had rubber heels and impressed on the heel was a trademark well known in the United States and England. No Frenchman has owned a pair of shoes like that for years."

"I know," Spencer answered softly. "He was trying to talk just before they killed him. He told me Fraser had been murdered, just as I thought. Did Anita tell you about Fraser? Good. This stranger also muttered something concerning a spy. We'll talk about it later on. Right now, I've got to get Anita out of here."

"She has already gone, Jack. I told her how to get away. In the confusion she found a perfect chance."

Spencer closed both eyes and breathed a long sigh of relief.

"Then you pack Anita's things. We're being taken to a train. I'm not in the clear yet, but I'd like to see those Nazis put me off once I'm aboard."

The military trucks, jammed with prisoners, pulled up to the small railroad station platform. Oddly enough, the platform was crowded and most of the prospective passengers were farmers. They milled around excitedly.

GESTAPO GUARDS cleared a path as the train began slowing up for the stop. But there were only thirty guards and more than two hundred prospective passengers. The guards were overwhelmed.

Spencer seized Valerie's arm and held her tightly. They were shoved around by the swarming crowd although everyone was good-natured about it and there were profuse apologies.

Brandt was there, roaring for order, but nobody paid any attention to him. He yelled commands. The Gestapo men drew guns and blackjacks.

Someone bumped violently against Jack Spencer. It was the farmer he had seen the night before, the man to whom he had sent Anita. Something white flashed and a hand dug into Spencer's coat pocket. Then the farmer was carried away by the crowd which retreated under the threats of the guards.

Suddenly the platform was clear except for the prisoners who were quickly herded into a group. The Gestapo agents stared in stunned surprise. Spencer barely noticed all this. He stepped behind Valerie, fished out the note which that farmer had placed in his pocket and was surprised to find it had been written by Anita. He ripped the paper into shreds and held them in one hand as he shuffled along toward the compartment assigned to him.

On his way he bent quickly, raised the iron lid of an axle bearing box and stuffed the papers inside. By the time they were found, they would either be ground to a pulp or so soaked with grease that they would hardly be noticed let alone read. He was the last person in line and none noticed this act.

Valerie wore a coat which belonged to Anita and kept the collar of it pulled high around her head. Anita had attracted some attention by fainting the night before, but Spencer doubted any of these Gestapo men would miss her or notice the presence of a new face. Nevertheless, it did no harm to be careful.

Papers were being examined as each prisoner was assigned a compartment. Directly ahead of Valerie was Ted Tannen and Don Leeds. They seemed friendly. Slightly to one side of them shuffled Armando, the Brazilian, and he was strangely quiet, depressed.

"Jack," Valerie whispered, "what on earth happened at the platform? All those people crowding and shoving, and then they disappeared as if by magic." After the dangers they had passed through together, ordinary things were waved. It was "Jack" and "Valerie" now.

"You just witnessed a minor demonstration of the French Underground," Spencer answered in a low voice. "It was carried out for one purpose—to plant a letter in my pocket."

"A letter?" Valerie asked quickly.

"From Anita. She wrote it at the farmhouse. Seems the French Underground knew something about the man who was killed in the hotel lobby last night. The Gestapo chased him clear from Paris because he knew what was going on and wanted to warn us."

"It must have been terribly important," Valerie opined. "They certainly killed him quickly enough."

"It was. Seems we have a Nazi spy in our midst. The cleverest one ever turned out by their espionage schools. He has been fitted out with passports and papers stolen from an American. In this identity he hopes to pass the usual F.B.I. scrutiny when we reach New York. Then he'll be free to carry on the work assigned to him."

Valerie gave Spencer a worried look. "If they thought you knew this, Jack, they'd—"

"Get rid of me just as they got rid of the man who did his best to warn us. I know, Val, but it doesn't make much difference. This is war and anything goes. I'll fight back with everything I have. That spy probably intends to rebuild the Nazi spy system in the United States. It has been pretty well smashed, you know. That's what makes him so dangerous. If he gets away with it, he'll accomplish his purpose."

CHAPTER VI

PITFALL

VALERIE DIDN'T comment because she and Jack Spencer were now at the head of the line. Tannen and Leeds climbed into a compartment. A Gestapo guard gave Spencer a push and indicated that he and Valerie were to share the compartment with Tannen and Leeds.

They climbed in and settled down across from the other two Americans. Tannen closed the door. Leeds shut the one leading into the aisle. Then Tannen leaned closer.

"I miss Anita, Jack," he said, "and I notice a new face among us. If it is something I should not know—"

"Anita didn't come with us," Spencer said. "She had other plans. Meet Valerie Cabot. She's British, was trapped in France and as a friendly gesture, Anita gave her the passport which Anita did not hope to use again. I'm depending on you two to keep this quiet."

"Absolutely," Leeds said, with a broad grin. "We're more than delighted to help, especially anyone as lovely as you, Miss Cabot. It's quite apparent you did not spend a long time in France or you would have lost that bloom in your cheeks."

"I lived in Paris before the war," Valerie said. "I—fled to the country and paid a farmer to hide me. There was plenty to eat."

Jack Spencer saw Brandt stalking down the platform, followed by several of his agents. They stopped at every compartment and slapped long pieces of paper across the door. One man wielded a paste brush.

"We're being sealed in," Spencer said. "They do that with diplomatic trains. Nobody can get off the train, nor on it. We're a long way from neutral territory so the ride should be quite interesting—and exciting perhaps."

"I've had enough excitement," Tannen said. "I can't wait to see that old lady with the torch in New York Harbor. Then I've another disagreeable job to do. Inform Ed Fraser's people about what happened. Spencer, they ought to get something out of those Nazi killers because of what happened to Fraser. It was their fault."

"We'll write Hitler personally." Jack Spencer laughed. "Just the same, I never was satisfied about Fraser's death. There was a door near that lion's cage. Someone could have slipped in, murdered him and got away before we knew what was going on."

"I'm not satisfied about it either," Tannen agreed. "Fraser knew about the lion, and he never took risks."

"Nonsense," Leeds commented dryly. "We all saw the blood on that lion's paw. The wound was caused by the lion's claws. Fraser just got lost in the dark, stumbled up against the cage and—"

The train gave a jerk and the railroad platform began to slip away. Throughout the train a cheer arose. A long, lingering cheer from the throats of people who had not believed this would ever happen. The first leg of a journey back home! Home where there was butter and coffee, warm clothing, newspapers that told the truth, and people who smiled and laughed. Even Valerie joined in the cheering.

French countryside whizzed past. Now and then they saw ruined houses and barns, token of the invader's wrath. Farmers in the fields never even looked up as the train passed. This was not the France of five years ago. This was a sullen, brooding France, barely held in check by the ruthlessness of the Nazis and their frequent firing squads. A France that was getting ready to leap over the traces at the first opportunity.

The inner door of their compartment was slid back and a uniformed guard spoke Jack Spencer's name. Spencer arose, wondering what this was all about.

"Come with me," the guard said.

SPENCER GRINNED at Valerie, waved a careless salute to Tannen and Leeds and stepped into the aisle. He was roughly shoved along by the guard. Every few steps the Gestapo man would bend down and peer out of windows as if to see where they were.

At the end of the car he elbowed in front of the American and seemed to have trouble opening the door. They passed through four more cars, going forward all the time. Obviously, that guard was stalling and Spencer tried to figure out why. He decided to stall too, and see what happened.

The guard appeared to be quite satisfied with this until they passed out of the last car and paused in front of a door marked "Baggage." Spencer steadied himself on the swaying platform. The train whistle hooted one short blast. That seemed to be a signal. The guard seized Spencer's arm and literally threw him against the baggage car door.

It opened and at that instant the train dived into a tunnel. Utter blackness descended. The train lights had been turned out. Spencer felt a big hand flat against the small of his back. That hand started to shove. He didn't wait for the act to be completed, but gave a flying leap into the baggage car.

Something crashed just behind him. He felt the breeze of the heavy object, felt the car floor jolt under its impact. Then he blundered against someone and the anger that surged through him took material form. He jabbed his fists forward—short, vicious punches that hurt.

He felt a fist whiz past his ear, turned and drove a straight right blindly into the darkness. It met flesh and drew a howl. To one side there was violent scuffling, curses, and the sound of blows being struck. Spencer grinned. Here was where he had a distinct advantage. Any man in this car was his enemy, but they were handicapped by the darkness and were fighting among themselves.

The American slowly moved back a few feet, crouched, and started swinging his arms in wide arcs until he encountered a pair of substantial hips. Both arms closed around this man and dragged him to the floor. Jack Spencer whaled the hardest punch he could summon and guided it more by instinct than anything else. It connected with a jaw and the form he straddled went suddenly limp.

Locating the Luger holstered at the man's hip, Spencer drew it free and scurried toward the further corner of the car. He recalled that these baggage cars all had narrow racks near the roof. By sense of feel, he located this and also encountered what felt like old rags or parts of a uniform. He slid the gun beneath these and left it there. An ace in the hole that might prove to be handy.

The car was fairly quiet now. He knew the men were moving forward slowly, trying to make sure they were not getting into any more fights among themselves. Spencer moved too, until he felt the door handle. This exit would take him still further toward the front of the train, but anything was better than facing the four or five Gestapo men who were actually panting in rage.

Spencer gave the handle a forward push. The door swung toward him. He opened it, slipped through, and let it close gently behind him.

The cool air seeping through the platform doors felt good. He had no doubts about the trouble he was in. Orders must have been given that he was to be killed. Purely by accident, of course. But now that he realized there was a dangerous spy aboard, traveling on the papers of an American, he had to come through.

A SPY like that could wreak havoc in the United States. Then there was Valerie. He had known her only a few hours, but that didn't seem to matter. He liked her—liked the calm with which she stood this ordeal. The way her blue eyes could crackle in fury; her smile and the soft roundness of her body. She was also worth living for.

Someone fumbled with the platform door of the baggage car. Jack Spencer quietly opened the other door and moved into the front car. He was surprised to find it Class A accommodations. The passageway was narrow and he moved sideward until he reached the main part of the car. A door blocked his way, but he had to go on.

Opening it, he blinked at the brilliant light that assailed his eyes. Then he made out the form of Brandt, slowly rising from a chair behind a small desk at the far end of the car. Brandt, now in full Gestapo uniform and scowling fiercely.

"Good afternoon, *Herr* Brandt." Spencer bowed slightly. "Should I have asked for an appointment?"

"What do you want?" Brandt demanded. "How did you get here?"

"Do you mean, how did I escape the pitfalls in my way, *Herr* Brandt? Perhaps I'm a soft, decadent American with a lot of luck. On the other hand, I may be tougher than I seem."

"I don't know what you are talking about," Brandt snapped. "Why did you come here?"

"To find out if I am permitted to remain with this party and be sent home." Jack Spencer shrugged. "After all, I have had some doubts. Did you contact the American Charge d'Affaires in Vichy? Did you discover that your ranking officer in the Foreign Ministry does have a nephew under arrest in Brazil?"

"You are permitted to go through," Brandt said surlily. "I myself am accompanying the party to see that everything is proper. Now get out of here."

Spencer did not move. One of the guards had silently slipped up behind him and a gun was drilling the small of his back. He raised his hands high.

"It seems you want me to leave, but someone else has other ideas," he said to Brandt slowly. "Has the gentleman with the gun a black eye? Or a bruised and swollen jaw? Your men were having quite a battle among themselves back in the baggage car."

CHAPTER VII

CHECKMATE

BRANDT BARKED an order in German. The gun was removed from Jack Spencer's back and the guard stepped forward. His uniform was torn and there was a little dried blood around the corners of his mouth. He gave Brandt a rapid report.

Brandt's face grew sterner, his eyes narrowed and he made fists out of his hands.

"Spencer," he said curtly, "my guard tells me you deliberately started fighting. That is not permitted. If you keep this up, I shall revoke the visa on your passport."

Spencer laughed a little. "You wouldn't dare, Brandt. I'm the only man in this party for whom the Brazilian Government will release that nephew of the Reich."

Brandt dropped a hand to the gun holstered at his hip. He whipped it out, leveled the weapon, and Jack Spencer wondered, with a shudder, if he had carried this game too far.

Then there was a commotion behind him. An angry voice spoke in English and Ted Tannen surged into the car with two Gestapo men hanging onto his arms.

"What is this?" Tannen yelled.

Brandt instantly lowered the gun. "I was merely trying to emphasize, for the benefit of Mr. Spencer, that we shall tolerate no fighting on this train. He was about to attack me so I drew my gun in self-defense."

Tannen glanced at the Gestapo man who stood with a pistol in his hand, trying to comprehend the sudden turn of events.

"It looks like it!" Tannen thundered. "I don't know who you are, sir. I don't give a hoot in Hades, but I hope you understand English enough to know that if anything happens to Jack Spencer, you'll be held accountable! Now, if you don't want us for anything else, we'll be going."

"Just a moment," Brandt barked. "Spencer, that woman Anita Clark—she seems to be in your company a great deal. Perhaps you are in love with her, eh?"

"It does happen," Spencer admitted, "but I fail to see how that concerns you. Come on, Tannen, there's a smell in this car I don't like."

No one attempted to stop them. On the platform in front of the baggage car door, Jack Spencer paused to wipe sweat off his face.

"Thanks, pal," he said. "I'm still doubtful whether or not Brandt was going to shoot. He didn't dare when you showed up."

Tannen scowled. "I followed you when that Gestapo monkey herded you to the front of the train. I saw him shove you into the baggage car, but when I reached it, the door was locked. They opened it later on and I banged right through."

Spencer led the way across the baggage car and winced at the sight of a long, narrow box lying on the floor. That was what had crashed down right behind him. He could have been crushed by the thing. He gave it an experimental shove with his foot. It didn't budge.

"I was supposed to be underneath that box," Spencer told Tannen. "Brandt doesn't like my company."

"We'd better stick close," Tannen said. "Brandt gave me the fish eye too. Maybe I'm on his list for extermination. Have you any idea why they'd prefer you dead?"

"Faintly," Spencer replied. "I think they suspect I may know that your partner's death in the lion house was not an accident."

Tannen gasped and stopped short. "Jack," he demanded, "have you anything to prove he was murdered? I've got to know. It's imperative. My own life may be in danger."

"I have no proof beyond a pretty good-sized hunch. What are you worried about?"

"Fraser and I used to get about Paris quite a lot. He had a knack for sticking his nose in the wrong places. A week ago both of us blundered into a hotel where Occupation Army officers are housed. We heard a group discussing certain weaknesses in the Nazi fortifications in Belgium. When I was arrested, I thought they were taking me in for that and I had visions of a bullet-scarred wall."

Spencer whistled. "Perhaps there is the motive. Tannen, whatever you know must be told to the others. Such information must go through. Come on back to our compartment."

THEY HURRIED through the cars. Spencer saw that the Brazilian, Armando, was not in his compartment. Then he had a second shock. Don Leeds was alone in their own quarters. Valerie had disappeared.

"She was here when I left," Tannen answered Spencer's unspoken question. "Wake up, Leeds, and find out where she went."

Leeds awoke with a start, blinked owlishly, and then jumped to his feet.

"What's wrong? Aren't we going to be allowed to finish the trip?"

"No reason why not," Spencer answered. "Where is Valerie?"

"Good gosh, I don't know." Leeds looked around. "Maybe she went out to wash up or something."

"She wouldn't dare leave this compartment for fear of being recognized," Tannen said tartly. "You know that, Don."

"We'll, I'm not her guardian," Leeds snapped. "If she wants to prowl, that's her business. You two act as though I might have tossed her out the door."

Spencer turned and headed for the rear of the train. He inspected every compartment in each car, but there was no trace of Val. He recalled Brandt's odd statement about his being in love with her. There was more than just idle curiosity to that remark.

And where was Armando, the Brazilian? Spencer started to retrace his steps and this time he looked in the wash rooms. Suddenly the train plunged into another tunnel. An instant later, Spencer heard a shrill scream of sheerest terror. He began running, heedless of the questions passengers flung at him. That scream sounded as though it came from directly outside the car through which he had been moving.

Reaching the platform, he felt cooler air than usual and realized that one of the doors must have been open for a moment. There was the smell of fumes from the engine, too. Oddly enough, that platform was dark.

Spencer reached up and found an overhead bulb loose in its socket. He tightened it and the platform was flooded with yellow light.

Both doors were equipped with inside seals. Spencer examined one, found it intact, and looked at the other. It was official, all right, but—the glue hadn't even hardened. This door had been opened, someone flung out to bounce against the tunnel wall, fly back and be ground to death under the wheels of the train.

The cry could have come from either a man or a woman. Jack Spencer felt all the horror of it still seeping through his brain. Lips tight, eyes sparkling dangerously, he proceeded through the whole train until he reached the baggage car. That long box had been propped up again and rocked gently with the rhythm of the train's movement.

That box! Easily large enough to accommodate a human being. Only one person had been thrown off the train. Two were missing, because Jack had seen no sign of Armando during his search, either. There was a fifty-fifty chance that he, and not Valerie, had been the victim.

At no time had any of the Gestapo guards tried to interfere with Jack Spencer. Right now, one of them stood with his back against the further baggage car door and he seemed to be smiling contemptuously.

Spencer gave the long box a hard shove. As it toppled over, he tried to stop it from crashing, but the heavy thing slid right through his grasp. It was equipped with a hinged lid which was screwed down. Spencer looked around, saw a kit of tools and seized a screw driver. Working furiously, while the guard stood by, he got the lid open, raised it—and groaned.

The case was jammed full of pamphlets. Nazi propaganda stuff. Spencer dropped the lid, walked slowly toward the car door and hoped that the guard would try to stop him. The Gestapo man did not; merely moved aside and even opened the door for him. He gave an exaggerated bow.

SPENCER RECOGNIZED these symptoms of Nazi confidence. They were laughing at him, knowing they held all the cards in the deck. He stepped into Brandt's private car. The Gestapo official looked up, his eyes challenging the American to start something.

Jack Spencer sat down. He had to know whether or not Valerie was dead. The only way was by admitting defeat, and the consular clerk felt no delusions about the fact that he was licked.

"What is your proposition, Brandt?" he asked bluntly.

"Proposition?" Brandt wrinkled his face. "Why should I make any proposition to you?"

"Lay off, will you? I know when I'm finished. Where is the girl?" Brandt leaned across the small desk.

"I'm afraid you speak in riddles. Someone is—missing, perhaps?"

"Look," Spencer said. "Let's drop pretenses. For some reason you don't want me to reach Lisbon and the United States. For that same reason I am going to my own country. You can't stop me—not even by murder—because if you do, the whole necessity for this transfer of prisoners falls flat."

"Now that I think of it," Brandt said, "we are one short. I counted the prisoners as they went aboard. Just a moment." Brandt glanced through several papers and then looked up again. "It is the woman Anita Clark. She did not board the train. Foolish of her to escape. There will not be another chance to go home."

"All right," Spencer admitted, "she did escape. By now, she is in Spain. But there is someone else missing—another girl who was in my compartment when your gorilla brought me to the baggage car as the guest star in an accident intended to be fatal. When I got back, she was gone."

"Too bad," Brandt said mockingly. "An American, of course?"

Jack sighed and closed both eyes wearily. "You know who she is, Brandt. You know blamed well where she is, too. I said I'd listen to a proposition, didn't I?"

Brandt arose. "Then you admit I have been too clever for you. Much too clever. You furnished Anita Clark with a passport. A blank one was missing from my desk at Moisdon. You were quite neat about that, Mr. Spencer. Of course, I learned what you had done. The stupid guard remembered your red hair, and you are the only prisoner with red hair."

"Where is she?" Jack repeated hollowly.

Brandt disregarded his question. "The guard remembered just before I shot him. People regain their memories when they face rifles. Very amazing. So now you come crawling to me, begging mercy for a British spy. A spy who was under arrest when you freed her. You want a proposition. Well, here it is. I shall give you a gun. You will do as I direct."

"Better not get too free with a weapon, Brandt," Spencer said. "I might succumb to temptation."

"And have the girl tortured and then shot? No, I have studied Americans. Where women are concerned, they are softer than usual. With this gun you will shoot Don Leeds. Then you will kill Ted Tannen and, finally send a bullet through your own head. I shall indicate that you went mad."

CHAPTER VIII

TIME TO DIE

MOTIONLESS, JACK Spencer looked at the proffered gun. This was a typical Nazi gesture—to get a man down and then trample on him. To take a hostage, and compel an enemy to obey the direct command. Any underhanded method of fighting was fair to these men without hearts or souls.

"Mr. Leeds first and then Tannen," Brandt repeated, with a smirk. "I shall provide you with privacy when you wish to—execute the third person I insist upon having removed."

"How do I know you'll keep your promise about the girl? How do I know she's even alive?"

Brandt shrugged. "A chance you will have to take. Here—this is the Clark woman's passport which the English girl used. It was in her handbag. Is that proof enough we have her?"

"I don't need proof of that," Spencer said. "The fact that she is missing indicates she has either been captured or murdered. Just why do you want Tannen and Leeds killed?"

Brandt fished a fingernail file out of his pocket and began working on his nails. He seemed extremely occupied by this. The gun lay on the edge of the desk within easy reach of where Jack Spencer was seated.

"It really makes no difference whom you kill," Brandt said, and the American knew he lied. "Tannen and Leeds seem to be your closest friends, the people to whom you may have confided certain things. Also, it is enough that you obey orders without questioning them. You are in no position to bargain."

Spencer picked up the gun. He had an idea that the moment his hand started moving toward the weapon, hidden guns were brought to bear on him. If he lifted the Luger quickly, aimed it at Brandt, he would probably be dead a fraction of a second later.

Calmly he removed the clip. There were three bullets in the gun.

"You certainly don't expect me to miss, do you?" he asked dryly.

Brandt looked up with a faint smile.

"Our firing squads have executed thousands of our enemies," he said. "You may not know it, but the firing squad of four men does its damage with only one bullet. Three of the rifles contain a blank. We cannot afford to be careless with bullets, you see. So if they can do it, you certainly will not fail."

Jack Spencer stuffed the gun into his pocket, arose and walked slowly toward the door. Brandt called him and he turned around.

Brandt waved the fingernail file as a teacher waves a pencil at some recalcitrant student.

"Mind you, Mr. Spencer, there is a time limit. Two hours and no more. Promptly at the end of one hundred and twenty minutes, the girl—well, use your imagination. Good hunting, Mr. Spencer."

The young American grimaced and headed back toward his own car. There were two men guarding the baggage car, but he paid no attention to them. It was dark outside now and they were not too far from a neutral border. Much more than two hours' journey though, and that was all the time allotted to Spencer for his murder task.

Somewhere on board this train was a spy. Leeds? Tannen? Armando, who was missing? Even Valerie herself? Or was it some insignificant person quietly merged with the main group of passengers?

Jack Spencer had little to go on. The murder of Ed Fraser in the lion house had something to do with it. So did the disappearance of Armando. Spencer firmly believed it had been the Brazilian who had been hurled off the train as it passed through the tunnel. Brandt would hardly have dared kill Valerie. She was much too useful a hostage.

SPENCER BEGAN walking faster as he neared his own car. He decided to be direct—to question Tannen and Leeds, put the whole thing squarely up to them. But Leeds was the only one in the compartment and he was busy staring out of the window into inky blackness, trying to figure out where they were.

"Oh, hello." He smiled at Spencer. "Tannen told me you had a bit of trouble with that Gestapo officer."

"Leeds," Spencer said, "until you approached me in the lobby of the hotel at Moisdon, I never saw you before. I've talked to you infrequently since then. Just who are you, anyway?"

"Why, I thought everyone knew that." Leeds looked out of the window again. "I was the business and advertising manager for an American newspaper in Paris. The *Sphere*.... We're going along at a pretty good clip. We're at least two hundred miles beyond Dentz already."

"How do you know?" Spencer queried.

Leeds gave him a peculiar glance. "I noticed the station as we passed through. The city also. We slowed up for it."

"We passed through Dentz just about the time that Valerie disappeared," Spencer accused. "You told me you'd been asleep all the time. Now you say you were awake. Leeds—you're a liar. I want to see your passport."

Leeds laughed. He seemed entirely at his ease. So much so that Jack Spencer's suspicions were rising fast. After all, a Nazi spy would feel perfectly safe while he was in German-conquered territory and protected by Gestapo guards. Leeds handed over his passport and Spencer examined it briefly. He gave it back without comment.

"Suppose we drop the matter," Leeds said. "I hate arguments. Why don't you pick on Tannen for a change?"

Spencer looked around. Tannen was leaning against the compartment door. He had apparently been there for some time without making his presence known. Spencer asked for his passport, too, and Tannen produced it. Receiving it back, Tannen gave a barely perceptible jerk of his head and went away.

"Why," Spencer asked, "does *Herr* Brandt want you killed, Mr. Leeds?"

Leeds gasped at that one and sat erect.

"Wants me killed? Good heavens, I don't know! Does he?"

"You have less than two hours to live," Spencer told him. "That warning should be worth something to you. Pay me back by truthfully answering one question. Were you, or were you not, asleep when Valerie left this compartment?"

Leeds was growing more and more nervous. He kept biting his lower lip and hardly seemed to hear the consular clerk's question. He recovered his wits with a start.

"I—was asleep," he declared. "Really, I was. Dozing perhaps and I did notice us pass through Dentz, but I don't know when Valerie departed, nor where she went."

Tannen was outside the compartment again, impatient to see Jack Spencer alone. Spencer walked out and Tannen led him to an empty compartment. He closed the door, sat down, and leaned forward eagerly.

"I overheard Leeds telling about his occupation in Paris. That's a lie. I knew the business manager of the *Sphere's* Paris Edition. His name was Leeds, too, but I never did find out his first name. Jack—the Don Leeds we know is a fake."

"So I'm beginning to comprehend," Spencer said slowly. "You are sure about this, Tannen?"

"I'm positive. The Leeds who worked for that newspaper died in Paris eight weeks ago. Of natural causes. Jack, I think Leeds turned Valerie over to the Gestapo. Probably tricked her into a trap of some kind. The same with Armando. He's gone also."

"Stay here," Spencer said. "I'll be right back."

HE HURRIED to the compartment which Armando had shared with two other men. He asked pertinent questions and got quick, honest replies.

"No, Armando hasn't returned yet," one man said. "He was talking to us when a girl went by—the one who was with you all the time in the hotel. Armando immediately arose, followed her, and that's the last we've seen of him. Is anything wrong, Mr. Spencer?"

"You are the only representative of the United States Government aboard this train," the other man broke in. "We must rely on you. There won't be any trouble getting to Lisbon, will there?"

"You'll get there," Spencer promised grimly, "if I have to kill a couple of men to make certain of it. Which of these suitcases belongs to Armando?"

He took the one they pointed out, carried it back to the compartment where Tannen waited and opened the locked suitcase by the simple method of cutting through its leather side. Clothing and papers spilled out. Spencer picked up several pieces of paper. They were advertising cuts.

"Look," he said, and showed them to Tannen. "Armando was a business representative and must have taken a lot of ads in the *Sphere*. A long time ago, I'll grant, because no newspaper except Nazi-inspired ones have been permitted to exist since the occupation. But these cuts prove that Armando had dealings with the real Don Leeds."

"That's it," Tannen grunted. "Armando knew this Don Leeds was a fake. He had reasons for not exposing him perhaps, but the false Leeds made certain that Armando would do no talking. In my opinion, the Brazilian has been murdered. Leeds is a Nazi. He must be so important that Brandt was willing to risk trouble by having one passenger missing. Jack, there is something going on. Something big, and Leeds is right in the middle of the web."

There was half a pack of American cigarettes in Armando's bag. Dry and carefully hoarded. Spencer gave half to Tannen, lighted one for himself and stuffed the rest into his pocket. He smoked slowly, enjoying every puff to its fullest. American cigarettes were as rare in Paris as were merciful Nazis.

The smoke helped him relax, steady his nerves. Then they were torn raw again. Brandt opened the compartment door and stuck his head in. He was smiling in high satisfaction.

"It is getting late, Mr. Spencer. In less than two hours we shall be at the Border and our little bargain must be completed before then. Can I depend on you?"

Spencer grasped the door handle and slid it shut so fast that Brandt had to leap back. His smile died away and he scowled. Then he disappeared.

"What did he mean?" Tannen asked. "Time is getting short? What is that bargain you two have?"

"I'm afraid you'll find out, Tannen," Spencer said. "Don't ask for unpleasant news. I've made up my mind, though. Leeds is going to tell me the truth. All of it—if I have to shoot him."

He drew the Luger and calmly pumped a bullet into the firing chamber. He dropped the gun into a side pocket, but before he could arise, Don Leeds hurried past the compartment without looking in. Spencer yanked the door open, and Tannen grabbed his arm.

"Jack, what the devil—"

Jack Spencer pulled himself free. "I said I was going to make Leeds talk. Valerie's life depends upon it. Don't try to stop me, Tannen, or you might—"

He didn't finish the threat, just hurried in the same direction which Leeds had taken. Tannen sat down slowly, remained seated for about a minute or two, then hurried in pursuit of Spencer. He was halfway through the car when a single shot rang out.

Tannen began running, paying no attention to the anxious queries of the passengers. He reached the platform between cars and stopped quickly. One of the platform doors was ajar. Neither Spencer nor Leeds were anywhere about. The seal on that door had been ruthlessly ripped off.

CHAPTER IX

THE STAMP
OF GUILT

TANNEN RAN forward again, passed through the baggage car and still saw nothing of Jack Spencer or Leeds. But suddenly, as he found himself in the passageway to Brandt's private quarters he could hear Spencer's voice. Tannen quickly stepped into the compartment.

"Brandt," Jack Spencer said coolly, "I've killed Leeds. I shot him through the head and pushed him out of a platform door. You'd better have that door resealed."

"Very good," Brandt said. "I shall have the train searched to see if you are telling the truth. What of *Herr* Tannen?"

"He's next," Spencer said grimly. "I'm beginning to find out how it feels to be a Nazi now. If I kept this up, I might discover I like to murder people, just as you and your kind do. Don't worry—Tannen will be taken care of, although I'm still wondering why you want those men executed."

Brandt leaned back and his chair squeaked dismally.

"I have told you—when people know too much, it is time for them to die."

Jack Spencer laughed bitterly. "Time to die! Brandt, you're right about me. I do know too much. For instance, I'm sure that either Leeds, Tannen or Armando is a spy. A Nazi agent on his way to the United States. What I can't get through my head is why on earth you want them murdered? After all, the one who is a spy is also a Nazi."

Brandt blanched when Spencer admitted his knowledge of a spy's presence on the train. For a moment it looked as if the Gestapo officer was going to take action. Spencer's hand slid into his side coat pocket and curled around the Luger.

"You are mistaken," Brandt said finally. "Why should we try to send one of our agents to the United States in such a foolish manner when a submarine could deposit him on the coast any time we chose?"

"Ah—you forget, *Herr* Brandt," Spencer reproved, "that I have been in Unoccupied France and able to listen to a short-wave radio. I got all the news from home. Eight of your spies tried that trick. Six are dead— two are in prison. Your espionage outfit in the United States has been crippled by the work of J. Edgar Hoover and his F.B.I. You need a leader there, someone to knit the loose threads together again and make a workable organization out of the remnants. Only a man who could enter the country legally would be able to do that."

"I have no time to talk," Brandt snapped. "It is enough that the girl will be spared only if you now kill Tannen and then yourself."

Jack Spencer took one of Armando's cigarettes from his pocket, lighted it and crossed his legs. Through a window behind Brandt, he could see that the train was moving at a terrific rate.

Brandt ordered him out, harshly. Spencer grinned and blew a mouthful of smoke into the Gestapo man's face. For half an hour he sat there while Brandt fumed. To all of the Nazi's threats, he had only one answer.

"My time limit isn't up yet and if I choose to stay here, that's my business. Kick me out and I'll yell the whole story all over the train. You know, Brandt, I don't think you like this spy—whoever he may be. I think you want him murdered because you may then take his place."

"Why should I ask for such a perilous job?" Brandt snarled.

"Ah," Spencer chuckled, "then it is true. Why, Brandt? Because the United States is a pretty good place. Even with its rubber and gas rationing, a little less meat perhaps, a few privations, but if that rationing was cut in half we'd still live ten times better than any Nazi, and fifty times better than those poor devils you conquered. Good heavens, man, ask me something difficult to answer."

Brandt arose menacingly. "You will go or I shall have you executed where you sit. Is that quite clear?"

SPENCER KNEW the game was over. He got up and sauntered in the direction of the baggage car. While he had been seated there, taunting Brandt, his mind had been extremely busy. First, with the idea that Valerie had been snatched from beneath Leeds' nose. That was impossible. She would have put up a terrific fuss. Therefore, she went willingly and Leeds knew why and where she was going.

Spencer tried to puzzle out just where Brandt could have hidden the girl. After all, hiding places on a speeding train are few. Wherever she was, that place must be thought secure by its simple obviousness.

Spencer walked across the baggage car. One Gestapo man was on duty there, eyeing him ominously. The big, coffinlike crate was standing on end once more. Spencer's eyes sparkled. He turned suddenly and threw himself at the Nazi guard.

This act was accomplished so fast the German didn't even have time to cry out an alarm. Spencer got the man's neck in a viselike grip, shoved a knee into his back and pulled him over. Gradually, the Nazi's face turned bluish. His struggles ceased and he slid limply to the floor when Jack Spencer let him go.

The American hurried to the big crate, tipped it over, and this time it wasn't quite so heavy. He found the same screw driver and set to work. When the lid came free, he saw Valerie inside, tied and gagged. Her eyes pleaded with him. Spencer leaned close and whispered:

"I don't know but I ought to let you stay there, darling. You got me into an awful mess."

She wagged her head energetically. He took out a knife, cut her loose, and she swayed a bit after he stood her up.

"Jack"—she wetted her lips between words—"I went for a walk and they seized me. I was rolled into a big blanket and two Gestapo men carried me right through the train. Nobody paid any attention."

"People being repatriated don't usually observe things too closely, Val," he said grimly. "They are more concerned with minding their own business and getting out of this Dark Age continent. I have no time for explanations now. How are you at riding the top of a train moving plenty of miles an hour?"

"I'll do anything if it means those—those beasts won't get me again, Jack!" she declared.

"Then come forward quickly. We'll open one of the platform doors between this baggage car and Brandt's private car. Nobody can see us there. Come on."

He got the door open, whispered instructions in Valerie's ear and gave her a boost up. She seized some projection on the roof of the car and he saw two lovely, silken-clad legs hurriedly vanish from sight. He closed the door, replaced the seal as well as he could and started walking toward the rear of the train. His plan was working out.

When he pushed open the door of the car to which he and his party had been assigned, he saw Tannen suddenly start moving back. Tannen held up both hands as if he hoped they would shield him from a bullet.

"No!" he half-screamed. "Jack, you can't do it. Jack—don't! I'm your friend. Don't kill me!"

Spencer kept on going, features impassive, steps almost robotlike in their steady advance. Suddenly Tannen changed his tactics and charged straight at the American. His frenzy lent him strength and speed. He brushed past Spencer and began running madly. The chase began.

Spencer went after him. Tannen kept yelling that he was to be murdered, but the passengers either decided this was some new form of entertainment or they trusted Jack Spencer enough to know that

Tannen must have gone stark mad. At least, no one made any attempt to hinder the consular clerk's progress.

When he reached the baggage car door and opened it, he saw Tannen crouched in a corner, shivering with terror. Slowly Spencer drew the Luger from his pocket. With the same motion he glanced at his wristwatch. By the planned speed of this train they should be streaking across a corner of neutral territory within twenty minutes now. Then there would be a stop at a neutral railroad station where the passengers would be transferred to another train. That was why Brandt had given him a time limit.

Jack Spencer saw that the Gestapo guard had been removed. He calmly locked the door behind him, kept his gun trained on Tannen and walked to the other door. He locked this one also.

Turning slowly, he leveled the Luger. His finger squeezed trigger. The gun bucked. Tannen gave a jerk and a howl of astonishment. Three or four inches to the left of his head was a small bullet-hole through the side of the car.

Spencer fired again and then twice more. Each time he came reasonably close, but managed to miss. Tannen's terror now became something to behold. He was waving his hands and trying to talk at the same time, but his throat had become too parched. Only unintelligible croaks came out.

Spencer kept the gun trained on him.

"Brandt isn't coming—did you notice that, Tannen?" he asked. "Brandt wants you killed. He's smart. If I kill you, his responsibility is gone. Both to the Reich and to the United States. He'll simply tell your superiors I got out of hand and tell United States officials that I went stark, raving mad. You thought the second bullet in the gun would either be a blank or have so little powder that the slug wouldn't harm you. Brandt loaded the gun to capacity, with real bullets. Like this one."

The gun blazed. Tannen shrieked a curse and plunged headlong toward Spencer. Instead of a bullet he met a hard fist that rocked him back on his heels. Then Spencer closed and punched until Tannen howled for mercy. He talked—mostly about the way Brandt had doublecrossed him. He swore a terrible vengeance, promising that both Spencer and Valerie should go free.

Then Tannen got to his feet. The train had stopped and he knew it. Brandt had not put in an appearance yet. He could not figure things out until the side doors of the baggage car slid back.

Four men, armed with tommy guns, jumped in. They were dressed in dark civilian clothes. Behind them came Don Leeds, similarly armed.

Jack Spencer dropped the Luger he held and stood aside. Tannen was tied up and swung like a sack of potatoes out the door. A moment later, a car motor started up.

"Brandt has been taken care of." Leeds grinned at Spencer. "I suppose you still can't imagine what we're up to."

"Oh, yes, I can," Spencer said. "You've just taken Tannen right out of my hands. He's the spy who was planted among us. You're another, Leeds, with one big difference. He is Nazi and you—are British. I knew this when I checked your passports. Tannen's was impressed with a stolen U.S. Government seal which was in Brandt's office at Maisdon. I impressed a blank piece of paper with that seal and kept the impression. Most of those seals have little peculiarities, like the print of a typewriter. Tannen's passport was faked and that seal used on it."

LEEDS CHUCKLED.

"I had an idea you were wise," he said, "and I thought you were about ready to get rough so I decided it was time to start things humming. I got past you, all right, reached the top of the train and made my way to the engine. I stuck up the crew and made them really shovel on the coal. We're two miles from a neutral Border. The area is deserted and we, as British subjects, are within our rights to attack this train."

"Nobody said you weren't," Jack Spencer told him. "It had to be Tannen, of course. Ed Fraser was murdered in that lion's house because he knew Tannen and would expose the man who was posing as Tannen. Armando died because he was too suspicious. Tannen believed that Armando was wise to him when really Armando was just trying to find out why you were posing as Don Leeds. You're not Leeds, of course."

"My name is Kincaid." The British agent nodded. "Oh, yes—Valerie is on her way to this car now. I left her to handle the train crew while I came back and pulverized Brandt. She's a British agent also. The two of us have been after von Graum—our mutual friend who took Tannen's identity—for weeks. He operated in London for a time and murdered two people there. We wanted him for that and we got him, even though we had practically to snatch him from the grasp of our ally. Thanks, Jack, you were helpful."

"Don't kid yourself," Jack Spencer said. "I was only helping myself. Brandt had me on a spot. I was supposed to kill you. They suspected you, of course. You arranged that for me nicely, by climbing to the top of the train. Tannen—or whatever his name is—really believed I had shot you. I let him think so, too—I let him hear me report the fact to Brandt. Then I went after Tannen."

"I heard the shots, Jack. Couldn't make up my mind if you really were finishing him off."

"Brandt gave me a prepared gun. The bullet meant for you would have done the job. The second—for Tannen—wouldn't even have wounded him. What neither of them knew was that I'd swiped another Luger and hidden it here in the baggage car. I switched guns, fired at Tannen and made him think Brandt was doublecrossing him. Tannen promptly confessed. Leeds—or Kincaid—who was that man they murdered in the hotel lobby?"

"One of our chaps," the British agent said. "He discovered who the spy was and came to tell us. Just pryor to that, they'd arrested Valerie. It was pure luck that you came along and got her out of it."

Jack Spencer swung out of the side door and dropped to the ground.

"This is going to create an awful smell in the State Department," he said, "but we'll iron it out. I'm going forward and see what's delaying Valerie."

"Good luck," the British agent called out. "If you don't mind, we'll let her continue the trip on Anita Clark's passport. Safer that way. She can come back from America by plane."

"If I don't mind?" Spencer shouted. "Brother, I was going to insist on the same thing. When you promise to commit two murders and then suicide for the sake of a girl, you really want to know her better."